FIVE SINISTER CHARACTERS

BY

RAYMOND CHANDLER

CONTENTS

1

Anna Halsey was about two hundred and forty pounds of middle-aged putty-faced woman in a black tailor-made suit. Her eyes were shiny black shoe buttons, her cheeks were as soft as suet and about the same color. She was sitting behind a black glass desk that looked like Napoleon's tomb and she was smoking a cigarette in a black holder that was not quite as long as a rolled umbrella. She said: "I need a man."

I watched her shake ash from the cigarette to the shiny top of the desk where flakes of it curled and crawled in the draft from an open window.

"I need a man good-looking enough to pick up a dame who has a sense of class, but he's got to be tough enough to swap punches with a power shovel. I need a guy who can act like a bar lizard and backchat like Fred Allen, only better, and get hit on the head with a beer truck and think some cutie in the leg-line topped him with a breadstick."

"It's a cinch," I said. "You need the New York Yankees, Robert Donat, and the Yacht Club Boys."

"You might do," Anna said, "cleaned up a little. Twenty bucks a day and ex's. I haven't brokered a job in years, but this one is out of my line. I'm in the smooth-angles of the detecting business and I make money without getting my can knocked off. Let's see how Gladys likes you."

She reversed the cigarette holder and tipped a key on a large black-and-chromium annunciator box. "Come in and empty Anna's ash tray, honey."

We waited.

The door opened and a tall blonde dressed better than the Duchess of Windsor strolled in.

She swayed elegantly across the room, emptied Anna's ash tray, patted her fat cheek, gave me a smooth rippling glance and went out again.

"I think she blushed," Anna said when the door closed. "I guess you still have it."

"She blushed--and I have a dinner date with Darryl Zanuck," I said. "Quit horsing around. What's the story?"

"It's to smear a girl. A redheaded number with bedroom eyes. She's shill for a gambler and she's got her hooks into a rich man's pup."

"What do I do to her?"

Anna sighed. "It's kind of a mean job, Philip, I guess. If she's got a record of any sort, you dig it up and toss it in her face. If she hasn't, which is more likely as she comes from good people, it's kind of up to you. You get an idea once in a while, don't you?"

"I can't remember the last one I had. What gambler and what rich man?"

"Marty Estel."

I started to get up from my chair, then remembered that business had been bad for a month and that I needed the money.

I sat down again.

"You might get into trouble, of course," Anna said. "I never heard of Marty bumping anybody off in the public square at high noon, but he don't play with cigar coupons."

"Trouble is my business," I said. "Twenty-five a day and guarantee of two-fifty, if I pull the job."

"I gotta make a little something for myself," Anna whined.

"O.K. There's plenty of coolie labor around town. Nice to have seen you looking so well. So long, Anna."

I stood up this time. My life wasn't worth much, but it was worth that much. Marty Estel was supposed to be pretty tough people, with the right helpers and the right protection behind him. His place was out in West Hollywood, on the Strip. He wouldn't pull anything crude, but if he pulled at all, something would pop.

"Sit down, it's a deal," Anna sneered. "I'm a poor old broken-down woman trying to run a high-class detective agency on nothing but fat and bad health, so take my last nickel and laugh at me."

"Who's the girl?" I had sat down again.

"Her name is Harriet Huntress--a swell name for the part too. She lives in the El Milano, nineteen-hundred block on North Sycamore, very high-class. Father went broke back in thirty-one and jumped out of his office window. Mother dead. Kid sister in boarding school back in Connecticut. That might make an angle."

"Who dug up all this?"

"The client got a bunch of photostats of notes the pup had given to Marty. Fifty grand worth. The pup-- he's an adopted son to the old man--denied the notes, as kids will. So the client had the photostats experted by a guy named Arbogast, who pretends to be good at that sort of thing. He said O.K. and dug around a bit, but he's too fat to do legwork, like me, and he's off the case now."

"But I could talk to him?"

"I don't know why not." Anna nodded several of her chins.

"This client--does he have a name?"

"Son, you have a treat coming. You can meet him in person--right now."

She tipped the key of her call box again. "Have Mr. Jeeter come in, honey."

"That Gladys," I said, "does she have a steady?"

"You lay off Gladys!" Anna almost screamed at me. "She's worth eighteen grand a year in divorce business to me. Any guy that lays a finger on her, Philip Marlowe, is practically cremated."

"She's got to fall some day," I said. "Why couldn't I catch her?"

The opening door stopped that.

I hadn't seen him in the paneled reception room, so he must have been waiting in a private office. He hadn't enjoyed it. He came in quickly, shut the door quickly, and yanked a thin octagonal platinum watch from his vest and glared at it. He was a tall white-blond type in pin-striped flannel of youthful cut. There was a small pink rosebud in his lapel. He had a keen frozen face, a little pouchy under the eyes, a little thick in the lips. He carried an ebony cane with a silver knob, wore spats and looked a smart sixty, but I gave him close to ten years more. I didn't like him.

"Twenty-six minutes, Miss Halsey," he said icily. "My time happens to be valuable. By regarding it as valuable I have managed to make a great deal of money."

"Well, we're trying to save you some of the money," Anna drawled. She didn't like him either. "Sorry to keep you waiting, Mr. Jeeter, but you wanted to see the operative I selected and I had to send for him."

"He doesn't look the type to me," Mr. Jeeter said, giving me a nasty glance. "I think more of a gentleman--"

5

"You're not the Jeeter of *Tobacco Road*, are you?" I asked him.

He came slowly towards me and half lifted the stick. His icy eyes tore at me like claws. "So you insult me," he said. "Me--a man in my position."

"Now wait a minute," Anna began.

"Wait a minute nothing," I said. "This party said I was not a gentleman. Maybe that's O.K. for a man in his position, whatever it is--but a man in my position doesn't take a dirty crack from anybody. He can't afford to. Unless, of course, it wasn't intended."

Mr. Jeeter stiffened and glared at me. He took his watch out again and looked at it. "Twenty-eight minutes," he said. "I apologize, young man. I had no desire to be rude."

"That's swell," I said. "I knew you weren't the Jeeter in *Tobacco Road* all along."

That almost started him again, but he let it go. He wasn't sure how I meant it.

"A question or two while we are together," I said. "Are you willing to give this Huntress girl a little money--for expenses?"

"Not one cent," he barked. "Why should I?"

"It's got to be a sort of custom. Suppose she married him. What would he have?"

"At the moment a thousand dollars a month from a trust fund established by his mother, my late wife." He dipped his head. "When he is twenty-eight years old, far too much money."

"You can't blame the girl for trying," I said. "Not these days. How about Marty Estel? Any settlement there?"

He crumpled his gray gloves with a purple-veined hand. "The debt is uncollectible. It is a gambling debt."

Anna sighed wearily and flicked ash around on her desk.

"Sure," I said. "But gamblers can't afford to let people welsh on them. After all, if your son had won, Marty would have paid *him.*"

"I'm not interested in that," the tall thin man said coldly.

"Yeah, but think of Marty sitting there with fifty grand in notes. Not worth a nickel. How will he sleep nights?"

Mr. Jeeter looked thoughtful. "You mean there is danger of violence?" he suggested, almost suavely.

"That's hard to say. He runs an exclusive place, gets a good movie crowd. He has his own reputation to think of. But he's in a racket and he knows people. Things can happen--a long way off from where Marty is. And Marty is no bathmat. He gets up and walks."

Mr. Jeeter looked at his watch again and it annoyed him. He slammed it back into his vest. "All that is your affair," he snapped. "The district attorney is a personal friend of mine. If this matter seems to be beyond your powers--"

"Yeah," I told him. "But you came slumming down our street just the same. Even if the D.A. is in your vest pocket--along with that watch."

He put his hat on, drew on one glove, tapped the edge of his shoe with his stick, walked to the door and opened it.

"I ask results and I pay for them," he said coldly. "I pay promptly. I even pay generously sometimes, although I am not considered a generous man. I think we all understand one another."

He almost winked then and went on out. The door closed softly against the cushion of air in the door-closer. I looked at Anna and grinned.

"Sweet, isn't he?" she said. "I'd like eight of him for my cocktail set."

I gouged twenty dollars out of her--for expenses.

2

The Arbogast I wanted was John D. Arbogast and he had an office on Sunset near Ivar. I called him up from a phone booth. The voice that answered was fat. It wheezed softly, like the voice of a man who had just won a pie-eating contest.

"Mr. John D. Arbogast?"

"Yeah."

"This is Philip Marlowe, a private detective working on a case you did some experting on. Party named Jeeter."

"Yeah?"

"Can I come up and talk to you about it--after I eat lunch?"

"Yeah." He hung up. I decided he was not a talkative man.

I had lunch and drove out there. It was east of Ivar, an old two-story building faced with brick which had been painted recently. The street floor was stores and a restaurant. The building entrance was the foot of a wide straight stairway to the second floor. On the directory at the bottom I read: John D. Arbogast, Suite 212. I went up the stairs and found myself in a wide straight hall that ran parallel with the street. A man in a smock was standing in an open doorway down to my right. He wore a round mirror strapped to his forehead and pushed back, and his face had a puzzled expression. He went back to his office and shut the door.

I went the other way, about half the distance along the hall. A door on the side away from Sunset was lettered: JOHN D. ARBOGAST, EXAMINER OF QUESTIONED DOCUMENTS. PRIVATE INVESTIGATOR. ENTER. The door opened without resistance onto a small windowless anteroom with a couple of easy chairs, some magazines, two chromium smoking stands. There were two floor lamps and a ceiling fixture, all lighted. A door on the other side of the cheap but thick new rug was lettered: JOHN D. ARBOGAST, EXAMINER OF QUESTIONED DOCUMENTS. PRIVATE.

A buzzer had rung when I opened the outer door and gone on ringing until it closed. Nothing happened. Nobody was in the waiting room. The inner door didn't open. I went over and listened at the panel--no sound of conversation inside. I knocked. That didn't buy me anything either. I tried the knob. It turned, so I opened the door and went in.

This room had two north windows, both curtained at the sides and both shut tight. There was dust on the sills. There was a desk, two filing cases, a carpet which was just a carpet, and walls which were just walls. To the left another door with a glass panel was lettered: JOHN D. ARBOGAST. LABORATORY. PRIVATE.

I had an idea I might be able to remember the name.

The room in which I stood was small. It seemed almost too small even for the pudgy hand that rested on the edge of the desk, motionless, holding a fat pencil like a carpenter's pencil. The hand had a wrist, hairless as a plate. A buttoned shirt cuff, not too clean,

9

came down out of a coat sleeve. The rest of the sleeve dropped over the far edge of the desk out of sight. The desk was less than six feet long, so he couldn't have been a very tall man. The hand and the ends of the sleeves were all I saw of him from where I stood. I went quietly back through the anteroom and fixed its door so that it couldn't be opened from the outside and put out the three lights and went back to the private office. I went around an end of the desk.

He was fat all right, enormously fat, fatter by far than Anna Halsey. His face, what I could see of it, looked about the size of a basket ball. It had a pleasant pinkness, even now. He was kneeling on the floor. He had his large head against the sharp inner corner of the kneehole of the desk, and his left hand was flat on the floor with a piece of yellow paper under it. The fingers were outspread as much as such fat fingers could be, and the yellow paper showed between. He looked as if he were pushing hard on the floor, but he wasn't really. What was holding him up was his own fat. His body was folded down against his enormous thighs, and the thickness and fatness of them held him that way, kneeling, poised solid. It would have taken a couple of good blocking backs to knock him over. That wasn't a very nice idea at the moment, but I had it just the same. I took time out and wiped the back of my neck, although it was not a warm day.

His hair was gray and clipped short and his neck had as many folds as a concertina. His feet were small, as the feet of fat men often are, and they were in black shiny shoes which were sideways on the carpet and close together and neat and nasty. He wore a dark suit that needed cleaning. I leaned down and buried my fingers in the bottomless fat of his neck. He had an artery in there somewhere, probably, but I couldn't find it and he didn't need it any more anyway. Between his bloated knees on the carpet a dark stain had spread and spread--

I knelt in another place and lifted the pudgy fingers that were holding down the piece of yellow paper. They were cool, but not cold, and soft and a little sticky. The paper was from a scratch pad. It would have been very nice if it had had a message on it, but it hadn't. There were vague meaningless marks, not words, not even letters. He had tried to write something after he was shot--perhaps even thought he *was* writing something--but all he managed was some hen scratches.

He had slumped down then, still holding the paper, pinned it to the floor with his fat hand, held on to the fat pencil with his other hand, wedged his torso against his huge thighs, and so died. John D. Arbogast. Examiner of Questioned Documents. Private. Very damned private. He had said "yeah" to me three times over the phone.

And here he was.

I wiped doorknobs with my handkerchief, put off the lights in the anteroom, left the outer door so that it was locked from the outside, left the hallway, left the building and left the neighborhood. So far as I could tell nobody saw me go. So far as I could tell.

3

The El Milano was, as Anna had told me, in the 1900 block on North Sycamore. It was most of the block. I parked fairly near the ornamental forecourt and went along to the pale blue neon sign over the entrance to the basement garage. I walked down a railed ramp into a bright space of glistening cars and cold air. A trim light-colored Negro in a spotless coverall suit with blue cuffs came out of a glass office. His black hair was as smooth as a bandleader's.

"Busy?" I asked him.

"Yes and no, sir."

"I've got a car outside that needs a dusting. About five bucks worth of dusting."

It didn't work. He wasn't the type. His chestnut eyes became thoughtful and remote. "That is a good deal of dusting, sir. May I ask if anything else would be included?"

"A little. Is Miss Harriet Huntress' car in?"

He looked. I saw him look along the glistening row at a canary-yellow convertible which was about as inconspicuous as a privy on the front lawn.

"Yes, sir. It is in."

"I'd like her apartment number and a way to get up there without going through the lobby. I'm a private detective." I showed him a buzzer. He looked at the buzzer. It failed to amuse him.

He smiled the faintest smile I ever saw. "Five dollars is nice money, sir, to a working man. It falls a little short of being nice enough to make me risk my position. About from here to Chicago short, sir. I suggest that you save your five dollars, sir, and try the customary mode of entry."

"You're quite a guy," I said. "What are you going to be when you grow up--a five-foot shelf?"

"I am already grown up, sir. I am thirty-four years old, married happily, and have two children. Good afternoon, sir."

He turned on his heel. "Well, goodbye," I said. "And pardon my whiskey breath. I just got in from Butte."

I went back up along the ramp and wandered along the street to where I should have gone in the first place. I might have known that five bucks and a buzzer wouldn't buy me anything in a place like the El Milano.

The Negro was probably telephoning the office right now.

The building was a huge white stucco affair, Moorish in style, with great fretted lanterns in the forecourt and huge date palms. The entrance was at the inside corner of an L, up marble steps, through an arch framed in California or dishpan mosaic.

A doorman opened the door for me and I went in. The lobby was not quite as big as the Yankee Stadium. It was floored with a pale blue carpet with sponge rubber underneath. It was so soft it made me want to lie down and roll. I waded over to the desk and put an elbow on it and was stared at by a pale thin clerk with one of those mustaches that get stuck under your fingernail. He toyed with it and looked past my shoulder at an Ali Baba oil jar big enough to keep a tiger in.

"Miss Huntress in?"

"Who shall I announce?"

"Mr. Marty Estel."

That didn't take any better than my play in the garage. He leaned on something with his left foot. A blue-and-gilt door opened at the end of the desk and a large sandy-haired man with cigar ash on his vest came out and leaned absently on the end of the desk and stared at the Ali Baba oil jar, as if trying to make up his mind whether it was a spittoon.

The clerk raised his voice. "You are Mr. Marty Estel?"

"From him."

"Isn't that a little different? And what is your name, sir, if one may ask?"

"One may ask," I said. "One may not be told. Such are my orders. Sorry to be stubborn and all that rot."

He didn't like my manner. He didn't like anything about me. "I'm afraid I can't announce you," he said coldly. "Mr. Hawkins, might I have your advice on a matter?"

The sandy-haired man took his eyes off the oil jar and slid along the desk until he was within blackjack range of me.

"Yes, Mr. Gregory?" he yawned.

"Nuts to both of you," I said. "And that includes your lady friends."

Hawkins grinned. "Come into my office, bo. We'll kind of see if we can get you straightened out."

I followed him into the doghole he had come out of. It was large enough for a pint-sized desk, two chairs, a knee-high cuspidor, and an open box of cigars. He placed his rear end against the desk and grinned at me sociably.

"Didn't play it very smooth, did you, bo? I'm the house man here. Spill it."

"Some days I feel like playing smooth," I said, "and some days I feel like playing it like a waffle iron." I got my wallet out and showed him the buzzer and the small photostat of my license behind a celluloid window.

"One of the boys, huh?" He nodded. "You ought to of asked for me in the first place."

"Sure. Only I never heard of you. I want to see this Huntress frail. She doesn't know me, but I have business with her, and it's not noisy business."

He made a yard and half sideways and cocked his cigar in the other corner of his mouth. He looked at my right eyebrow. "What's the gag? Why try to apple-polish the dinge downstairs? You gettin' any expense money?"

"Could be."

"I'm nice people," he said. "But I gotta protect the guests."

"You're almost out of cigars," I said, looking at the ninety or so in the box. I lifted a couple, smelled them, tucked a folded ten-dollar bill below them and put them back.

"That's cute," he said. "You and me could get along. What you want done?"

"Tell her I'm from Marty Estel. She'll see me."

"It's the job if I get a kickback."

"You won't. I've got important people behind me."

I started to reach for my ten, but he pushed my hand away. "I'll take a chance," he said. He reached for his phone and asked for Suite 814 and began to hum. His humming sounded like a cow being sick. He leaned forward suddenly and his face became a honeyed smile. His voice dripped.

"Miss Huntress? This is Hawkins, the house man. Hawkins. Yeah...Hawkins. Sure, you meet a lot of people, Miss Huntress. Say, there's a gentleman in my office wanting to see you with a message from Mr. Estel. We can't let him up without your say so, because he don't want to give us no name...Yeah, Hawkins, the house detective, Miss Huntress. Yeah, he says you don't know him personal, but he looks O.K. to

15

me...O.K. Thanks a lot, Miss Huntress. Serve him right up."

He put the phone down and patted it gently.

"All you needed was some background music," I said.

"You can ride up," he said dreamily. He reached absently into his cigar box and removed the folded bill. "A darb," he said softly. "Every time I think of that dame I have to go out and walk around the block. Let's go."

We went out to the lobby again and Hawkins took me to the elevator and high-signed me in.

As the elevator doors closed I saw him on his way to the entrance, probably for his walk around the block.

The elevator had a carpeted floor and mirrors and indirect lighting. It rose as softly as the mercury in a thermometer. The doors whispered open, I wandered over the moss they used for a hall carpet and came to a door marked 814. I pushed a little button beside it, chimes rang inside and the door opened.

She wore a street dress of pale green wool and a small cockeyed hat that hung on her ear like a butterfly. Her eyes were wide-set and there was thinking room between them. Their color was lapis-lazuli blue and the color of her hair was dusky red, like a fire under control but still dangerous. She was too tall to be cute. She wore plenty of make-up in the right places and the cigarette she was poking at me had a built-on mouthpiece about three inches long. She didn't look hard, but she looked as if she had heard all the answers and remembered the ones she thought she might be able to use sometime.

She looked me over coolly. "Well, what's the message, brown-eyes?"

"I'd have to come in," I said. "I never could talk on my feet."

She laughed disinterestedly and I slid past the end of her cigarette into a long rather narrow room with plenty of nice furniture, plenty of windows, plenty of drapes, plenty of everything. A fire blazed behind a screen, a big log on top of a gas teaser. There was a silk Oriental rug in front of a nice rose davenport in front of the nice fire, and beside that there was Scotch and swish on a tabouret, ice in a bucket, everything to make a man feel at home.

"You'd better have a drink," she said. "You probably can't talk without a glass in your hand."

I sat down and reached for the Scotch. The girl sat in a deep chair and crossed her knees. I thought of Hawkins walking around the block. I could see a little something in his point of view.

"So you're from Marty Estel," she said, refusing a drink.

"Never met him."

"I had an idea to that effect. What's the racket, bum? Marty will love to hear how you used his name."

"I'm shaking in my shoes. What made you let me up?"

"Curiosity. I've been expecting lads like you any day. I never dodge trouble. Some kind of a dick, aren't you?"

I lit a cigarette and nodded. "Private. I have a little deal to propose."

"Propose it." She yawned.

"How much will you take to lay off young Jeeter?"

She yawned again. "You interest me--so little I could hardly tell you."

"Don't scare me to death. Honest, how much are you asking? Or is that an insult?"

She smiled. She had a nice smile. She had lovely teeth. "I'm a bad girl now," she said. "I don't have to ask. They bring it to me, tied up with ribbon."

"The old man's a little tough. They say he draws a lot of water."

"Water doesn't cost much."

I nodded and drank some more of my drink. It was good Scotch. In fact it was perfect. "His idea is you get nothing. You get smeared. You get put in the middle. I can't see it that way."

"But you're working for him."

"Sounds funny, doesn't it? There's probably a smart way to play this, but I just can't think of it at the moment. How much would you take--or would you?"

"How about fifty grand?"

"Fifty grand for you and another fifty for Marty?"

She laughed. "Now, you ought to know Marty wouldn't like me to mix in his business. I was just thinking of my end."

She crossed her legs the other way. I put another lump of ice in my drink.

"I was thinking of five hundred," I said.

"Five hundred what?" She looked puzzled.

"Dollars--not Rolls-Royces."

She laughed heartily. "You amuse me. I ought to tell you to go to hell, but I like brown eyes. Warm brown eyes with flecks of gold in them."

"You're throwing it away. I don't have a nickel."

She smiled and fitted a fresh cigarette between her lips. I went over to light it for her. Her eyes came up and looked into mine. Hers had sparks in them.

"Maybe I have a nickel already," she said softly.

18

"Maybe that's why he hired the fat boy--so you couldn't make him dance." I sat down again.

"Who hired what fat boy?"

"Old Jeeter hired a fat boy named Arbogast. He was on the case before me. Didn't you know? He got bumped off this afternoon."

I said it quite casually for the shock effect, but she didn't move. The provocative smile didn't leave the corners of her lips. Her eyes didn't change. She made a dim sound with her breath.

"Does it have to have something to do with me?" she asked quietly.

"I don't know. I don't know who murdered him. It was done in his office, around noon or a little later. It may not have anything to do with the Jeeter case. But it happened pretty pat--just after I had been put on the job and before I got a chance to talk to him."

She nodded. "I see. And you think Marty does things like that. And of course you told the police?"

"Of course I did not."

"You're giving away a little weight there, brother."

"Yeah. But let's get together on a price and it had better be low. Because whatever the cops do to me they'll do plenty to Marty Estel and you when they get the story--if they get it."

"A little spot of blackmail," the girl said coolly. "I think I might call it that. Don't go too far with me, brown-eyes. By the way, do I know your name?"

"Philip Marlowe."

"Then listen, Philip. I was in the Social Register once. My family were nice people. Old man Jeeter ruined my father-- all proper and legitimate, the way that kind of heel ruins people--but he ruined him, and my father committed suicide, and my mother died and

19

I've got a kid sister back East in school and perhaps I'm not too damn particular how I get the money to take care of her. And maybe I'm going to take care of old Jeeter one of these days, too--even if I have to marry his son to do it."

"Stepson, adopted son," I said. "No relation at all."

"It'll hurt him just as hard, brother. And the boy will have plenty of the long green in a couple of years. I could do worse--even if he does drink too much."

"You wouldn't say that in front of him, lady."

"No? Take a look behind you, gumshoe. You ought to have the wax taken out of your ears."

I stood up and turned fast. He stood about four feet from me. He had come out of some door and sneaked across the carpet and I had been too busy being clever with nothing on the ball to hear him. He was big, blond, dressed in a rough sporty suit, with a scarf and open-necked shirt. He was red-faced and his eyes glittered and they were not focusing any too well. He was a bit drunk for that early in the day.

"Beat it while you can still walk," he sneered at me. "I heard it. Harry can say anything she likes about me. I like it. Dangle, before I knock your teeth down your throat!"

The girl laughed behind me. I didn't like that. I took a step towards the big blond boy. His eyes blinked. Big as he was, he was a pushover.

"Ruin him, baby," the girl said coldly behind my back. "I love to see these hard numbers bend at the knees."

I looked back at her with a leer. That was a mistake. He was wild, probably, but he could still hit a wall that didn't jump. He hit me while I was looking back over my shoulder. It hurts to be hit that way. He hit me plenty hard, on the back end of the jawbone.

I went over sideways, tried to spread my legs, and slid on the silk rug. I did a nose dive somewhere or other and my head was not as hard as the piece of furniture it smashed into.

For a brief blurred moment I saw his red face sneering down at me in triumph. I think I was a little sorry for him--even then.

Darkness folded down and I went out.

4

When I came to, the light from the windows across the room was hitting me square in the eyes. The back of my head ached. I felt it and it was sticky. I moved around slowly, like a cat in a strange house, got up on my knees and reached for the bottle of Scotch on the tabouret at the end of the davenport. By some miracle I hadn't knocked it over. Falling I had hit my head on the clawlike leg of a chair. That had hurt me a lot more than young Jeeter's haymaker. I could feel the sore place on my jaw all right, but it wasn't important enough to write in my diary.

I got up on my feet, took a swig of the Scotch and looked around. There wasn't anything to see. The room was empty. It was full of silence and the memory of a nice perfume. One of those perfumes you don't notice until they are almost gone, like the last leaf on a tree. I felt my head again, touched the sticky place with my handkerchief, decided it wasn't worth yelling about, and took another drink.

I sat down with the bottle on my knees, listening to traffic noise somewhere, far off. It was a nice room.

Miss Harriet Huntress was a nice girl. She knew a few wrong numbers, but who didn't? I should criticize a little thing like that. I took another drink. The level in the bottle was a lot lower now. It was smooth and you hardly noticed it going down. It didn't take half your tonsils with it, like some of the stuff I had to drink. I took some more. My head felt all right now. I felt fine. I felt like singing the Prologue to Pagliacci. Yes, she was a nice girl. If she was paying her own rent, she was doing right well. I was for her. She was swell. I used some more of her Scotch.

The bottle was still half full. I shook it gently, stuffed it in my overcoat pocket, put my hat somewhere on my head and left. I made the elevator without hitting the walls on either side of the corridor, floated downstairs, strolled out into the lobby.

Hawkins, the house dick, was leaning on the end of the desk again, staring at the Ali Baba oil jar. The same clerk was nuzzling at the same itsy-bitsy mustache. I smiled at him. He smiled back. Hawkins smiled at me. I smiled back. Everybody was swell.

I made the front door the first time and gave the doorman two bits and floated down the steps and along the walk to the street and my car. The swift California twilight was falling. It was a lovely night. Venus in the west was as bright as a street lamp, as bright as life, as bright as Miss Huntress' eyes, as bright as a bottle of Scotch. That reminded me. I got the square bottle out and tapped it with discretion, corked it, and tucked it away again. There was still enough to get home on.

I crashed five red lights on the way back but my luck was in and nobody pinched me. I parked more or less in front of my apartment house and more or less near the curb. I rode to my floor in the elevator, had a little trouble opening the doors and helped myself out with my bottle. I got the key into my door and unlocked it and stepped inside and found the light switch. I took a little more of my medicine before exhausting myself any further. Then I started for the kitchen to get some ice and ginger ale for a real drink.

I thought there was a funny smell in the apartment-- nothing I could put a name to offhand--a sort of medicinal smell. I hadn't put it there and it hadn't been there when I went out. But I felt too well to argue about it. I started for the kitchen, got about halfway there.

They came out at me, almost side by side, from the dressing room beside the wall bed--two of them--with guns. The tall one was grinning. He had his hat low on his forehead and he had a wedge-shaped face that ended in a point, like the bottom half of the ace of diamonds. He had dark moist eyes and a nose so bloodless that it might have been made of white wax. His gun was a Colt Woodsman with a long barrel and the front sight filed off. That meant he thought he was good.

The other was a little terrier-like punk with bristly reddish hair and no hat and watery blank eyes and bat ears and small feet in dirty white sneakers. He had an automatic that looked too heavy for him to hold up, but he seemed to like holding it. He breathed open- mouthed and noisily and the smell I had noticed came from him in waves--menthol.

"Reach, you bastard," he said.

I put my hands up. There was nothing else to do.

The little one circled around to the side and came at me from the side. "Tell us we can't get away with it," he sneered.

"You can't get away with it," I said.

The tall one kept on grinning loosely and his nose kept on looking as if it was made of white wax. The little one spat on my carpet. "Yah!" He came close to me, leering, and made a pass at my chin with the big gun.

I dodged. Ordinarily that would have been just something which, in the circumstances, I had to take and like. But I was feeling better than ordinary. I was a world-beater. I took them in sets, guns and all. I took the little man around the throat and jerked him hard against my stomach, put a hand over his little gun hand and knocked the gun to the floor. It was easy. Nothing was bad about it but his breath. Blobs of saliva came out on his lips. He spit curses.

The tall man stood and leered and didn't shoot. He didn't move. His eyes looked a little anxious, I thought, but I was too busy to make sure. I went down behind the little punk, still holding him, and got hold of his gun. That was wrong. I ought to have pulled my own.

I threw him away from me and he reeled against a chair and fell down and began to kick the chair savagely. The tall man laughed.

"It ain't got any firing pin in it," he said.

"Listen," I told him earnestly, "I'm half full of good Scotch and ready to go places and get things done. Don't waste much of my time. What do you boys want?"

"It still ain't got any firing pin in it," Waxnose said. "Try and see. I don't never let Frisky carry a loaded rod. He's too impulsive. You got a nice arm action there, pal. I will say that for you."

Frisky sat up on the floor and spat on the carpet again and laughed. I pointed the muzzle of the big automatic at the floor and squeezed the trigger. It clicked dryly, but from the balance it felt as if it had cartridges in it.

"We don't mean no harm," Waxnose said. "Not this trip. Maybe next trip? Who knows? Maybe you're a guy that will take a hint. Lay off the Jeeter kid is the word. See?"

"No."

"You won't do it?"

"No, I don't see. Who's the Jeeter kid?"

Waxnose was not amused. He waved his long .22 gently. "You oughta get your memory fixed, pal, about the same time you get your door fixed. A pushover that was. Frisky just blew it in with his breath."

"I can understand that," I said.

"Gimme my gat," Frisky yelped. He was up off the floor again, but this time he rushed his partner instead of me.

"Lay off, dummy," the tall one said. "We just got a message for a guy. We don't blast him. Not today."

"Says you!" Frisky snarled and tried to grab the .22 out of Waxnose's hand. Waxnose threw him to one side without trouble but the interlude allowed me to switch the big automatic to my left hand and jerk out my Luger. I showed it to Waxnose. He nodded, but did not seem impressed.

"He ain't got no parents," he said sadly. "I just let him run around with me. Don't pay him no attention unless he bites you. We'll be on our way now. You get the idea. Lay off the Jeeter kid."

"You're looking at a Luger," I said. "Who is the Jeeter kid? And maybe we'll have some cops before you leave."

He smiled wearily. "Mister, I pack this small-bore because I can shoot. If you think you can take me, go to it."

"O.K.," I said. "Do you know anybody named Arbogast?"

"I meet such a lot of people," he said, with another weary smile. "Maybe yes, maybe no. So long, pal. Be pure."

He strolled over to the door, moving a little sideways, so that he had me covered all the time, and I had him covered, and it was just a case of who shot first and straightest, or whether it was worthwhile to shoot at all, or whether I could hit anything with so much nice warm Scotch in me. I let him go. He didn't look like a killer to me, but I could have been wrong.

The little man rushed me again while I wasn't thinking about him. He clawed his big automatic out of my left hand, skipped over to the door, spat on the carpet again, and slipped out. Waxnose backed after him--long sharp face, white nose, pointed chin, weary expression. I wouldn't forget him.

He closed the door softly and I stood there, foolish, holding my gun. I heard the elevator come up and go down again and stop. I still stood there. Marty Estel wouldn't be very likely to hire a couple of comics like that to throw a scare into anybody. I thought about that, but thinking got me nowhere. I remembered the half-bottle of Scotch I had left and went into executive session with it.

An hour and a half later I felt fine, but I still didn't have any ideas. I just felt sleepy.

The jarring of the telephone bell woke me. I had dozed off in the chair, which was a bad mistake, because I woke up with two flannel blankets in my mouth, a splitting headache, a bruise on the back of my head and another on my jaw, neither of them larger than a Yakima apple, but sore for all that. I felt terrible. I felt like an amputated leg.

I crawled over to the telephone and humped myself in a chair beside it and answered it. The voice dripped icicles.

"Mr. Marlowe? This is Mr. Jeeter. I believe we met this morning. I'm afraid I was a little stiff with you."

"I'm a little stiff myself. Your son poked me in the jaw. I mean your stepson, or your adopted son--or whatever he is."

"He is both my stepson and my adopted son. Indeed?" He sounded interested. "And where did you meet him?"

"In Miss Huntress' apartment."

"Oh I see." There had been a sudden thaw. The icicles had melted. "Very interesting. What did Miss Huntress have to say?"

"She liked it. She liked him poking me in the jaw."

"I see. And why did he do that?"

"She had him hid out. He overheard some of our talk. He didn't like it."

"I see. I have been thinking that perhaps some consideration--not large, of course--should be granted to her for her co-operation. That is, if we can secure it."

"Fifty grand is the price."

"I'm afraid I don't--"

"Don't kid me," I snarled. "Fifty thousand dollars. Fifty grand. I offered her five hundred--just for a gag."

"You seem to treat this whole business in a spirit of considerable levity," he snarled back. "I am not accustomed to that sort of thing and I don't like it."

I yawned. I didn't give a damn if school kept in or not. "Listen, Mr. Jeeter, I'm a great guy to horse around, but I have my mind on the job just the same. And there are some very unusual angles to this case. For instance a couple of gunmen just stuck me up in my apartment here and told me to lay off the Jeeter case. I don't see why it should get so tough."

"Good heavens!" He sounded shocked. "I think you had better come to my house at once and we will discuss matters. I'll send my car for you. Can you come right away?"

"Yeah. But I can drive myself. I--"

"No. I'm sending my car and chauffeur. His name is George; you may rely upon him absolutely. He should be there in about twenty minutes."

"O.K.," I said. "That just gives me time to drink my dinner. Have him park around the corner of Kenmore, facing towards Franklin." I hung up.

When I'd had a hot-and-cold shower and put on some clean clothes I felt more respectable. I had a couple of drinks, small ones for a change, and put a light overcoat on and went down to the street.

The car was there already. I could see it half a block down the side street. It looked like a new market opening. It had a couple of headlamps like the one on the front end of a streamliner, two amber foglights hooked to the front fender, and a couple of sidelights as big as ordinary headlights. I came up beside it and stopped and a man stepped out of the shadows, tossing a cigarette over his shoulder with a neat flip of the wrist. He was tall, broad, dark, wore a peaked cap, a Russian tunic with a Sam Browne belt, shiny leggings and breeches that flared like an English staff major's whipcords.

"Mr. Marlowe?" He touched the peak of his cap with a gloved forefinger.

"Yeah," I said. "At ease. Don't tell me that's old man Jeeter's car."

"One of them." It was a cool voice that could get fresh.

He opened the rear door and I got in and sank down into the cushions and George slid under the wheel and started the big car. It moved away from the curb and around the corner with as much noise as a bill makes in a wallet. We went west. We seemed to be drifting with the current, but we passed everything. We slid through the heart of Hollywood, the west end of it, down to the Strip and along the glitter of that to the cool quiet of Beverly Hills where the bridle path divides the boulevard.

We gave Beverly Hills the swift and climbed along the foothills, saw the distant lights of the university buildings and swung north into Bel-Air. We began to slide up long narrow streets with high walls and no sidewalks and big gates. Lights on mansions glowed politely through the early night. Nothing stirred. There was no sound but the soft purr of the tires on concrete. We swung left again and I caught a sign which read Calvello Drive. Halfway up this George started to swing the car wide to make a left turn in at a pair of twelve-foot wrought-iron gates. Then something happened.

A pair of lights flared suddenly just beyond the gates and a horn screeched and a motor raced. A car charged at us fast. George straightened out with a flick of the wrist, braked the car and slipped off his right glove, all in one motion.

The car came on, the lights swaying. "Damn drunk," George swore over his shoulder.

It could be. Drunks in cars go all kinds of places to drink. It could be. I slid down onto the floor of the car and yanked the Luger from under my arm and reached up to open the catch. I opened the door a little and held it that way, looking over the sill. The headlights hit me in the face and I ducked, then came up again as the beam passed.

The other car jammed to a stop. Its door slammed open and a figure jumped out of it, waving a gun and shouting. I heard the voice and knew.

"Reach, you bastards!" Frisky screamed at us.

George put his left hand on the wheel and I opened my door a little more. The little man in the street was bouncing up and down and yelling. Out of the small dark car from which he had jumped came no sound except the noise of its motor.

"This is a heist!" Frisky yelled. "Out of there and line up, you sons of bitches!"

I kicked my door open and started to get out, the Luger down at my side.

"You asked for it!" the little man yelled.

I dropped--fast. The gun in his hand belched flame. Somebody must have put a firing pin in it. Glass smashed behind my head. Out of the corner of my eye, which oughtn't to have had any corners at that particular moment, I saw George make a movement as smooth as a ripple of water. I brought the Luger up and started to squeeze the trigger, but a shot crashed beside me--George.

I held my fire. It wasn't needed now.

The dark car lurched forward and started down the hill furiously. It roared into the distance while the little man out in the middle of the pavement was still reeling grotesquely in the light reflected from the walls.

There was something dark on his face that spread. His gun bounded along the concrete. His little legs buckled and he plunged sideways and rolled and then, very suddenly, became still.

George said, "Yah!" and sniffed at the muzzle of his revolver.

"Nice shooting." I got out of the car, stood there looking at the little man--a crumpled nothing. The dirty white of his sneakers gleamed a little in the side glare of the car's lights.

George got out beside me. "Why me, brother?"

"I didn't fire. I was watching that pretty hip draw of yours. It was sweeter than honey."

"Thanks, pal. They were after Mister Gerald, of course. I usually ferry him home from the club about this time, full of liquor and bridge losses."

We went over to the little man and looked down at him. He wasn't anything to see. He was just a little man who was dead, with a big slug in his face and blood on him.

"Turn some of those damn lights off," I growled. "And let's get away from here fast."

"The house is just across the street." George sounded as casual as if he had just shot a nickel in a slot machine instead of a man.

"The Jeeters are out of this, if you like your job. You ought to know that. We'll go back to my place and start all over."

"I get it," he snapped, and jumped back into the big car. He cut the foglights and the sidelights and I got in beside him in the front seat.

We straightened out and started up the hill, over the brow. I looked back at the broken window. It was the small one at the extreme back of the car and it wasn't shatterproof. A large piece was gone from it. They could fit that, if they got around to it, and make some evidence. I didn't think it would matter, but it might.

At the crest of the hill a large limousine passed us going down. Its dome light was on and in the interior, as in a lighted showcase, an elderly couple sat stiffly, taking the royal salute. The man was in evening clothes, with a white scarf and a crush hat. The woman was in furs and diamonds.

George passed them casually, gunned the car and we made a fast right turn into a dark street. "There's a couple of good dinners all shot to hell," he drawled, "and I bet they don't even report it."

"Yeah. Let's get back home and have a drink," I said. "I never really got to like killing people."

5

We sat with some of Miss Harriet Huntress' Scotch in our glasses and looked at each other across the rims. George looked nice with his cap off. His head was clustered over with wavy dark-brown hair and his teeth were very white and clean. He sipped his drink and nibbled a cigarette at the same time. His snappy black eyes had a cool glitter in them.

"Yale?" I asked.

"Dartmouth, if it's any of your business."

"Everything's my business. What's a college education worth these days?"

"Three squares and a uniform," he drawled.

"What kind of guy is young Jeeter?"

"Big blond bruiser, plays a fair game of golf, thinks he's hell with the women, drinks heavy but hasn't sicked up on the rugs so far."

"What kind of guy is old Jeeter?"

"He'd probably give you a dime--if he didn't have a nickel with him."

"Tsk, tsk, you're talking about your boss."

George grinned. "He's so tight his head squeaks when he takes his hat off. I always took chances. Maybe that's why I'm just somebody's driver. This is good Scotch."

I made another drink, which finished the bottle. I sat down again.

"You think those two gunnies were stashed out for Mister Gerald?"

"Why not? I usually drive him home about that time. Didn't today. He had a bad hangover and didn't go out until late. You're a dick, you know what it's all about, don't you?"

"Who told you I was a dick?"

"Nobody but a dick ever asked so goddam many questions."

I shook my head. "Uh-uh. I've asked you just six questions. Your boss has a lot of confidence in you. He must have told you."

The dark man nodded, grinned faintly and sipped. "The whole set-up is pretty obvious," he said. "When the car started to swing for the turn into the driveway these boys went to work. I don't figure they meant to kill anybody, somehow. It was just a scare. Only that little guy was nuts."

I looked at George's eyebrows. They were nice black eyebrows, with a gloss on them like horsehair.

"It doesn't sound like Marty Estel to pick that sort of helpers."

"Sure. Maybe that's why he picked that sort of helpers."

"You're smart. You and I can get along. But shooting that little punk makes it tougher. What will you do about that?"

"Nothing."

"O.K. If they get to you and tie it to your gun, if you still have the gun, which you probably won't, I suppose it will be passed off as an attempted stick-up. There's just one thing."

"What?" George finished his second drink, laid the glass aside, lit a fresh cigarette and smiled.

"It's pretty hard to tell a car from in front--at night. Even with all those lights. It might have been a visitor."

He shrugged and nodded. "But if it's a scare, that would do just as well. Because the family would hear about it and the old man would guess whose boys they were--and why."

"Hell, you really are smart," I said admiringly, and the phone rang.

It was an English-butler voice, very clipped and precise, and it said that if I was Mr. Philip Marlowe, Mr. Jeeter would like to speak to me. He came on at once, with plenty of frost.

"I must say that you take your time about obeying orders," he barked. "Or hasn't that chauffeur of mine--"

"Yeah, he got here, Mr. Jeeter," I said. "But we ran into a little trouble. George will tell you."

"Young man, when I want something done--"

"Listen, Mr. Jeeter, I've had a hard day. Your son punched me on the jaw and I fell and cut my head open. When I staggered back to my apartment, more dead than alive, I was stuck up by a couple of hard guys with guns who told me to lay off the Jeeter case. I'm doing my best but I'm feeling a little frail, so don't scare me."

"Young man--"

"Listen," I told him earnestly, "if you want to call all the plays in this game, you can carry the ball yourself. Or you can save yourself a lot of money and hire an order taker. I have to do things my way. Any cops visit you tonight?"

"Cops?" he echoed in a sour voice. "You mean policemen?"

"By all means--I mean policemen."

"And why should I see any policemen?" he almost snarled.

"There was a stiff in front of your gates half an hour ago. Stiff meaning dead man. He's quite small. You could sweep him up in a dustpan, if he bothers you."

"My God! Are you serious?"

"Yes. What's more he took a shot at George and me. He recognized the car. He must have been all set for your son, Mr. Jeeter."

A silence with barbs on it. "I thought you said a dead man," Mr. Jeeter's voice said very coldly. "Now you say he shot at you."

"That was while he wasn't dead," I said. "George will tell you. George--"

"You come out here at once!" he yelled at me over the phone. "At once, do you hear? At once!"

"George will tell you," I said softly and hung up.

George looked at me coldly. He stood up and put his cap on. "O.K., pal," he said. "Maybe some day I can put you on to a soft thing." He started for the door.

"It had to be that way. It's up to him. He'll have to decide."

"Nuts," George said, looking back over his shoulder. "Save your breath, shamus. Anything you say to me is just so much noise in the wrong place."

He opened the door, went out, shut it, and I sat there still holding the telephone, with my mouth open and nothing in it but my tongue and a bad taste on that.

I went out to the kitchen and shook the Scotch bottle, but it was still empty. I opened some rye and swallowed a drink and it tasted sour. Something was bothering me. I had a feeling it was going to bother me a lot more before I was through.

They must have missed George by a whisker. I heard the elevator come up again almost as soon as it had stopped going down. Solid steps grew louder along the hallway. A fist hit the door. I went over and opened it.

One was in brown, one in blue, both large, hefty and bored.

The one in brown pushed his hat back on his head with a freckled hand and said: "You Philip Marlowe?"

"Me," I said.

They rode me back into the room without seeming to. The one in blue shut the door. The one in brown palmed a shield and let me catch a glint of the gold and enamel.

"Finlayson, Detective Lieutenant working out of Central Homicide," he said. "This is Sebold, my partner. We're a couple of swell guys not to get funny with. We hear you're kind of sharp with a gun."

Sebold took his hat off and dusted his salt-and-pepper hair back with the flat of his hand. He drifted noiselessly out to the kitchen.

Finlayson sat down on the edge of a chair and flicked his chin with a thumbnail as square as an ice cube and yellow as a mustard plaster. He was older than Sebold, but not so good-looking. He had the frowsy expression of a veteran cop who hadn't got very far.

I sat down. I said: "How do you mean, sharp with a gun?"

"Shooting people is how I mean."

I lit a cigarette. Sebold came out of the kitchen and went into the dressing room behind the wall bed.

"We understand you're a private-license guy," Finlayson said heavily.

"That's right."

"Give." He held his hand out. I gave him my wallet. He chewed it over and handed it back. "Carry a gun?"

I nodded. He held out his hand for it. Sebold came out of the dressing room. Finlayson sniffed at the Luger, snapped the magazine out, cleared the breech and held the gun so that a little light shone up through the magazine opening into the breech end of the barrel. He looked down the muzzle, squinting. He handed the gun to Sebold. Sebold did the same thing.

"Don't think so," Sebold said. "Clean, but not that clean. Couldn't have been cleaned within the hour. A little dust."

"Right."

Finlayson picked the ejected shell off the carpet, pressed it into the magazine and snapped the magazine back in place. He handed me the gun. I put it back under my arm.

"Been out anywhere tonight?" he asked tersely.

"Don't tell me the plot," I said. "I'm just a bit-player."

37

"Smart guy," Sebold said dispassionately. He dusted his hair again and opened a desk drawer. "Funny stuff. Good for a column. I like 'em that way--with my blackjack."

Finlayson sighed. "Been out tonight, shamus?"

"Sure. In and out all the time. Why?"

He ignored the question. "Where you been?"

"Out to dinner. Business call or two."

"Where at?"

"I'm sorry, boys. Every business has its private files."

"Had company, too," Sebold said, picking up George's glass and sniffing it. "Recent--within the hour."

"You're not that good," I told him sourly.

"Had a ride in a big Caddy?" Finlayson bored on, taking a deep breath. "Over West L. A. direction?"

"Had a ride in a Chrysler--over Vine Street direction."

"Maybe we better just take him down," Sebold said, looking at his fingernails.

"Maybe you better skip the gang-buster stuff and tell me what's stuck in your nose. I get along with cops-- except when they act as if the law is only for citizens."

Finlayson studied me. Nothing I had said made an impression on him. Nothing Sebold said made any impression on him. He had an idea and he was holding it like a sick baby.

"You know a little rat named Frisky Lavon?" he sighed. "Used to be a dummy-chucker, then found out he could bug his way outa raps. Been doing that for say twelve years. Totes a gun and acts simple. But he quit acting tonight at seven thirty about. Quit cold-- with a slug in his head."

"Never heard of him," I said.

"You bumped anybody off tonight?"

"I'd have to look at my notebook."

Sebold leaned forward politely. "Would you care for a smack in the kisser?" he inquired.

Finlayson held his hand out sharply. "Cut it, Ben. Cut it. Listen, Marlowe. Maybe we're going at this wrong. We're not talking about murder. Could have been legitimate. This Frisky Lavon got froze off tonight on Calvello Drive in Bel-Air. Out in the middle of the street. Nobody seen or heard anything. So we kind of want to know."

"All right," I growled. "What makes it my business? And keep that piano tuner out of my hair. He has a nice suit and his nails are clean, but he bears down on his shield too hard."

"Nuts to you," Sebold said.

"We got a funny phone call," Finlayson said. "Which is where you come in. We ain't just throwing our weight around. And we want a forty-five. They ain't sure what kind yet."

"He's smart. He threw it under the bar at Levy's," Sebold sneered.

"I never had a forty-five," I said. "A guy who needs that much gun ought to use a pick."

Finlayson scowled at me and counted his thumbs. Then he took a deep breath and suddenly went human on me. "Sure, I'm just a dumb flatheel," he said. "Anybody could pull my ears off and I wouldn't even notice it. Let's all quit horsing around and talk sense.

"This Frisky was found dead after a no-name phone call to West L. A. police. Found dead outside a big house belonging to a man named Jeeter who owns a string of investment companies. He wouldn't use a guy

39

like Frisky for a pen-wiper, so there's nothing in that. The servants didn't hear nothing, nor the servants at any of the four houses on the block. Frisky is lying in the street and somebody run over his foot, but what killed him was a forty-five slug smack in his face. West L. A. ain't hardly started the routine when some guy calls up Central and says to tell Homicide if they want to know who got Frisky Lavon, ask a private eye named Philip Marlowe, complete with address and everything, then a quick hang-up.

"O.K. The guy on the board gives me the dope and I don't know Frisky from a hole in my sock, but I ask Identification and sure enough they have him and just about the time I'm looking it over the flash comes from West L. A. and the description seems to check pretty close. So we get together and it's the same guy all right and the chief of detectives has us drop around here. So we drop around."

"So here you are," I said. "Will you have a drink?"

"Can we search the joint, if we do?"

"Sure. It's a good lead--that phone call, I mean--if you put in about six months on it."

"We already got that idea," Finlayson growled. "A hundred guys could have chilled this little wart, and two-three of them maybe could have thought it was a smart rib to pin it on you. Them two-three is what interests us."

I shook my head.

"No ideas at all, huh?"

"Just for wisecracks," Sebold said.

Finlayson lumbered to his feet. "Well, we gotta look around."

"Maybe we had ought to have brought a search warrant," Sebold said, tickling his upper lip with the end of his tongue.

"I don't *have* to fight this guy, do I?" I asked Finlayson. "I mean, is it all right if I leave him his gag lines and just keep my temper?"

Finlayson looked at the ceiling and said dryly: "His wife left him day before yesterday. He's just trying to compensate, as the fellow says."

Sebold turned white and twisted his knuckles savagely. Then he laughed shortly and got to his feet.

They went at it. Ten minutes of opening and shutting drawers and looking at the backs of shelves and under seat cushions and letting the bed down and peering into the electric refrigerator and the garbage pail fed them up.

They came back and sat down again. "Just a nut," Finlayson said wearily. "Some guy that picked your name outa the directory maybe. Could be anything."

"Now I'll get that drink."

"I don't drink," Sebold snarled.

Finlayson crossed his hands on his stomach. "That don't mean any liquor gets poured in the flowerpot, son."

I got three drinks and put two of them beside Finlayson. He drank half of one of them and looked at the ceiling. "I got another killing, too," he said thoughtfully. "A guy in your racket, Marlowe. A fat guy on Sunset. Name of Arbogast. Ever hear of him?"

"I thought he was a handwriting expert," I said.

"You're talking about police business," Sebold told his partner coldly.

"Sure. Police business that's already in the morning paper. This Arbogast was shot three times with a

41

twenty-two. Target gun. You know any crooks that pack that kind of heat?"

I held my glass tightly and took a long slow swallow. I hadn't thought Waxnose looked dangerous enough, but you never knew.

"I did," I said slowly. "A killer named Al Tessilore. But he's in Folsom. He used a Colt Woodsman."

Finlayson finished the first drink, used the second in about the same time, and stood up. Sebold stood up, still mad.

Finlayson opened the door. "Come on, Ben." They went out.

I heard their steps along the hall, the clang of the elevator once more. A car started just below in the street and growled off into the night.

"Clowns like that don't kill," I said out loud. But it looked as if they did.

I waited fifteen minutes before I went out again. The phone rang while I was waiting, but I didn't answer it.

I drove towards the El Milano and circled around enough to make sure I wasn't followed.

6

The lobby hadn't changed any. The blue carpet still tickled my ankles while I ambled over to the desk, the same pale clerk was handing a key to a couple of horse-faced females in tweeds, and when he saw me he put his weight on his left foot again and the door at the end of the desk popped open and out popped the fat and erotic Hawkins, with what looked like the same cigar stub in his face.

He hustled over and gave me a big warm smile this time, took hold of my arm. "Just the guy I was hoping to see," he chuckled. "Let's us go upstairs a minute."

"What's the matter?"

"Matter?" His smile became broad as the door to a two-car garage. "Nothing ain't the matter. This way."

He pushed me into the elevator and said "Eight" in a fat cheerful voice and up we sailed and out we got and slid along the corridor. Hawkins had a hard hand and knew where to hold an arm. I was interested enough to let him get away with it. He pushed the buzzer beside Miss Huntress' door and Big Ben chimed inside and the door opened and I was looking at a deadpan in a derby hat and a dinner coat. He had his right hand in the side pocket of the coat, and under the derby a pair of scarred eyebrows and under the eyebrows a pair of eyes that had as much expression as the cap on a gas tank.

The mouth moved enough to say: "Yeah?"

"Company for the boss," Hawkins said expansively.

"What company?"

"Let me play too," I said. "Limited Liability Company. Gimme the apple."

"Huh?" The eyebrows went this way and that and the jaw came out. "Nobody ain't kiddin' anybody, I hope."

"Now, now, gents--" Hawkins began.

A voice behind the derby-hatted man interrupted him. "What's the matter, Beef?"

"He's in a stew," I said.

"Listen, mugg--"

"Now, now, gents--" as before.

"Ain't nothing the matter," Beef said, throwing his voice over his shoulder as if it were a coil of rope.

43

"The hotel dick got a guy up here and he says he's company."

"Show the company in, Beef." I liked this voice. It was smooth quiet, and you could have cut your name in it with a thirty-pound sledge and a cold chisel.

"Lift the dogs," Beef said, and stood to one side.

We went in. I went first, then Hawkins, then Beef wheeled neatly behind us like a door. We went in so close together that we must have looked like a three-decker sandwich.

Miss Huntress was not in the room. The log in the fireplace had almost stopped smoldering. There was still that smell of sandalwood on the air. With it cigarette smoke blended.

A man stood at the end of the davenport, both hands in the pockets of a blue camel's hair coat with the collar high to a black snap-brim hat. A loose scarf hung outside his coat. He stood motionless, the cigarette in his mouth lisping smoke. He was tall, black-haired, suave, dangerous. He said nothing.

Hawkins ambled over to him. "This is the guy I was telling you about, Mr. Estel," the fat man burbled. "Come in earlier today and said he was from you. Kinda fooled me."

"Give him a ten, Beef."

The derby hat took its left hand from somewhere and there was a bill in it. It pushed the bill at Hawkins. Hawkins took the bill, blushing.

"This ain't necessary, Mr. Estel. Thanks a lot just the same."

"Scram."

"Huh?" Hawkins looked shocked.

"You heard him," Beef said truculently. "Want your fanny out the door first, huh?"

Hawkins drew himself up. "I gotta protect the tenants. You gentlemen know how it is. A man in a job like this."

"Yeah. Scram," Estel said without moving his lips.

Hawkins turned and went out quickly, softly. The door clicked gently shut behind him. Beef looked back at it, then moved behind me.

"See if he's rodded, Beef."

The derby hat saw if I was rodded. He took the Luger and went away from me. Estel looked casually at the Luger, back at me. His eyes held an expression of indifferent dislike.

"Name's Philip Marlowe, eh? A private dick."

"So what?" I said.

"Somebody's goin' to get somebody's face pushed into somebody's floor," Beef said coldly.

"Aw, keep that crap for the boiler room," I told him. "I'm sick of hard guys for this evening. I said 'so what,' and 'so what' is what I said."

Marty Estel looked mildly amused. "Hell, keep your shirt in. I've got to look after my friends, don't I? You know who I am. O.K., I know what you talked to Miss Huntress about. And I know something about you that you don't know I know."

"All right," I said. "This fat slob Hawkins collected ten from me for letting me up here this afternoon-- knowing perfectly well who I was--and he has just collected ten from your iron man for slipping me the nasty. Give me back my gun and tell me what makes my business your business."

"Plenty. First off, Harriet's not home. We're waiting for her on account of a thing that happened. I can't wait any longer. Got to go to work at the club. So what did you come after this time?"

45

"Looking for the Jeeter boy. Somebody shot at his car tonight. From now on he needs somebody to walk behind him."

"You think I play games like that?" Estel asked me coldly.

I walked over to a cabinet and opened it and found a bottle of Scotch. I twisted the cap off, lifted a glass from the tabouret and poured some out. I tasted it. It tasted all right.

I looked around for ice, but there wasn't any. It had all melted long since in the bucket.

"I asked you a question," Estel said gravely.

"I heard it. I'm making my mind up. The answer is, I wouldn't have thought it--no. But it happened. I was there. I was in the car--instead of young Jeeter. His father had sent for me to come to the house to talk things over."

"What things?"

I didn't bother to look surprised. "You hold fifty grand of the boy's paper. That looks bad for you, if anything happens to him."

"I don't figure it that way. Because that way I would lose my dough. The old man won't pay--granted. But I wait a couple of years and I collect from the kid. He gets his estate out of trust when he's twenty-eight. Right now he gets a grand a month and he can't even will anything, because it's still in trust. Savvy?"

"So you wouldn't knock him off," I said, using my Scotch. "But you might throw a scare into him."

Estel frowned. He discarded his cigarette into a tray and watched it smoke a moment before he picked it up again and snubbed it out. He shook his head.

"If you're going to bodyguard him, it would almost pay me to stand part of your salary, wouldn't it?

Almost. A man in my racket can't take care of everything. He's of age and it's his business who he runs around with. For instance, women. Any reason why a nice girl shouldn't cut herself a piece of five million bucks?"

I said: "I think it's a swell idea. What was it you knew about me that I didn't know you knew?"

He smiled, faintly. "What was it you were waiting to tell Miss Huntress--the thing that happened?"

He smiled faintly again.

"Listen, Marlowe, there are lots of ways to play any game. I play mine on the house percentage, because that's all I need to win. What makes me get tough?"

I rolled a fresh cigarette around in my fingers and tried to roll it around my glass with two fingers. "Who said you were tough? I always heard the nicest things about you."

Marty Estel nodded and looked faintly amused. "I have sources of information," he said quietly. "When I have fifty grand invested in a guy, I'm apt to find out a little about him. Jeeter hired a man named Arbogast to do a little work. Arbogast was killed in his office today--with a twenty-two. That could have nothing to do with Jeeter's business. But there was a tail on you when you went there and you didn't give it to the law. Does that make you and me friends?"

I licked the edge of my glass, nodded. "It seems it does."

"From now on just forget about bothering Harriet, see?"

"O.K."

"So we understand each other real good, now."

"Yeah."

"Well, I'll be going. Give the guy back his Luger, Beef."

The derby hat came over and smacked my gun into my hand hard enough to break a bone.

"Staying?" Estel asked, moving towards the door.

"I guess I'll wait a little while. Until Hawkins comes up to touch me for another ten."

Estel grinned. Beef walked in front of him wooden-faced to the door and opened it. Estel went out. The door closed. The room was silent. I sniffed at the dying perfume of sandalwood and stood motionless, looking around.

Somebody was nuts. I was nuts. Everybody was nuts. None of it fitted together worth a nickel. Marty Estel, as he said, had no good motive for murdering anybody, because that would be the surest way to kill chances to collect his money. Even if he had a motive for murdering anybody, Waxnose and Frisky didn't seem like the team he would select for the job. I was in bad with the police, I had spent ten dollars of my twenty expense money, and I didn't have enough leverage anywhere to lift a dime off a cigar counter.

I finished my drink, put the glass down, walked up and down the room, smoked a third cigarette, looked at my watch, shrugged and felt disgusted. The inner doors of the suite were closed. I went across to the one out of' which young Jeeter must have sneaked that afternoon. Opening it I looked into a bedroom done in ivory and ashes of roses. There was a big double bed with no footboard, covered with figured brocade. Toilet articles glistened on a built-in dressing table with a panel light. The light was lit. A small lamp on a table beside the door was lit also. A door near the dressing table showed the cool green of bathroom tiles.

I went over and looked in there. Chromium, a glass stall shower, monogrammed towels on a rack, a glass shelf for perfume and bath salts at the foot of the tub, everything nice and refined. Miss Huntress did herself well. I hoped she was paying her own rent. It didn't make any difference to me--I just liked it that way.

I went back towards the living room, stopped in the doorway to take another pleasant look around, and noticed something I ought to have noticed the instant I stepped into the room. I noticed the sharp tang of cordite on the air, almost, but not quite gone. And then I noticed something else.

The bed had been moved over until its head overlapped the edge of a closet door which was not quite closed. The weight of the bed was holding it from opening. I went over there to find out why it wanted to open. I went slowly and about halfway there I noticed that I was holding a gun in my hand.

I leaned against the closet door. It didn't move. I threw more weight against it. It still didn't move. Braced against it I pushed the bed away with my foot, gave ground slowly.

A weight pushed against me hard. I had gone back a foot or so before anything else happened. Then it happened suddenly. He came out--sideways, in a sort of roll. I put some more weight back on the door and held him like that a moment, looking at him.

He was still big, still blond, still dressed in rough sporty material, with scarf and open-necked shirt. But his face wasn't red any more.

I gave ground again and he rolled down the back of the door, turning a little like a swimmer in the surf, thumped the floor and lay there, almost on his back, still looking at me. Light from the bedside lamp glittered on his head. There was a scorched and soggy stain on the rough coat--about where his heart would be. So he wouldn't get that five million after all. And nobody would get anything and Marty Estel wouldn't get his fifty grand. Because young Mister Gerald was dead.

I looked back into the closet where he had been. Its door hung wide open now. There were clothes on racks, feminine clothes, nice clothes. He had been backed in among them, probably with his hands in the air and a gun against his chest. And then he had been shot dead, and whoever did it hadn't been quite quick enough or quite strong enough to get the door shut. Or had been scared and had just yanked the bed over against the door and left it that way.

Something glittered down on the floor. I picked it up. A small automatic, .25 caliber, a woman's purse gun with a beautifully engraved butt inlaid with silver and ivory. I put the gun in my pocket. That seemed a funny thing to do, too.

I didn't touch him. He was as dead as John D. Arbogast and looked a whole lot deader. I left the door open and listened, walked quickly back across the room and into the living room and shut the bedroom door, smearing the knob as I did it.

A lock was being tinkled at with a key. Hawkins was back again, to see what delayed me. He was letting himself in with his passkey.

I was pouring a drink when he came in.

He came well into the room, stopped with his feet planted and surveyed me coldly.

"I seen Estel and his boy leave," he said. "I didn't see you leave. So I come up. I gotta--"

"You gotta protect the guests," I said.

"Yeah. I gotta protect the guests. You can't stay up here, pal. Not without the lady of the house home."

"But Marty Estel and his hard boy can."

He came a little closer to me. He had a mean look in his eye. He had always had it, probably, but I noticed it more now.

"You don't want to make nothing of that, do you?" he asked me.

"No. Every man to his own chisel. Have a drink."

"That ain't your liquor."

"Miss Huntress gave me a bottle. We're pals. Marty Estel and I are pals. Everybody is pals. Don't you want to be pals?"

"You ain't trying to kid me, are you?"

"Have a drink and forget it."

I found a glass and poured him one. He took it.

"It's the job if anybody smells it on me," he said.

"Uh-huh."

He drank slowly, rolling it around on his tongue. "Good Scotch."

"Won't be the first time you tasted it, will it?"

He started to get hard again, then relaxed. "Hell, I guess you're just a kidder." He finished the drink, put the glass down, patted his lips with a large and very crumpled handkerchief and sighed.

"O.K.," he said. "But we'll have to leave now."

"All set. I guess she won't be home for a while. You see them go out?"

"Her and the boy friend. Yeah, long time ago."

I nodded. We went towards the door and Hawkins saw me out. He saw me downstairs and off the premises. But he didn't see what was in Miss Huntress' bedroom. I wondered if he would go back up. If he did, the Scotch bottle would probably stop him.

I got into my car and drove off home--to talk to Anna Halsey on the phone. There wasn't any case any more--for us. I parked close to the curb this time. I wasn't feeling gay any more. I rode up in the elevator and unlocked the door and clicked the light on.

Waxnose sat in my best chair, an unlit hand-rolled brown cigarette between his fingers, his bony knees crossed, and his long Woodsman resting solidly on his leg. He was smiling. It wasn't the nicest smile I ever saw.

"Hi, pal," he drawled. "You still ain't had that door fixed. Kind of shut it, huh?" His voice, for all the drawl, was deadly.

I shut the door, stood looking across the room at him.

"So you killed my pal," he said.

He stood up slowly, came across the room slowly and leaned the .22 against my throat. His smiling thin-lipped mouth seemed as expressionless, for all its smile, as his wax-white nose. He reached quietly under my coat and took the Luger. I might as well leave it home from now on. Everybody in town seemed to be able to take it away from me.

He stepped back across the room and sat down again in the chair.

"Steady does it," he said almost gently. "Park the body, friend. No false moves. No moves at all. You and me are at the jumping-off place. The clock's tickin' and we're waiting to go.

I sat down and stared at him. A curious bird. I moistened my dry lips. "You told me his gun had no firing pin," I said.

"Yeah. He fooled me on that, the little so-and-so. And I told you to lay off the Jeeter kid. That's cold

52

now. It's Frisky I'm thinking about. Crazy, ain't it? Me bothering about a dimwit like that, packin' him around with me, and letting him get hisself bumped off." He sighed and added simply, "He was my kid brother."

"I didn't kill him," I said.

He smiled a little more. He had never stopped smiling. The corners of his mouth just tucked in a little deeper.

"Yeah?"

He slid the safety catch off the Luger, laid it carefully on the arm of the chair at his right, and reached into his pocket. What he brought out made me as cold as an ice bucket.

It was a metal tube, dark and rough-looking, about four inches long and drilled with a lot of small holes. He held his Woodsman in his left hand and began to screw the tube casually on the end of it.

"Silencer," he said. "They're the bunk, I guess you smart guys think. This one ain't the bunk--not for three shots. I oughta know. I made it myself."

I moistened my lips again. "It'll work for one shot," I said. "Then it jams your action. That one looks like cast-iron. It will probably blow your hand off."

He smiled his waxy smile, screwed it on, slowly, lovingly, gave it a last hard turn and sat back relaxed. "Not this baby. She's packed with steel wool and that's good for three shots, like I said. Then you got to repack it. And there ain't enough back pressure to jam the action on this gun. You feel good? I'd like you to feel good."

"I feel swell, you sadistic son of a bitch," I said.

"I'm having you lie down on the bed after a while. You won't feel nothing. I'm kind of fussy about my killings. Frisky didn't feel nothing, I guess. You got him neat."

"You don't see good," I sneered. "The chauffeur got him with a Smith & Wesson forty-four. I didn't even fire."

"Uh-huh."

"O.K., you don't believe me," I said. "What did you kill Arbogast for? There was nothing fussy about that killing. He was just shot at his desk, three times with a twenty-two and he fell down on the floor. What did he ever do to your filthy little brother?"

He jerked the gun up, but his smile held. "You got guts," he said. "Who is this here Arbogast?"

I told him. I told him slowly and carefully, in detail. I told him a lot of things. And he began in some vague way to look worried. His eyes flickered at me, away, back again, restlessly, like a hummingbird.

"I don't know any party named Arbogast, pal," he said slowly. "Never heard of him. And I ain't shot any fat guys today."

"You killed him," I said. "And you killed young Jeeter--in the girl's apartment at the El Milano. He's lying there dead right now. You're working for Marty Estel. He's going to be awfully damn sorry about that kill. Go ahead and make it three in a row."

His face froze. The smile went away at last. His whole face looked waxy now. He opened his mouth and breathed through it, and his breath made a restless worrying sound. I could see the faint glitter of sweat on his forehead, and I could feel the cold from the evaporation of sweat on mine.

Waxnose said very gently: "I ain't killed anybody at all, friend. Not anybody. I wasn't hired to kill people.

54

Until Frisky stopped that slug I didn't have no such ideas. That's straight."

I tried not to stare at the metal tube on the end of the Woodsman.

A flame flickered at the back of his eyes, a small, weak, smoky flame. It seemed to grow larger and clearer. He looked down at the floor between his feet. I looked around at the light switch, but it was too far away. He looked up again. Very slowly he began to unscrew the silencer. He had it loose in his hand. He dropped it back into his pocket, stood up, holding the two guns, one in each hand. Then he had another idea. He sat down again, took all the shells out of the Luger quickly and threw it on the floor after them.

He came towards me softly across the room. "I guess this is your lucky day," he said. "I got to go a place and see a guy."

"I knew all along it was my lucky day. I've been feeling so good."

He moved delicately around me to the door and opened it a foot and started through the narrow opening, smiling again.

"I gotta see a guy," he said very gently, and his tongue moved along his lips.

"Not yet," I said, and jumped.

His gun hand was at the edge of the door, almost beyond the edge. I hit the door hard and he couldn't bring it in quickly enough. He couldn't get out of the way. I pinned him in the doorway, and used all the strength I had. It was a crazy thing. He had given me a break and all I had to do was to stand still and let him go. But I had a guy to see too--and I wanted to see him first.

Waxnose leered at me. He grunted. He fought with his hand beyond the door edge. I shifted and hit his jaw with all I had. It was enough. He went limp. I hit him again. His head bounced against the wood. I heard a light thud beyond the door edge. I hit him a third time. I never bit anything any harder.

I took my weight back from the door then and he slid towards me, blank-eyed, rubber-kneed and I caught him and twisted his empty hands behind him and let him fall. I stood over him panting. I went to the door. His Woodsman lay almost on the sill. I picked it up, dropped it into my pocket--not the pocket that held Miss Huntress' gun. He hadn't even found that.

There he lay on the floor. He was thin, he had no weight, but I panted just the same. In a little while his eyes flickered open and looked up at me.

"Greedy guy," he whispered wearily. "Why did I ever leave Saint Looey?"

I snapped handcuffs on his wrists and pulled him by the shoulders into the dressing room and tied his ankles with a piece of rope. I left him laying on his back, a little sideways, his nose as white as ever, his eyes empty now, his lips moving a little as if he were talking to himself. A funny lad, not all bad, but not so pure I had to weep over him either.

I put my Luger together and left with my three guns. There was nobody outside the apartment house.

7

The Jeeter mansion was on a nine- or ten-acre knoll, a big colonial pile with fat white columns and dormer windows and magnolias and a four-car garage. There was a circular parking space at the top of the driveway with two cars parked in it-- one was the big dreadnaught in which I'd ridden and the other a canary-yellow sports convertible I had seen before.

I rang a bell the size of a silver dollar. The door opened and a tall narrow cold-eyed bird in dark clothes looked out at me.

"Mr. Jeeter home? Mr. Jeeter, Senior?"

"May I ask who is calling?" The accent was a little too thick, like cut Scotch.

"Philip Marlowe. I'm working for him. Maybe I had ought to of gone to the servant's entrance."

He hitched a finger at a wing collar and looked at me without pleasure. "Aw, possibly. You may step in. I shall inform Mr. Jeeter. I believe he is engaged at the moment. Kindly wait 'ere in the 'all."

"The act stinks," I said. "English butlers aren't dropping their h's this year."

"Smart guy, huh?" he snarled, in a voice from not any farther across the Atlantic than Hoboken. "Wait here." He slid away.

I sat down in a carved chair and felt thirsty. After a while the butler came cat-footing back along the hall and jerked his chin at me unpleasantly.

We went along a mile of hallway. At the end it broadened without any doors into a huge sunroom. On the far side of the sunroom the butler opened a wide door and I stepped past him into an oval room with a black-and-silver oval rug, a black marble table in the middle of the rug, stiff high-backed carved chairs against the walls, a huge oval mirror with a rounded surface that made me look like a pygmy with water on the brain, and in the room three people.

By the door opposite where I came in, George the chauffeur stood stiffly in his neat dark uniform, with his peaked cap in his hand. In the least uncomfortable of the chairs sat Miss Harriet Huntress holding a glass in which there was half a drink. And around the silver margin of the oval rug, Mr. Jeeter, Senior, was trying his legs out in a brisk canter, still under wraps, but mad inside. His face was red and the veins on his nose were distended. His hands were in the pockets of a velvet smoking jacket. He wore a pleated shirt with a black pearl in the bosom, a batwing black tie and one of his patent-leather oxfords was unlaced.

He whirled and yelled at the butler behind me: "Get out and keep those doors shut! And I'm not at home to anybody, understand? Nobody!"

The butler closed the doors. Presumably, he went away. I didn't hear him go.

George gave me a cool one-sided smile and Miss Huntress gave me a bland stare over her glass. "You made a nice comeback," she said demurely.

"You took a chance leaving me alone in your apartment," I told her. "I might have sneaked some of your perfume.'

"Well, what do you want?" Jeeter yelled at me. "A nice sort of detective you turned out to be. I put you on a confidential job and you walk right in on Miss Huntress and explain the whole thing to her."

"It worked, didn't it?"

He stared. They all stared. "How do you know that?" he barked.

"I know a nice girl when I see one. She's here telling you she had an idea she got not to like, and for you to quit worrying about it. Where's Mister Gerald?"

Old man Jeeter stopped and gave me a hard level stare. "I still regard you as incompetent," he said. "My son is missing."

"I'm not working for you. I'm working for Anna Halsey. Any complaints you have to make should be addressed to her, Do I pour my own drink or do you have a flunky in a purple suit to do it? And what do you mean, your son is missing?"

"Should I give him the heave, sir?" George asked quietly.

Jeeter waved his hand at a decanter and siphon and glasses on the black marble table and started around the rug again. "Don't be silly," he snapped at George.

George flushed a little, high on his cheekbones. His mouth looked tough.

I mixed myself a drink and sat down with it and tasted it and asked again: "What do you mean your son is missing, Mr. Jeeter?"

"I'm paying you good money," he started to yell at me, still mad.

"When?"

He stopped dead in his canter and looked at me again. Miss Huntress laughed lightly. George scowled.

"What do you suppose I mean--my son is missing?" he snapped. "I should have thought that would be clear enough even to you. Nobody knows where he is. Miss Huntress doesn't know. I don't know. No one at any of the places where he might be known."

"But I'm smarter than they are," I said. "*I* know."

Nobody moved for a long minute. Jeeter stared at me fish-eyed. George stared at me. The girl stared at me. She looked puzzled. The other two just stared.

I looked at her. "Where did you go when you went out, if you're telling?"

Her dark blue eyes were water-clear. "There's no secret about it. We went out together--in a taxi. Gerald had had his driving license suspended for a month. Too

59

many tickets. We went down towards the beach and I had a change of heart, as you guessed. I decided I was just being a chiseler after all. I didn't want Gerald's money really. What I wanted was revenge. On Mr. Jeeter here for ruining my father. Done all legally of course, but done just the same. But I got myself in a spot where I couldn't have my revenge and not look like a cheap chiseler. So I told Gerald to find some other girl to play with. He was sore and we quarreled. I stopped the taxi and got out in Beverly Hills. He went on. I don't know where. Later I went back to the El Milano and got my car out of the garage and came here. To tell Mr. Jeeter to forget the whole thing and not bother to sick sleuths on to me."

"You say you went with him in a taxi," I said. "Why wasn't George driving him, if he couldn't drive himself?"

I stared at her, but I wasn't talking to her. Jeeter answered me, frostily. "George drove me home from the office, of course. At that time Gerald had already gone out. Is there anything important about that?"

I turned to him. "Yeah. There's going to be. Mister Gerald is at the El Milano. Hawkins the house dick told me. He went back there to wait for Miss Huntress and Hawkins let him into her apartment. Hawkins will do you those little favors--for ten bucks. He may be there still and he may not."

I kept on watching them. It was hard to watch all three of them. But they didn't move. They just looked at me.

"Well--I'm glad to hear it," old man Jeeter said. "I was afraid he was off somewhere getting drunk."

"No. He's not off anywhere getting drunk," I said. "By the way, among these places you called to see if he was there, you didn't call the El Milano?"

George nodded. "Yes, I did. They said he wasn't there. Looks like this house peeper tipped the phone girl off not to say anything."

"He wouldn't have to do that. She'd just ring the apartment and he wouldn't answer--naturally." I watched old man Jeeter hard then, with a lot of interest. It was going to be hard for him to take that up, but he was going to have to do it.

He did. He licked his lips first. "Why--naturally, if I may ask?" he said coldly.

I put my glass down on the marble table and stood against the wall, with my hands hanging free. I still tried to watch them--all three of them.

"Let's go back over this thing a little," I said. "We're all wise to the situation. I know George is, although he shouldn't be, being just a servant. I know Miss Huntress is. And of course you are, Mr. Jeeter. So let's see what we have got. We have a lot of things that don't add up, but I'm smart. I'm going to add them up anyhow. First-off a handful of photostats of notes from Marty Estel. Gerald denies having given these and Mr. Jeeter won't pay them, but he has a handwriting man named Arbogast check the signatures, to see if they look genuine. They do. They are. This Arbogast may have done other things. I don't know. I couldn't ask him. When I went to see him, he was dead--shot three times--as I've since heard-- with a twenty-two. No, I didn't tell the police, Mr. Jeeter."

The tall silver-haired man looked horribly shocked. His lean body shook like a bullrush. "Dead?" he whispered. "Murdered?"

61

I looked at George. George didn't move a muscle. I looked at the girl. She sat quietly, waiting, tight-lipped.

I said: "There's only one reason to suppose his killing had anything to do with Mr. Jeeter's affairs. He was shot with a twenty-two--and there is a man in this case who wears a twenty-two."

I still had their attention. And their silence.

"Why he was shot I haven't the faintest idea. He was not a dangerous man to Miss Huntress or Marty Estel. He was too fat to get around much. My guess is he was a little too smart. He got a simple case of signature identification and he went on from there to find out more than he should. And after he had found out more than he should--he guessed more than he ought--and maybe he even tried a little blackmail. And somebody rubbed him out this afternoon with a twenty-two. O.K., I can stand it. I never knew him.

"So I went over to see Miss Huntress and after a lot of finagling around with this itchy-handed house dick I got to see her and we had a chat, and then Mister Gerald stepped neatly out of hiding and bopped me a nice one on the chin and over I went and hit my head on a chair leg. And when I came out of that the joint was empty. So I went on home.

"And home I found the man with the twenty-two and with him a dimwit called Frisky Lavon, with a bad breath and a very large gun, neither of which matters now as he was shot dead in front of your house tonight, Mr. Jeeter--shot trying to stick up your car. The cops know about that one--they came to see me about it--because the other guy, the one that packs the twenty-two, is the little dimwit's brother and he thought I shot Dimwit and tried to put the bee on me. But it didn't work. That's two killings.

"We now come to the third and most important. I went back to the El Milano because it no longer seemed a good idea for Mister Gerald to be running around casually. He seemed to have a few enemies. It even seemed that he was supposed to be in the car this evening when Frisky Lavon shot at it--but of course that was just a plant."

Old Jeeter drew his white eyebrows together in an expression of puzzlement. George didn't look puzzled. He didn't look anything. He was as wooden-faced as a cigar-store Indian. The girl looked a little white now, a little tense. I plowed on.

"Back at the El Milano I found that Hawkins had let Marty Estel and his bodyguard into Miss Huntress' apartment to wait for her. Marty had something to tell her--that Arbogast had been killed. That made it a good idea for her to lay off young Jeeter for a while-- until the cops quieted down anyhow. A thoughtful guy, Marty. A much more thoughtful guy than you would suppose. For instance, he knew about Arbogast and he knew Mr. Jeeter went to Anna Halsey's office this morning and he knew somehow--Anna might have told him herself, I wouldn't put it past her--that I was working on the case now. So he had me tailed to Arbogast's place and away, and he found out later from his cop friends that Arbogast had been murdered, and he knew I hadn't given it out. So he had me there and that made us pals. He went away after telling me this and once more I was left alone in Miss Huntress' apartment. But this time for no reason at all I poked around. And I found young Mister Gerald, in the bedroom, in a closet."

I stepped quickly over to the girl and reached into my pocket and took out the small fancy .25 automatic and laid it down on her knee.

"Ever see this before?"

Her voice had a curious tight sound, but her dark blue eyes looked at me levelly.

"Yes. It's mine."

"You kept it where?"

"In the drawer of a small table beside the bed."

"Sure about that?"

She thought. Neither of the two men stirred.

George began to twitch the corner of his mouth. She shook her head suddenly, sideways.

"No. I have an idea now I took it out to show somebody--because I don't know much about guns-- and left it lying on the mantel in the living room. In fact, I'm almost sure I did. It was Gerald I showed it to."

"So he might have reached for it there, if anybody tried to make a wrong play at him?"

She nodded, troubled. "What do you mean--he's in the closet?" she asked in a small quick voice.

"You know. Everybody in this room knows what I mean. They know that I showed you that gun for a purpose." I stepped away from her and faced George and his boss. "He's dead, of course. Shot through the heart--probably with this gun. It was left there with him. That's why it would be left."

The old man took a step and stopped and braced himself against the table. I wasn't sure whether he had turned white or whether he had been white already. He stared stonily at the girl. He said very slowly, between his teeth: "You damned murderess!"

"Couldn't it have been suicide?" I sneered.

He turned his head enough to look at me. I could see that the idea interested him. He half nodded.

"No," I said. "It couldn't have been suicide."

He didn't like that so well. His face congested with blood and the veins on his nose thickened. The girl touched the gun lying on her knee, then put her hand loosely around the butt. I saw her thumb slide very gently towards the safety catch. She didn't know much about guns, but she knew that much.

"It couldn't be suicide," I said again, very slowly. "As an isolated event--maybe. But not with all the other stuff that's been happening. Arbogast, the stick-up down on Calvello Drive outside this house, the thugs planted in my apartment, the job with the twenty-two."

I reached into my pocket again and pulled out Waxnose's Woodsman. I held it carelessly on the flat of my left hand. "And curiously enough, I don't think it was *this*twenty-two--although this happens to be the gunman's twenty-two. Yeah, I have the gunman, too. He's tied up in my apartment. He came back to knock me off, but I talked him out of it. I'm a swell talker."

"Except that you overdo it," the girl said coolly, and lifted the gun a little.

"It's obvious who killed him, Miss Huntress," I said. "It's simply a matter of motive and opportunity. Marty Estel didn't, and didn't have it done. That would spoil his chances to get his fifty grand. Frisky Lavon's pal didn't, regardless of who he was working for, and I don't think he was working for Marty Estel. He couldn't have got into the El Milano to do the job, and certainly not into Miss Huntress' apartment. Whoever did it had something to gain by it and an opportunity to get to the place where it was done. Well, who had something to gain? Gerald had five million coming to him in two years out of a trust fund. He couldn't will it until he got it. So if he died, his natural heir got it. Who's his natural heir? You'd be surprised. Did you know that in the state of California and some others, but not in all, a man can by his own act become a natural heir? Just by adopting somebody who has money and no heirs!"

George moved then. His movement was once more as smooth as a ripple of water. The Smith & Wesson gleamed dully in his hand, but he didn't fire it. The small automatic in the girl's hand cracked. Blood spurted from George's brown hard hand. The Smith & Wesson dropped to the floor. He cursed. She didn't know much about guns--not very much.

"Of course!" she said grimly. "George could get into the apartment without any trouble, if Gerald was there. He would go in through the garage, a chauffeur in uniform, ride up in the elevator and knock at the door. And when Gerald opened it, George would back him in with that Smith & Wesson. But how did he know Gerald was there?"

I said: "He must have followed your taxi. We don't know where he has been all evening since he left me. He had a car with him. The cops will find out. How much was in it for you, George?"

George held his right wrist with his left hand, held it tightly, and his face was twisted, savage. He said nothing.

"George would back him in with the Smith & Wesson," the girl said wearily. "Then he would see my gun on the mantelpiece. That would be better. He would use that. He would back Gerald into the bedroom, away from the corridor, into the closet, and there, quietly, calmly, he would kill him and drop the gun on the floor."

"George killed Arbogast, too. He killed him with a twenty-two because he knew that Frisky Lavon's brother had a twenty-two, and he knew that because he had hired Frisky and his brother to put over a big scare on Gerald--so that when he was murdered it would look as if Marty Estel had had it done. That was why I was brought out here tonight in the Jeeter car--so that the two thugs who had been warned and planted could pull their act and maybe knock me off, if I got too tough. Only George likes to kill people. He made a neat shot at Frisky. He hit him in the face. It was so good a shot I think he meant it to be a miss. How about it, George?"

Silence.

I looked at old Jeeter at last. I had been expecting him to pull a gun himself, but he hadn't. He just stood there, open mouthed, appalled, leaning against the black marble table, shaking.

"My God!" he whispered. "My God!"

"You don't have one--except money."

A door squeaked behind me. I whirled, but I needn't have bothered. A hard voice, about as English as Amos and Andy, said: "Put 'em up, bud."

The butler, the very English butler, stood there in the doorway, a gun in his hand, tight-lipped. The girl turned her wrist and shot him just kind of casually, in the shoulder or something. He squealed like a stuck pig.

"Go away, you're intruding," she said coldly.

He ran. We heard his steps running.

"He's going to fall," she said.

I was wearing my Luger in my right hand now, a little late in the season, as usual. I came around with it. Old man Jeeter was holding on to the table, his face gray as a paving block. His knees were giving. George stood cynically, holding a handkerchief around his bleeding wrist, watching him.

"Let him fall," I said. "Down is where he belongs."

He fell. His head twisted. His mouth went slack. He hit the carpet on his side and rolled a little and his knees came up. His mouth drooled a little. His skin turned violet.

"Go call the law, angel," I said. "I'll watch them now."

"All right," she said standing up. "But you certainly need a lot of help in your private-detecting business, Mr. Marlowe."

8

I had been in there for a solid hour, alone. There was the scarred desk in the middle, another against the wall, a brass spittoon on a mat, a police loudspeaker box on the wall, three squashed flies, a smell of cold cigars and old clothes. There were two hard armchairs with felt pads and two hard straight chairs without pads. The electric-light fixture had been dusted about Coolidge's first term.

The door opened with a jerk and Finlayson and Sebold came in. Sebold looked as spruce and nasty as ever, but Finlayson looked older, more worn, mousier. He held a sheaf of papers in his hand. He sat down across the desk from me and gave me a hard bleak stare.

"Guys like you get in a lot of trouble," Finlayson said sourly. Sebold sat down against the wall and tilted his hat over his eyes and yawned and looked at his new stainless-steel wrist watch.

"Trouble is my business," I said. "How else would I make a nickel?"

"We oughta throw you in the can for all this cover-up stuff. How much you making on this one?"

"I was working for Anna Halsey who was working for old man Jeeter. I guess I made a bad debt."

Sebold smiled his blackjack smile at me. Finlayson lit a cigar and licked at a tear on the side of it and pasted it down, but it leaked smoke just the same when he drew on it. He pushed papers across the desk at me.

"Sign three copies."

I signed three copies.

He took them back, yawned and rumpled his old gray head. "The old man's had a stroke," he said. "No dice there. Probably won't know what time it is when he comes out. This George Hasterman, this chauffeur guy, he just laughs at us. Too bad he got pinked. I'd like to wrastle him a bit."

"He's tough," I said.

"Yeah. O.K., you can beat it for now."

I got up and nodded to them and went to the door. "Well, good night, boys."

Neither of them spoke to me.

I went out, along the corridor and down in the night elevator to the City Hall lobby. I went out the Spring Street side and down the long flight of empty steps and the wind blew cold. I lit a cigarette at the bottom. My car was still out at the Jeeter place. I lifted a foot to start walking to a taxi half a block down across the street. A voice spoke sharply from a parked car.

69

"Come here a minute."

It was a man's voice, tight, hard. It was Marty Estel's voice. It came from a big sedan with two men in the front seat. I went over there. The rear window was down and Marty Estel leaned a gloved hand on it.

"Get in." He pushed the door open. I got in. I was too tired to argue. "Take it away, Skin."

The car drove west through dark, almost quiet streets, almost clean streets. The night air was not pure but it was cool. We went up over a hill and began to pick up speed.

"What they get?" Estel asked coolly.

"They didn't tell me. They didn't break the chauffeur yet."

"You can't convict a couple million bucks of murder in this man's town." The driver called Skin laughed without turning his head. "Maybe I don't even touch my fifty grand now...she likes you."

"Uh-huh. So what?"

"Lay off her."

"What will it get me?"

"It's what it'll get you if you don't."

"Yeah, sure," I said. "Go to hell, will you please. I'm tired." I shut my eyes and leaned in the corner of the car and just like that went to sleep. I can do that sometimes, after a strain.

A hand shaking my shoulder woke me. The car had stopped. I looked out at the front of my apartment house.

"Home," Marty Estel said. "And remember. Lay off her."

"Why the ride home? Just to tell me that?"

"She asked me to look out for you. That's why you're loose. She likes you. I like her. See? You don't want any more trouble."

"Trouble--" I started to say, and stopped. I was tired of that gag for that night. "Thanks for the ride, and apart from that, nuts to you." I turned away and went into the apartment house and up.

The door lock was still loose but nobody waited for me this time. They had taken Waxnose away long since. I left the door open and threw the windows up and I was still sniffing at policemen's cigar butts when the phone rang. It was her voice, cool, a little hard, not touched by anything, almost amused. Well, she'd been through enough to make her that way, probably.

"Hello, brown-eyes. Make it home all right?"

"Your pal Marty brought me home. He told me to lay off you. Thanks with all my heart, if I have any, but don't call me up any more."

"A little scared, Mr. Marlowe?"

"No. Wait for me to call you," I said. "Good night, angel."

"Good night, brown-eyes."

The phone clicked. I put it away and shut the door and pulled the bed down. I undressed and lay on it for a while in the cold air.

Then I got up and had a drink and a shower and went to sleep.

They broke George at last, but not enough. He said there had been a fight over the girl and young Jeeter had grabbed the gun off the mantel and George had fought with him and it had gone off. All of which, of course, looked possible--in the papers. They never pinned the Arbogast killing on him or on anybody. They never found the gun that did it, but it was not

Waxnose's gun. Waxnose disappeared--I never heard where. They didn't touch old man Jeeter, because he never came out of his stroke, except to lie on his back and have nurses and tell people how he hadn't lost a nickel in the depression.

Marty Estel called me up four times to tell me to lay off Harriet Huntress. I felt kind of sorry for the poor guy. He had it bad. I went out with her twice and sat with her twice more at home, drinking her Scotch. It was nice, but I didn't have the money, the clothes, the time or the manners. Then she stopped being at the El Milano and I heard she had gone to New York.

I was glad when she left--even though she didn't bother to tell me goodbye.

PEARLS ARE A NUISANCE

1

I t is quite true that I wasn't doing anything that morning except looking at a blank sheet of paper in my typewriter and thinking about writing a letter. It is also quite true that I don't have a great deal to do any morning. But that is no reason why I should have to go out hunting for old Mrs. Penruddock's pearl necklace. I don't happen to be a policeman.

It was Ellen Macintosh who called me up, which made a difference, of course. "How are you, darling?" she asked. "Busy?"

"Yes and no," I said. "Mostly no. I am very well. What is it now?"

"I don't think you love me, Walter. And anyway you ought to get some work to do. You have too much money. Somebody has stolen Mrs. Penruddock's pearls and I want you to find them."

"Possibly you think you have the police department on the line," I said coldly. "This is the residence of Walter Gage. Mr. Gage talking."

"Well, you can tell Mr. Gage from Miss Ellen Macintosh," she said, "that if he is not out here in half an hour, he will receive a small parcel by registered mail containing one diamond engagement ring."

"And a lot of good it did me," I said. "That old crow will live for another fifty years."

But she had already hung up so I put my hat on and went down and drove off in the Packard. It was a nice late April morning, if you care for that sort of thing. Mrs. Penruddock lived on a wide quiet street in Carondelet Park. The house had probably looked

73

exactly the same for the last fifty years, but that didn't make me any better pleased that Ellen Macintosh might live in it another fifty years, unless old Mrs. Penruddock died and didn't need a nurse any more. Mr. Penruddock had died a few years before, leaving no will, a thoroughly tangled-up estate, and a list of pensioners as long as a star boarder's arm.

I rang the front doorbell and the door was opened, not very soon, by a little old woman with a maid's apron and a strangled knot of gray hair on the top of her head. She looked at me as if she had never seen me before and didn't want to see me now.

"Miss Ellen Macintosh, please," I said. "Mr. Walter Gage calling."

She sniffed, turned without a word and we went back into the musty recesses of the house and came to a glassed-in porch full of wicker furniture and the smell of Egyptian tombs. She went away, with another sniff.

In a moment the door opened again and Ellen Macintosh came in. Maybe you don't like tall girls with honey-colored hair and skin like the first strawberry peach the grocer sneaks out of the box for himself. If you don't, I'm sorry for you.

"Darling, so you did come," she cried. "That was nice of you, Walter. Now sit down and I'll tell you all about it."

We sat down.

"Mrs. Penruddock's pearl necklace has been stolen, Walter."

"You told me that over the telephone. My temperature is still normal."

"If you will excuse a professional guess," she said, "it is probably subnormal--permanently. The pearls are a string of forty-nine matched pink ones which Mr.

74

Penruddock gave to Mrs. Penruddock for her golden wedding present. She hardly ever wore them lately, except perhaps on Christmas or when she had a couple of very old friends in to dinner and was well enough to sit up. And every Thanksgiving she gives a dinner to all the pensioners and friends and old employees Mr. Penruddock left on her hands, and she wore them then."

"You are getting your verb tenses a little mixed," I said, "but the general idea is clear. Go on."

"Well, Walter," Ellen said, with what some people call an arch look, "the pearls have been stolen. Yes, I know that is the third time I told you that, but there's a strange mystery about it. They were kept in a leather case in an old safe which was open half the time and which I should judge a strong man could open with his fingers even when it was locked. I had to go there for a paper this morning and I looked in at the pearls just to say hello--"

"I hope your idea in hanging on to Mrs. Penruddock has not been that she might leave you that necklace," I said stiffly. "Pearls are all very well for old people and fat blondes, but for tall willowy--"

"Oh shut up, darling," Ellen broke in. "I should certainly not have been waiting for these pearls-- because they were false."

I swallowed hard and stared at her. "Well," I said, with a leer, "I have heard that old Penruddock pulled some cross-eyed rabbits out of the hat occasionally, but giving his own wife a string of phony pearls on her golden wedding gets my money."

"Oh, don't be such a fool, Walter! They were real enough then. The fact is Mrs. Penruddock sold them and had imitations made. One of her old friends, Mr.

Lansing Gallemore of the Gallemore Jewelry Company, handled it all for her very quietly, because of course she didn't want anyone to know. And that is why the police have not been called in. You *will* find them for her, won't you, Walter?"

"How? And what did she sell them for?"

"Because Mr. Penruddock died suddenly without making any provision for all these people he had been supporting. Then the depression came, and there was hardly any money at all. Only just enough to carry on the household and pay the servants, all of whom have been with Mrs. Penruddock so long that she would rather starve than let any of them go."

"That's different," I said. "I take my hat off to her. But how the dickens am I going to find them, and what does it matter anyway--if they were false?"

"Well, the pearls--imitations, I mean--cost two hundred dollars and were specially made in Bohemia and it took several months and the way things are over there now she might never be able to get another set of really good imitations. And she is terrified somebody will find out they were false, or that the thief will blackmail her, when he finds out they were false. You see, darling, I know who stole them."

I said, "Huh?" a word I very seldom use as I do not think it part of the vocabulary of a gentleman.

"The chauffeur we had here a few months, Walter--a horrid big brute named Henry Eichelberger. He left suddenly the day before yesterday, for no reason at all. Nobody ever leaves Mrs. Penruddock. Her last chauffeur was a very old man and he died. But Henry Eichelberger left without a word and I'm sure he had stolen the pearls. He tried to kiss me once, Walter."

"Oh, he did," I said in a different voice. "Tried to kiss you, eh? Where is this big slab of meat, darling? Have you any idea at all? It seems hardly likely he would be hanging around on the street corner for me to punch his nose for him."

Ellen lowered her long silky eyelashes at me--and when she does that I go limp as a scrubwoman's back hair.

"He didn't run away. He must have known the pearls were false and that he was safe enough to blackmail Mrs. Penruddock. I called up the agency he came from and he has been back there and registered again for employment. But they said it was against their rules to give his address."

"Why couldn't somebody else have taken the pearls? A burglar, for instance?"

"There is no one else. The servants are beyond suspicion and the house is locked up as tight as an icebox every night and there were no signs of anybody having broken in. Besides Henry Eichelberger knew where the pearls were kept, because he saw me putting them away after the last time she wore them--which was when she had two very dear friends in to dinner on the occasion of the anniversary of Mr. Penruddock's death."

"That must have been a pretty wild party," I said. "All right, I'll go down to the agency and make them give me his address. Where is it?"

"It is called the Ada Twomey Domestic Employment Agency, and it is in the two-hundred block on East Second, a very unpleasant neighborhood."

"Not half as unpleasant as my neighborhood will be to Henry Eichelberger," I said. "So he tried to kiss you, eh?"

"The pearls, Walter," Ellen said gently, "are the important thing. I do hope he hasn't already found out they are false and thrown them in the ocean."

"If he has, I'll make him dive for them."

"He is six feet three and very big and strong, Walter," Ellen said coyly. "But not handsome like you, of course."

"Just my size," I said. "It will be a pleasure. Good-bye, darling."

She took hold of my sleeve. "There is just one thing, Walter. I don't mind a little fighting because it is manly. But you mustn't cause a disturbance that would bring the police in, you know. And although you are very big and strong and played right tackle at college, you are a little weak about one thing. Will you promise me not to drink any whiskey?"

"This Eichelberger," I said, "is all the drink I want."

2

The Ada Twomey Domestic Employment Agency on East Second Street proved to be all that the name and location implied. The odor of the anteroom, in which I was compelled to wait for a short time, was not at all pleasant. The agency was presided over by a hard-faced middle-aged woman who said that Henry Eichelberger was registered with them for employment as a chauffeur, and that she could arrange to have him call upon me, or could bring him there to the office for an interview. But when I placed a ten-dollar bill on her desk and indicated that it was merely an earnest of good faith, without prejudice to any commission which might become due to her agency, she relented and gave me his address, which was out west on Santa Monica

Boulevard, near the part of the city which used to be called Sherman.

I drove out there without delay, for fear that Henry Eichelberger might telephone in and be informed that I was coming. The address proved to be a seedy hotel, conveniently close to the interurban car tracks and having its entrance adjoining a Chinese laundry. The hotel was upstairs, the steps being covered--in places--with strips of decayed rubber matting to which were screwed irregular fragments of unpolished brass. The smell of the Chinese laundry ceased about halfway up the stairs and was replaced by a smell of kerosene, cigar butts, slept-in air and greasy paper bags. There was a register at the head of the stairs on a wooden shelf. The last entry was in pencil, three weeks previous as to date, and had been written by someone with a very unsteady hand. I deduced from this that the management was not over-particular.

There was a bell beside the book and a sign reading: MANAGER. I rang the bell and waited. Presently a door opened down the hall and feet shuffled towards me without haste. A man appeared wearing frayed leather slippers and trousers of a nameless color, which had the two top buttons unlatched to permit more freedom to the suburbs of his extensive stomach. He also wore red suspenders, his shirt was darkened under the arms, and elsewhere, and his face badly needed a thorough laundering and trimming.

He said, "Full-up, bud," and sneered.

I said: "I am not looking for a room. I am looking for one Eichelberger, who, I am informed lives here, but who, I observe, has not registered in your book. And this, as of course you know, is contrary to the law."

"A wise guy," the fat man sneered again. "Down the hall, bud. Two-eighteen." He waved a thumb the color and almost the size of a burnt baked potato.

"Have the kindness to show me the way," I said.

"Geez, the lootenant-governor," he said, and began to shake his stomach. His small eyes disappeared in folds of yellow fat. "O.K., bud. Follow on."

We went into the gloomy depths of the back hall and came to a wooden door at the end with a closed wooden transom above it. The fat man smote the door with a fat hand. Nothing happened.

"Out," he said.

"Have the kindness to unlock the door," I said. "I wish to go in and wait for Eichelberger."

"In a pig's valise," the fat man said nastily, "Who the hell you think you are, bum?"

This angered me. He was a fair-sized man, about six feet tall, but too full of the memories of beer. I looked up and down the dark hall. The place seemed utterly deserted.

I hit the fat man in the stomach.

He sat down on the floor and belched and his right kneecap came into sharp contact with his jaw. He coughed and tears welled up in his eyes.

"Cripes, bud," he whined. "You got twenty years on me. That ain't fair."

"Open the door," I said. "I have no time to argue with you."

"A buck," he said, wiping his eyes on his shirt. "Two bucks and no tip-off."

I took two dollars out of my pocket and helped the man to his feet. He folded the two dollars and produced an ordinary passkey which I could have purchased for five cents.

"Brother, you sock," he said. "Where you learn it? Most big guys are muscle-bound." He unlocked the door.

"If you hear any noises later on," I said, "ignore them. If there is any damage, it will be paid for generously."

He nodded and I went into the room. He locked the door behind me and his steps receded. There was silence.

The room was small, mean and tawdry. It contained a brown chest of drawers with a small mirror hanging over it, a straight wooden chair, a wooden rocking chair, a single bed of chipped enamel, with a much mended cotton counterpane. The curtains at the single window had fly marks on them and the green shade was without a slat at the bottom. There was a wash bowl in the corner with two paper-thin towels hanging beside it. There was, of course, no bathroom, and there was no closet. A piece of dark figured material hanging from a shelf made a substitute for the latter. Behind this I found a gray business suit of the largest size made, which would be my size, if I wore ready-made clothes, which I do not. There was a pair of black brogues on the floor, size number twelve at least. There was also a cheap fiber suitcase, which of course I searched, as it was not locked.

I also searched the bureau and was surprised to find that everything in it was neat and clean and decent. But there was not much in it. Particularly there were no pearls in it. I searched in all other likely and unlikely places in the room but I found nothing of interest.

I sat on the side of the bed and lit a cigarette and waited. It was now apparent to me that Henry Eichelberger was either a very great fool or entirely innocent. The room and the open trail he had left behind him did not suggest a man dealing in operations like stealing pearl necklaces.

I had smoked four cigarettes, more than I usually smoke in an entire day, when approaching steps sounded. They were light quick steps but not at all clandestine. A key was thrust into the door and turned and the door swung carelessly open. A man stepped through it and looked at me.

I am six feet three inches in height and weigh over two hundred pounds. This man was tall, but he seemed lighter. He wore a blue serge suit of the kind which is called neat for lack of anything better to say about it. He had thick wiry blond hair, a neck like a Prussian corporal in a cartoon, very wide shoulders and large hard hands, and he had a face that had taken much battering in its time. His small greenish eyes glinted at me with what I then took to be evil humor. I saw at once that he was not a man to trifle with, but I was not afraid of him. I was his equal in size and strength, and, I had small doubt, his superior in intelligence.

I stood up off the bed calmly and said: "I am looking for one Eichelberger."

"How you get in here, bud?" It was a cheerful voice, rather heavy, but not unpleasant to the ear.

"The explanation of that can wait," I said stiffly. "I am looking for one Eichelberger. Are you he?"

"Haw," the man said. "A gut-buster. A comedian. Wait'll I loosen my belt." He took a couple of steps farther into the room and I took the same number towards him.

"My name is Walter Gage," I said. "Are you Eichelberger?"

"Gimme a nickel," he said, "and I'll tell you."

I ignored that. "I am the fiancé of Miss Ellen Macintosh," I told him coldly. "I am informed that you tried to kiss her."

He took another step towards me and I another towards him. "Whaddaya mean--tried?" he sneered.

I led sharply with my right and it landed flush on his chin. It seemed to me a good solid punch, but it scarcely moved him. I then put two hard left jabs into his neck and landed a second hard right at the side of his rather wide nose. He snorted and hit me in the solar plexus.

I bent over and took hold of the room with both hands and spun it. When I had it nicely spinning I gave it a full swing and hit myself on the back of the head with the floor. This made me lose my balance temporarily and while I was thinking about how to regain it a wet towel began to slap at my face and I opened my eyes. The face of Henry Eichelberger was close to mine and bore a certain appearance of solicitude.

"Bud," his voice said, "your stomach is as weak as a Chinaman's tea."

"Brandy!" I croaked. "What happened?"

"You tripped on a little tear in the carpet, bud. You really got to have liquor?"

"Brandy," I croaked again, and closed my eyes.

"I hope it don't get me started," his voice said.

A door opened and closed. I lay motionless and tried to avoid being sick at my stomach. The time passed slowly, in a long gray veil. Then the door of the room opened and closed once more and a moment later something hard was being pressed against my lips. I opened my mouth and liquor poured down my throat. I coughed, but the fiery liquid coursed through my veins and strengthened me at once. I sat up.

"Thank you, Henry," I said. "May I call you Henry?"

"No tax on it, bud."

I got to my feet and stood before him. He stared at me curiously. "You look O.K.," he said. "Why'n't you told me you was sick?"

"Damn you, Eichelberger!" I said and hit with all my strength on the side of his jaw. He shook his head and his eyes seemed annoyed. I delivered three more punches to his face and jaw while he was still shaking his head.

"So you wanta play for keeps!" he yelled and took hold of the bed and threw it at me.

I dodged the corner of the bed, but in doing so I moved a little too quickly and lost my balance and pushed my head about four inches into the baseboard under the window.

A wet towel began to slap at my face. I opened my eyes.

"Listen, kid. You got two strikes and no balls on you. Maybe you oughta try a lighter bat."

"Brandy," I croaked.

"You'll take rye." He pressed a glass against my lips and I drank thirstily. Then I climbed to my feet again.

The bed, to my astonishment, had not moved. I sat down on it and Henry Eichelberger sat down beside me and patted my shoulder.

"You and me could get along," he said. "I never kissed your girl, although I ain't saying I wouldn't like to. Is that all is worrying at you?"

He poured himself half a water glassful of the whiskey out of the pint bottle which he had gone out to buy. He swallowed the liquor thoughtfully.

"No, there is another matter," I said.

"Shoot. But no more haymakers. Promise?"

I promised him rather reluctantly. "Why did you leave the employ of Mrs. Penruddock?" I asked him.

He looked at me from under his shaggy blond eyebrows. Then he looked at the bottle he was holding in his hand. "Would you call me a looker?" he asked.

"Well, Henry--"

"Don't pansy up on me," he snarled.

"No, Henry, I should not call you very handsome. But unquestionably you are virile."

He poured another half-waterglassful of whiskey and handed it to me. "Your turn," he said. I drank it down without fully realizing what I was doing. When I had stopped coughing Henry took the glass out of my hand and refilled it. He took his own drink moodily. The bottle was now nearly empty.

"Suppose you fell for a dame with all the looks this side of heaven. With a map like mine. A guy like me, a guy from the stockyards that played himself a lot of very tough left end at a cow college and left his looks and education on the scoreboard. A guy that has fought everything but whales and freight hogs--engines to you--and licked 'em all, but naturally had to take a sock now and then. Then I get a job where I see this lovely all the time and every day and know it's no dice. What would you do, pal? Me, I just quit the job."

"Henry, I'd like to shake your hand," I said.

He shook hands with me listlessly. "So I ask for my time," he said. "What else would I do?" He held the bottle up and looked at it against the light. "Bo, you made an error when you had me get this. When I start drinking it's a world cruise. You got plenty dough?"

"Certainly," I said. "If whiskey is what you want, Henry, whiskey is what you shall have. I have a very nice apartment on Franklin Avenue in Hollywood and while I cast no aspersions on your own humble and of course quite temporary abode, I now suggest we repair to my apartment, which is a good deal larger and gives one more room to extend one's elbow." I waved my hand airily.

"Say, you're drunk," Henry said, with admiration in his small green eyes.

"I am not yet drunk, Henry, although I do in fact feel the effect of that whiskey and very pleasantly. You must not mind my way of talking which is a personal matter, like your own clipped and concise method of speech. But before we depart there is one other rather insignificant detail I wish to discuss with you. I am empowered to arrange for the return of Mrs. Penruddock's pearls. I understand there is some possibility that you may have stolen them."

"Son, you take some awful chances," Henry said softly.

"This is a business matter, Henry, and plain talk is the best way to settle it. The pearls are only false pearls, so we should very easily be able to come to an agreement. I mean you no ill will, Henry, and I am obliged to you for procuring the whiskey, but business is business. Will you take fifty dollars and return the pearls and no questions asked?"

Henry laughed shortly and mirthlessly, but he seemed to have no animosity in his voice when he said: "So you think I stole some marbles and am sitting around here waiting for a flock of dicks to swarm me?"

"No police have been told, Henry, and you may not have known the pearls were false. Pass the liquor, Henry."

He poured me most of what was left in the bottle, and I drank it down with the greatest good humor. I threw the glass at the mirror, but unfortunately missed. The glass, which was of heavy and cheap construction, fell on the floor and did not break. Henry Eichelberger laughed heartily.

"What are you laughing at, Henry?"

"Nothing," he said. "I was just thinking what a sucker some guy is finding out he is--about them marbles."

"You mean you did not steal the pearls, Henry?"

He laughed again, a little gloomily. "Yeah," he said, "meaning no. I oughta sock you, but what the hell? Any guy can get a bum idea. No, I didn't steal no pearls, bud. If they was ringers, I wouldn't be bothered, and if they was what they looked like the one time I saw them on the old lady's neck, I wouldn't decidedly be holed up in no cheap flat in L.A. waiting for a couple carloads of johns to put the sneeze on me."

I reached for his hand again and shook it.

"That is all I required to know," I said happily. "Now I am at peace. We shall now go to my apartment and consider ways and means to recover these pearls. You and I together should make a team that can conquer any opposition, Henry."

"You ain't kidding me, huh?"

I stood up and put my hat on--upside down. "No, Henry. I am making you an offer of employment which I understand you need, and all the whiskey you can drink. Let us go. Can you drive a car in your condition?"

"Hell, I ain't drunk," Henry said, looking surprised.

We left the room and walked down the dark hallway. The fat manager very suddenly appeared from some nebulous shade and stood in front of us rubbing his stomach and looking at me with small greedy expectant eyes. "Everything okey?" he inquired, chewing on a time-darkened toothpick.

"Give him a buck," Henry said.

"What for, Henry?"

"Oh, I dunno. Just give him a buck."

I withdrew a dollar bill from my pocket and gave it to the fat man.

"Thanks, pal," Henry said. He chucked the fat man under the Adam's apple, and removed the dollar bill deftly from between his fingers. "That pays for the hooch," he added. "I hate to have to bum dough."

We went down the stairs arm in arm, leaving the manager trying to cough the toothpick up from his esophagus.

3

At five o'clock that afternoon I awoke from slumber and found that I was lying on my bed in my apartment in the Chateau Moraine, on Franklin Avenue near Ivar Street, in Hollywood. I turned my head, which ached, and saw that Henry Eichelberger was lying beside me in his undershirt and trousers. I then perceived that I also was as lightly attired. On the table near by there stood an almost full bottle of Old Plantation rye whiskey, the full quart size, and on the floor lay an entirely empty bottle of the same excellent brand. There were garments lying here and there on the floor, and a cigarette had burned a hole in the brocaded arm of one of my easy chairs.

I felt myself over carefully. My stomach was stiff and sore and my jaw seemed a little swollen on one side. Otherwise I was none the worse for wear. A sharp pain darted through my temples as I stood up off the bed, but I ignored it and walked steadily to the bottle on the table and raised it to my lips. After a steady draught of the fiery liquid I suddenly felt much better. A hearty and cheerful mood came over me and I was ready for any adventure. I went back to the bed and shook Henry firmly by the shoulder.

"Wake up, Henry," I said. "The sunset hour is nigh. The robins are calling and the squirrels are scolding and the morning glories furl themselves in sleep."

Like all men of action Henry Eichelberger came awake with his fist doubled. "What was that crack?" he snarled. "Oh, yeah. Hi, Walter. How you feel?"

"I feel splendid. Are you rested?"

"Sure." He swung his shoeless feet to the floor and rumpled his thick blond hair with his fingers. "We was going swell until you passed out," he said. "So I had me a nap. I never drink solo. You O.K.?"

"Yes, Henry, I feel very well indeed. And we have work to do."

"Swell." He went to the whiskey bottle and quaffed from it freely. He rubbed his stomach with the flat of his hand. His green eyes shone peacefully. "I'm a sick man," he said, "and I got to take my medicine." He put the bottle down on the table and surveyed the apartment. "Geez," he said, "we thrown it into us so fast I ain't hardly looked at the dump. You got a nice little place here, Walter. Geez, a white typewriter and a white telephone. What's the matter, kid--you just been confirmed?"

"Just a foolish fancy, Henry," I said, waving an airy hand. Henry went over and looked at the typewriter and the telephone side by side on my writing desk, and the silver-mounted desk set, each piece chased with my initials.

"Well fixed, huh?" Henry said, turning his green gaze on me.

"Tolerably so, Henry," I said modestly;

"Well, what next pal? You got any ideas or do we just drink some?"

"Yes, Henry, I do have an idea. With a man like you to help me I think it can be put into practice. I feel that we must, as they say, tap the grapevine. When a string of pearls is stolen, all the underworld knows it at once. Pearls are hard to sell, Henry, inasmuch as they cannot be cut and can be identified by experts, I have read. The underworld will be seething with activity. It should not be too difficult for us to find someone who would send a message to the proper quarter that we are willing to pay a reasonable sum for their return."

"You talk nice--for a drunk guy," Henry said, reaching for the bottle. "But ain't you forgot these marbles are phonies?"

"For sentimental reasons I am quite willing to pay for their return, just the same."

Henry drank some whiskey, appeared to enjoy the flavor of it and drank some more. He waved the bottle at me politely.

"That's O.K.--as far as it goes," he said. "But this underworld that's doing all this here seething you spoke of ain't going to seethe a hell of a lot over a string of glass beads. Or am I screwy?"

"I was thinking, Henry, that the underworld probably has a sense of humor and the laugh that would go around would be quite emphatic.'

"There's an idea in that," Henry said. "Here's some mug finds out lady Penruddock has a string of oyster fruit worth oodles of kale, and he does hisseif a neat little box job and trots down to the fence. And the fence gives him the belly laugh. I would say something like that could get around the poolrooms and start a little idle chatter. So far, so nutty. But this box man is going to dump them beads in a hurry, because he has a three-to-ten on him even if they are only worth a nickel plus sales tax. Breaking and entering is the rap, Walter."

"However, Henry," I said, "there is another element in the situation. If this thief is very stupid, it will not, of course, have much weight. But if he is even moderately intelligent, it will. Mrs. Penruddock is a very proud woman and lives in a very exclusive section of the city. If it should become known that she wore imitation pearls, and above all, if it should be even hinted in the public press that these were the very pearls her own husband had given her for her golden wedding present--well, I am sure you see the point, Henry."

"Box guys ain't too bright," he said and rubbed his stony chin. Then he lifted his right thumb and bit it thoughtfully. He looked at the windows, at the corner of the room, at the floor. He looked at me from the corners of his eyes.

"Blackmail, huh?" he said. "Maybe. But crooks don't mix their rackets much. Still, the guy might pass the word along. There's a chance, Walter. I wouldn't care to hock my gold fillings to buy me a piece of it, but there's a chance. How much you figure to put out?"

"A hundred dollars should be ample, but I am willing to go as high as two hundred, which is the actual cost of the imitations."

Henry shook his head and patronized the bottle. "Nope. The guy wouldn't uncover hisself for that kind of money. Wouldn't be worth the chance he takes. He'd dump the marbles and keep his nose clean."

"We can at least try, Henry."

"Yeah, but where? And we're getting low on liquor. Maybe I better put my shoes on and run out, huh?"

At that very moment, as if in answer to my unspoken prayer, a soft dull thump sounded on the door of my apartment. I opened it and picked up the final edition of the evening paper. I closed the door again and carried the paper back across the room, opening it up as I went. I touched it with my right forefinger and smiled confidently at Henry Eichelberger.

"Here. I will wager you a full quart of Old Plantation that the answer will be on the crime page of this paper."

"There ain't any crime page," Henry chortled. "This is Los Angeles. I'll fade you."

I opened the paper to page three with some trepidation, for, although I had already seen the item I was looking for in an early edition of the paper while waiting in Ada Twomey's Domestic Employment Agency, I was not certain it would appear intact in the later editions. But my faith was rewarded. It had not been removed, but appeared midway of column three exactly as before. The paragraph, which was quite short, was headed: LOU GANDESI QUESTIONED

IN GEM THEFTS. "Listen to this, Henry," I said, and began to read.

Acting on an anonymous tip police late last night picked up Louis C. (Lou) Gandesi, proprietor of a well-known Spring Street tavern, and quizzed him intensively concerning the recent wave of dinner party hold-ups in an exclusive western section of this city, hold-ups during which, it is alleged, more than two hundred thousand dollars' worth of valuable jewels have been torn at gun's point from women guests in fashionable homes. Gandesi was released at a late hour and refused to make any statement to reporters. "I never kibitz the cops," he said modestly. Captain William Norgaard, of the General Robbery Detail, announced himself as satisfied that Gandesi had no connection with the robberies, and that the tip was merely an act of personal spite.

I folded the paper and threw it on the bed.

"You win, ho," Henry said, and handed me the bottle. I took a long drink and returned it to him. "Now what? Brace this Gandesi and take him through the hoops?"

"He may be a dangerous man, Henry. Do you think we are equal to it?"

Henry snorted contemptuously. "Yah, a Spring Street punk. Some fat slob with a phony ruby on his mitt. Lead me to him. We'll turn the slob inside out and drain his liver. But we're just about fresh out of liquor. All we got is maybe a pint." He examined the bottle against the light.

"We have had enough for the moment, Henry."

"We ain't drunk, are we? I only had seven drinks since I got here, maybe nine."

"Certainly we are not drunk, Henry, but you take very large drinks, and we have a difficult evening before us. I think we should now get shaved and dressed, and I further think that we should wear dinner clothes. I have an extra suit which will fit you admirably, as we are almost exactly the same size. It is certainly a remarkable omen that two such large men should be associated in the same enterprise. Evening clothes impress these low characters, Henry."

"Swell," Henry said. "They'll think we're mugs workin' for some big shot. This Gandesi will be scared enough to swallow his necktie."

We decided to do as I had suggested and I laid out clothes for Henry, and while he was bathing and shaving I telephoned to Ellen Macintosh.

"Oh, Walter, I am so glad you called up," she cried. "Have you found anything?"

"Not yet, darling," I said. "But we have an idea. Henry and I are just about to put it into execution."

"Henry, Walter? Henry who?"

"Why, Henry Eichelberger, of course, darling. Have you forgotten him so soon? Henry and I are warm friends and we--"

She interrupted me coldly. "Are you drinking, Walter?" she demanded in a very distant voice.

"Certainly not, darling. Henry is a teetotaler."

She sniffed sharply. I could hear the sound distinctly over the telephone. "But didn't Henry take the pearls?" she asked, after quite a long pause.

"Henry, angel? Of course not. Henry left because he was in love with you."

"Oh, Walter. That ape? I'm sure you're drinking terribly. I don't ever want to speak to you again.

Goodbye." And she hung the phone up very sharply so that a painful sensation made itself felt in my ear.

I sat down in a chair with a bottle of Old Plantation in my hand wondering what I had said that could be construed as offensive or indiscreet. As I was unable to think of anything, I consoled myself with the bottle until Henry came out of the bathroom looking extremely personable in one of my pleated shirts and a wing collar and black bow tie.

It was dark when we left the apartment and I, at least, was full of hope and confidence, although a little depressed by the way Ellen Macintosh had spoken to me over the telephone.

4

Mr. Gandesi's establishment was not difficult to find, inasmuch as the first taxicab driver Henry yelled at on Spring Street directed us to it. It was called the Blue Lagoon and its interior was bathed in an unpleasant blue light. Henry and I entered it steadily, since we had consumed a partly solid meal at Mandy's Caribbean Grotto before starting out to find Mr. Gandesi. Henry looked almost handsome in my second-best dinner suit, with a fringed white scarf hanging over his shoulder, a lightweight black felt hat on the back of his head (which was only a little larger than mine), and a bottle of whiskey in each of the side pockets of the summer overcoat he was wearing.

The bar of the Blue Lagoon was crowded, but Henry and I went on back to the small dim dining room behind it. A man in a dirty dinner suit came up to us and Henry asked him for Gandesi, and he pointed out a fat man who sat alone at a small table in the far corner of the room. We went that way.

The man sat with a small glass of red wine in front of him and slowly twisted a large green stone on his finger. He did not look up. There were no other chairs at the table, so Henry leaned on it with both elbows.

"You Gandesi?" he said.

The man did not look up even then. He moved his thick black eyebrows together and said in an absent voice: "Si. Yes."

"We got to talk to you in private," Henry told him. Where we won't be disturbed."

Gandesi looked up now and there was extreme boredom in his flat black almond-shaped eyes. "So?" he asked and shrugged. "Eet ees about what?"

"About some pearls," Henry said. "Forty-nine on the string, matched and pink."

"You sell--or you buy?" Gandesi inquired and his chin began to shake up and down as if with amusement.

"Buy," Henry said.

The man at the table crooked his finger quietly and a very large waiter appeared at his side. "Ees dronk," he said lifelessly. "Put dees men out."

The waiter took hold of Henry's shoulder. Henry reached up carelessly and took hold of the waiter's hand and twisted it. The waiter's face in that bluish light turned some color I could not describe, but which was not at all healthy. He let out a low moan. Henry dropped the hand and said to me: "Put a C-note on the table."

I took my wallet out and extracted from it one of the two hundred-dollar bills I had taken the precaution to obtain from the cashier at the Chateau Moraine.

Gandesi stared at the bill and made a gesture to the large waiter, who went away rubbing his hand and holding it tight against his chest.

"What for?" Gandesi asked.

"Five minutes of your time alone."

"Ees very fonny. O.K., I bite." Gandesi took the bill and folded it neatly and put it in his vest pocket. Then he put both hands on the table and pushed himself heavily to his feet. He started to waddle away without looking at us.

Henry and I followed him among the crowded tables to the far side of the dining room and through a door in the wainscoting and then down a narrow dim hallway. At the end of this Gandesi opened a door into a lighted room and stood holding it for us, with a grave smile on his olive face. I went in first.

As Henry passed in front of Gandesi into the room the latter, with surprising agility, took a small shiny black leather club from his clothes and hit Henry on the head with it very hard. Henry sprawled forward on his hands and knees. Gandesi shut the door of the room very quickly for a man of his build and leaned against it with the small club in his left hand. Now, very suddenly, in his right hand appeared a short but heavy black revolver.

"Ees very fonny," he said politely, and chuckled to himself.

Exactly what happened then I did not see clearly. Henry was at one instant on his hands and knees with his back to Gandesi. In the next, or possibly even in the same instant, something swirled like a big fish in water and Gandesi grunted. I then saw that Henry's hard blond head was buried in Gandesi's stomach and that Henry's large hands held both of Gandesi's hairy

97

wrists. Then Henry straightened his body to its full height and Gandesi was high up in the air balanced on top of Henry's head, his mouth strained wide open and his face a dark purple color. Then Henry shook himself, as it seemed, quite lightly, and Gandesi landed on his back on the floor with a terrible thud and lay gasping. Then a key turned in the door and Henry stood with his back to it, holding both the club and the revolver in his left hand, and solicitously feeling the pockets which contained our supply of whiskey. All this happened with such rapidity that I leaned against the side wall and felt a little sick at my stomach.

"A gut-buster," Henry drawled. "A comedian. Wait'll I loosen my belt."

Gandesi rolled over and got to his feet very slowly and painfully and stood swaying and passing his hand up and down his face. His clothes were covered with dust.

"This here's a sap," Henry said, showing me the small black club. "He hit me with it, didn't he?"

"Why, Henry, don't you know?" I inquired.

"I just wanted to be sure," Henry said. "You don't do that to the Eichelbergers."

"O.K., what you boys want?" Gandesi asked abruptly, with no trace whatever of his Italian accent.

"I told you what we wanted, dough-face."

"I don't think I know you boys," Gandesi said and lowered his body with care into a wooden chair beside a shabby office desk. He mopped his face and neck and felt himself in various places.

"You got the wrong idea, Gandesi. A lady living in Carondelet Park lost a forty-nine bead pearl necklace a couple of days back. A box job, but a pushover. Our

outfit's carrying a little insurance on those marbles.
And I'll take that C note."

He walked over to Gandesi and Gandesi quickly
reached the folded bill from his pocket and handed it to
him. Henry gave me the bill and I put it back in my
wallet.

"I don't think I hear about it," Gandesi said carefully.

"You hit me with a sap," Henry said. "Listen kind of
hard."

Gandesi shook his head and then winced. "I don't
back no petermen," he said, "nor no heist guys. You
got me wrong."

"Listen hard," Henry said in a low voice. "You might
hear something." He swung the small black club
lightly in front of his body with two fingers of his right
hand. The slightly too small hat was still on the back of
his head, although a little crumpled.

"Henry," I said, "you seem to be doing all the work
this evening. Do you think that is quite fair?"

"O.K., work him over," Henry said. "These fat guys
bruise something lovely."

By this time Gandesi had become a more natural
color and was gazing at us steadily. "Insurance guys,
huh?" he inquired dubiously.

"You said it, dough-face."

"You try Melachrino?" Gandesi asked.

"Haw," Henry began raucously, "a gut-buster. A--"
but I interrupted him sharply.

"One moment, Henry," I said. Then turning to
Gandesi, "Is this Melachrino a person?" I asked him.

Gandesi's eyes rounded in surprise. "Sure--a guy.
You don't know him, huh?" A look of dark suspicion
was born in his shoeblack eyes, but vanished almost as
soon as it appeared.

"Phone him," Henry said, pointing to the instrument which stood on the shabby office desk.

"Phone is bad," Gandesi objected thoughtfully.

"So is sap poison," Henry said.

Gandesi sighed and turned his thick body in the chair and drew the telephone towards him. He dialed a number with an inky nail and listened. After an interval he said: "Joe?...Lou. Couple insurance guys tryin' to deal on a Carondelet Park job...Yeah...No, marbles...You ain't heard a whisper, huh?...O.K., Joe."

Gandesi replaced the phone and swung around in the chair again. He studied us with sleepy eyes. "No soap. What insurance outfit you boys work for?"

"Give him a card," Henry said to me.

I took my wallet out once more and withdrew one of my cards from it. It was an engraved calling card and contained nothing but my name. So I used my pocket pencil to write, Chateau Moraine Apartments, Franklin near Ivar, below the name. I showed the card to Henry and then gave it to Gandesi.

Gandesi read the card and quietly bit his finger. His face brightened suddenly. "You boys better see Jack Lawler," he said.

Henry stared at him closely. Gandesi's eyes were now bright and unblinking and guileless.

"Who's he?" Henry asked.

"Runs the Penguin Club. Out on the Strip--Eighty-six Forty-four Sunset or some number like that. He can find out, if any guy can."

"Thanks," Henry said quietly. He glanced at me. "You believe him?"

"Well, Henry," I said, "I don't really think he would be above telling us an untruth."

"Haw!" Gandesi began suddenly. "A gut-buster! A--
"

"Can it!" Henry snarled. "That's my line. Straight goods, is it, Gandesi? About this Jack Lawler?"

Gandesi nodded vigorously. "Straight goods, absolute. Jack Lawler got a finger in everything high class that's touched. But he ain't easy to see."

"Don't worry none about that. Thanks, Gandesi."

Henry tossed the black club into the corner of the room and broke open the breech of the revolver he had been holding all this time in his left hand. He ejected the shells and then bent down and slid the gun along the floor until it disappeared under the desk. He tossed the cartridges idly in his hand for a moment and then let them spill on the floor.

So long, Gandesi," he said coldly. "And keep that schnozzle of yours clean, if you don't want to be looking for it under the bed."

He opened the door then and we both went out quickly and left the Blue Lagoon without interference from any of the employees.

5

My car was parked a short distance away down the block. We entered it and Henry leaned his arms on the wheel and stared moodily through the windshield.

"Well, what you think, Walter?" he inquired at length.

"If you ask my opinion, Henry, I think Mr. Gandesi told us a cock-and-bull story merely to get rid of us. Furthermore I do not believe he thought we were insurance agents."

"Me too, and an extra helping," Henry said. "I don't figure there's any such guy as this Melachrino or this Jack Lawler and this Gandesi called up some dead number and had himself a phony chin with it. I oughta go back there and pull his arms and legs off. The hell with the fat slob."

"We had the best idea we could think of, Henry, and we executed it to the best of our ability. I now suggest that we return to my apartment and try to think of something else."

"And get drunk," Henry said, starting the car and guiding it away from the curb.

"We could perhaps have a small allowance of liquor, Henry."

"Yah!" Henry snorted. "A stall. I oughta go back there and wreck the joint."

He stopped at the intersection, although no traffic signal was in operation at the time; and raised a bottle of whiskey to his lips. He was in the act of drinking when a car came up behind us and collided with our car, but not very severely. Henry choked and lowered his bottle, spilling some of the liquor on his garments.

"This town's getting too crowded," he snarled. "A guy can't take hisself a drink without some smart monkey bumps his elbow."

Whoever it was in the car behind us blew a horn with some insistence, inasmuch as our car had not yet moved forward. Henry wrenched the door open and got out and went back. I heard voices of considerable loudness, the louder being Henry's voice. He came back after a moment and got into the car and drove on.

"I oughta have pulled his mush off," he said, "but I went soft," He drove rapidly the rest of the way to Hollywood and the Chateau Moraine and we went up to my apartment and sat down with large glasses in our hands.

"We got better than a quart and a half of hooch," Henry said, looking at the two bottles which he had placed on the table beside others which had long since been emptied. "That oughta be good for an idea."

"If it isn't enough, Henry, there is an abundant further supply where it came from," I drained my glass cheerfully.

"You seem a right guy," Henry said. "What makes you always talk so funny?"

"I cannot seem to change my speech, Henry. My father and mother were both severe purists in the New England tradition, and the vernacular has never come naturally to my lips, even while I was in college."

Henry made an attempt to digest this remark, but I could see that it lay somewhat heavily on his stomach.

We talked for a time concerning Gandesi and the doubtful quality of his advice, and thus passed perhaps half an hour. Then rather suddenly the white telephone on my desk began to ring. I hurried over to it, hoping that it was Ellen Macintosh and that she had recovered from her ill humor. But it proved to be a male voice and a strange one to me. It spoke crisply, with an unpleasant metallic quality of tone.

"You Walter Gage?"

"This is Mister Gage speaking."

"Well, *Mister* Gage, I understand you're in the market for some jewelry."

I held the phone very tightly and turned my body and made grimaces to Henry over the top of the instrument. But he was moodily pouring himself another large portion of Old Plantation.

"That is so," I said into the telephone, trying to keep my voice steady, although my excitement was almost too much for me. "If by jewelry you mean pearls."

"Forty-nine in a rope, brother, And five grand is the price."

"Why that is entirely absurd," I gasped. "Five thousand dollars for those--"

The voice broke in on me rudely. "You heard me, brother. Five grand. Just hold up the hand and count the fingers. No more, no less. Think it over. I'll call you later."

The phone clicked dryly and I replaced the instrument shakily in its cradle. I was trembling. I walked back to my chair and sat down and wiped my face with my handkerchief.

"Henry," I said in a low tense voice, "it worked. But how strangely."

Henry put his empty glass down on the floor. It was the first time that I had ever seen him put an empty glass down and leave it empty. He stared at me closely with his tight unblinking green eyes.

"Yeah?" he said gently. "What worked, kid?" He licked his lips slowly with the tip of his tongue.

"What we accomplished down at Gandesi's place, Henry. A man just called me on the telephone and asked me if I was in the market for pearls."

"Geez." Henry pursed his lips and whistled gently. "That damn dago had something after all."

"But the price is five thousand dollars, Henry. That seems beyond reasonable explanation."

"Huh?" Henry's eyes seemed to bulge as if they were about to depart from their orbits. "Five grand for them ringers? The guy's nuts. They cost two C's, you said. Bugs completely is what the guy is. Five grand? Why, for five grand I could buy me enough phony pearls to cover an elephant's caboose."

I could see that Henry seemed puzzled. He refilled our glasses silently and we stared at each other over them. "Well, what the heck can you do with that, Walter?" he asked after a long silence.

"Henry," I said firmly, "there is only one thing to do. It is true that Ellen Macintosh spoke to me in confidence, and as she did not have Mrs. Penruddock's express permission to tell me about the pearls, I suppose I should respect that confidence. But Ellen is now angry with me and does not wish to speak to me, for the reason that I am drinking whiskey in considerable quantities, although my speech and brain are still reasonably clear. This last is a very strange development and I think, in spite of everything, some close friend of the family should be consulted. Preferably of course, a man, someone of large business experience, and in addition to that a man who understands about jewels. There is such a man, Henry, and tomorrow morning I shall call upon him."

"Geez," Henry said. "You coulda said all that in nine words, bo. Who is this guy?"

"His name is Mr. Lansing Gallemore, and he is president of the Gallemore Jewelry Company on Seventh Street. He is a very old friend of Mrs. Penruddock--Ellen has often mentioned him--and is, in fact, the very man who procured for her the imitation pearls."

"But this guy will tip the bulls," Henry objected.

"I do not think so, Henry. I do not think he will do anything to embarrass Mrs. Penruddock in any way."

Henry shrugged. "Phonies are phonies," he said. "You can't make nothing else outa them. Not even no president of no jewlery store can't."

"Nevertheless, there must be a reason why so large a sum is demanded, Henry. The only reason that occurs to me is blackmail and, frankly, that is a little too much for me to handle alone, because I do not know enough about the background of the Penruddock family."

"Okey," Henry said, sighing. "If that's your hunch, you better follow it, Walter. And I better breeze on home and flop so as to be in good shape for the rough work, if any."

"You would not care to pass the night here, Henry?"

"Thanks, pal, but I'm O.K. back at the hotel. I'll just take this spare bottle of the tiger sweat to put me to sleep. I might happen to get a call from the agency in the A.M. and would have to brush my teeth and go after it. And I guess I better change my duds back to where I can mix with the common people."

So saying he went into the bathroom and in a short time emerged wearing his own blue serge suite. I urged him to take my car, but he said it would not be safe in his neighborhood. He did, however, consent to use the topcoat he had been wearing and, placing in it carefully the unopened quart of whiskey, he shook me warmly by the hand.

"One moment, Henry," I said and took out my wallet. I extended a twenty-dollar bill to him.

"What's that in favor of?" he growled.

"You are temporarily out of employment, Henry, and you have done a noble piece of work this evening, puzzling as are the results. You should be rewarded and I can well afford this small token."

"Well, thanks, pal," Henry said. "But it's just a loan." His voice was gruff with emotion. "Should I give you a buzz in the A.M.?"

"By all means. And there is one thing more that has occurred to me. Would it not be advisable for you to change your hotel? Suppose, through no fault of mine, the police learn of this theft. Would they not at least suspect you?"

"Hell, they'd bounce me up and down for hours," Henry said. "But what'll it get them? I ain't no ripe peach."

"It is for you to decide, of course, Henry."

"Yeah. Good night, pal, and don't have no nightmares."

He left me then and I felt suddenly very depressed and lonely. Henry's company had been very stimulating to me, in spite of his rough way of talking. He was very much of a man. I poured myself a rather large drink of whiskey from the remaining bottle and drank it quickly but gloomily.

The effect was such that I had an overmastering desire to speak to Ellen Macintosh at all costs. I went to the telephone and called her number. After a long wait a sleepy maid answered. But Ellen, upon hearing my name, refused to come to the telephone. That depressed me still further and I finished the rest of the whiskey almost without noticing what I was doing. I then lay down on the bed and fell into fitful slumber.

6

The busy ringing of the telephone awoke me and I saw that the morning sunlight was streaming into the room. It was nine o'clock and all the lamps were still burning. I arose feeling a little stiff and dissipated, for I was still wearing my dinner suit. But I am a healthy man with very steady nerves and I did not feel as badly as I expected. I went to the telephone and answered it.

Henry's voice said: "How you feel, pal? I got a hangover like twelve Swedes."

"Not too badly, Henry."

"I got a call from the agency about a job. I better go down and take a gander at it. Should I drop around later?"

"Yes, Henry, by all means do that. By eleven o'clock I should be back from the errand about which I spoke to you last night."

"Any more calls from you know?"

"Not yet, Henry."

"Check. Abyssinia." He hung up and I took a cold shower and shaved and dressed. I donned a quiet brown business suit and had some coffee sent up from the coffee shop downstairs. I also had the waiter remove the empty bottles from my apartment and gave him a dollar for his trouble. After drinking two cups of black coffee I felt my own man once more and drove downtown to the Gallemore Jewelry Company's large and brilliant store on West Seventh Street.

It was another bright, golden morning and it seemed that somehow things should adjust themselves on so pleasant a day.

Mr. Lansing Gallemore proved to be a little difficult to see, so that I was compelled to tell his secretary that it was a matter concerning Mrs. Penruddock and of a confidential nature. Upon this message being carried in to him I was at once ushered into a long paneled office, at the far end of which Mr. Gallemore stood behind a massive desk. He extended a thin pink hand to me.

"Mr. Gage? I don't believe we have met, have we?"

"No, Mr. Gallemore, I do not believe we have. I am the fiancé--or was until last night--of Miss Ellen Macintosh, who, as you probably know, is Mrs. Penruddock's nurse. I am come to you upon a very delicate matter and it is necessary that I ask for your confidence before I speak."

He was a man of perhaps seventy-five years of age, and very thin and tall and correct and well preserved. He had cold blue eyes but a warming smile. He was attired youthfully enough in a gray flannel suit with a red carnation at his lapel.

"That is something I make it a rule never to promise, Mr. Gage," he said. "I think it is almost always a very unfair request. But if you assure me the matter concerns Mrs. Penruddock and is really of a delicate and confidential nature, I will make an exception."

"It is indeed, Mr. Gallemore," I said, and thereupon told him the entire story, concealing nothing, not even the fact that I had consumed far too much whiskey the day before.

He stared at me curiously at the end of my story. His finely shaped hand picked up an old-fashioned white quill pen and he slowly tickled his right ear with the feather of it.

"Mr. Gage," he said, "can't you guess why they ask five thousand dollars for that string of pearls?"

"If you permit me to guess, in a matter of so personal a nature, I could perhaps hazard an explanation, Mr. Gallemore."

He moved the white feather around to his left ear and nodded. "Go ahead, son."

"The pearls are in fact real, Mr. Gallemore. You are a very old friend of Mrs. Penruddock--perhaps even a

109

childhood sweetheart. When she gave you her pearls, her golden wedding present, to sell because she was in sore need of money for a generous purpose, you did not sell them, Mr. Gallemore. You only pretended to sell them. You gave her twenty thousand dollars of your own money, and you returned the real pearls to her, pretending that they were an imitation made in Czechoslovakia."

"Son, you think a lot smarter than you talk," Mr. Gallemore said. He arose and walked to a window, pulled aside a fine net curtain and looked down on the bustle of Seventh Street. He came back to his desk and seated himself and smiled a little wistfully.

"You are almost embarrassingly correct, Mr. Gage," he said, and sighed. "Mrs. Penruddock is a very proud woman, or I should simply have offered her the twenty thousand dollars as an unsecured loan. I happened to be the co-administrator of Mr. Penruddock's estate and I knew that in the condition of the financial market at that time it would be out of the question to raise enough cash, without damaging the corpus of the estate beyond reason, to care for all those relatives and pensioners. So Mrs. Penruddock sold her pearls--as she thought--but she insisted that no one should know about it. And I did what you have guessed. It was unimportant. I could afford the gesture. I have never married, Gage, and I am rated a wealthy man. As a matter of fact, at that time, the pearls would not have fetched more than half of what I gave her, or of what they should bring today."

I lowered my eyes for fear this kindly old gentleman might be troubled by my direct gaze.

"So I think we had better raise that five thousand, son," Mr. Gallemore at once added in a brisk voice.

"The price is pretty low, although stolen pearls are a great deal more difficult to deal in than cut stones. If I should care to trust you that far on your face, do you think you could handle the assignment?"

"Mr. Gallemore," I said firmly but quietly, "I am a total stranger to you and I am only flesh and blood. But I promise you by the memories of my dead and revered parents that there will be no cowardice."

"Well, there is a good deal of the flesh and blood, son," Mr. Gallemore said kindly. "And I am not afraid of your stealing the money, because possibly I know a little more about Miss Ellen Macintosh and her boy friend than you might suspect. Furthermore, the pearls are insured, in my name, of course, and the insurance company should really handle this affair. But you and your funny friend seem to have got along very nicely so far, and I believe in playing out a hand. This Henry must be quite a man."

"I have grown very attached to him, in spite of his uncouth ways," I said.

Mr. Gallemore played with his white quill pen a little longer and then he brought out a large checkbook and wrote a check, which he carefully blotted and passed across the desk.

"If you get the pearls, I'll see that the insurance people refund this to me," he said. "If they like my business, there will be no difficulty about that. The bank is down at the corner and I will be waiting for their call. They won't cash the check without telephoning me, probably. Be careful, son, and don't get hurt."

He shook hands with me once more and I hesitated. "Mr. Gallemore, you are placing a greater trust in me than any man ever has," I said. "With the exception, of course, of my own father."

"I am acting like a damn fool," he said with a peculiar smile. "It is so long since I heard anyone talk the way Jane Austen writes that it is making a sucker out of me."

"Thank you, sir. I know my language is a bit stilted. Dare I ask you to do me a small favor, sir?"

"What is it, Gage?"

"To telephone Miss Ellen Macintosh, from whom I am now a little estranged, and tell her that I am not drinking today, and that you have entrusted me with a very delicate mission."

He laughed aloud. "I'll be glad to, Walter. And as I know she can be trusted, I'll give her an idea of what's going on."

I left him then and went down to the bank with the check, and the teller, after looking at me suspiciously, then absenting himself from his cage for a long time, finally counted out the money in hundred-dollar bills with the reluctance one might have expected, if it had been his own money.

I placed the flat packet of bills in my pocket and said: "Now give me a roll of quarters, please."

"A roll of quarters, sir?" His eyebrows lifted.

"Exactly. I use them for tips. And naturally I should prefer to carry them home in the wrappings."

"Oh, I see. Ten dollars, please."

I took the fat hard roll of coins and dropped it into my pocket and drove back to Hollywood.

Henry was waiting for me in the lobby of the Chateau Moraine, twirling his hat between his rough hard hands. His face looked a little more deeply lined than it had the day before and I noticed that his breath smelled of whiskey. We went up to my apartment and he turned to me eagerly.

"Any luck, pal?"

"Henry," I said, "before we proceed further into this day I wish it clearly understood that I am not drinking. I see that already you have been at the bottle."

"Just a pick-up, Walter," he said a little contritely. "That job I went out for was gone before I got there. What's the good word?"

I sat down and lit a cigarette and stared at him evenly. "Well, Henry, I don't really know whether I should tell you or not. But it seems a little petty not to do so after all you did last night to Gandesi." I hesitated a moment longer while Henry stared at me and pinched the muscles of his left arm. "The pearls are real, Henry. And I have instructions to proceed with the business and I have five thousand dollars in cash in my pocket at this moment."

I told him briefly what had happened.

He was more amazed than words could tell. "Cripes!" he exclaimed, his mouth hanging wide open. "You mean you got the five grand from this Gallemore--just like that?"

"Precisely that, Henry."

"Kid," he said earnestly, "You got something with that daisy pan and that fluff talk that a lot of guys would give important dough to cop. Five grand--out of a business guy--just like that. Why, I'll be a monkey's uncle. I'll be a snake's daddy. I'll be a mickey finn at a woman's-club lunch."

At that exact moment, as if my entrance to the building had been observed, the telephone rang again and I sprang to answer it.

It was one of the voices I was awaiting, but not the one I wanted to hear with the greater longing. "How's it looking to you this morning, Gage?"

"It is looking better," I said. "If I can have any assurance of honorable treatment, I am prepared to go through with it."

"You mean you got the dough?"

"In my pocket at this exact moment."

The voice seemed to exhale a slow breath. "You'll get your marbles O.K.--if we get the price, Gage. We're in this business for a long time and we don't welsh. If we did, it would soon get around and nobody would play with us any more."

"Yes, I can readily understand that," I said. "Proceed with your instructions," I added coldly.

"Listen close, Gage. Tonight at eight sharp you be in Pacific Palisades. Know where that is?"

"Certainly. It is a small residential section west of the polo fields on Sunset Boulevard."

"Right. Sunset goes slap through it. There's one drugstore there--open till nine. Be there waiting a call at eight sharp tonight. Alone. And I mean alone, Gage. No cops and no strongarm guys. It's rough country down there and we got a way to get you to where we want you and know if you're alone. Get all this?"

"I am not entirely an idiot," I retorted.

"No dummy packages, Gage. The dough will be checked. No guns. You'll be searched and there's enough of us to cover you from all angles. We know your car. No funny business, no smart work, no slip-up and nobody hurt. That's the way we do business. How's the dough fixed?"

"One-hundred-dollar bills," I said. "And only a few of them are new."

"Attaboy. Eight o'clock then. Be smart, Gage."

The phone clicked in my ear and I hung up. It rang again almost instantly. This time it was the one voice.

"Oh, Walter," Ellen cried, "I was so mean to you! Please forgive me, Walter. Mr. Gallemore has told me everything and I'm so frightened."

"There is nothing of which to be frightened," I told her warmly. "Does Mrs. Penruddock know, darling?"

"No, darling. Mr. Gallemore told me not to tell her. I am phoning from a store down on Sixth Street. Oh, Walter, I really am frightened. Will Henry go with you?"

"I am afraid not, darling. The arrangements are all made and they will not permit it. I must go alone."

"Oh, Walter! I'm terrified. I can't bear the suspense."

"There is nothing to fear," I assured her. "It is a simple business transaction. And I am not exactly a midget."

"But, Walter--oh, I *will* try to be brave, Walter. Will you promise me just one teensy-weensy little thing?"

"Not a drop, darling," I said firmly. "Not a single solitary drop."

"Oh, Walter!"

There was a little more of that sort of thing, very pleasant to me in the circumstances, although possibly not of great interest to others. We finally parted with my promise to telephone as soon as the meeting between the crooks and myself had been consummated.

I turned from the telephone to find Henry drinking deeply from a bottle he had taken from his hip pocket.

"Henry!" I cried sharply.

He looked at me over the bottle with a shaggy determined look. 'Listen, pal," he said in a low hard voice. "I got enough of your end of the talk to figure the set-up. Some place out in the tall weeds and you go alone and they feed you the old sap poison and take your dough and leave you lying--with the marbles still in their kitty. Nothing doing, pal. I said--nothing doing!" He almost shouted the last words.

"Henry, it is my duty and I must do it," I said quietly.

"Haw!" Henry snorted. "I say no. You're a nut, but you're a sweet guy on the side. I say no. Henry Eichelberger of the Wisconsin Eichelbergers--in fact, I might just as leave say of the Milwaukee Eichelbergers--says no. And he says it with both hands working." He drank again from his bottle.

"You certainly will not help matters by becoming intoxicated," I told him rather bitterly.

He lowered the bottle and looked at me with amazement written all over his rugged features. "Drunk, Walter?" he boomed. "Did I hear you say drunk? An Eichelberger drunk? Listen, son. We ain't got a lot of time now. It would take maybe three months. Some day when you got three months and maybe five thousand gallons of whiskey and a funnel, I would be glad to take my own time and show you what an Eichelberger looks like when drunk. You wouldn't believe it. Son, there wouldn't be nothing left of this town but a few sprung girders and a lot of busted bricks, in the middle of which--Geez, I'll get talking English myself if I hang around you much longer--in the middle of which, peaceful, with no human life nearer than maybe fifty miles, Henry Eichelberger will be on his back smiling at the sun. Drunk, Walter. Not stinking drunk, not even country-club drunk. But you could use the word drunk and I wouldn't take no offense."

He sat down and drank again. I stared moodily at the floor. There was nothing for me to say.

"But that," Henry said, "is some other time. Right now I am just taking my medicine. I ain't myself without a slight touch of delirium tremens, as the guy says. I was brought up on it. And I'm going with you, Walter. Where is this place at?"

"It's down near the beach, Henry, and you are not going with me. If you must get drunk--get drunk, but you are not going with me."

"You got a big car, Walter. I'll hide in back on the floor under a rug. It's a cinch."

"No, Henry."

"Walter, you are a sweet guy," Henry said, "and I am going with you into this frame. Have a smell from the barrel, Walter. You look to me kind of frail."

We argued for an hour and my head ached and I began to feel very nervous and tired. It was then that I made what might have been a fatal mistake. I succumbed to Henry's blandishments and took a small portion of whiskey, purely for medicinal purposes. This made me feel so much more relaxed that I took another and larger portion. I had had no food except coffee that morning and only a very light dinner the evening before. At the end of another hour Henry had been out for two more bottles of whiskey and I was as bright as a bird. All difficulties had now disappeared and I had agreed heartily that Henry should lie in the back of my car hidden by a rug and accompany me to the rendezvous.

We had passed the time very pleasantly until two o'clock, at which hour I began to feel sleepy and lay down on the bed, and fell into a deep slumber.

7

When I awoke again it was almost dark. I rose from
the bed with panic in my heart, and also a sharp shoot
of pain through my temples. It was only six-thirty,
however. I was alone in the apartment and lengthening
shadows were stealing across the floor. The display of
empty whiskey bottles on the table was very
disgusting. Henry Eichelberger was nowhere to be
seen. With an instinctive pang, of which I was almost
immediately ashamed, I hurried to my jacket hanging
on the back of a chair and plunged my hand into the
inner breast pocket. The packet of bills was there
intact. After a brief hesitation, and with a feeling of
secret guilt, I drew them out and slowly counted them
over. Not a bill was missing. I replaced the money and
tried to smile at myself for this lack of trust, and then
switched on a light and went into the bathroom to take
alternate hot and cold showers until my brain was once
more comparatively clear.

I had done this and was dressing in fresh linen when
a key turned in the lock and Henry Eichelberger
entered with two wrapped bottles under his arm. He
looked at me with what I thought was genuine
affection.

"A guy that can sleep it off like you is a real champ,
Walter," he said admiringly. "I snuck your keys so as
not to wake you. I had to get some eats and some more
hooch. I done a little solo drinking, which as I told you
is against my principles, but this is a big day.
However, we take it easy from now on as to the hooch.
We can't afford no jitters till it's all over."

He had unwrapped a bottle while he was speaking and poured me a small drink. I drank it gratefully and immediately felt a warm glow in my veins.

"I bet you looked in your poke for that deck of mazuma," Henry said, grinning at me.

I felt myself reddening, but I said nothing. "Okay, pal, you done right. What the heck do you know about Henry Eichelberger anyways? I done something else." He reached behind him and drew a short automatic from his hip pocket. "If these boys wanta play rough," he said, "I got me five bucks worth of iron that don't mind playin' rough a little itself. And the Eichelbergers ain't missed a whole lot of the guys they shot at."

"I don't like that, Henry," I said severely. "That is contrary to the agreement."

"Nuts to the agreement," Henry said. "The boys get their dough and no cops. I'm out to see that they hand over them marbles and don't pull any fast footwork."

I saw there was no use arguing with him, so I completed my dressing and prepared to leave the apartment. We each took one more drink and then Henry put a full bottle in his pocket and we left.

On the way down the hall to the elevator he explained in a low voice: "I got a hack out front to tail you, just in case these boys got the same idea. You might circle a few quiet blocks so as I can find out. More like they don't pick you up till down close to the beach."

"All this must be costing you a great deal of money, Henry," I told him, and while we were waiting for the elevator to come up I took another twenty-dollar bill from my wallet and offered it to him. He took the money reluctantly, but finally folded it and placed it in his pocket.

I did as Henry had suggested, driving up and down a number of the hilly streets north of Hollywood Boulevard, and presently I heard the unmistakable hoot of a taxicab horn behind me. I pulled over to the side of the road. Henry got out of the cab and paid off the driver and got into my car beside me.

"All clear," he said. "No tail. I'll just keep kind of slumped down and you better stop somewhere for some groceries on account of if we have to get rough with these mugs, a full head of steam will help."

So I drove westward and dropped down to Sunset Boulevard and presently stopped at a crowded drive-in restaurant where we sat at the counter and ate a light meal of omelette and black coffee. We then proceeded on our way. When we reached Beverly Hills, Henry again made me wind in and out through a number of residential streets where he observed very carefully through the rear window of the car.

Fully satisfied at last we drove back to Sunset, and without incident onwards through Bel-Air and the fringes of Westwood, almost as far as the Riviera Polo field. At this point, down in the hollow, there is a canyon called Mandeville Canyon, a very quiet place. Henry had me drive up this for a short distance. We then stopped and had a little whiskey from his bottle and he climbed into the back of the car and curled his big body up on the floor, with the rug over him and his automatic pistol and his bottle down on the floor conveniently to his hand. That done I once more resumed my journey.

Pacific Palisades is a district whose inhabitants seem to retire rather early. When I reached what might be called the business center nothing was open but the drugstore beside the bank. I parked the car, with Henry

120

remaining silent under the rug in the back, except for a slight gurgling noise I noticed as I stood on the dark sidewalk. Then I went into the drugstore and saw by its clock that it was now fifteen minutes to eight. I bought a package of cigarettes and lit one and took up my position near the open telephone booth.

The druggist, a heavy-set red-faced man of uncertain age, had a small radio up very loud and was listening to some foolish serial. I asked him to turn it down, as I was expecting an important telephone call. This he did, but not with any good grace, and immediately retired to the back part of his store whence I saw him looking out at me malignantly through a small glass window.

At precisely one minute to eight by the drugstore clock the phone rang sharply in the booth. I hastened into it and pulled the door tight shut. I lifted the receiver, trembling a little in spite of myself.

It was the same cool metallic voice. "Gage?"

"This is Mr. Gage."

"You done just what I told you?"

"Yes," I said. "I have the money in my pocket and I am entirely alone." I did not like the feeling of lying so brazenly, even to a thief, but I steeled myself to it.

"Listen, then. Go back about three hundred feet the way you come. Beside the firehouse there's a service station, closed up, painted green and red and white. Beside that, going south, is a dirt road. Follow it three quarters of a mile and you come to a white fence of four-by-four built almost across the road. You can just squeeze your car by at the left side. Dim your lights and get through there and keep going down the little hill into a hollow with sage all around. Park there, cut your lights, and wait. Get it?"

"Perfectly," I said coldly, "and it shall be done exactly that way."

"And listen, pal. There ain't a house in half a mile, and there ain't any folks around at all. You got ten minutes to get there. You're watched right this minute. You get there fast and you get there alone--or you got a trip for biscuits. And don't light no matches or pills nor use no flashlights. On your way."

The phone went dead and I left the booth. I was scarcely outside the drugstore before the druggist rushed at his radio and turned it up to a booming blare. I got into my car and turned it and drove back along Sunset Boulevard, as directed. Henry was as still as the grave on the floor behind me.

I was now very nervous and Henry had all the liquor which we had brought with us. I reached the firehouse in no time at all and through its front window I could see four firemen playing cards. I turned to the right down the dirt road past the red-and-green-and-white service station and almost at once the night was so still, in spite of the quiet sound of my car, that I could hear the crickets and tree-frogs chirping and trilling in all directions, and from some nearby watery spot came the hoarse croak of a solitary bullfrog.

The road dipped and rose again and far off there was a yellow window. Then ahead of me, ghostly in the blackness of the moonless night, appeared the dim white barrier across the road. I noted the gap at the side and then dimmed my headlamps and steered carefully through it and so on down a rough short hill into an oval-shaped hollow space surrounded by low brush and plentifully littered with empty bottles and cans and pieces of paper. It was entirely deserted, however, at this dark hour. I stopped my car and shut off the ignition, and the lights, and sat there motionless, hands on the wheel.

Behind me I heard no murmur of sound from Henry. I waited possibly five minutes, although it seemed much longer, but nothing happened. It was very still, very lonely, and I did not feel happy.

Finally there was a faint sound of movement behind me and I looked back to see the pale blur of Henry's face peering at me from under the rug.

His voice whispered huskily. "Anything stirring, Walter?"

I shook my head at him vigorously and he once more pulled the rug over his face. I heard a faint sound of gurgling.

Fully fifteen minutes passed before I dared to move again. By this time the tensity of waiting had made me stiff. I therefore boldly unlatched the door of the car and stepped out upon the rough ground. Nothing happened. I walked slowly back and forth with my hands in my pockets. More and more time dragged by. More than half an hour had now elapsed and I became impatient. I went to the rear window of the car and spoke softly into the interior.

"Henry, I fear we have been victimized in a very cheap way. I fear very much that this is nothing but a low practical joke on the part of Mr. Gandesi in retaliation for the way you handled him last night. There is no one here and only one possible way of arriving. It looks to me like a very unlikely place for the sort of meeting we have been expecting."

"The son of a bitch!" Henry whispered back, and the gurgling sound was repeated in the darkness of the car. Then there was movement and he appeared free of the rug. The door opened against my body. Henry's head

123

emerged. He looked in all directions his eyes could command. "Sit down on the running board," he whispered. "I'm getting out, If they got a bead on us from them bushes, they'll only see one head."

I did what Henry suggested and turned my collar up high and pulled my hat down over my eyes. As noiselessly as a shadow Henry stepped out of the car and shut the door without sound and stood before me ranging the limited horizon with his eyes. I could see the dim reflection of light on the gun in his hand. We remained thus for ten more minutes.

Henry then got angry and threw discretion to the winds. "Suckered!" he snarled. "You know what happened, Walter?"

"No, Henry. I do not."

"It was just a tryout, that's what it was. Somewhere along the line these dirty-so-and-so's checked on you to see did you play ball, and then again they checked on you at that drugstore back there. I bet you a pair of solid platinum bicycle wheels that was a long-distance call you caught back there."

"Yes, Henry, now that you mention it, I am sure it was," I said sadly.

"There you are, kid. The bums ain't even left town. They are sitting back there beside their plush-lined spittoons giving you the big razzoo. And tomorrow this guy calls you again on the phone and says O.K. so far, but they had to be careful and they will try again tonight maybe out in San Fernando Valley and the price will be upped to ten grand, on account of their extra trouble. I oughta go back there and twist that Gandesi so he would be lookin' up his left pants leg."

"Well, Henry," I said, "after all, I did not do exactly what they told me to, because you insisted on coming with me. And perhaps they are more clever than you think. So I think the best thing now is to go back to town and hope there will be a chance tomorrow to try again. And you must promise me faithfully not to interfere."

"Nuts!" Henry said angrily. "Without me along they would take you the way the cat took the canary. You are a sweet guy, Walter, but you don't know as many answers as Baby Leroy. These guys are thieves and they have a string of marbles that might probably bring them twenty grand with careful handling. They are out for a quick touch, but they will squeeze all they can just the same. I oughta go back to that fat wop Gandesi right now. I could do things to that slob that ain't been invented yet."

"Now, Henry, don't get violent," I said.

"Haw," Henry snarled. "Them guys give me an ache in the back of my lap." He raised his bottle to his lips with his left hand and drank thirstily. His voice came down a few tones and sounded more peaceful. "Better dip the bill, Walter. The party's a flop."

"Perhaps you are right, Henry," I sighed. "I will admit that my stomach has been trembling like an autumn leaf for all of half an hour."

So I stood up boldly beside him and poured a liberal portion of the fiery liquid down my throat. At once my courage revived. I handed the bottle back to Henry and he placed it carefully down on the running board. He stood beside me dancing the short automatic pistol up and down on the broad palm of his hand.

"I don't need no tools to handle that bunch. The hell with it." And with a sweep of his arm he hurled the pistol off among the bushes, where it fell to the ground with a muffled thud. He walked away from the car and stood with his arms akimbo, looking up at the sky.

I moved over beside him and watched his averted face, insofar as I was able to see it in that dim light. A strange melancholy came over me. In the brief time I had known Henry I had grown very fond of him.

"Well, Henry," I said at last, "what is the next move?"

"Beat it on home, I guess," he said slowly and mournfully. "And get good and drunk." He doubled his hands into fists and shook them slowly. Then he turned to face me. "Yeah," he said. "Nothing else to do. Beat it on home, kid, is all that is left to us."

"Not quite yet, Henry," I said softly.

I took my right hand out of my pocket. I have large hands. In my right hand nestled the roll of wrapped quarters which I had obtained at the bank that morning. My hand made a large fist around them.

"Good night, Henry," I said quietly, and swung my fist with all the weight of my arm and body. "You had two strikes on me, Henry," I said. "The big one is still left."

But Henry was not listening to me. My fist with the wrapped weight of metal inside it had caught him fairly and squarely on the point of his jaw. His legs became boneless and he pitched straight forward, brushing my sleeve as he fell. I stepped quickly out of his way.

Henry Eichelberger lay motionless on the ground, as limp as a rubber glove.

I looked down at him a little sadly, waiting for him to stir, but he did not move a muscle. He lay inert, completely unconscious. I dropped the roll of quarters back into my pocket, bent over him, searched him thoroughly, moving him around like a sack of meal, but it was a long time before I found the pearls. They were twined around his ankle inside his left sock.

"Well, Henry," I said, speaking to him for the last time, although he could not hear me, "you are a gentleman, even if you are a thief. You could have taken the money a dozen times this afternoon and given me nothing. You could have taken it a little while ago when you had the gun in your hand, but even that repelled you. You threw the gun away and we were man to man, far from help, far from interference. And even then you hesitated, Henry. In fact, Henry, I think for a successful thief you hesitated just a little too long. But as a man of sporting feelings I can only think the more highly of you. Goodbye, Henry, and good luck."

I took my wallet out and withdrew a one-hundred-dollar bill and placed it carefully in the pocket where I had seen Henry put his money. Then I went back to the car and took a drink out of the whiskey bottle and corked it firmly and laid it beside him, convenient to his right hand.

I felt sure that when he awakened he would need it.

8

It was past ten o'clock when I returned home to my apartment, but I at once went to the telephone and called Ellen Macintosh. "Darling!" I cried. "I have the pearls."

I caught the sound of her indrawn breath over the wire. "Oh darling," she said tensely and excitedly, "and you are not hurt? They did not hurt you, darling? They just took the money and let you go?"

"There were no 'they,' darling," I said proudly. "I still have Mr. Gallemore's money intact. There was only Henry."

"Henry!" she cried in a very strange voice. "But I thought--Come over here at once, Walter Gage, and tell me--"

"I have whiskey on my breath, Ellen."

"Darling! I'm sure you needed it. Come at once."

So once more I went down to the street and hurried to Carondelet Park and in no time at all was at the Penruddock residence. Ellen came out on the porch to meet me and we talked there quietly in the dark, holding hands, for the household had gone to bed. As simple as I could I told her my story.

"But darling," she said at last, "how did you know it was Henry? I thought Henry was your friend. And this other voice on the telephone--"

"Henry *was* my friend," I said a little sadly, "and that is what destroyed him. As to the voice on the telephone, that was a small matter and easily arranged. Henry was away from me a number of times to arrange it. There was just one small point that gave me thought. After I gave Gandesi my private card with the name of my apartment house scribbled upon it, it was necessary for Henry to communicate to his confederate that we had seen Gandesi and given him my name and address. For of course when I had this foolish, or perhaps not so very foolish idea of visiting some well-known underworld character in order to send a message that we would buy back the pearls, this was Henry's opportunity to make me think the telephone message came as a result of our talking to Gandesi, and telling him our difficulty. But since the first call came to me at my apartment before Henry had had a chance to inform his confederate of our meeting with Gandesi, it was obvious that a trick had been employed.

"Then I recalled that a car had bumped into us from behind and Henry had gone back to abuse the driver. And of course the bumping was deliberate, and Henry had made the opportunity for it on purpose, and his confederate was in the car. So Henry, while pretending to shout at him, was able to convey the necessary information."

"But, Walter," Ellen said, having listened to this explanation a little impatiently, "that is a very small matter. What I really want to know is how you decided that Henry had the pearls at all."

"But you told me he had them," I said. "You were quite sure of it. Henry is a very durable character. It would be just like him to hide the pearls somewhere, having no fear of what the police might do to him, and get another position and then after perhaps quite a long time, retrieve the pearls and quietly leave this part of the country."

Ellen shook her head impatiently in the darkness of the porch. "Walter," she said sharply, "you are hiding something. You could not have been sure and you would not have hit Henry in that brutal way, unless you had been sure. I know you well enough to know that."

"Well, darling," I said modestly, "there was indeed another small indication, one of those foolish trifles which the cleverest men overlook. As you know, I do not use the regular apartment house telephone, not wishing to be annoyed by solicitors and such people. The phone which I use is a private line and its number is unlisted. But the calls I received from Henry's confederate came over that phone, and Henry had been in my apartment a great deal, and I had been careful not to give Mr. Gandesi that number, because of course I did not expect anything from Mr. Gandesi, as I was perfectly sure from the beginning that Henry had the pearls, if only I could get him to bring them out of hiding."

"Oh, darling," Ellen cried, and threw her arms around me. "How brave you are, and I really think that you are actually clever in your own peculiar way. Do you believe that Henry was in love with me?"

But that was a subject in which I had no interest whatever. I left the pearls in Ellen's keeping and late as the hour now was I drove at once to the residence of Mr. Lansing Gallemore and told him my story and gave him back his money.

A few months later I was happy to receive a letter postmarked in Honolulu and written on a very inferior brand of paper.

Well, pal, that Sunday punch of yours was the money and I did not think you had it in you, altho of course I was not set for it. But it was a pip and made me think of you for a week every time I brushed my teeth. It was too bad I had to scram because you are a sweet guy altho a little on the goofy side and I'd like to be getting plastered with you right now instead of wiping oil valves where I am at which is not where this letter is mailed by several thousand miles. There is just two things I would like you to know and they are both kosher. I did fall hard for that tall blonde and this was the main reason I took my time from the old lady. Glomming the pearls was just one of those screwy ideas a guy can get when he is dizzy with a dame. It was a crime the way they left them marbles lying around in that bread box and I worked for a Frenchy once in Djibouty and got to know pearls enough to tell them from snowballs. But when it came to the clinch down there in that brush with us two alone and no holds barred I just was too soft to go through with the deal. Tell that blonde you got a loop on I was asking for her.

YRS. as ever,

HENRY EICHELBERGER (Alias)

P. S. What do you know, that punk that did the phone work on you tried to take me for a fifty cut on that C note you tucked in my vest. I had to twist the sucker plenty.

Yrs. H. E. (Alias)

At one o'clock in the morning, Carl, the night porter, turned down the last of three table lamps in the main lobby of the Windermere Hotel. The blue carpet darkened a shade or two and the walls drew back into remoteness. The chairs filled with shadowy loungers. In the corners were memories like cobwebs.

Tony Reseck yawned. He put his head on one side and listened to the frail, twittery music from the radio room beyond a dim arch at the far side of the lobby. He frowned. That should be his radio room after one A.M. Nobody should be in it. That red-haired girl was spoiling his nights.

The frown passed and a miniature of a smile quirked at the corners of his lips. He sat relaxed, a short, pale, paunchy, middle-aged man with long, delicate fingers clasped on the elk's tooth on his watch chain; the long delicate fingers of a sleight-of-hand artist, fingers with shiny, molded nails and tapering first joints, fingers a little spatulate at the ends. Handsome fingers. Tony Reseck rubbed them gently together and there was peace in his quiet sea-gray eyes.

The frown came back on his face. The music annoyed him. He got up with a curious litheness, all in one piece, without moving his clasped hands from the watch chain. At one moment he was leaning back relaxed, and the next he was standing balanced on his feet, perfectly still, so that the movement of rising seemed to be a thing perfectly perceived, an error of vision.

He walked with small, polished shoes delicately across the blue carpet and under the arch. The music was louder. It contained the hot, acid blare, the frenetic, jittering runs of a jam session. It was too loud. The red-haired girl sat there and stared silently at the fretted part of the big radio cabinet as though she could see the band with its fixed professional grin and the sweat running down its back. She was curled up with her feet under her on a davenport which seemed to contain most of the cushions in the room. She was tucked among them carefully, like a corsage in the florist's tissue paper.

She didn't turn her head. She leaned there, one hand in a small fist on her peach-colored knee. She was wearing lounging pajamas of heavy ribbed silk embroidered with black lotus buds.

"You like Goodman, Miss Cressy?" Tony Reseck asked.

The girl moved her eyes slowly. The light in there was dim, but the violet of her eyes almost hurt. They were large, deep eyes without a trace of thought in them. Her face was classical and without expression.

She said nothing.

Tony smiled and moved his fingers at his sides, one by one, feeling them move. "You like Goodman, Miss Cressy?" he repeated gently.

"Not to cry over," the girl said tonelessly.

Tony rocked back on his heels and looked at her eyes. Large, deep, empty eyes. Or were they? He reached down and muted the radio.

"Don't get me wrong," the girl said. "Goodman makes money, and a lad that makes legitimate money these days is a lad you have to respect. But this jitterbug music gives me the backdrop of a beer flat. I like something with roses in it."

"Maybe you like Mozart," Tony said.

"Go on, kid me," the girl said.

"I wasn't kidding you, Miss Cressy. I think Mozart was the greatest man that ever lived--and Toscanini is his prophet."

"I thought you were the house dick." She put her head back on a pillow and stared at him through her lashes. "Make me some of that Mozart," she added.

"It's too late," Tony sighed. "You can't get it now."

She gave him another long lucid glance. "Got the eye on me, haven't you, flatfoot?" She laughed a little, almost under her breath. "What did I do wrong?"

Tony smiled his toy smile. "Nothing, Miss Cressy. Nothing at all. But you need some fresh air. You've been five days in this hotel and you haven't been outdoors. And you have a tower room."

She laughed again. "Make me a story about it. I'm bored."

"There was a girl here once had your suite. She stayed in the hotel a whole week, like you. Without going out at all, I mean. She didn't speak to anybody hardly. What do you think she did then?"

The girl eyed him gravely. "She jumped her bill."

He put his long delicate hand out and turned it slowly, fluttering the fingers, with an effect almost like a lazy wave breaking. 'Unh-uh. She sent down for her bill and paid it. Then she told the hop to be back in half an hour for her suitcases. Then she went out on her balcony."

The girl leaned forward a little, her eyes still grave, one hand capping her peach-colored knee. "What did you say your name was?"

"Tony Reseck."

"Sounds like a flunky."

"Yeah," Tony said. "Polish."

"Go on, Tony."

"All the tower suites have private balconies, Miss Cressy. The walls of them are too low for fourteen stories above the street. It was a dark night, that night, high clouds." He dropped his hand with a final gesture, a farewell gesture. "Nobody saw her jump. But when she hit, it was like a big gun going off."

"You're making it up, Tony." Her voice was a clean dry whisper of sound.

He smiled his toy smile. His quiet sea gray eyes seemed almost to be smoothing the long waves of her hair. "Eve Cressy," he said musingly. "A name waiting for lights to be in."

"Waiting for a tall dark guy that's no good, Tony. You wouldn't care why. I was married to him once. I might be married to him again. You can make a lot of mistakes in just one lifetime." The hand on her knee opened slowly until the fingers were strained back as far as they would go. Then they closed quickly and tightly, and even in that dim light the knuckles shone like the little polished bones. "I played him a low trick once. I put him in a bad place--without meaning to. You wouldn't care about that either. It's just that I owe him something."

He leaned over softly and turned the knob on the radio. A waltz formed itself dimly on the warm air. A tinsel waltz, but a waltz. He turned the volume up. The music gushed from the loudspeaker in a swirl of shadowed melody. Since Vienna died, all waltzes are shadowed.

The girl put her hand on one side and hummed three or four bars and stopped with a sudden tightening of her mouth.

"Eve Cressy," she said. "It was in lights once. At a bum night club. A dive. They raided it and the lights went out."

He smiled at her almost mockingly. "It was no dive while you were there, Miss Cressy...That's the waltz the orchestra always played when the old porter walked up and down in front of the hotel entrance, all swelled up with his medals on his chest. *The Last Laugh.* Emil Jannings. You wouldn't remember that one, Miss Cressy."

"'Spring, Beautiful Spring,'" she said. "No, I never saw it."

He walked three steps away from her and turned. "I have to go upstairs and palm doorknobs. I hope I didn't bother you. You ought to go to bed now. It's pretty late."

The tinsel waltz stopped and a voice began to talk. The girl spoke through the voice. "You really thought something like that--about the balcony?"

He nodded. "I might have," he said softly. "I don't any more."

"No chance, Tony." Her smile was a dim lost leaf. "Come and talk to me some more. Redheads don't jump, Tony. They hang on--and wither."

He looked at her gravely for a moment and then moved away over the carpet. The porter was standing in the archway that led to the main lobby. Tony hadn't looked that way yet, but he knew somebody was there. He always knew if anybody was close to him. He could hear the grass grow, like the donkey in *The Blue Bird.*

The porter jerked his chin at him urgently. His broad face above the uniform collar looked sweaty and excited. Tony stepped up close to him and they went together through the arch and out to the middle of the dim lobby.

"Trouble?" Tony asked wearily.

"There's a guy outside to see you, Tony. He won't come in. I'm doing a wipe--off on the plate glass of the doors and he comes up beside me, a tall guy. 'Get Tony,' he says, out of the side of his mouth."

Tony said: "Uh-huh," and looked at the porter's pale blue eyes. "Who was it?"

"Al, he said to say he was."

Tony's face became as expressionless as dough. "Okey." He started to move off.

The porter caught his sleeve. "Listen, Tony. You got any enemies?"

Tony laughed politely, his face still like dough.

"Listen, Tony." The porter held his sleeve tightly. "There's a big black car down the block, the other way from the hacks. There's a guy standing beside it with his foot on the running board. This guy that spoke to me, he wears a dark-colored, wrap-around overcoat with a high collar turned up against his ears. His hat's way low, You can't hardly see his face. He says, 'Get Tony,' out of the side of his mouth. You ain't got any enemies, have you, Tony?"

"Only the finance company," Tony said. "Beat it."

He walked slowly and a little stiffly across the blue carpet, up the three shallow steps to the entrance lobby with the three elevators on one side and the desk on the other. Only one elevator was working. Beside the open doors, his arms folded, the night operator stood silent in a neat blue uniform with silver facings. A lean, dark Mexican named Gomez. A new boy, breaking in on the night shift.

The other side was the desk, rose marble, with the night clerk leaning on it delicately. A small neat man with a wispy reddish mustache and cheeks so rosy they looked roughed. He stared at Tony and poked a nail at his mustache.

Tony pointed a stiff index finger at him, folded the other three fingers tight to his palm, and flicked his thumb up and down on the stiff finger. The clerk touched the other side of his mustache and looked bored.

Tony went on past the closed and darkened newsstand and the side entrance to the drugstore, out to the brassbound plate-glass doors. He stopped just inside them and took a deep, hard breath. He squared his shoulders, pushed the doors open and stepped out into the cold damp night air.

The street was dark, silent. The rumble of traffic on Wilshire, two blocks away, had no body, no meaning. To the left were two taxis. Their drivers leaned against a fender, side by side, smoking. Tony walked the other way. The big dark car was a third of a block from the hotel entrance. Its lights were dimmed and it was only when he was almost up to it that he heard the gentle sound of its engine turning over.

A tall figure detached itself from the body of the car and strolled toward him, both hands in the pockets of the dark overcoat with the high collar. From the man's mouth a cigarette tip glowed faintly, a rusty pearl.

They stopped two feet from each other.

The tall man said, "Hi, Tony. Long time no see."

"Hello, Al. How's it going?"

"Can't complain." The tall man started to take his right hand out of his overcoat pocket, then stopped and laughed quietly. "I forgot. Guess you don't want to shake hands."

"That don't mean anything," Tony said. "Shaking hands. Monkeys can shake hands. What's on your mind, Al?"

"Still the funny little fat guy, eh, Tony?"

"I guess." Tony winked his eyes tight. His throat felt tight.

"You like your job back there?"

"It's a job."

Al laughed his quiet laugh again. "You take it slow, Tony. I'll take it fast. So it's a job and you want to hold it. Okey. There's a girl named Eve Cressy flopping in your quiet hotel. Get her out. Fast and right now."

"What's the trouble?"

The tall man looked up and down the street. A man behind in the car coughed lightly. "She's hooked with a wrong number. Nothing against her personal, but she'll lead trouble to you. Get her out, Tony. You got maybe an hour."

"Sure," Tony said aimlessly, without meaning.

Al took his hand out of his pocket and stretched it against Tony's chest. He gave him a light lazy push. "I wouldn't be telling you just for the hell of it, little fat brother. Get her out of there."

"Okey," Tony said, without any tone in his voice.

The tall man took back his hand and reached for the car door. He opened it and started to slip in like a lean black shadow.

Then he stopped and said something to the men in the car and got out again. He came back to where Tony stood silent, his pale eyes catching a little dim light from the street.

"Listen, Tony. You always kept your nose clean. You're a good brother, Tony."

Tony didn't speak.

Al leaned toward him, a long urgent shadow, the high collar almost touching his ears. "It's trouble business, Tony. The boys won't like it, but I'm telling you just the same. This Cressy was married to a lad named Johnny Rails. Rails is out of Quentin two, three days, or a week. He did a three-spot for manslaughter. The girl put him there. He ran down an old man one night when he was drunk, and she was with him. He wouldn't stop. She told him to go in and tell it, or else. He didn't go in. So the Johns come for him."

Tony said, "That's too bad."

"It's kosher, kid. It's my business to know. This Rails flapped his mouth in stir about how the girl would be waiting for him when he got out, all set to forgive and forget, and he was going straight to her."

Tony said, "What's he to you?" His voice had a dry, stiff crackle, like thick paper.

Al laughed. "The trouble boys want to see him. He ran a table at a spot on the Strip and figured out a scheme. He and another guy took the house for fifty grand. The other lad coughed up, but we still need Johnny's twenty-five. The trouble boys don't get paid to forget."

Tony looked up and down the dark street. One of the taxi drivers flicked a cigarette stub in a long arc over the top of one of the cabs. Tony watched it fall and spark on the pavement. He listened to the quiet sound of the big car's motor.

"I don't want any part of it," he said. "I'll get her out."

Al backed away from him, nodding. "Wise kid. How's mom these days?"

"Okey," Tony said.

"Tell her I was asking for her."

"Asking for her isn't anything," Tony said.

Al turned quickly and got into the car. The car curved lazily in the middle of the block and drifted back toward the corner. Its lights went up and sprayed on a wall. It turned a corner and was gone. The lingering smell of its exhaust drifted past Tony's nose. He turned and walked back to the hotel and into it. He went along to the radio room.

The radio still muttered, but the girl was gone from the davenport in front of it. The pressed cushions were hollowed out by her body. Tony reached down and touched them. He thought they were still warm. He turned the radio off and stood there, turning a thumb slowly in front of his body, his hand flat against his stomach. Then he went back through the lobby toward the elevator bank and stood beside a majolica jar of white sand. The clerk fussed behind a pebbled-glass screen at one end of the desk. The air was dead.

The elevator bank was dark. Tony looked at the indicator of the middle car and saw that it was at 14.

"Gone to bed," he said under his breath.

The door of the porter's room beside the elevators opened and the little Mexican night operator came out in street clothes. He looked at Tony with a quiet sidewise look out of eyes the color of dried-out chestnuts.

"Good night, boss."

"Yeah," Tony said absently.

He took a thin dappled cigar out of his vest pocket and smelled it. He examined it slowly, turning it around in his neat fingers. There was a small tear along the side. He frowned at that and put the cigar away.

There was a distant sound and the hand on the indicator began to steal around the bronze dial. Light glittered up in the shaft and the straight line of the car floor dissolved the darkness below. The car stopped and the doors opened, and Carl came out of it.

His eyes caught Tony's with a kind of jump and he walked over to him, his head on one side, a thin shine along his pink upper lip.

"Listen, Tony."

Tony took his arm in a hard swift hand and turned him. He pushed him quickly, yet somehow casually, down the steps to the dim main lobby and steered him into a corner. He let go of the arm. His throat tightened again, for no reason he could think of.

"Well?" he said darkly. "Listen to what?"

The porter reached into a pocket and hauled out a dollar bill. "He gimme this," he said loosely. His glittering eyes looked past Tony's shoulder at nothing. They winked rapidly. "Ice and ginger ale."

"Don't stall," Tony growled.

"Guy in Fourteen-B," the porter said.

"Lemme smell your breath."

The porter leaned toward him obediently.

"Liquor," Tony said harshly.

"He gimme a drink."

Tony looked down at the dollar bill. "Nobody's in Fourteen. Not on my list," he said.

"Yeah. There is." The porter licked his lips and his eyes opened and shut several times. "Tall dark guy."

"All right," Tony said crossly. "All right. There's a tall dark guy in Fourteen-B and he gave you a buck and a drink. Then what?"

"Gat under his arm," Carl said, and blinked.

Tony smiled, but his eyes had taken on the lifeless glitter of thick ice. "You take Miss Cressy up to her room?"

Carl shook his head. "Gomez. I saw her go up."

"Get away from me," Tony said between his teeth. "And don't accept any more drinks from the guests."

He didn't move until Carl had gone back into his cubbyhole by the elevators and shut the door. Then he moved silently up the three steps and stood in front of the desk, looking at the veined rose marble, the onyx pen set, the fresh registration card in its leather frame. He lifted a hand and smacked it down hard on the marble. The clerk popped out from behind the glass screen like a chipmunk coming out of its hole.

Tony took a flimsy out of his breast pocket and spread it on the desk. "No Fourteen-B on this," he said in a bitter voice.

The clerk wisped politely at his mustache. "So sorry. You must have been out to supper when he checked in."

"Who?"

"Registered as James Watterson, San Diego." The clerk yawned.

"Ask for anybody?"

The clerk stopped in the middle of the yawn and looked at the top of Tony's head. "Why yes. He asked for a swing band. Why?"

"Smart, fast and funny," Tony said. "If you like 'em that way." He wrote on his flimsy and stuffed it back into his pocket. "I'm going upstairs and palm doorknobs. There's four tower rooms you ain't rented yet. Get up on your toes, son. You're slipping."

"I made out," the clerk drawled, and completed his yawn. "Hurry back, pop. I don't know how I'll get through the time."

"You could shave that pink fuzz off your lip," Tony said, and went across to the elevators.

He opened up a dark one and lit the dome light and shot the car up to fourteen. He darkened it again, stepped out and closed the doors. This lobby was smaller than any other, except the one immediately below it. It had a single blue-paneled door in each of the walls other than the elevator wall. On each door was a gold number and letter with a gold wreath around it. Tony walked over to 14A and put his ear to the panel. He heard nothing. Eve Cressy might be in bed asleep, or in the bathroom, or out on the balcony. Or she might be sitting there in the room, a few feet from the door, looking at the wall. Well, he wouldn't expect to be able to hear her sit and look at the wall. He went over to 14B and put his ear to that panel. This was different. There was a sound in there. A man coughed. It sounded somehow like a solitary cough. There were no voices. Tony pressed the small nacre button beside the door.

Steps came without hurry. A thickened voice spoke through the panel. Tony made no answer, no sound. The thickened voice repeated the question. Lightly, maliciously, Tony pressed the bell again.

Mr. James Watterson, of San Diego, should now open the door and give forth noise. He didn't. A silence fell beyond that door that was like the silence of a glacier. Once more Tony put his ear to the wood. Silence utterly.

He got out a master key on a chain and pushed it delicately into the lock of the door. He turned it,

144

pushed the door inward three inches and withdrew the key. Then he waited.

"All right," the voice said harshly. "Come in and get it."

Tony pushed the door wide and stood there, framed against the light from the lobby. The man was tall, black-haired, angular and white-faced. He held a gun. He held it as though he knew about guns.

"Step right in," he drawled.

Tony went in through the door and pushed it shut with his shoulder. He kept his hands a little out from his sides, the clever fingers curled and slack. He smiled his quiet little smile.

"Mr. Watterson?"

"And after that what?"

"I'm the house detective here."

"It slays me."

The tall, white-faced, somehow handsome and somehow not handsome man backed slowly into the room. It was a large room with a low balcony around two sides of it. French doors opened out on the little private open-air balcony that each of the tower rooms had. There was a grate set for a log fire behind a paneled screen in front of a cheerful davenport. A tall misted glass stood on a hotel tray beside a deep, cozy chair. The man backed toward this and stood in front of it. The large, glistening gun drooped and pointed at the floor.

"It slays me," he said. "I'm in the dump an hour and the house copper gives me the bus. Okey, sweetheart, look in the closet and bathroom. But she just left."

"You didn't see her yet," Tony said.

145

The man's bleached face filled with unexpected lines. His thickened voice edged toward a snarl. "Yeah? Who didn't I see yet?"

"A girl named Eve Cressy."

The man swallowed. He put his gun down on the table beside the tray. He let himself down into the chair backwards, stiffly, like a man with a touch of lumbago. Then he leaned forward and put his hands on his kneecaps and smiled brightly between his teeth. "So she got here, huh? I didn't ask about her yet. I'm a careful guy. I didn't ask yet."

"She's been here five days," Tony said. "Waiting for you. She hasn't left the hotel a minute."

The man's mouth worked a little. His smile had a knowing tilt to it. "I got delayed a little up north," he said smoothly. "You know how it is. Visiting old friends. You seem to know a lot about my business, copper."

"That's right, Mr. Rails."

The man lunged to his feet and his hand snapped at the gun. He stood leaning over, holding it on the table, staring. "Dames talk too much," he said with a muffled sound in his voice as though he held something soft between his teeth and talked through it.

"Not dames, Mr. Rails."

"Huh?" The gun slithered on the hard wood of the table. "Talk it up, copper. My mind reader just quit."

"Not dames, guys. Guys with guns."

The glacier silence fell between them again. The man straightened his body out slowly. His face was washed clean of expression, but his eyes were haunted. Tony leaned in front of him, a shortish plump man with a quiet, pale, friendly face and eyes as simple as forest water.

"They never run out of gas--those boys," Johnny Rails said, and licked at his lip. "Early and late, they work. The old firm never sleeps."

"You know who they are?" Tony said softly.

"I could maybe give nine guesses. And twelve of them would be right."

"The trouble boys," Tony said, and smiled a brittle smile.

"Where is she?" Johnny Rails asked harshly.

"Right next door to you."

The man walked to the wall and left his gun lying on the table. He stood in front of the wall, studying it. He reached up and gripped the grillwork of the balcony railing. When he dropped his hand and turned, his face had lost some of its lines. His eyes had a quieter glint. He moved back to Tony and stood over him.

"I've got a stake," he said. "Eve sent me some dough and I built it up with a touch I made up north. Case dough, what I mean. The trouble boys talk about twenty-five grand." He smiled crookedly. "Five C's I can count. I'd have a lot of fun making them believe that, I would."

"What did you do with it?" Tony asked indifferently.

"I never had it, copper. Leave that lay. I'm the only guy in the world that believes it. It was a little deal that I got suckered on."

"I'll believe it," Tony said.

"They don't kill often. But they can be awful tough."

"Mugs," Tony said with a sudden bitter contempt. "Guys with guns. Just mugs."

Johnny Rails reached for his glass and drained it empty. The ice cubes tinkled softly as he put it down. He picked his gun up, danced it on his palm, then tucked it, nose down, into an inner breast pocket. He stared at the carpet.

"How come you're telling me this, copper?"

"I thought maybe you'd give her a break."

"And if I wouldn't?"

"I kind of think you will," Tony said.

Johnny Rails nodded quietly. "Can I get out of here?"

"You could take the service elevator to the garage. You could rent a car. I can give you a card to the garage man."

"You're a funny little guy," Johnny Rails said.

Tony took out a worn ostrich-skin billfold and scribbled on a printed card. Johnny Rails read it, and stood holding it, tapping it against a thumbnail.

"I could take her with me," he said, his eyes narrow. "You could take a ride in a basket too," Tony said. "She's been here five days, I told you. She's been spotted. A guy I know called me up and told me to get her out of here. Told me what it was all about. So I'm getting you out instead."

"They'll love that," Johnny Rails said. "They'll send you violets."

"I'll weep about it on my day off."

Johnny Rails turned his hand over and stared at the palm. "I could see her, anyway. Before I blow. Next door to here, you said?"

Tony turned on his heel and started for the door. He said over his shoulder, "Don't waste a lot of time, handsome. I might change my mind."

The man said, almost gently: "You might be spotting me right now, for all I know."

Tony didn't turn his head. "That's a chance you have to take."

He went on to the door and passed out of the room. He shut it carefully, silently, looked once at the door of 14A and got into his dark elevator. He rode it down to the linen-room floor and got out to remove the basket that held the service elevator open at that floor. The door slid quietly shut. He held it so that it made no noise. Down the corridor, light came from the open door of the housekeeper's office. Tony got back into his elevator and went on down to the lobby.

The little clerk was out of sight behind his pebbled-glass screen, auditing accounts. Tony went through the main lobby and turned into the radio room. The radio was on again, soft. She was there, curled on the davenport again. The speaker hummed to her, a vague sound so low that what it said was as wordless as the murmur of trees. She turned her head slowly and smiled at him.

"Finished palming doorknobs? I couldn't sleep worth a nickel. So I came down again. Okey?"

He smiled and nodded. He sat down in a green chair and patted the plump brocade arms of it. "Sure, Miss Cressy."

"Waiting is the hardest kind of work, isn't it? I wish you'd talk to that radio. It sounds like a pretzel being bent."

Tony fiddled with it, got nothing he liked, set it back where it had been.

"Beer-parlor drunks are all the customers now."

She smiled at him again.

"I don't bother you being here, Miss Cressy?"

"I like it. You're a sweet little guy, Tony."

He looked stiffly at the floor and a ripple touched his spine. He waited for it to go away. It went slowly. Then he sat back, relaxed again, his neat fingers clasped on his elk's tooth. He listened. Not to the radio--to far-off, uncertain things, menacing things. And perhaps to just the safe whir of wheels going away into a strange night.

"Nobody's all bad," he said out loud.

The girl looked at him lazily. "I've met two or three I was wrong on, then."

He nodded. "Yeah," he admitted judiciously. "I guess there's some that are."

The girl yawned and her deep violet eyes half closed. She nestled back into the cushions. "Sit there for a while, Tony. Maybe I could nap."

"Sure. Not a thing for me to do. Don't know why they pay me."

She slept quickly and with complete stillness, like a child. Tony hardly breathed for ten minutes. He just watched her, his mouth a little open. There was a quiet fascination in his limpid eyes, as if he was looking at an altar.

Then he stood up with infinite care and padded away under the arch to the entrance lobby and the desk. He stood at the desk listening for a little while. He heard a pen rustling out of sight. He went around the corner to the row of house phones in little glass cubbyholes. He lifted one and asked the night operator for the garage.

It rang three or four times and then a boyish voice answered: "Windermere Hotel. Garage speaking."

"This is Tony Reseck. That guy Watterson I gave a card to. He leave?"

"Sure, Tony. Half an hour almost. Is it your charge?"

"Yeah," Tony said. "My party. Thanks. Be seein' you."

He hung up and scratched his neck. He went back to the desk and slapped a hand on it. The clerk wafted himself around the screen with his greeter's smile in place. It dropped when he saw Tony.

"Can't a guy catch up on his work?" he grumbled.

"What's the professional rate on Fourteen-B?"

The clerk stared morosely. "There's no professional rate in the tower."

"Make one. The fellow left already. Was there only an hour."

"Well, well," the clerk said airily. "So the personality didn't click tonight. We get a skip-out."

"Will five bucks satisfy you?

"Friend of yours?"

"No. Just a drunk with delusions of grandeur and no dough."

"Guess we'll have to let it ride, Tony. How did he get out?"

"I took him down the service elevator. You was asleep. Will five bucks satisfy you?"

"Why?"

The worn ostrich-skin wallet came out and a weedy five slipped across the marble. "All I could shake him for," Tony said loosely.

The clerk took the five and looked puzzled. "You're the boss," he said, and shrugged. The phone shrilled on the desk and he reached for it. He listened and then pushed it toward Tony. "For you."

Tony took the phone and cuddled it close to his chest. He put his mouth close to the transmitter. The voice was strange to him. It had a metallic sound. Its syllables were meticulously anonymous.

"Tony? Tony Reseck?"

"Talking."

"A message from Al. Shoot?"

Tony looked at the clerk. "Be a pal," he said over the mouthpiece. The clerk flicked a narrow smile at him and went away. "Shoot," Tony said into the phone.

"We had a little business with a guy in your place. Picked him up scramming. Al had a hunch you'd run him out. Tailed him and took him to the curb. Not so good. Backfire."

Tony held the phone very tight and his temples chilled with the evaporation of moisture. "Go on," he said. "I guess there's more."

"A little. The guy stopped the big one. Cold. Al--Al said to tell you goodbye."

Tony leaned hard against the desk. His mouth made a sound that was not speech.

"Get it?" The metallic voice sounded impatient, a little bored. "This guy had him a rod. He used it. Al won't be phoning anybody any more."

Tony lurched at the phone, and the base of it shook on the rose marble. His mouth was a hard dry knot.

The voice said: "That's as far as we go, hub. G'night." The phone clicked dryly, like a pebble hitting a wall.

Tony put the phone down in its cradle very carefully, so as not to make any sound. He looked at the clenched palm of his left hand. He took a handkerchief out and rubbed the palm softly and straightened the fingers out with his other hand. Then he wiped his forehead. The clerk came around the screen again and looked at him with glinting eyes.

"I'm off Friday. How about lending me that phone number?"

Tony nodded at the clerk and smiled a minute frail smile. He put his handkerchief away and patted the pocket he had put it in. He turned and walked away

152

from the desk, across the entrance lobby, down the three shallow steps, along the shadowy reaches of the main lobby, and so in through the arch to the radio room once more. He walked softly, like man moving in a room where somebody is very sick. He reached the chair he had sat in before and lowered himself into it inch by inch. The girl slept on, motionless, in that curled-up looseness achieved by some women and all cats. Her breath made no slightest sound against the vague murmur of the radio.

Tony Reseck leaned back in the chair and clasped his hands on his elk's tooth and quietly closed his eyes.

THE KING IN YELLOW

1

George Millar, night auditor at the Carlton Hotel, was a dapper wiry little man, with a soft deep voice like a torch singer's. He kept it low, but his eyes were sharp and angry, as he said into the PBX mouthpiece: "I'm very sorry. It won't happen again. I'll send up at once."

He tore off the headpiece, dropped it on the keys of the switchboard and marched swiftly from behind the pebbled screen and out into the entrance lobby. It was past one and the Carlton was two thirds residential. In the main lobby, down three shallow steps, lamps were dimmed and the night porter had finished tidying up. The place was deserted--a wide space of dim furniture, rich carpet. Faintly in the distance a radio sounded. Millar went down the steps and walked quickly towards the sound, turned through an archway and looked at a man stretched out on a pale green davenport and what looked like all the loose cushions in the hotel. He lay on his side dreamy-eyed and listened to the radio two yards away from him.

Millar barked: "Hey, you! Are you the house dick here or the house cat?"

Steve Grayce turned his head slowly and looked at Millar. He was a long black-haired man, about twenty-eight, with deep-set silent eyes and a rather gentle mouth. He jerked a thumb at the radio and smiled. "King Leopardi, George. Hear that trumpet tone. Smooth as an angel's wing, boy."

"Swell! Goon back upstairs and get him out of the corridor!"

Steve Grayce looked shocked. "What--again? I thought I had those birds put to bed long ago." He swung his feet to the floor and stood up. He was at least a foot taller than Millar.

"Well, Eight-sixteen says no. Eight-sixteen says he's out in the hall with two of his stooges. He's dressed in yellow satin shorts and a trombone and he and his pals are putting on a jam session. And one of those hustlers Quillan registered in Eight-eleven is out there truckin' for them. Now get on to it, Steve--and this time make it stick."

Steve Grayce smiled wryly. He said: "Leopardi doesn't belong here anyway. Can I use chloroform or just my blackjack?"

He stepped long legs over the pale-green carpet, through the arch and across the main lobby to the single elevator that was open and lighted. He slid the doors shut and ran it up to Eight, stopped it roughly and stepped out into the corridor.

The noise hit him like a sudden wind. The walls echoed with it. Half a dozen doors were open and angry guests in night robes stood in them peering.

"It's O.K. folks," Steve Grayce said rapidly. "This is absolutely the last act. Just relax."

He rounded a corner and the hot music almost took him off his feet. Three men were lined up against the wall, near an open door from which light streamed. The middle one, the one with the trombone, was six feet tall, powerful and graceful, with a hairline mustache. His face was flushed and his eyes had an alcoholic glitter. He wore yellow satin shorts with large initials embroidered in black on the left leg--nothing more. His torso was tanned and naked.

155

The two with him were in pajamas, the usual halfway-good-looking band boys, both drunk, but not staggering drunk. One jittered madly on a clarinet and the other on a tenor saxophone.

Back and forth in front of them, strutting, trucking, preening herself like a magpie, arching her arms and her eyebrows, bending her fingers back until the carmine nails almost touched her arms, a metallic blonde swayed and went to town on the music. Her voice was a throaty screech, without melody, as false as her eyebrows and as sharp as her nails. She wore high-heeled slippers and black pajamas with a long purple sash.

Steve Grayce stopped dead and made a sharp downward motion with his hand. "Wrap it up!" he snapped. "Can it.. Put it on ice. Take it away and bury it. The show's out. Scram, now--scram!"

King Leopardi took the trombone from his lips and bellowed: "Fanfare to a house dick!"

The three drunks blew a stuttering note that shook the walls. The girl laughed foolishly and kicked out. Her slipper caught Steve Grayce in the chest. He picked it out of the air, jumped towards the girl and took hold of her wrist.

"Tough, eh?" he grinned. "I'll take you first."

"Get him!" Leopardi yelled. "Sock him low! Dance the gumheel on his neck!"

Steve swept the girl off her feet, tucked her under his arm and ran. He carried her as easily as a parcel. She tried to kick his legs. He laughed and shot a glance through a lighted doorway. A man's brown brogues lay under a bureau. He went on past that to a second lighted doorway, slammed through and kicked the door shut, turned far enough to twist the tabbed key in the

156

lock. Almost at once a fist hit the door. He paid no
attention to it.

He pushed the girl along the short passage past the
bathroom, and let her go. She reeled away from him
and put her back to the bureau, panting, her eyes
furious. A lock of damp gold-dipped hair swung down
over one eye. She shook her head violently and bared
her teeth.

"How would you like to get vagged, sister?"

"Go to hell!" she spit out. "The King's a friend of
mine, see? You better keep your paws off me, copper."

"You run the circuit with the boys?"

She spat at him again.

"How'd you know they'd be here?"

Another girl was sprawled across the bed, her head
to the wall, tousled black hair over a white face. There
was a tear in the leg of her pajamas. She lay limp and
groaned.

Steve said harshly: "Oh, oh, the torn-pajama act. It
flops here, sister, it flops hard. Now listen, you kids.
You can go to bed and stay till morning or you can
take the bounce. Make up your minds."

The black-haired girl groaned. The blonde said:
"You get out of my room, you damned gum-heel!"

She reached behind her and threw a hand mirror.
Steve ducked. The mirror slammed against the wall
and fell without breaking. The black-haired girl rolled
over on the bed and said wearily: "Oh lay off. I'm
sick."

She lay with her eyes closed, the lids fluttering.

The blonde swiveled her hips across the room to a
desk by the window, poured herself a full half-glass of
Scotch in a water glass and gurgled it down before

Steve could get to her. She choked violently, dropped the glass and went down on her hands and knees.

Steve said grimly: "That's the one that kicks you in the face, sister."

The girl crouched, shaking her head. She gagged once, lifted the carmine nails to paw at her mouth. She tried to get up, and her foot skidded out from under her and she fell down on her side and went fast asleep.

Steve sighed, went over and shut the window and fastened it. He rolled the black-haired girl over and straightened her on the bed and got the bedclothes from under her, tucked a pillow under her head. He picked the blonde bodily off the floor and dumped her on the bed and covered both girls to the chin. He opened the transom, switched off the ceiling light and unlocked the door. He relocked it from the outside, with a master key on a chain.

"Hotel business," he said under his breath. "Phooey."

The corridor was empty now. One lighted door still stood open. Its number was 815, two doors from the room the girls were in. Trombone music came from it softly--but not softly enough for 1:25 AM.

Steve Grayce turned into the room, crowded the door shut with his shoulder and went along past the bathroom. King Leopardi was alone in the room.

The bandleader was sprawled out in an easy chair, with a tall misted glass at his elbow. He swung the trombone in a tight circle as he played it and the lights danced in the horn.

Steve lit a cigarette, blew a plume of smoke and stared through it at Leopardi with a queer, half-admiring, half-contemptuous expression.

He said softly: "Lights out, yellow-pants. You play a sweet trumpet and your trombone don't hurt either. But

158

we can't use it here. I already told you that once. Lay off. Put that thing away."

Leopardi smiled nastily and blew a stuttering raspberry that sounded like a devil laughing.

"Says you," he sneered. "Leopardi does what he likes, where he likes, when he likes. Nobody's stopped him yet, gum-shoe. Take the air."

Steve hunched his shoulders and went close to the tall dark man. He said patiently: "Put that bazooka down, big-stuff. People are trying to sleep. They're funny that way. You're a great guy on a band shell. Everywhere else you're just a guy with a lot of jack and a personal reputation that stinks from here to Miami and back. I've got a job to do and I'm doing it. Blow that thing again and I'll wrap it around your neck."

Leopardi lowered the trombone and took a long drink from the glass at his elbow. His eyes glinted nastily. He lifted the trombone to his lips again, filled his lungs with air and blew a blast that rocked the walls. Then he stood up very suddenly and smoothly and smashed the instrument down on Steve's head.

"I never did like house peepers," he sneered. "They smell like public toilets."

Steve took a short step back and shook his head. He leered, slid forward on one foot and smacked Leopardi open-handed. The blow looked light, but Leopardi reeled all the way across the room and sprawled at the foot of the bed, sitting on the floor, his right arm draped in an open suitcase.

For a moment neither man moved. Then Steve kicked the trombone away from him and squashed his cigarette in a glass tray. His black eyes were empty but his mouth grinned whitely.

"If you want trouble," he said, "I come from where they make it."

Leopardi smiled, thinly, tautly, and his right hand came up out of the suitcase with a gun in it. His thumb snicked the safety catch. He held the gun steady, pointing.

"Make some with this," he said, and fired.

The bitter roar of the gun seemed a tremendous sound in the closed room. The bureau mirror splintered and glass flew. A sliver cut Steve's cheek like a razor blade. Blood oozed in a small narrow line on his skin.

He left his feet in a dive. His right shoulder crushed against Leopardi's bare chest and his left hand brushed the gun away from him, under the bed. He rolled swiftly to his right and came up on his knees spinning.

He said thickly, harshly: "You picked the wrong gee, brother."

He swarmed on Leopardi and dragged him to his feet by his hair, by main strength. Leopardi yelled and hit him twice on the jaw and Steve grinned and kept his left hand twisted in the bandleader's long sleek black hair. He turned his hand and the head twisted with it and Leopardi's third punch landed on Steve's shoulder. Steve took hold of the wrist behind the punch and twisted that and the bandleader went down on his knees yowling. Steve lifted him by the hair again, let go of his wrist and punched him three times in the stomach, short terrific jabs. He let go of the hair then as he sank the fourth punch almost to his wrist.

Leopardi sagged blindly to his knees and vomited.

Steve stepped away from him and went into the bathroom and got a towel off the rack. He threw it at Leopardi, jerked the open suitcase onto the bed and started throwing things into it.

Leopardi wiped his face and got to his feet still gagging. He swayed, braced himself on the end of the bureau. He was white as a sheet.

Steve Grayce said: "Get dressed, Leopardi. Or go out the way you are. It's all one to me.

Leopardi stumbled into the bathroom, pawing the wall like a blind man

2

Millar stood very still behind the desk as the elevator opened. His face was white and scared and his cropped black mustache was a smudge across his upper lip. Leopardi came out of the elevator first, a muffler around his neck, a lightweight coat tossed over his arm, a hat tilted on his head. He walked stiffly, bent forward a little, his eyes vacant. His face had a greenish pallor.

Steve Grayce stepped out behind him carrying a suitcase, and Carl, the night porter, came last with two more suitcases and two instrument cases in black leather. Steve marched over to the desk and said harshly: "Mr. Leopardi's bill--if any. He's checking out."

Millar goggled at him across the marble desk. "I--I don't think, Steve--"

"O.K. I thought not."

Leopardi smiled very thinly and unpleasantly and walked out through the brass-edged swing doors the porter held open for him. There were two nighthawk cabs in the line. One of them came to life and pulled up to the canopy and the porter loaded Leopardi's stuff into it. Leopardi got into the cab and leaned forward to put his head to the open window. He said slowly and thickly: "I'm sorry for you, gum-heel. I mean sorry."

Steve Grayce stepped back and looked at him woodenly. The cab moved off down the street, rounded a corner and was gone. Steve turned on his heel, took a quarter from his pocket and tossed it up in the air. He slapped it into the night porter's hand.

"From the King," he said. "Keep it to show your grandchildren."

He went back into the hotel, got into the elevator without looking at Millar, shot it up to Eight again and went along the corridor, master-keyed his way into Leopardi's room. He relocked it from the inside, pulled the bed out from the wall and went in behind it. He got a .32 automatic off the carpet, put it in his pocket and prowled the floor with his eyes looking for the ejected shell. He found it against the wastebasket, reached to pick it up, and stayed bent over, staring into the basket. His mouth tightened. He picked up the shell and dropped it absently into his pocket, then reached a questing finger into the basket and lifted out a torn scrap of paper on which a piece of newsprint had been pasted. Then he picked up the basket, pushed the bed back against the wall and dumped the contents of the basket out on it.

From the trash of torn papers and matches he separated a number of pieces with newsprint pasted to them. He went over to the desk with them and sat down. A few minutes later he had the torn scraps put together like a jigsaw puzzle and could read the message that had been made by cutting words and letters from magazines and pasting them on a sheet.

TEN GRAND BY TH U RS DAY NI GHT, LEO PAR DI. DAY AFTER YOU OPEN AT T HE CL U B

SHAL OTTE. OR EL SE--CURTAINS. FROM HER
BROTHER.

Steve Grayce said: "Huh." He scooped the torn
pieces into a hotel envelope, put that in his inside
breast pocket and lit a cigarette. "The guy had guts," he
said. "I'll grant him that--and his trumpet."

He locked the room, listened a moment in the now
silent corridor, then went along to the room occupied
by the two girls. He knocked softly and put his ear to
the panel. A chair squeaked and feet came towards the
door.

"What is it?" The girl's voice was cool, wide awake.
It was not the blonde's voice.

"The house man. Can I speak to you a minute?"

"You're speaking to me."

"Without the door between, lady."

"You've got the passkey. Help yourself." The steps
went away. He unlocked the door with his master key,
stepped quietly inside, and shut it. There was a dim
light in a lamp with a shirred shade on the desk. On the
bed the blonde snored heavily, one hand clutched in
her brilliant metallic hair. The black-haired girl sat in
the chair by the window, her legs crossed at right
angles like a man's and stared at Steve emptily.

He went close to her and pointed to the long tear in
her pajama leg. He said softly: "You're not sick. You
were not drunk. That tear was done a long time ago.
What's the racket? A shakedown on the King?"

The girl stared at him coolly, puffed at a cigarette
and said nothing.

"He checked out," Steve said. "Nothing doing in that
direction now, sister." He watched her like a hawk, his
black eyes hard and steady on her face.

"Aw, you house dicks make me sick!" the girl said with sudden anger. She surged to her feet and went past him into the bathroom, shut and locked the door.

Steve shrugged and felt the pulse of the girl asleep in the bed--a thumpy, draggy pulse, a liquor pulse.

"Poor damn hustlers," he said under his breath.

He looked at a large purple bag that lay on the bureau, lifted it idly and let it fall. His face stiffened again. The bag made a heavy sound on the glass top, as if there were a lump of lead inside it. He snapped it open quickly and plunged a hand in. His fingers touched the cold metal of a gun. He opened the bag wide and stared down into it at a small .25 automatic. A scrap of white paper caught his eye. He fished it out and held it to the light--a rent receipt with a name and address. He stuffed it into his pocket, closed the bag and was standing by the window when the girl came out of the bathroom.

"Hell, are you still haunting me?" she snapped. "You know what happens to hotel dicks that master-key their way into ladies' bedrooms at night?"

Steve said loosely: "Yeah. They get in trouble. They might even get shot at."

The girl's face became set, but her eyes crawled sideways and looked at the purple bag. Steve looked at her. "Know Leopardi in Frisco?" he asked. "He hasn't played here in two years. Then he was just a trumpet player in Vane Utigore's band--a cheap outfit."

The girl curled her lip, went past him and sat down by the window again. Her face was white, stiff. She said dully: "Blossom did. That's Blossom on the bed."

"Know he was coming to this hotel tonight?"

"What makes it your business?"

"I can't figure him coming here at all," Steve said. "This is a quiet place. So I can't figure anybody coming here to put the bite on him."

"Go somewhere else and figure. I need sleep."

Steve said: "Good night, sweetheart--and keep your door locked."

A thin man with thin blond hair and thin face was standing by the desk, tapping on the marble with thin fingers. Millar was still behind the desk and he still looked white and scared. The thin man wore a dark gray suit with a scarf inside the collar of the coat. He had a look of having just got up. He turned seagreen eyes slowly on Steve as he got out of the elevator, waited for him to come up to the desk and throw a tabbed key on it.

Steve said: "Leopardi's key, George. There's a busted mirror in his room and the carpet has his dinner on it--mostly Scotch." He turned to the thin man.

"You want to see me, Mr. Peters?"

"What happened, Grayce?" The thin man had a tight voice that expected to be lied to.

"Leopardi and two of his boys were on Eight, the rest of the gang on Five. The bunch on Five went to bed. A couple of obvious hustlers managed to get themselves registered just two rooms from Leopardi. They managed to contact him and everybody was having a lot of nice noisy fun out in the hall. I could only stop it by getting a little tough."

"There's blood on your cheek," Peters said coldly. "Wipe it off."

Steve scratched at his cheek with a handkerchief. The thin thread of blood had dried. "I got the girls tucked away in their room," he said. "The two stooges took the hint and holed up, but Leopardi still thought

165

the guests wanted to hear trombone music. I threatened to wrap it around his neck and he beaned me with it. I slapped him open-handed and he pulled a gun and took a shot at me. Here's the gun."

He took the .32 automatic out of his pocket and laid it on the desk. He put the used shell beside it. "So I beat some sense into him and threw him out," he added.

Peters tapped on the marble. "Your usual tact seems to have been well in evidence."

Steve stared at him. "He shot at me," he repeated quietly. "With a gun. This gun. I'm tender to bullets. He missed, but suppose he hadn't? I like my stomach the way it is, with just one way in and one way out."

Peters narrowed his tawny eyebrows. He said very politely: "We have you down on the payroll here as a night clerk, because we don't like the name house detective. But neither night clerks nor house detectives put guests out of the hotel without consulting me. Not ever, Mr. Grayce."

Steve said: "The guy shot at me, pal. With a gun. Catch on? I don't have to take that without a kickback, do I?" His face was a little white.

Peters said: "Another point for your consideration. The controlling interest in this hotel is owned by Mr. Halsey G. Walters. Mr. Walters also owns the Club Shalotte, where King Leopardi is opening on Wednesday night. And that, Mr. Grayce, is why Leopardi was good enough to give us his business. Can you think of anything else I should like to say to you?"

"Yeah. I'm canned," Steve said mirthlessly.

"Very correct, Mr. Grayce. Good-night, Mr. Grayce."

The thin blond man moved to the elevator and the night porter took him up.

Steve looked at Millar.

"Jumbo Walters, huh?" he said softly. "A tough, smart guy. Much too smart to think this dump and the Club Shalotte belong to the same sort of customers. Did Peters write Leopardi to come here?"

"I guess he did, Steve." Millar's voice was low and gloomy.

"Then why wasn't he put in a tower suite with a private balcony to dance on, at twenty-eight bucks a day? Why was he put on a medium-priced transient floor? And why did Quillan let those girls get so close to him?"

Millar pulled at his black mustache. "Tight with money--as well as with Scotch, I suppose. As to the girls, I don't know."

Steve slapped the counter open-handed. "Well, I'm canned, for not letting a drunken heel make a parlor house and a shooting gallery out of the eighth floor. Nuts! Well, I'll miss the joint at that."

"I'll miss you too, Steve," Millar said gently. "But not for a week. I take a week off starting tomorrow. My brother has a cabin at Crestline."

"Didn't know you had a brother," Steve said absently. He opened and closed his fist on the marble desk top.

"He doesn't come into town much. A big guy. Used to be a fighter."

Steve nodded and straightened from the counter. "Well, I might as well finish out the night," he said. "On my back. Put this gun away somewhere, George."

He grinned coldly and walked away, down the steps into the dim main lobby and across to the room where the radio was. He punched the pillows into shape on the pale green davenport, then suddenly reached into his pocket and took out the scrap of white paper he had lifted from the black-haired girl's purple handbag. It was a receipt for a week's rent, to a Miss Marilyn Delorme, Apt. 211, Ridgeland Apartments, 118 Court Street.

He tucked it into his wallet and stood staring at the silent radio. "Steve, I think you got another job," he said under his breath. "Something about this set-up smells."

He slipped into a closet-like phone both in the corner of the room, dropped a nickel and dialed an all-night radio station. He had to dial four times before he got a clear line to the Owl Program announcer.

"How's to play King Leopardi's record of 'Solitude' again?" he asked him.

"Got a lot of requests piled up. Played it twice already. Who's calling?"

"Steve Grayce, night man at the Carlton Hotel."

"Oh, a sober guy on his job. For you, pal, anything."

Steve went back to the davenport, snapped the radio on and lay down on his back, with his hands clasped behind his head.

Ten minutes later the high, piercingly sweet trumpet notes of King Leopardi came softly from the radio, muted almost to a whisper, and sustaining E above high C for an almost incredible period of time.

"Shucks," Steve grumbled, when the record ended. "A guy that can play like that--maybe I was too tough with him."

3

Court Street was old town, wop town, crook town, arty town. It lay across the top of Bunker Hill and you could find anything there from down-at-heels ex-Greenwich-villagers to crooks on the lam, from ladies of anybody's evening to County Relief clients brawling with haggard landladies in grand old houses with scrolled porches, parquetry floors, and immense sweeping banisters of white oak, mahogany and Circassian walnut.

It had been a nice place once, had Bunker Hill, and from the days of its niceness there still remained the funny little funicular railway, called the Angel's Flight, which crawled up and down a yellow clay bank from Hill Street. It was afternoon when Steve Grayce got off the car at the top, its only passenger. He walked along in the sun, a tall, wide-shouldered, rangy-looking man in a well-cut blue suit.

He turned west at Court and began to read the numbers. The one he wanted was two from the corner, across the street from a red brick funeral parlor with a sign in gold over it: Paolo Perrugini Funeral Home. A swarthy iron-gray Italian in a cutaway coat stood in front of the curtained door of the red brick building, smoking a cigar and waiting for somebody to die.

One-eighteen was a three-storied frame apartment house. It had a glass door, well masked by a dirty net curtain, a hall runner eighteen inches wide, dim doors with numbers painted on them with dim-paint, a staircase halfway back. Brass stair rods glittered in the dimness of the hallway.

Steve Grayce went up the stairs and prowled back to the front. Apartment 211, Miss Marilyn Delorme, was on the right, a front apartment. He tapped lightly on the wood, waited, tapped again. Nothing moved beyond the silent door, or in the hallway. Behind another door across the hall somebody coughed and kept on coughing.

Standing there in the half-light Steve Grayce wondered why he had come. Miss Delorme had carried a gun. Leopardi had received some kind of a threat letter and torn it up and thrown it away. Miss Delorme had checked out of the Carlton about an hour after Steve told her Leopardi was gone. Even at that--

He took out a leather keyholder and studied the lock of the door. It looked as if it would listen to reason. He tried a pick on it, snicked the bolt back and stepped softly into the room. He shut the door, but the pick wouldn't lock it.

The room was dim with drawn shades across two front windows. The air smelled of face powder. There was light-painted furniture, a pull-down double bed which was pulled down but had been made up. There was a magazine on it, a glass tray full of cigarette butts, a pint bottle half full of whiskey, and a glass on a chair beside the bed. Two pillows had been used for a back rest and were still crushed in the middle.

On the dresser there was a composition toilet set, neither cheap nor expensive, a comb with black hair in it, a tray of manicuring stuff, plenty of spilled powder--in the bathroom, nothing. In a closet behind the bed a lot of clothes and two suitcases. The shoes were all one size.

Steve stood beside the bed and pinched his chin. "Blossom, the spitting blonde, doesn't live here," he said under his breath. "Just Marilyn the torn-pants brunette."

He went back to the dresser and pulled drawers out. In the bottom drawer, under the piece of wall paper that lined it, he found a box of .25 copper-nickel automatic shells. He poked at the butts in the ash tray. All had lipstick on them. He pinched his chin again, then feathered the air with the palm of his hand, like an oarsman with a scull.

"Bunk," he said softly. "Wasting your time, Stevie."

He walked over to the door and reached for the knob, then turned back to the bed and lifted it by the footrail.

Miss Marilyn Delorme was in.

She lay on her side on the floor under the bed, long legs scissored out as if in running. One mule was on, one off. Garters and skin showed at the tops of her stockings, and a blue rose on something pink. She wore a square-necked, short-sleeved dress that was not too clean. Her neck above the dress was blotched with purple bruises.

Her face was a dark plum color, her eyes had the faint stale glitter of death, and her mouth was open so far that it foreshortened her face. She was colder than ice, and still quite limp. She had been dead two or three hours at least, six hours at most.

The purple bag was beside her, gaping like her mouth. Steve didn't touch any of the stuff that had been emptied out on the floor. There was no gun and there were no papers.

He let the bed down over her again, then made the rounds of the apartment, wiping everything he had touched and a lot of things he couldn't remember whether he had touched or not.

He listened at the door and stepped out. The hall was still empty. The man behind the opposite door still coughed. Steve went down the stairs, looked at the mailboxes and went back along the lower hall to a door.

Behind this door a chair creaked monotonously. He knocked and a woman's sharp voice called out. Steve opened the door with his handkerchief and stepped in.

In the middle of the room a woman rocked in an old Boston rocker, her body in the slack boneless attitude of exhaustion. She had a mud-colored face, stringy hair, gray cotton stockings--everything a Bunker Hill landlady should have. She looked at Steve with the interested eye of a dead goldfish.

"Are you the manager?"

The woman stopped rocking, screamed, "Hi, Jake! Company!" at the top of her voice, and started rocking again.

An icebox door thudded shut behind a partly open inner door and a very big man came into the room carrying a can of beer. He had a doughy mooncalf face, a tuft of fuzz on top of an otherwise bald head, a thick brutal neck and chin, and brown pig eyes about as expressionless as the woman's. He needed a shave-- had needed one the day before--and his collarless shirt gaped over a big hard hairy chest. He wore scarlet suspenders with large gilt buckles on them.

He held the can of beer out to the woman. She clawed it out of his hand and said bitterly: "I'm so tired I ain't got no sense."

The man said: "Yah. You ain't done the halls so good at that."

The woman snarled: "I done 'em as good as I aim to." She sucked the beer thirstily.

Steve looked at the man and said: "Manager?"

"Yah. 'S me. Jake Stoyanoff. Two hun'erd eighty-six stripped, and still plenty tough."

Steve said: "Who lives in Two-eleven?"

The big man leaned forward a little from the waist and snapped his suspenders. Nothing changed in his eyes. The skin along his big jaw may have tightened a little. "A dame," he said.

"Alone?"

"Go on--ask me," the big man said. He stuck his hand out and lifted a cigar off the edge of a stained-wood table. The cigar was burning uncvcnly and it smelled as if somebody had set fire to the doormat. He pushed it into his mouth with a hard, thrusting motion, as if he expected his mouth wouldn't want it to go in.

"I'm asking you," Steve said.

"Ask me out in the kitchen," the big man drawled.

He turned and held the door open. Steve went past him.

The big man kicked the door shut against the squeak of the rocking chair, opened up the icebox and got out two cans of beer. He opened them and handed one to Steve.

"Dick?"

Steve drank some of the beer, put the can down on the sink, got a brand-new card out of his wallet--a business card printed that morning. He handed it to the man.

The man read it, put it down on the sink, picked it up and read it again. "One of them guys," he growled over his beer. "What's she pulled this time?"

Steve shrugged and said: "I guess it's the usual. The torn pajama act. Only there's a kickback this time."

"How come? You handling it, huh? Must be a nice cozy one."

Steve nodded. The big man blew smoke from his mouth. "Go ahead and handle it," he said.

"You don't mind a pinch here?"

The big man laughed heartily. "Nuts to you, brother," he said pleasantly enough. "You're a private dick. So it's a hush. O.K. Go out and hush it. And if it was a pinch--that bothers me like a quart of milk. Go into your act. Take all the room you want. Cops don't bother Jake Stoyanoff."

Steve stared at the man. He didn't say anything. The big man talked it up some more, seemed to get more interested. "Besides," he went on, making motions with the cigar, "I'm softhearted. I never turn up a dame. I never put a frill in the middle." He finished his beer and threw the can in a basket under the sink, and pushed his hand out in front of him, revolving the large thumb slowly against the next two fingers. "Unless there's some of that," he added.

Steve said softly: "You've got big hands. You could have done it."

"Huh?" His small brown leathery eyes got silent and stared. Steve said: "Yeah. You might be clean. But with those hands the cops'd go round and round with you just the same."

The big man moved a little to his left, away from the sink. He let his right hand hang down at his side, loosely. His mouth got so tight that the cigar almost touched his nose.

"What's the beef, huh?" he barked. "What you shovin' at me, guy? What--"

"Cut it," Steve drawled. "She's been croaked. Strangled. Upstairs, on the floor under her bed. About midmorning, I'd say. Big hands did it--hands like yours."

174

The big man did a nice job of getting the gun off his hip. It arrived so suddenly that it seemed to have grown in his hand and been there all the time.

Steve frowned at the gun and didn't move. The big man looked him over. "You're tough," he said. "I been in the ring long enough to size up a guy's meat. You're plenty hard, boy. But you ain't as hard as lead. Talk it up fast."

"I knocked at her door. No answer. The lock was a pushover. I went in. I almost missed her because the bed was pulled down and she had been sitting on it, reading a magazine. There was no sign of struggle. I lifted the bed just before I left--and there she was. Very dead, Mr. Stoyanoff. Put the gat away. Cops don't bother you, you said a minute ago."

The big man whispered: "Yes and no. They don't make me happy neither. I get a bump once'n a while. Mostly a Dutch. You said something about my hands, mister."

Steve shook his head. "That was a gag," he said. "Her neck has nail marks. You bite your nails down close. You're clean."

The big man didn't look at his fingers. He was very pale. There was sweat on his lower lips, in the black stubble of his beard. He was still leaning forward, still motionless, when there was a knocking beyond the kitchen door, the door from the living room to the hallway. The creaking chair stopped and the woman's sharp voice screamed: "Hi, Jake! Company!"

The big man cocked his head. "That old slut wouldn't climb off'n her fanny if the house caught fire," he said thickly.

He stepped to the door and slipped through it, locking it behind him.

Steve ranged the kitchen swiftly with his eyes. There was a small high window beyond the sink, a trap low down for a garbage pail and parcels, but no other door. He reached for his card Stoyanoff had left lying on the drainboard and slipped it back into his pocket. Then he took a short-barreled Detective Special out of his left breast pocket where he wore it nose down, as in a holster.

He had got that far when the shots roared beyond the wall--muffled a little, but still loud--four of them blended in a blast of sound.

Steve stepped back and hit the kitchen door with his leg out straight. It held and jarred him to the top of his head and in his hip joint. He swore, took the whole width of the kitchen and slammed into it with his left shoulder. It gave this time. He pitched into the living room. The mud-faced woman sat leaning forward in her rocker, her head to one side and a lock of mousy hair smeared down over her bony forehead.

"Backfire, huh?" she said stupidly. "Sounded kinda close. Musta been in the alley."

Steve jumped across the room, yanked the outer door open and plunged out into the hall.

The big man was still on his feet, a dozen feet down the hallway, in the direction of a screen door that opened flush on an alley. He was clawing at the wall. His gun lay at his feet. His left knee buckled and he went down on it.

A door was flung open and a hard-looking woman peered out, and instantly slammed her door shut again. A radio suddenly gained in volume beyond her door.

The big man got up off his left knee and the leg shook violently inside his trousers. He went down on both knees and got the gun into his hand and began to crawl towards the screen door. Then, suddenly he went down flat on his face and tried to crawl that way, grinding his face into the narrow hall runner.

Then he stopped crawling and stopped moving altogether. His body went limp and the hand holding the gun opened and the gun rolled out of it.

Steve hit the screen door and was out in the alley. A gray sedan was speeding towards the far end of it. He stopped, steadied himself and brought his gun up level, and the sedan whisked out of sight around the corner.

A man boiled out of another apartment house across the alley. Steve ran on, gesticulating back at him and pointing ahead. As he ran he slipped the gun back into his pocket. When he reached the end of the alley, the gray sedan was out of sight. Steve skidded around the wall onto the sidewalk, slowed to a walk and then stopped.

Half a block down a man finished parking a car, got out and went across the sidewalk to a lunchroom. Steve watched him go in, then straightened his hat and walked along the wall to the lunchroom.

He went in, sat at the counter and ordered coffee. In a little while there were sirens.

Steve drank his coffee, asked for another cup and drank that. He lit a cigarette and walked down the long hill to Fifth, across to Hill, back to the foot of the Angel's Flight, and got his convertible out of a parking lot.

He drove out west, beyond Vermont, to the small hotel where he had taken a room that morning.

4

Bill Dockery, floor manager of the Club Shalotte, teetered on his heels and yawned in the unlighted entrance to the dining room. It was a dead hour for business, late cocktail time, too early for dinner, and much too early for the real business of the club, which was high-class gambling.

Dockery was a handsome mug in a midnight-blue dinner jacket and a maroon carnation. He had a two-inch forehead under black lacquer hair, good features a little on the heavy side, alert brown eyes and very long curly eyelashes which he liked to let down over his eyes, to fool troublesome drunks into taking a swing at him.

The entrance door of the foyer was opened by the uniformed doorman and Steve Grayce came in.

Dockery said, "Ho, hum," tapped his teeth and leaned his weight forward. He walked across the lobby slowly to meet the guest. Steve stood just inside the doors and ranged his eyes over the high foyer walled with milky glass, lighted softly from behind. Molded in the glass were etchings of sailing ships, beasts of the jungle, Siamese pagodas, temples of Yucatan. The doors were square frames of chromium, like photo frames. The Club Shalotte had all the class there was, and the mutter of voices from the bar lounge on the left was not noisy. The faint Spanish music behind the voices was delicate as a carved fan.

Dockery came up and leaned his sleek head forward an inch. "May I help you?"

"King Leopardi around?"

Dockery leaned back again. He looked less interested. "The bandleader? He opens tomorrow night."

"I thought he might be around--rehearsing or something."

"Friend of his?"

"I know him. I'm not job-hunting, and I'm not a song plugger if that's what you mean."

Dockery teetered on his heels. He was tone-deaf and Leopardi meant no more to him than a bag of peanuts. He half smiled. "He was in the bar lounge a while ago." He pointed with his square rock-like chin. Steve Grayce went into the bar lounge.

It was about a third full, warm and comfortable and not too dark nor too light. The little Spanish orchestra was in an archway, playing with muted strings small seductive melodies that were more like memories than sounds. There was no dance floor. There was a long bar with comfortable seats, and there were small round composition-top tables, not too close together. A wall seat ran around three sides of the room. Waiters flitted among the tables like moths.

Steve Grayce saw Leopardi in the far corner, with a girl. There was an empty table on each side of him. The girl was a knockout.

She looked tall and her hair was the color of a brush fire seen through a dust cloud. On it, at the ultimate rakish angle, she wore a black velvet double-pointed beret with two artificial butterflies made of polka-dotted feathers and fastened on with tall silver pins. Her dress was burgundy-red wool and the blue fox draped over one shoulder was at least two feet wide. Her eyes were large, smoke-blue, and looked bored. She slowly turned a small glass on the table top with a gloved left hand.

Leopardi faced her, leaning forward, talking. His shoulders looked very big in a shaggy, cream-colored

179

sports coat. Above the neck of it his hair made a point on his brown neck. He laughed across the table as Steve came up and his laugh had a confident, sneering sound.

Steve stopped, then moved behind the next table. The movement caught Leopardi's eye. His head turned, he looked annoyed, and then his eyes got very wide and brilliant and his whole body turned slowly, like a mechanical toy.

Leopardi put both his rather small well-shaped hands down on the table, on either side of a highball glass. He smiled. Then he pushed his chair back and stood up. He put one finger up and touched his hairline mustache, with theatrical delicacy. Then he said drawlingly, but distinctly: "You son of a bitch!"

A man at a nearby table turned his head and scowled. A waiter who had started to come over stopped in his tracks, then faded back among the tables. The girl looked at Steve Grayce and then leaned back against the cushions of the wall seat and moistened the end of one bare finger on her right hand and smoothed a chestnut eyebrow.

Steve stood quite still. There was a sudden high flush on his cheekbones. He said softly: "You left something at the hotel last night. I think you ought to do something about it. Here."

He reached a folded paper out of his pocket and held it out. Leopardi took it, still smiling, opened it and read it. It was a sheet of yellow paper with torn pieces of white paper pasted on it. Leopardi crumpled the sheet and let it drop at his feet.

He took a smooth step towards Steve and repeated more loudly: "You son of a bitch!"

The man who had first looked around stood up sharply and turned. He said clearly: "I don't like that sort of language in front of my wife."

Without even looking at the man Leopardi said: "To hell with you and your wife."

The man's face got a dusky red. The woman with him stood up and grabbed a bag and a coat and walked away. After a moment's indecision the man followed her. Everybody in the place was staring now. The waiter who had faded back among the tables went through the doorway into the entrance foyer, walking very quickly.

Leopardi took another, longer step and slammed Steve Grayce on the jaw. Steve rolled with the punch and stepped back and put his hand down on another table and upset a glass. He turned to apologize to the couple at the table. Leopardi jumped forward very fast and hit him behind the ear.

Dockery came through the doorway, split two waiters like a banana skin and started down the room showing all his teeth.

Steve gagged a little and ducked away. He turned and said thickly: "Wait a minute, you fool--that isn't all of it--there's--"

Leopardi closed in fast and smashed him full on the mouth. Blood oozed from Steve's lip and crawled down the line at the corner of his mouth and glistened on his chin. The girl with the red hair reached for her bag, white-faced with anger, and started to get up from behind her table.

Leopardi turned abruptly on his heel and walked away. Dockery put out a hand to stop him. Leopardi brushed it aside and went on, went out of the lounge.

The tall red-haired girl put her bag down on the table again and dropped her handkerchief on the floor. She looked at Steve quietly, spoke quietly. "Wipe the blood off your chin before it drips on your shirt." She had a soft, husky voice with a trill in it.

Dockery came up harsh-faced, took Steve by the arm and put weight on the arm. "All right, you! Let's go!"

Steve stood quite still, his feet planted, staring at the girl. He dabbed at his mouth with a handkerchief. He half smiled. Dockery couldn't move him an inch. Dockery dropped his hand, signaled two waiters and they jumped behind Steve, but didn't touch him.

Steve felt his lip carefully and looked at the blood on his handkerchief. He turned to the people at the table behind him and said: "I'm terribly sorry. I lost my balance."

The girl whose drink he had spilled was mopping her dress with a small fringed napkin. She smiled up at him and said: "It wasn't your fault."

The two waiters suddenly grabbed Steve's arms from behind. Dockery shook his head and they let go again. Dockery said tightly: "You hit him?"

"No."

"You say anything to make him hit you?"

"No."

The girl at the corner table bent down to get her fallen handkerchief. It took her quite a time. She finally got it and slid into the corner behind the table again. She spoke coldly.

"Quite right, Bill. It was just some more of the King's sweet way with his public."

Dockery said "Huh?" and swiveled his head on his thick hard neck. Then he grinned and looked back at Steve.

182

Steve said grimly: "He gave me three good punches, one from behind, without a return. You look pretty hard. See can you do it."

Dockery measured him with his eyes. He said evenly: "You win. I couldn't...Beat it!" he added sharply to the waiters. They went away. Dockery sniffed his carnation, and said quietly: "We don't go for brawls in here." He smiled at the girl again and went away, saying a word here and there at the tables. He went out through the foyer doors.

Steve tapped his lip, put his handkerchief in his pocket and stood searching the floor with his eyes.

The red-haired girl said calmly: "I think I have what you want--in my handkerchief. Won't you sit down?"

Her voice had a remembered quality, as if he had heard it before.

He sat down opposite her, in the chair where Leopardi had been sitting.

The red-haired girl said: "The drink's on me. I was with him."

Steve said, "Coke with a dash of bitters," to the waiter.

The waiter said: "Madame?"

"Brandy and soda. Light on the brandy, please." The waiter bowed and drifted away. The girl said amusedly: "Coke with a dash of bitters. That's what I love about Hollywood. You meet so many neurotics."

Steve stared into her eyes and said softly: "I'm an occasional drinker, the kind of guy who goes out for a beer and wakes up in Singapore with a full beard."

"I don't believe a word of it. Have you known the King long?"

"I met him last night. I didn't get along with him."

"I sort of noticed that." She laughed. She had a rich low laugh, too.

"Give me that paper, lady."

"Oh, one of these impatient men. Plenty of time." The handkerchief with the crumpled yellow sheet inside it was clasped tightly in her gloved hand. Her middle right finger played with an eyebrow. "You're not in pictures, are you?"

"Hell, no."

"Same here, Me, I'm too tall. The beautiful men have to wear stilts in order to clasp me to their bosoms."

The waiter set the drinks down in front of them, made a grace note in the air with his napkin and went away.

Steve said quietly, stubbornly: "Give me that paper, lady."

"I don't like that 'lady' stuff. It sounds like cop to me."

"I don't know your name."

"I don't know yours. Where did you meet Leopardi?" Steve sighed. The music from the little Spanish orchestra had a melancholy minor sound now and the muffled clicking of gourds dominated it.

Steve listened to it with his head on one side. He said: "The E string is a half-tone flat. Rather cute effect."

The girl stared at him with new interest. "I'd never have noticed that," she said. "And I'm supposed to be a pretty good singer. But you haven't answered my question."

He said slowly: "Last night I was house dick at the Carlton Hotel. They called me night clerk, but house dick was what I was. Leopardi stayed there and cut up too rough. I threw him out and got canned."

184

The girl said: "Ah. I begin to get the idea. He was being the King and you were being--if I might guess--a pretty tough order of house detective."

"Something like that. Now will you please--"

"You still haven't told me your name."

He reached for his wallet, took one of the brand-new cards out of it and passed it across the table. He sipped his drink while she read it.

"A nice name," she said slowly. "But not a very good address. And *Private investigator* is bad. It should have been *Investigations,* very small, in the lower left-hand corner."

"They'll be small enough," Steve grinned. "Now will you please--"

She reached suddenly across the table and dropped the crumpled ball of paper in his hand.

"Of course I haven't read it--and of course I'd like to. You do give me that much credit, I hope"--she looked at the card again, and added--Steve. Yes, and your office should be in a Georgian or very modernistic building in the Sunset Eighties. Suite Something-or-other. And your clothes should be very jazzy. Very jazzy indeed, Steve. To be inconspicuous in this town is to be a busted flush."

He grinned at her. His deep-set black eyes had lights in them. She put the card away in her bag, gave her fur piece a yank, and drank about half of her drink. "I have to go." She signaled the waiter and paid the check. The waiter went away and she stood up.

Steve said sharply: "Sit down."

She stared at him wonderingly. Then she sat down again and leaned against the wall, still staring at him. Steve leaned across the table, asked "How well do you know Leopardi?"

"Off and on for years. If it's any of your business. Don't go masterful on me, for God's sake. I loathe masterful men. I once sang for him, but not for long. You can't just sing for Leopardi--if you get what I mean."

"You were having a drink with him."

She nodded slightly and shrugged. "He opens here tomorrow night. He was trying to talk me into singing for him again. I said no, but I may have to, for a week or two anyway. The man who owns the Club Shalotte also owns my contract--and the radio station where I work a good deal."

"Jumbo Walters," Steve said. "They say he's tough but square. I never met him, but I'd like to. After all I've got a living to get. Here."

He reached back across the table and dropped the crumpled paper. "The name was--"

"Dolores Chiozza."

Steve repeated it lingeringly. "I like it. I like your singing too. I've heard a lot of it. You don't oversell a song, like most of these high-money torchers." His eyes glistened.

The girl spread the paper on the table and read it slowly, without expression. Then she said quietly: "Who tore it up?"

"Leopardi, I guess. The pieces were in his wastebasket last night. I put them together, after he was gone. The guy has guts--or else he gets these things so often they don't register any more."

"Or else he thought it was a gag." She looked across the table levelly, then folded the paper and handed it back.

186

"Maybe. But if he's the kind of guy I hear he is--one of them is going to be on the level and the guy behind it is going to do more than just shake him down."

Dolores Chiozza said: "He's the kind of guy you hear he is."

"It wouldn't be hard for a woman to get to him then--would it--a woman with a gun?"

She went on staring at him. "No. And everybody would give her a big hand, if you ask me. If I were you, I'd just forget the whole thing. If he wants protection--Walters can throw more around him than the police. If he doesn't--who cares? I don't. I'm damn sure I don't."

"You're kind of tough yourself, Miss Chiozza--over some things."

She said nothing. Her face was a little white and more than a little hard.

Steve finished his drink, pushed his chair back and reached for his hat. He stood up. "Thank you very much for the drink, Miss Chiozza. Now that I've met you I'll look forward all the more to hearing you sing again."

"You're damn formal all of a sudden," she said.

He grinned. "So long, Dolores."

"So long, Steve. Good luck--in the sleuth racket. If I hear of anything--"

He turned and walked among the tables out of the bar lounge.

5

In the crisp fall evening the lights of Hollywood and Los Angeles winked at him. Searchlight beams probed the cloudless sky as if searching for bombing-planes.

Steve got his convertible out of the parking lot and drove it east along Sunset. At Sunset and Fairfax he bought an evening paper and pulled over to the curb to look through it. There was nothing in the paper about 118 Court Street.

He drove on and ate dinner at the little coffee shop beside his hotel and went to a movie. When he came out he bought a Home Edition of the *Tribune,* a morning sheet. They were in that--both of them.

Police thought Jake Stoyanoff might have strangled the girl, but she had not been attacked. She was described as a stenographer, unemployed at the moment. There was no picture of her. There was a picture of Stoyanoff that looked like a touched up police photo. Police were looking for a man who had been talking to Stoyanoff just before he was shot. Several people said he was a tall man in a dark suit. That was all the description the police got--or gave out.

Steve grinned sourly, stopped at the coffee shop for a goodnight cup of coffee and then went up to his room. It was a few minutes to eleven o'clock. As he unlocked his door the telephone started to ring.

He shut the door and stood in the darkness remembering where the phone was. Then he walked straight to it, catlike in the dark room, sat in an easy chair and reached the phone up from the lower shelf of a small table. He held the one-piece to his ear and said: "Hello."

"Is this Steve?" It was a rich, husky voice, low, vibrant. It held a note of strain.

"Yeah, this is Steve. I can hear you. I know who you are."

There was a faint dry laugh. "You'll make a detective after all. And it seems I'm to give you your first case.

Will you come over to my place at once? It's Twenty-four twelve Renfrew--North, there isn't any South--just half a block below Fountain. It's a sort of bungalow court. My house is the last in line, at the back."

Steve said: "Yes. Sure. What's the matter?"

There was a pause. A horn blared in the street outside the hotel. A wave of white light went across the ceiling from some car rounding the corner uphill. The low voice said very slowly: "Leopardi. I can't get rid of him. He's--he's passed out in my bedroom." Then a tinny laugh that didn't go with the voice at all.

Steve held the phone so tight his hand ached. His teeth clicked in the darkness. He said flatly, in a dull, brittle voice: "Yeah. It'll cost you twenty bucks."

"Of course. Hurry, please."

He hung up, sat there in the dark room breathing hard. He pushed his hat back on his head, then yanked it forward again with a vicious jerk and laughed out loud. "Hell," he said, "That kind of a dame."

Twenty-four-twelve Renfrew was not strictly a bungalow court. It was a staggered row of six bungalows, all facing the same way, but so-arranged that no two of their front entrances overlooked each other. There was a brick wall at the back and beyond the brick wall a church. There was a long smooth lawn, moon-silvered.

The door was up two steps, with lanterns on each side and an iron-work grill over the peep hole. This opened to his knock and a girl's face looked out, a small oval face with a Cupid's bow mouth, arched and plucked eyebrows, wavy brown hair. The eyes were like two fresh and shiny chestnuts.

Steve dropped a cigarette and put his foot on it. "Miss Chiozza. She's expecting me. Steve Grayce."

"Miss Chiozza has retired, sir," the girl said with a half insolent twist to her lips.

"Break it up, kid. You heard me, I'm expected."

The wicket slammed shut. He waited, scowling back along the narrow moonlit lawn towards the street. O.K. So it was like that--well, twenty bucks was worth a ride in the moonlight anyway.

The lock clicked and the door opened wide. Steve went past the maid into a warm cheerful room, old-fashioned with chintz. The lamps were neither old nor new and there were enough of them--in the right places. There was a hearth behind a paneled copper screen, a davenport close to it, a bar-top radio in the corner.

The maid said stiffly: "I'm sorry, sir. Miss Chiozza forgot to tell me. Please have a chair." The voice was soft, and it might be cagey. The girl went off down the room--short skirts, sheer silk stockings, and four-inch spike heels.

Steve sat down and held his hat on his knee and scowled at the wall. A swing door creaked shut. He got a cigarette out and rolled it between his fingers and then deliberately squeezed it to a shapeless flatness of white paper and ragged tobacco. He threw it away from him, at the fire screen.

Dolores Chiozza came towards him. She wore green velvet lounging pajamas with a long gold-fringed sash. She spun the end of the sash as if she might be going to throw a loop with it. She smiled a slight artificial smile. Her face had a clean scrubbed look and her eyelids were bluish and they twitched.

Steve stood up and watched the green morocco slippers peep out under the pajamas as she walked.

When she was close to him he lifted his eyes to her face and said dully: "Hello."

She looked at him very steadily, then spoke in a high, carrying voice. "I know it's late, but I knew you were used to being up all night. So I thought what we had to talk over--Won't you sit down?"

She turned her head very slightly, seemed to be listening for something.

Steve said: "I never go to bed before two. Quite all right."

She went over and pushed a bell beside the hearth. After a moment the maid came through the arch.

"Bring some ice cubes, Agatha. Then go along home. It's getting pretty late."

"Yes'm." The girl disappeared.

There was a silence then that almost howled till the tall girl took a cigarette absently out of a box, put it between her lips and Steve struck a match clumsily on his shoe. She pushed the end of the cigarette into the flame and her smoke-blue eyes were very steady on his black ones. She shook her head very slightly.

The maid came back with a copper ice bucket. She pulled a low Indian-brass tray-table between them before the davenport, put the ice bucket on it, then a siphon, glasses and spoons, and a triangular bottle that looked like good Scotch had come in it except that it was covered with silver filigree work and fitted with a stopper.

Dolores Chiozza said, "Will you mix a drink?" in a formal voice.

He mixed two drinks, stirred them, handed her one. She sipped it, shook her head. "Too light," she said. He put more whiskey in it and handed it back. She said,

"Better," and leaned back against the corner of the davenport.

The maid came into the room again. She had a small rakish red hat on her wavy brown hair and was wearing a gray coat trimmed with nice fur. She carried a black brocade bag that could have cleaned out a fair-sized icebox. She said: "Good night, Miss Dolores."

"Good night, Agatha."

The girl went out the front door, closed it softly. Her heels clicked down the walk. A car door opened and shut distantly and a motor started. Its sound soon dwindled away. It was a very quiet neighborhood.

Steve put his drink down on the brass tray and looked levelly at the tall girl, said harshly: "That means she's out of the way?"

"Yes. She goes home in her own car. She drives me home from the studio in mine--when I go to the studio, which I did tonight. I don't like to drive a car myself."

"Well, what are you waiting for?"

The red-haired girl looked steadily at the paneled fire screen and the unlit log fire behind it. A muscle twitched in her cheek.

After a moment she said: "Funny that I called you instead of Walters. He'd have protected me better than you can. Only he wouldn't have believed me. I thought perhaps you would. I didn't invite Leopardi here. So far as I know--we two are the only people in the world who know he's here."

Something in her voice jerked Steve upright.

She took a small crisp handkerchief from the breast pocket of the green velvet pajama-suit, dropped it on the floor, picked it up swiftly and pressed it against her mouth. Suddenly, without making a sound, she began to shake like a leaf.

Steve said swiftly: "What the hell--I can handle that heel in my hip pocket. I did last night--and last night he had a gun and took a shot at me."

Her head turned. Her eyes were very wide and staring. "But it couldn't have been my gun," she said in a dead voice.

"Huh? Of course not--what--?"

"It's my gun tonight," she said and stared at him. "You said a woman could get to him with a gun very easily."

He just stared at her. His face was white now and he made a vague sound in his throat.

"He's not drunk, Steve," she said gently. "He's dead. In yellow pajamas--in my bed. With my gun in his hand. You didn't think he was just drunk--did you, Steve?"

He stood up in a swift lunge, then became absolutely motionless, staring down at her. He moved his tongue on his lips and after a long time he formed words with it. "Let's go look at him," he said in a hushed voice.

6

The room was at the back of the house to the left. The girl took a key out of her pocket and unlocked the door. There was a low light on a table, and the venetian blinds were drawn. Steve went in past her silently, on cat feet.

Leopardi lay squarely in the middle of the bed, a large smooth silent man, waxy and artificial in death. Even his mustache looked phony. His half-open eyes, sightless as marbles, looked as if they had never seen. He lay on his back, on the sheet, and the bedclothes were thrown over the foot of the bed.

The King wore yellow silk pajamas, the slip-on kind, with a turned collar. They were loose and thin. Over his breast they were dark with blood that had seeped into the silk as if into blotting-paper. There was a little blood on his bare brown neck.

Steve stared at him and said tonelessly: "The King in Yellow. I read a book with that title once. He liked yellow, I guess. I packed some of his stuff last night. And he wasn't yellow either. Guys like him usually are--or are they?"

The girl went over to the corner and sat down in a slipper chair and looked at the floor. It was a nice room, as modernistic as the living room was casual. It had a chenille rug, café-au-lait color, severely angled furniture in inlaid wood, and a trick dresser with a mirror for a top, a kneehole and drawers like a desk. It had a box mirror above and a semi-cylindrical frosted wall light set above the mirror, In the corner there was a glass table with a crystal greyhound on top of it, and a lamp with the deepest drum shade Steve had ever seen.

He stopped looking at all this and looked at Leopardi again. He pulled the King's pajamas up gently and examined the wound. It was directly over the heart and the skin was scorched and mottled there. There was not so very much blood. He had died in a fraction of a second.

A small Mauser automatic lay cuddled in his right hand, on top of the bed's second pillow.

"That's artistic," Steve said and pointed. "Yeah, that's a nice touch. Typical contact wound, I guess. He even pulled his pajama shirt up. I've heard they do that. A Mauser seven-six-three about. Sure it's your gun?"

"Yes." She kept on looking at the floor. "It was in a desk in the living room--not loaded. But there were shells. I don't know why. Somebody gave it to me once. I didn't even know how to load it."

Steve smiled. Her eyes lifted suddenly and she saw his smile and shuddered. "I don't expect anybody to believe that," she said. "We may as well call the police, I suppose."

Steve nodded absently, put a cigarette in his mouth and flipped it up and down with his lips that were still puffy from Leopardi's punch. He lit a match on his thumbnail, puffed a small plume of smoke and said quietly: "No cops. Not yet. Just tell it.'

The red-haired girl said: "I sing at KFQC, you know. Three nights a week--on a quarter-hour automobile program. This was one of the nights. Agatha and I got home--oh, close to half-past ten. At the door I remembered there was no fizzwater in the house, so I sent her back to the liquor store three blocks away, and came in alone. There was a queer smell in the house. I don't know what it was. As if several men had been in here, somehow. When I came in the bedroom--he was exactly as he is now. I saw the gun and I went and looked and then I knew I was sunk. I didn't know what to do. Even if the police cleared me, everywhere I went from now on--"

Steve said sharply: "He got in here--how?"

"I don't know."

"Goon," he said.

"I locked the door. Then I undressed--with that on my bed. I went into the bathroom to shower and collect my brains, if any. I locked the door when I left the room and took the key. Agatha was back then, but I don't think she saw me. Well, I took the shower and it braced me up a bit. Then I had a drink and then I came in here and called you."

She stopped and moistened the end of a finger and smoothed the end of her left eyebrow with it. "That's all, Steve--absolutely all."

"Domestic help can be pretty nosy. This Agatha's nosier than most--or I miss my guess." He walked over to the door and looked at the lock. "I bet there are three or four keys in the house that knock this over." He went to the windows and felt the catches, looked down at the screens through the glass. He said over his shoulder, casually: "Was the King in love with you?"

Her voice was sharp, almost angry. "He never was in love with any woman. A couple of years back in San Francisco, when I was with his band for a while, there was some slap-silly publicity about us. Nothing to it. It's been revived here in the hand-outs to the press, to build up his opening. I was telling him this afternoon I wouldn't stand for it, that I wouldn't be linked with him in anybody's mind. His private life was filthy. It reeked. Everybody in the business knows that. And it's not a business where daisies grow very often."

Steve said: "Yours was the only bedroom he couldn't make?"

The girl flushed to the roots of her dusky red hair.

"That sounds lousy," he said. "But I have to figure the angles. That's about true, isn't it?"

"Yes--I suppose so. I wouldn't say the only one."

"Go on out in the other room and buy yourself a drink."

She stood up and looked at him squarely across the bed. "I didn't kill him, Steve. I didn't let him into this house tonight. I didn't know he was coming here, or had any reason to come here. Believe that or not. But

196

something about this is wrong. Leopardi was the last man in the world to take his lovely life himself."

Steve said: "He didn't, angel. Go buy that drink. He was murdered. The whole thing is a frame--to get a cover-up from Jumbo Walters. Go on out."

He stood silent, motionless, until sounds he heard from the living room told him she was out there. Then he took out his handkerchief and loosened the gun from Leopardi's right hand and wiped it over carefully on the outside, broke out the magazine and wiped that off, spilled out all the shells and wiped every one, ejected the one in the breech and wiped that. He reloaded the gun and put it back in Leopardi's dead hand and closed his fingers around it and pushed his index finger against the trigger. Then he let the hand fall naturally back on the bed.

He pawed through the bedclothes and found an ejected shell and wiped that off, put it back where he had found it. He put the handkerchief to his nose, sniffed it wryly, went around the bed to a clothes closet and opened the door.

"Careless of your clothes, boy," he said softly.

The rough cream-colored coat hung in there, on a hook, over dark gray slacks with a lizard-skin belt. A yellow satin shirt and a wine-colored tie dangled alongside. A handkerchief to match the tie flowed loosely four inches from the breast pocket of the coat. On the floor lay a pair of gazelle-leather nutmeg-brown sports shoes, and socks without garters. And there were yellow satin shorts with heavy black initials on them lying close by.

Steve felt carefully in the gray slacks and got out a leather keyholder. He left the room, went along the cross-hall and into the kitchen. It had a solid door, a good spring lock with a key stuck in it. He took it out and tried keys from the bunch in the keyholder, found none that fitted, put the other key back and went into the living room. He opened the front door, went outside and shut it again without looking at the girl huddled in a corner of the davenport. He tried keys in the lock, finally found the right one. He let himself back into the house, returned to the bedroom and put the keyholder back in the pocket of the gray slacks again. Then he went to the living room.

The girl was still huddled motionless, staring at him.

He put his back to the mantel and puffed at cigarette. "Agatha with you all the time at the studio?"

She nodded. "I suppose so. So he had a key. That was what you were doing, wasn't it?"

"Yes. Had Agatha long?"

"About a year."

"She steal from you? Small stuff, I mean?"

Dolores Chiozza shrugged wearily. "What does it matter? Most of them do. A little face cream or powder, a handkerchief, a pair of stockings once in a while. Yes, I think she stole from me. They look on that sort of thing as more or less legitimate."

"Not the nice ones, angel."

"Well--the hours were a little trying, I work at night, often get home very late. She's a dresser as well as a maid."

"Anything else about her? She use cocaine or weed. Hit the bottle? Ever have laughing fits?"

"I don't think so. What has she got to do with it, Steve?"

"Lady, she sold somebody a key to your apartment. That's obvious. You didn't give him one, the landlord wouldn't give him one, but Agatha had one. Check?"

198

Her eyes had a stricken look. Her mouth trembled a little, not much. A drink was untasted at her elbow. Steve bent over and drank some of it.

She said slowly: "We're wasting time, Steve. We have to call the police. There's nothing anybody can do. I'm done for as a nice person, even if not as a lady at large. They'll think it was a lovers' quarrel and I shot him and that's that. If I could convince them I didn't, then he shot himself in my bed, and I'm still ruined. So I might as well make up my mind to face the music."

Steve said softly: "Watch this. My mother used to do it."

He put a finger to his mouth, bent down and touched her lips at the same spot with the same finger. He smiled, said: "We'll go to Walters--or you will. He'll pick his cops and the ones he picks won't go screaming through the night with reporters sitting in their laps. They'll sneak in quiet, like process servers. Walters can handle this. That was what was counted on. Me, I'm going to collect Agatha. Because I want a description of the guy she sold that key to--and I want it fast. And by the way, you owe me twenty bucks for coming over here. Don't let that slip your memory."

The tall girl stood up, smiling. "You're a kick, you are," she said. "What makes you so sure he was murdered?"

"He's not wearing his own pajamas. His have his initials on them. I packed his stuff last night--before I threw him out of the Carlton, Get dressed, angel--and get me Agatha's address."

He went into the bedroom and pulled a sheet over Leopardi's body, held it a moment above the still, waxen face before letting it fall.

"So long, guy," he said gently. "You were a louse--but you sure had music in you."

It was a small frame house on Brighton Avenue near Jefferson, in a block of small frame houses, all old-fashioned, with front porches. This one had a narrow concrete walk which the moon made whiter than it was.

Steve mounted the steps and looked at the light-edged shade of the wide front window. He knocked. There were shuffling steps and a woman opened the door and looked at him through the hooked screen--a dumpy elderly woman with frizzled gray hair. Her body was shapeless in a wrapper and her feet slithered in loose slippers. A man with a polished bald head and milky eyes sat in a wicker chair beside a table. He held his hands in his lap and twisted the knuckles aimlessly. He didn't look towards the door.

Steve said: "I'm from Miss Chiozza. Are you Agatha's mother?"

The woman said dully: "I reckon. But she ain't home, mister." The man in the chair got a handkerchief from somewhere and blew his nose. He snickered darkly.

Steve said: "Miss Chiozza's not feeling so well tonight. She was hoping Agatha would come back and stay the night with her."

The milky-eyed man snickered again, sharply. The woman said: "We dunno where she is. She don't come home. Pa'n me waits up for her to come home. She stays out till we're sick."

The old man snapped in a reedy voice: "She'll stay out till the cops get her one of these times."

"Pa's half blind," the woman said. "Makes him kinda mean. Won't you step in?"

Steve shook his head and turned his hat around in his hands like a bashful cowpuncher in a horse opera. "I've got to find her," he said. "Where would she go?"

"Out drinkin' liquor with cheap spenders," Pa cackled. "Pantywaists with silk handkerchiefs 'stead of neckties. If I had eyes, I'd strap her till she dropped." He grabbed the arms of his chair and the muscles knotted on the backs of his hands. Then he began to cry. Tears welled from his milky eyes and started through the white stubble on his cheeks, The woman went across and took the handkerchief out of his fist and wiped his face with it, Then she blew her nose on it and came back to the door.

"Might be anywhere," she said to Steve, "This is a big town, mister, I dunno where at to say."

Steve said dully: "I'll call back. If she comes in, will you hang onto her, What's your phone number?"

"What's the phone number, Pa?" the woman called back over her shoulder.

"I ain't sayin'," Pa snorted.

The woman said: "I remember now. South Two-four-five-four. Call any time. Pa'n me ain't got nothing to do."

Steve thanked her and went back down the white walk to the street and along the walk half a block to where he had left his car. He glanced idly across the way and started to get into his car, then stopped moving suddenly with his hand gripping the car door. He let go of that, took three steps sideways and stood looking across the street tight-mouthed.

All the houses in the block were much the same, but the one opposite had a FOR RENT placard stuck in the front window and a real-estate sign spiked into the small patch of front lawn. The house itself looked neglected, utterly empty, but in its little driveway stood a small neat black coupe.

Steve said under his breath: "Hunch. Play it up, Stevie."

He walked almost delicately across the wide dusty street, his hand touching the hard metal of the gun in his pocket, and came up behind the little car, stood and listened. He moved silently along its left side, glanced back across the street, then looked in the car's open left-front window.

The girl sat almost as if driving, except that her head was tipped a little too much into the corner. The little red hat was still on her head, the gray coat, trimmed with fur, still around her body. In the reflected moonlight her mouth was strained open. Her tongue stuck out. And her chestnut eyes stared at the roof of the car.

Steve didn't touch her. He didn't have to touch her to look any closer to know there would be heavy bruises on her neck.

"Tough on women, these guys," he muttered.

The girl's big black brocade bag lay on the seat beside her, gaping open like her mouth--like Miss Marilyn Delorme's mouth, and Miss Marilyn Delorme's purple bag.

"Yeah--tough on women."

He backed away till he stood under a small palm tree by the entrance to the driveway. The street was as empty and deserted as a closed theater, He crossed silently to his car, got into it and drove away.

Nothing to it. A girl coming home alone late at night, stuck up and strangled a few doors from her own home by some tough guy. Very simple. The first prowl car that cruised that block--if the boys were half awake--

202

would take a look the minute they spotted the FOR RENT sign. Steve tramped hard on the throttle and went away from there.

At Washington and Figueroa he went into an all-night drugstore and pulled shut the door of the phone booth at the back. He dropped his nickel and dialed the number of police headquarters.

He asked for the desk and said: "Write this down, will you, sergeant? Brighton Avenue, thirty-two-hundred block, west side, in driveway of empty house. Got that much?"

"Yeah. So what?"

"Car with dead woman in it," Steve said, and hung up.

7

Quillan, head day clerk and assistant manager of the Carlton Hotel, was on night duty, because Millar, the night auditor, was off for a week. It was half-past one and things were dead and Quillan was bored. He had done everything there was to do long ago, because he had been a hotel man for twenty years and there was nothing to it.

The night porter had finished cleaning up and was in his room beside the elevator bank. One elevator was lighted and open, as usual. The main lobby had been tidied up and the lights had been properly dimmed. Everything was exactly as usual.

Quillan was a rather short, rather thickset man with clear bright toadlike eyes that seemed to hold a friendly expression without really having any expression at all. He had pale sandy hair and not much of it. His pale hands were clasped in front of him on the marble top of the desk. He was just the right height to put his weight on the desk without looking as if he were sprawling. He was looking at the wall across the entrance lobby, but he wasn't seeing it, He was half asleep, even though his eyes were wide open, and if the night porter struck a match behind his door, Quillan would know it and bang on his bell.

The brass-trimmed swing doors at the street entrance pushed open and Steve Grayce came in, a summer-weight coat turned up around his neck, his hat yanked low and a cigarette wisping smoke at the corner of his mouth. He looked very casual, very alert, and very much at ease. He strolled over to the desk and rapped on it.

"Wake up!" he snorted.

Quillan moved his eyes an inch and said: "All outside rooms with bath. But positively no parties on the eighth floor. Hiyah, Steve. So you finally got the axe. And for the wrong thing. That's life."

Steve said: "O.K. Have you got a new night man here?"

"Don't need one, Steve. Never did, in my opinion."

"You'll need one as long as old hotel men like you register floozies on the same corridor with people like Leopardi."

Quillan half closed his eyes and then opened them to where they had been before. He said indifferently: "Not me, pal. But anybody can make a mistake. Millar's really an accountant--not a desk man."

Steve leaned back and his face became very still. The smoke almost hung at the tip of his cigarette. His eyes were like black glass now. He smiled a little dishonestly.

"And why was Leopardi put in an eight-dollar room on Eight instead of in a tower suite at twenty-eight per?"

Quillan smiled back at him. "I didn't register Leopardi, old sock. There were reservations in. I supposed they were what he wanted. Some guys don't spend. Any other questions, Mr. Grayce?"

"Yeah. Was Eight-fourteen empty last night?"

"It was on change, so it was empty. Something about the plumbing. Proceed."

"Who marked it on change?"

Quillan's bright fathomless eyes turned and became curiously fixed. He didn't answer.

Steve said: "Here's why. Leopardi was in Eight-fifteen and the two girls in Eight-eleven. Just Eight-thirteen between. A lad with a passkey could have gone into Eight-thirteen and turned both the bolt locks on the communicating doors. Then, if the folks in the two other rooms had done the same thing on their side, they'd have a suite set up."

"So what?" Quillan asked. "We got chiseled out of eight bucks, eh? Well, it happens, in better hotels than this." His eyes looked sleepy now.

Steve said: "Millar could have done that. But hell, it doesn't make sense. Millar's not that kind of a guy. Risk a job for a buck tip--phooey. Millar's no dollar pimp."

Quillan said: "All right, policeman. Tell me what's really on your mind."

"One of the girls in Eight-eleven had a gun. Leopardi got a threat letter yesterday--I don't know where or how. It didn't faze him, though. He tore it up. That's how I know. I collected the pieces from his basket. I suppose Leopardi's boys all checked out of here."

"Of course. They went to the Normandy."

"Call the Normandy, and ask to speak to Leopardi. If he's there, he'll still be at the bottle. Probably with a gang."

"Why?" Quillan asked gently.

"Because you're a nice guy. If Leopardi answers-- just hang up." Steve paused and pinched his chin hard. "If he went out, try to find out where."

Quillan straightened, gave Steve another long quiet look and went behind the pebbled-glass screen. Steve stood very still, listening, one hand clenched at his side, the other tapping noiselessly on the marble desk.

In about three minutes Quillan came back and leaned on the desk again and said: "Not there. Party going on in his suite--they sold him a big one--and sounds loud. I talked to a guy who was fairly sober. He said Leopardi got a call around ten--some girl. He went out preening himself, as the fellow says. Hinting about a very juicy date. The guy was just lit enough to hand me all this."

Steve said: "You're a real pal. I hate not to tell you the rest. Well, I liked working here. Not much work at that."

He started towards the entrance doors again. Quillan let him get his hand on the brass handle before he called out. Steve turned and came back slowly.

Quillan said: "I heard Leopardi took a shot at you. I don't think it was noticed. It wasn't reported down here. And I don't think Peters fully realized that until he saw the mirror in Eight fifteen. If you care to come back, Steve--"

Steve shook his head. "Thanks for the thought."

"And hearing about that shot," Quillan added, "made me remember something. Two years ago a girl shot herself in Eight fifteen."

Steve straightened his back so sharply that he almost jumped. "What girl?"

Quillan looked surprised. "I don't know. I don't remember her real name. Some girl who had been kicked around all she could stand and wanted to die in a clean bed--alone."

Steve reached across and took hold of Quillan's arm. "The hotel files," he rasped. "The clippings, whatever there was in the papers will be in them. I want to see those clippings."

Quillan stared at him for a long moment. Then he said: "Whatever game you're playing, kid--you're playing it damn close to your vest. I will say that for you. And me bored stiff with a night to kill."

He reached along the desk and thumped the call bell. The door of the night porter's room opened and the porter came across the entrance lobby. He nodded and smiled at Steve.

Quillan said: "Take the board, Carl. I'll be in Mr. Peters' office for a little while."

He went to the safe and got keys out of it.

8

The cabin was high up on the side of the mountain, against a thick growth of digger pine, oak and incense cedar. It was solidly built, with a stone chimney, shingled all over and heavily braced against the slope of the hill. By daylight the roof was green and the sides dark reddish brown and the window frames and draw curtains red. In the uncanny brightness of an all-night mid-October moon in the mountains, it stood out sharply in every detail, except color.

It was at the end of a road, a quarter of a mile from any other cabin. Steve rounded the bend towards it without lights, at five in the morning. He stopped his car at once, when he was sure it was the right cabin, got out and walked soundlessly along the side of the gravel road, on a carpet of wild iris.

On the road level there was a rough pine board garage, and from this a path went up to the cabin porch. The garage was unlocked. Steve swung the door open carefully, groped in past the dark bulk of a car and felt the top of the radiator. It was still warmish. He got a small flash out of his pocket and played it over the car. A gray sedan, dusty, the gas gauge low. He snapped the flash off, shut the garage door carefully and slipped into place the piece of wood that served for a hasp. Then he climbed the path to the house.

There was light behind the drawn red curtains. The porch was high and juniper logs were piled on it, with the bark still on them. The front door had a thumb latch and a rustic door handle above.

He went up, neither too softly nor too noisily, lifted his hand, sighed deep in his throat, and knocked, His hand touched the butt of the gun in the inside pocket of his coat, once, then came away empty.

A chair creaked and steps padded across the floor and a voice called out softly: "What is it?" Millar's voice.

Steve put his lips close to the wood and said: "This is Steve, George. You up already?"

The key turned, and the door opened. George Millar, the dapper night auditor of the Carlton House, didn't look dapper now. He was dressed in old trousers and a thick blue sweater with a roll collar. His feet were in ribbed wool socks and fleece-lined slippers. His clipped black mustache was a curved smudge across his pale face. Two electric bulbs burned in their sockets in a low beam across the room, below the slope of the high roof. A table lamp was lit and its shade was tilted to throw light on a big Morris chair with a leather seat and back-cushion. A fire burned lazily in a heap of soft ash on the big open hearth.

Millar said in his low, husky voice: "Hell's sake, Steve. Glad to see you. How'd you find us anyway? Come on in, guy."

Steve stepped through the door and Millar locked it. "City habit," he said grinning. "Nobody locks anything in the mountains. Have a chair. Warm your toes. Cold out at this tune of night."

Steve said: "Yeah, Plenty cold."

He sat down in the Morris chair and put his hat and coat on the end of the solid wood table behind it. He leaned forward and held his hands out to the fire.

Millar said: "How the hell did you find us, Steve?"

Steve didn't look at him. He said quietly: "Not so easy at that. You told me last night your brother had a cabin up here--remember? So I had nothing to do, so I thought I'd drive up and bum some breakfast. The guy in the inn at Crestline didn't know who had cabins where. His trade is with people passing through. I rang up a garage man and he didn't know any Millar cabin. Then I saw a light come on down the street in a coal-and-wood yard and a little guy who is forest ranger and deputy sheriff and wood-and-gas dealer and half a dozen other things was getting his car out to go down to San Bernardino for some tank gas. A very smart little guy. The minute I said your brother had been a fighter he wised up. So here I am."

Millar pawed at his mustache. Bedsprings creaked at the back of the cabin somewhere. "Sure, he still goes under his fighting name--Gaff Talley. I'll get him up and we'll have some coffee. I guess you and me are both in the same boat. Used to working at night and can't sleep. I haven't been to bed at all."

Steve looked at him slowly and looked away. A burly voice behind them said: "Gaff is up. Who's your pal, George?"

Steve stood up casually and turned. He looked at the man's hands first. He couldn't help himself. They were large hands, well kept as to cleanliness, but coarse and ugly. One knuckle had been broken badly. He was a big man with reddish hair. He wore a sloppy bathrobe over outing-flannel pajamas. He had a leathery expressionless face, scarred over the cheekbones. There were fine white scars over his eyebrows and at the corners of his mouth. His nose was spread and thick. His whole face looked as if it had caught a lot of gloves. His eyes alone looked vaguely like Millar's eyes.

Millar said: "Steve Grayce. Night man at the hotel-- until last night." His grin was a little vague.

Gaff Talley came over and shook hands. "Glad to meet you," he said. "I'll get some duds on and we'll scrape a breakfast off the shelves. I slept enough. George ain't slept any, the poor sap."

He went back across the room towards the door through which he'd come. He stopped there and leaned on an old phonograph, put his big hand down behind a pile of records in paper envelopes. He stayed just like that, without moving.

Millar said: "Any luck on a job, Steve? Or did you try yet?"

"Yeah. In a way. I guess I'm a sap, but I'm going to have a shot at the private-agency racket. Not much in it unless I can land some publicity." He shrugged. Then he said very quietly: "King Leopardi's been bumped off."

Millar's mouth snapped wide open. He stayed like that for almost a minute--perfectly still, with his mouth open. Gaff Tailey leaned against the wall and stared without showing anything in his face. Millar finally said: "Bumped off? Where? Don't tell me--"

"Not in the hotel, George. Too bad, wasn't it? In a girl's apartment. Nice girl too. She didn't entice him there. The old suicide gag--only it won't work. And the girl is my client."

Millar didn't move. Neither did the big man. Steve leaned his shoulders against the stone mantel. He said softly: "I went out to the Club Shalotte this afternoon to apologize to Leopardi. Silly idea, because I didn't owe him an apology. There was a girl there in the bar lounge with him. He took three socks at me and left. The girl didn't like that. We got rather clubby. Had a drink together. Then late tonight--last night--she called me up and said Leopardi was over at her place and--he was drunk and she couldn't get rid of him. I went there. Only he wasn't drunk. He was dead, in her bed, in yellow pajamas."

The big man lifted his left hand and roughed back his hair. Millar leaned slowly against the edge of the table, as if he were afraid the edge might be sharp enough to cut him. His mouth twitched under the clipped black mustache.

He said huskily: "That's lousy."

The big man said: "Well, for cryin' into a milk bottle."

Steve said: "Only they weren't Leopardi's pajamas. His had initials on them--big black initials. And his were satin, not silk. And although he had a gun in his hand--this girl's gun by the way--*he* didn't shoot himself in the heart. The cops will determine that. Maybe you birds never heard of the Lund test, with paraffin wax, to find out who did or didn't fire a gun recently. The kill ought to have been pulled in the hotel last night, in Room Eight-fifteen. I spoiled that by heaving him out on his neck before that black-haired girl in Eight-eleven could get to him. Didn't I, George?"

Millar said: "I guess you did--if I know what you're talking about."

Steve said slowly: "I think you know what I'm talking about, George. It would have been a kind of poetic justice if King Leopardi had been knocked off in Room Eight-fifteen. Because that was the room where a girl shot herself two years ago. A girl who registered as Mary Smith--but whose usual name was Eve Talley. And whose real name was Eve Millar."

The big man leaned heavily on the victrola and said thickly: "Maybe I ain't woke up yet. That sounds like it might grow up to be a dirty crack, We had a sister named Eve that shot herself in the Carlton. So what?"

Steve smiled a little crookedly. He said: "Listen, George. You told me Quillan registered those girls in Eight-eleven. You did. You told me Leopardi registered on Eight, instead of in a good suite, because he was tight. He wasn't tight. He just didn't care where he was put, as long as female company was handy. And you saw to that. You planned the whole thing,

George. You even got Peters to write Leopardi at the Raleigh in Frisco and ask him to use the Carlton when he came down--because the same man owned it who owned the Club Shalotte. As if a guy like Jumbo Walters would care where a bandleader registered."

Millar's face was dead white, expressionless. His voice cracked. "Steve--for God's sake, Steve, what are you talking about? How the hell could I--"

"Sorry, kid. I liked working with you. I liked you a lot. I guess I still like you. But I don't like people who strangle women--or people who smear women in order to cover up a revenge murder."

His hand shot up--and stopped. The big man said: "Take it easy--and look at this one."

Gaff's hand had come up from behind the pile of records. A Colt .45 was in it. He said between his teeth: "I always thought house dicks were just a bunch of cheap grafters. I guess I missed out on you. You got a few brains. Hell, I bet you even run out to One-eighteen Court Street. Right?"

Steve let his hand fall empty and looked straight at the big Colt. "Right. I saw the girl--dead--with your fingers marked into her neck. They can measure those, fella. Killing Dolores Chiozza's maid the same way was a mistake. They'll match up the two sets of marks, find out that your black-haired gun girl was at the Carlton last night, and piece the whole story together. With the information they get at the hotel they can't miss. I give you two weeks, if you beat it quick. And I mean quick."

Millar licked his dry lips and said softly: "There's no hurry, Steve. No hurry at all. Our job is done. Maybe not the best way, maybe not the nicest way, but it wasn't a nice job. And Leopardi was the worst kind of a louse. We loved our sister, and he made a tramp out of her. She was a wide-eyed kid that fell for a flashy greaseball, and the greaseball went up in the world and threw her out on her ear for a red-headed torcher who was more his kind. He threw her out and broke her heart and she killed herself."

Steve said harshly: "Yeah--and what were you doing all that time--manicuring your nails?"

"We weren't around when it happened. It took us a little time to find out the why of it."

Steve said: "So that was worth killing four people for, was it? And as for Dolores Chiozza, she wouldn't have wiped her feet on Leopardi--then, or any time since. But you had to put her in the middle too, with your rotten little revenge murder. You make me sick, George. Tell your big tough brother to get on with his murder party."

The big man grinned and said: "Nuff talk, George. See has he a gat--and don't get behind him or in front of him. This bean-shooter goes on through."

Steve stared at the big man's .45. His face was hard as white bone. There was a thin cold sneer on his lips and his eyes were cold and dark.

Millar moved softly in his fleece-lined slippers. He came around the end of the table and went close to Steve's side and reached out a hand to tap his pockets. He stepped back and pointed: "In there."

Steve said softly: "I must be nuts. I could have taken you then, George."

Gaff Talley barked: "Stand away from him."

He walked solidly across the room and put the big Colt against Steve's stomach hard. He reached up with his left hand and worked the Detective Special from the inside breast pocket. His eyes were sharp on

214

Steve's eyes. He held Steve's gun out behind him. "Take this, George."

Millar took the gun and went over beyond the big table again and stood at the far corner of it. Gaff Talley backed away from Steve.

"You're through, wise guy," he said. "You got to know that. There's only two ways outa these mountains and we gotta have time. And maybe you didn't tell nobody. See?"

Steve stood like a rock, his face white, a twisted half-smile working at the corners of his lips. He stared hard at the big man's gun and his stare was faintly puzzled.

Millar said: "Does it have to be that way, Gaff?" His voice was a croak now, without tone, without its usual pleasant huskiness.

Steve turned his head a little and looked at Millar. "Sure it has, George. You're just a couple of cheap hoodlums after all. A couple of nasty-minded sadists playing at being revengers of wronged girlhood. Hillbilly stuff. And right this minute you're practically cold meat--cold, rotten meat."

Gaff Talley laughed and cocked the big revolver with his thumb. "Say your prayers, guy," he jeered.

Steve said grimly: "What makes you think you're going to bump me off with that thing? No shells in it, strangler. Better try to take me the way you handle women--with your hands."

The big man's eyes flicked down, clouded. Then he roared with laughter. "Geez, the dust on that one must be a foot thick," he chuckled. "Watch."

He pointed the big gun at the floor and squeezed the trigger. The firing pin clicked dryly--on an empty chamber. The big man's face convulsed.

215

For a short moment nobody moved. Then Gaff turned slowly on the balls of his feet and looked at his brother. He said almost gently: "You, George?"

Millar licked his lips and gulped. He had to move his mouth in and out before he could speak.

"Me. Gaff. I was standing by the window when Steve got out of his car down the road, I saw him go into the garage. I knew the car would still be warm. There's been enough killing, Gaff. Too much. So I took the shells out of your gun."

Millar's thumb moved back the hammer on the Detective Special. Gaff's eyes bulged. He stared fascinated at the snub nosed gun. Then he lunged violently towards it, flailing with the empty Colt. Millar braced himself and stood very still and said dimly, like an old man: "Goodbye, Gaff."

The gun jumped three times in his small neat hand. Smoke curled lazily from its muzzle. A piece of burned log fell over in the fireplace.

Gaff Talley smiled queerly and stooped and stood perfectly still. The gun dropped at his feet. He put his big heavy hands against his stomach, said slowly, thickly: " 'S all right, kid. 'S all right, I guess...I guess I
.

His voice trailed off and his legs began to twist under him. Steve took three long quick silent steps, and slammed Millar hard on the angle of the jaw. The big man was still falling--as slowly as a tree falls.

Millar spun across the room and crashed against the end wall and a blue-and-white plate fell off the plate-molding and broke. The gun sailed from his fingers. Steve dived for it and came up with it. Millar crouched and watched his brother.

Gaff Talley bent his head to the floor and braced his hands and then lay down quietly, on his stomach, like a man who was very tired. He made no sound of any kind.

Daylight showed at the windows, around the red glass-curtains. The piece of broken log smoked against the side of the hearth and the rest of the fire was a heap of soft gray ash with a glow at its heart.

Steve said dully: "You saved my life, George--or at least you saved a lot of shooting. I took the chance because what I wanted was evidence. Step over there to the desk and write it all out and sign it."

Millar said: "Is he dead?"

"He's dead, George. You killed him. Write that too."

Millar said quietly: "It's funny. I wanted to finish Leopardi myself, with my own hands, when he was at the top, when he had the farthest to fall. Just finish him and then take what came. But Gaff was the guy who wanted it done cute. Gaff, the tough mug who never had any education and never dodged a punch in his life, wanted to do it smart and figure angles. Well, maybe that's why he owned property, like that apartment house on Court Street that Jake Stoyanoff managed for him. I don't know how he got to Dolores Chiozza's maid. It doesn't matter much, does it?"

Steve said: "Go and write it. You were the one called Leopardi up and pretended to be the girl, huh?"

Millar said: "Yes. I'll write it all down, Steve. I'll sign it and then you'll let me go--just for an hour. Won't you, Steve? Just an hour's start. That's not much to ask of an old friend, is it, Steve?"

Millar smiled. It was a small, frail, ghostly smile. Steve bent beside the big sprawled man and felt his neck artery. He looked up, said: "Quite dead...Yes, you get an hour's start, George--if you write it all out."

Millar walked softly over to a tall oak highboy desk, studded with tarnished brass nails. He opened the flap and sat down and reached for a pen. He unscrewed the top from a bottle of ink and began to write in his neat, clear accountant's handwriting.

Steve Grayce sat down in front of the fire and lit a cigarette and stared at the ashes. He held the gun with his left hand on his knee. Outside the cabin, birds began to sing. Inside there was no sound but the scratching pen.

9

The sun was well up when Steve left the cabin, locked it up, walked down the steep path and along the narrow gravel road to his car. The garage was empty now. The gray sedan was gone. Smoke from another cabin floated lazily above the pines and oaks half a mile away. He started his car, drove it around a bend, past two old boxcars that had been converted into cabins, then on to a main road with a stripe down the middle and so up the hill to Crestline.

He parked on the main street before the Rim-of-the-World Inn, had a cup of coffee at the counter, then shut himself in a phone booth at the back of the empty lounge. He had the long distance operator get Jumbo Walters' number in Los Angeles, then called the owner of the Club Shalotte.

A voice said silkily: "This is Mr. Walters' residence."

"Steve Grayce. Put him on, if you please."

"One moment, please." A click, another voice, not so smooth and much harder. "Yeah?"

"Steve Grayce. I want to speak to Mr. Walters."

"Sorry. I don't seem to know you. It's a little early, amigo. What's your business?"

"Did he go to Miss Chiozza's place?"

"Oh." A pause. "The shamus. I get it. Hold the line, pal."

Another voice now--lazy, with the faintest color of Irish in it. "You can talk, son. This is Walters."

"I'm Steve Grayce. I'm the man--"

"I know all about that, son. The lady is O.K., by the way. I think she's asleep upstairs. Go on."

"I'm at Crestline--top of the Arrowhead grade. Two men murdered Leopardi. One was George Millar, night auditor at the Carlton Hotel. The other his brother, an ex-fighter named Gaff Talley. Talley's dead--shot by his brother. Millar got away--but he left me a full confession signed, detailed, complete."

Walters said slowly: "You're a fast worker, son-- unless you're just plain crazy. Better come in here fast. Why did they do it?"

"They had a sister."

Walters repeated quietly: "They had a sister...What about this fellow that got away? We don't want some hick sheriff or publicity-hungry county attorney to get ideas--"

Steve broke in quietly: "I don't think you'll have to worry about that, Mr. Walters. I think I know where he's gone."

He ate breakfast at the inn, not because he was hungry, but because he was weak. He got into his car again and started down the long smooth grade from Crestline to San Bernardino, a broad paved boulevard skirting the edge of a sheer drop into the deep valley.

There were places where the road went close to the edge, white guard-fences alongside.

Two miles below Crestline was the place. The road made a sharp turn around a shoulder of the mountain. Cars were parked on the gravel off the pavement-- several private cars, an official car, and a wrecking car. The white fence was broken through and men stood around the broken place looking down.

Eight hundred feet below, what was left of a gray sedan lay silent and crumpled in the morning sunshine.

BAY CITY BLUES

One--Cinderella Suicide

It must have been Friday because the fish smell from the Mansion House coffee-shop next door was strong enough to build a garage on. Apart from that it was a nice warm day in spring, the tail of the afternoon, and there hadn't been any business in a week. I had my heels in the groove on my desk and was sunning my ankles in a wedge of sunlight when the phone rang. I took my hat off it and made a yawning sound into the mouthpiece.

A voice said: "I heard that. You oughta be ashamed of yourself, Johnny Dalmas. Ever hear of the Austrian case?"

It was Violets M'Gee, a homicide dick in the sheriff's office and a very nice guy except for one bad habit-- passing me cases where I got tossed around and didn't make enough money to buy a secondhand corset.

"No."

"One of those things down at the beach--Bay City. I hear the little burg went sour again the last time they elected themselves a mayor, but the sheriff lives down there and we like to be nice. We ain't tramped on it. They say the gambling boys put up thirty grand campaign money, so now you get a racing form with the bill of fare in the hash houses."

I yawned again.

"I heard that, too," M'Gee barked, "If you ain't interested I'll just bite my other thumbnail and let the whole thing go. The guy's got a little dough to spend, he says."

"What guy?"

"This Matson, the guy that found the stiff."

"What stiff?"

"You don't know nothing about the Austrian case, huh?"

"Didn't I say I didn't?"

"You ain't done nothing but yawn and say 'What.' Okay. We'll just let the poor guy get bumped off and City Homicide can worry about that one, now he's up here in town."

"This Matson? Who's going to bump him off?"

"Well, if he knew that, he wouldn't want to hire no shamus to find out, would he? And him in your own racket until they bust him a while back and now he can't go out hardly, on account of these guys with guns are bothering him."

"Come on over," I said. "My left arm is getting tired."

"I'm on duty."

"I was just going down to the drugstore for a quart of V.O. Scotch."

"That's me you hear knocking on the door," M'Gee said.

He arrived in less than half an hour--a large, pleasant-faced man with silvery hair and a dimpled chin and a tiny little mouth made to kiss babies with. He wore a well-pressed blue suit, polished square-toed shoes, and an elk's tooth on a gold chain hung across his stomach.

He sat down carefully, the way a fat man sits down, and unscrewed the top of the whisky bottle and sniffed it carefully, to make sure I hadn't refilled a good bottle with ninety-eight cent hooch, the way they do in the bars. Then he poured himself a big drink and rolled some of it around on his tongue and pawed my office with his eyes.

"No wonder you sit around waiting for jobs," he said. "You gotta have front these days."

"You could spare me a little," I said. "What about this Matson and this Austrian case?"

M'Gee finished his drink and poured another, not so large. He watched me play with a cigarette.

"A monoxide Dutch," he said. "A blond bim named Austrian, wife of a doctor down at Bay City. A guy that runs around all night keeping movie hams from having pink elephants for breakfast. So the frill went around on her own. The night she croaked herself she was over to Vance Conried's club on the bluff north of there. Know it?"

"Yeah. It used to be a beach club, with a nice private beach down below and the swellest legs in Hollywood in front of the cabanas. She went there to play roulette, huh?"

"Well, if we had any gambling joints in this county," M'Gee said, "I'd say the Club Conried would be one of them and there would be roulette. Say she played roulette. They tell me she had more personal games she played with Conried, but say she played roulette on the side. She loses, which is what roulette is for. That night she loses her shirt and she gets sore and throws a wingding all over the house. Conried gets her into his private room and pages the doc, her husband, through the Physicians' Exchange. So then the doe--"

"Wait a minute," I said. "Don't tell me all this was in evidence--not with the gambling syndicate we would have in this county, if we had a gambling syndicate."

M'Gee looked at me pityingly. "My wife's got a kid brother works on a throw-away paper down there. They didn't have no inquest. Well, the doc steams over to Conricd's joint and pokcs his wifc in thc arm with a needle to quiet her down. But he can't take her home on account of he has a babe case in Brentwood Heights. So Vance Conried gets his personal car out and takes her home and meantime the doc has called up his office nurse and asked her to go over to the house and see that his wife is all right. Which is all done, and Conried goes back to his chips and the nurse sees her in bed and leaves, and the maid goes back to bed. This is maybe midnight, or just a little after.

"Well, along about 2 A.M. this Harry Matson happens by. He's running a night-watchman service down there and that night he's out making rounds himself. On the street where Austrian lives he hears a car engine running in a dark garage, and he goes in to investigate. He finds the blond frail on the floor on her back, in peekaboo pajamas and slippers, with soot from the exhaust all over her hair."

M'Gee paused to sip a little more whisky and stare around my office again. I watched the last of the sunlight sneak over my windowsill and drop into the dark slit of the alley.

"So what does the chump do?" M'Gee said, wiping his lips on a silk handkerchief. "He decides the bim is dead, which maybe she is, but you can't always be sure

223

in a gas case, what with this new methylene-blue treatment--"

"For God's sake," I said. "What does he do?"

"He don't call no law," M'Gee said sternly. "He kills the car motor and douses his flash and beats it home to where he lives a few blocks away. He pages the doc from there and after a while they're both back at the garage. The doc says she's dead. He sends Matson in at a side door to call the local chief of police personal, at his home. Which Matson does, and after a while the chief buzzes over with a couple of stooges, and a little while after them the body snatcher from the undertaker, whose turn it is to be deputy coroner that week. They cart the stiff away and some lab man takes a blood sample and says it's full of monoxide. The coroner gives a release and the dame is cremated and the case is closed."

"Well, what's the matter with it?" I asked.

M'Gee finished his second drink and thought about having a third. He decided to have a cigar first. I didn't have any cigars and that annoyed him slightly, but he lit one of his own.

"I'm just a cop," he said, blinking at me calmly through the smoke. "I wouldn't know. All I know is, this Matson got bust loose from his licence and run out of town and he's scared."

"The hell with it," I said. "The last time I muscled into a small-town setup I got a fractured skull. How do I contact Matson?"

"I give him your number. He'll contact you."

"How well do you know him?"

"Well enough to give him your name," M'Gee said. "Of course, if anything comes up I should look into--"

224

"Sure," I said. "I'll put it on your desk. Bourbon or rye?"

"Go to hell," M'Gee said. "Scotch."

"What does Matson look like?"

"He's medium heavy, five-seven, one-seventy, gray hair."

He had another short, quick drink and left.

I sat there for an hour and smoked too many cigarettes. It got dark and my throat felt dry. Nobody called me up. I went over and switched the lights on, washed my hands, tucked away a small drink and locked the bottle up. It was time to eat.

I had my hat on and was going through the door when the Green Feather messenger boy came along the hallway looking at numbers. He wanted mine. I signed for a small irregular shaped parcel done up in the kind of flimsy yellowish paper laundries use. I put the parcel on my desk and cut the string. Inside there was tissue paper and an envelope with a sheet of paper and a flat key in it. The note began abruptly:

A friend in the sheriff's office gave me your name as a man I could trust. I have been a heel and am in a jam and all I want now is to get clear. Please come after dark to 524 Tennyson Arms Apartments, Harvard near Sixth, and use key to enter if I am out. Look out for Pat Reel, the manager, as I don't trust him. Please put the slipper in a safe place and keep it clean. P.S. They call him Violets, I never knew why.

I knew why. It was because he chewed violet-scented breath purifiers. The note was unsigned. It sounded a little jittery to me. I unwound the tissue paper. It contained a green velvet pump, size about 4A lined with white kid. The name *Verschoyle* was stamped in flowing gold script on the white kid insole.

On the side a number was written very small in indelible ink--*S465*--where a size number would be, but I knew it wasn't a size number because Verschoyle, Inc., on Cherokee Street in Hollywood made only custom shoes from individual lasts, and theatrical footwear and riding boots.

I leaned back and lit a cigarette and thought about it for a while. Finally I reached for the phone book and looked up the number of Verschoyle, Inc., and dialed it. The phone rang several times before a chirpy voice said: "Hello? Yes?"

"Verschoyle--in person," I said. "This is Peters, Identification Bureau." I didn't say what identification bureau.

"Oh, Mr. Verschoyle has gone home. We're closed, you know. We close at five-thirty. I'm Mr. Pringle, the bookkeeper. Is there anything--"

"Yeah. We got a couple of your shoes in some stolen goods. The mark is S-Four-Six-Five. That mean anything to you?"

"Oh yes, of course. That's a last number. Shall I look it up for you?"

"By all means," I said.

He was back in no time at all. "Oh yes, indeed, that is Mrs. Leland Austrian's number. Seven-thirty-six Altair Street, Bay City. We made all her shoes. Very sad. Yes. About two months ago we made her two pairs of emerald velvet pumps."

"What do you mean, sad?"

"Oh, she's dead, you know. Committed suicide."

"The hell you say. Two pairs of pumps, huh?"

"Oh yes, both the same you know. People often order delicate colors in pairs like that. You know a

226

spot or stain of any kind--and they might be made to match a certain dress--"

"Well, thanks a lot and take care of yourself," I said, and gave the phone back to him.

I picked up the slipper again and looked it over carefully. It hadn't been worn. There was no sign of rubbing on the buffed leather of the thin sole. I wondered what Harry Matson was doing with it. I put it in my office safe and went out to dinner.

Two--Murder On The Cuff

The Tennyson Arms was an old-fashioned dump, about eight stories high, faced with dark red brick. It had a wide center court with palm trees and a concrete fountain and some prissy-looking flower beds. Lanterns hung beside the Gothic door and the lobby inside was paved with red plush. It was large and empty except for a bored canary in a gilt cage the size of a barrel. It looked like the sort of apartment house where widows would live on the life insurance--not very young widows. The elevator was the self-operating kind that opens both doors automatically when it stops.

I walked along the narrow maroon carpet of the fifth-floor hallway and didn't see anybody, hear anybody, or smell anybody's cooking. The place was as quiet as a minister's study. Apartment 524 must have opened on the center court because a stained-glass window was right beside its door. I knocked, not loud, and nobody came to the door so I used the flat key and went in, and shut the door behind me.

A mirror glistened in a wall bed across the room. Two windows in the same wall as the entrance door were shut and dark drapes were drawn half across them, but enough light from some apartment across the

227

court drifted in to show the dark bulk of heavy, overstuffed furniture, ten years out of date, and the shine of two brass doorknobs. I went over to the windows and pulled the drapes closed, then used my pocket flash to find my way back to the door. The light switch there set off a big cluster of flame-colored candles in the ceiling fixture. They made the room look like a funeral-chapel annex. I put the light on in a red standing lamp, doused the ceiling light and started to give the place the camera eye.

In the narrow dressing room behind the wall bed there was a built-in bureau with a black brush and comb on it and gray hairs in the comb. There was a can of talcum, a flashlight, a crumpled man's handkerchief, a pad of writing paper, a bank pen and a bottle of ink on a blotter--about what one suitcase would hold in the drawers. The shirts had been bought in a Bay City men's furnishing store. There was a dark gray suit on a hanger and a pair of black brogues on the floor. In the bathroom there was a safety razor, a tube of brushless cream, some blades, three bamboo toothbrushes in a glass, a few other odds and ends. On the porcelain toilet tank there was a book bound in red cloth-- Dorsey's *Why We Behave Like Human Beings*. It was marked at page 116 by a rubber band. I had it open and was reading about the Evolution of Earth, Life and Sex when the phone started to ring in the living room.

I snicked off the bathroom light and padded across the carpet to the davenport. The phone was on a stand at one end. It kept on ringing and a horn tooted outside in the street, as if answering it. When it had rung eight times I shrugged and reached for it.

"Pat? Pat Reel?" the voice said.

I didn't know how Pat Reel would talk. I grunted. The voice at the other end was hard and hoarse at the same time. It sounded like a tough-guy voice.

"Pat?"

"Sure," I said.

There was silence. It hadn't gone over. Then the voice said: "This is Harry Matson. Sorry as all hell I can't make it back tonight. Just one of those things. That bother you much?"

"Sure," I said.

"What's that?"

"Sure."

"Is 'sure' all the words you know, for God's sake?"

"I'm a Greek."

The voice laughed. It seemed pleased with itself.

I said: "What kind of toothbrushes do you use, Harry?"

"Huh?"

This was a startled explosion of breath--not so pleased now.

"Toothbrushes--the little dinguses some people brush their teeth with. What kind do you use?"

"Aw, go to hell."

"Meet you on the step," I said.

The voice got mad now. "Listen, smart monkey! You ain't pulling nothin', see? We got your name, we got your number, and we got a place to put you if you don't keep your nose clean, see? And Harry don't live there any more, ha, ha."

"You picked him off, huh?"

"I'll say we picked him off. What do you think we done, took him to a picture show?"

"That's bad," I said. "The boss won't like that."

I hung up in his face and put the phone down on the table at the end of the davenport and rubbed the back of my neck. I took the door key out of my pocket and polished it on my handkerchief and laid it down carefully on the table. I got up and walked across to one of the windows and pulled the drapes aside far enough to look out into the court. Across its palm dotted oblong, on the same floor level I was on, a bald-headed man sat in the middle of a room under a hard, bright light, and didn't move a muscle. He didn't look like a spy.

I let the drapes fall together again and settled my hat on my head and went over and put the lamp out. I put my pocket flash down on the floor and palmed my handkerchief on the doorknob and quietly opened the door.

Braced to the door frame by eight hooked fingers, all but one of which were white as wax, there hung what was left of a man.

He had eyes an eighth of an inch deep, china-blue, wide open. They looked at me but they didn't see me. He had coarse gray hair on which the smeared blood looked purple. One of his temples was a pulp, and the tracery of blood from it reached clear to the point of his chin. The one straining finger that wasn't white had been pounded to shreds as far as the second joint. Sharp splinters of bone stuck out of the mangled flesh. Something that might once have been a fingernail looked now like a ragged splinter of glass.

The man wore a brown suit with patch pockets, three of them. They had been torn off and hung at odd angles showing the dark alpaca lining beneath.

He breathed with a faraway unimportant sound, like distant footfalls on dead leaves. His mouth was strained open like a fish's mouth, and blood bubbled from it. Behind him the hallway was empty as a new-dug grave.

Rubber heels squeaked suddenly on the bare space of wood beside the hall runner. The man's straining fingers slipped from the door frame and his body started to wind up on his legs. The legs couldn't hold it. They scissored and the body turned in mid-air, like a swimmer in a wave, and then jumped at me.

I clamped my teeth hard and spread my feet and caught him from behind, after his torso had made a half turn. He weighed enough for two men. I took a step back and nearly went down, took two more and then I had his dragging heels clear of the doorway. I let him down on his side as slowly as I could, crouched over him panting. After a second I straightened, went over to the door and shut and locked it. Then I switched the ceiling light on and started for the telephone.

He died before I reached it. I heard the rattle, the spent sigh, then silence. An out flung hand, the good one, twitched once and the fingers spread out slowly into a loose curve and stayed like that. I went back and felt his carotid artery, digging my fingers in hard. Not a flicker of a pulse. I got a small steel mirror out of my wallet and held it against his open mouth for a long minute. There was no trace of mist on it when I took it away. Harry Matson had come home from his ride.

A key tickled at the outside of the door lock and I moved fast. I was in the bathroom when the door opened, with a gun in my hand and my eyes to the crack of the bathroom door.

This one came in quickly, the way a wise cat goes through a swing door. His eyes flicked up at the ceiling

231

lights, then down at the floor. After that they didn't move at all. All his big body didn't move a muscle. He just stood and looked.

He was a big man in an unbuttoned overcoat, as if he had just come in or was just going out. He had a gray felt hat on the back of a thick creamy-white head. He had the heavy black eyebrows and broad pink face of a boss politician, and his mouth looked as if it usually had the smile--but not now. His face was all bone and his mouth jiggled a half-smoked cigar along his lips with a sucking noise.

He put a bunch of keys back in his pocket and said "God!" very softly, over and over again. Then he took a step forward and went down beside the dead man with a slow, clumsy motion. He put large fingers into the man's neck, took them away again, shook his head, looked slowly around the room. He looked at the bathroom door behind which I was hiding, but nothing changed in his eyes.

"Fresh dead," he said, a little louder. "Beat to a pulp."

He straightened up slowly and rocked on his heels. He didn't like the ceiling light any better than I had. He put the standing lamp on and switched the ceiling light off, rocked on his heels some more. His shadow crawled up the end wall, started across the ceiling, paused and dropped back again. He worked the cigar around in his mouth, dug a match out of his pocket and relit the butt carefully, turning it around and around in the flame. When he blew the match out he put it in his pocket. He did all this without once taking his eyes off the dead man on the floor.

He moved sideways over to the davenport and let himself down on the end of it. The springs squeaked dismally. He reached for the phone without looking at it, eyes still on the dead man.

He had the phone in his hand when it started to ring again. That jarred him. His eyes rolled and his elbows jerked against the sides of his thick over-coated body. Then he grinned very carefully and lifted the phone off the cradle and said in a rich, fruity voice: "Hello. Yeah, this is Pat."

I heard a dry, inarticulate croaking noise on the wire, and I saw Pat Reel's face slowly congest with blood until it was the color of fresh beef liver. His big hand shook the phone savagely.

"So it's Mister Big Chin!" he blared. "Well, listen here, saphead, you know something? Your stiff is right here on my carpet, that's where he is...How did he get here? How the hell would I know? Ask me, you croaked him here, and lemme tell you something. It's costing you plenty, see, plenty. No murder on the cuff in my house. I spot a guy for you and you knock him off in my lap, damn you! I'll take a grand and not a cent less, and you come and get what's here and I mean get it, see?"

There was more croaking on the wire. Pat Reel listened. His eyes got almost sleepy and the purple died out of his face. He said more steadily: "Okay. Okay. I was only kidding...Call me in half an hour downstairs."

He put down the phone and stood up. He didn't look towards the bathroom door, he didn't look anywhere. He began to whistle. Then he scratched his chin and took a step towards the door, stopped to scratch his chin again. He didn't know there was anybody in the apartment, he didn't know there wasn't anybody in the apartment--and he didn't have a gun. He took another step towards the door. Big Chin had told him something and the idea was to get out. He took a third step, then he changed his mind.

"Aw hell," he said out loud. "That screwy mug." Then his eyes ranged round the apartment swiftly. "Tryin' to kid me, huh?"

His hand raised to the chain switch. Suddenly he let it fall and knelt beside the dead man again. He moved the body a little, rolling it without effort on the carpet, and put his face down close to squint at the spot where the head had lain. Pat Reel shook his head in displeasure, got to his feet and put his hands under the dead man's armpits. He threw a glance over his shoulder at the dark bathroom and started to back towards me, dragging the body, grunting, the cigar butt still clamped in his mouth. His creamy-white hair glistened cleanly in the lamplight.

He was still bent over with his big legs spraddled when I stepped out behind him. He may have heard me at the last second but it didn't matter. I had shifted the gun to my left hand and I had a small pocket sap in my right. I laid the sap against the side of his head, just behind his right ear, and I laid it as though I loved it.

Pat Reel collapsed forward across the sprawled body he was dragging, his head down between the dead man's legs. His hat rolled gently off to the side. He didn't move. I stepped past him to the door and left.

Three--Gentleman Of The Press

Over on Western Avenue I found a phone booth and called the sheriff's office. Violets M'Gee was still there, just ready to go home.

I said: "What was the name of your kid brother-in-law that works on the throw-away paper down at Bay City?"

234

"Kincaid. They call him Dolly Kincaid. A little feller."

"Where would he be about now?"

"He hangs around the city hall. Think he's got a police beat. Why?"

"I saw Matson," I said. "Do you know where he's staying?"

"Naw. He just called me on the phone. What you think of him?"

"I'll do what I can for him. Will you be home tonight?"

"I don't know why not. Why?"

I didn't tell him why. I got into my car and pointed it towards Bay City. I got down there about nine. The police department was half a dozen rooms in a city hall that belonged in the hookworm-and-Bible belt. I pushed past a knot of smoothies into an open doorway where there was light and a counter. There was a PBX board in the corner and a uniformed man behind it.

I put an arm on the counter and a plainclothes man with his coat off and an under-arm holster looking the size of a wooden leg against his ribs took one eye off his paper and said, "Yeah?" and bonged a spittoon without moving his head more than an inch.

I said: "I'm looking for a fellow named Dolly Kincaid."

"Out to eat. I'm holdin' down his beat," he said in a solid, unemotional voice.

"Thanks. You got a pressroom here?"

"Yeah. Got a toilet, too. Wanta see?"

"Take it easy," I said. "I'm not trying to get fresh with your town."

He bonged the spittoon again. "Pressroom's down the hall. Nobody in it. Dolly's due back, if he don't get drowned in a pop bottle."

A small-boned, delicate-faced young man with a pink complexion and innocent eyes strolled into the room with a half-eaten hamburger sandwich in his left hand. His hat, which looked like a reporters hat in a movie, was smashed on the back of his small blond head. His shirt collar was unbuttoned at the neck and his tie was pulled to one side. The ends of it hung out over his coat. The only thing the matter with him for a movie news hawk was that he wasn't drunk. He said casually: "Anything stirring, boys?"

The big black-haired plainclothes man bonged his private spittoon again and said: "I hear the mayor changed his underpants, but it's just a rumor."

The small young man smiled mechanically and turned away. The cop said: "This guy wants to see you, Dolly."

Kincaid munched his hamburger and looked at me hopefully. I said: "I'm a friend of Violets'. Where can we talk?"

"Let's go into the pressroom," he said. The black-haired cop studied me as we went out. He had a look in his eyes as if he wanted to pick a fight with somebody, and he thought I would do.

We went along the hall towards the back and turned into a room with a long, bare, scarred table, three or four wooden chairs and a lot of newspapers on the floor. There were two telephones on one end of the table, and a flyblown framed picture in the exact center of each wall--Washington, Lincoln, Horace Greeley, and the other one somebody I didn't recognize. Kincaid shut the door and sat on one end of the table and swung his leg and bit into the last of his sandwich.

I said: "I'm John Dalmas, a private dick from L.A. How's to take a ride over to Seven thirty-six Altair Street and tell me what you know about the Austrian case? Maybe you better call M'Gee up and get him to introduce us." I pushed a card at him.

The pink young man slid down off the table very rapidly and stuffed the card into his pocket without looking at it and spoke close to my ear. "Hold it."

Then he walked softly over to the framed picture of Horace Greeley and lifted it off the wall and pressed on a square of paint behind it. The paint gave--it was painted over fabric. Kincaid looked at me and raised his eyebrows. I nodded. He hung the picture back on the wall and came back to me. "Mike," he said under his breath. "Of course I don't know who listens or when, or even whether the damn thing still works."

"Horace Greeley would have loved it," I said.

"Yeah. The beat's pretty dead tonight. I guess I could go out. Al De Spain will cover for me anyway." He was talking loud now.

"The big black-haired cop?"

"Yeah."

"What makes him sore?"

"He's been reduced to acting patrolman. He ain't even working tonight. Just hangs around and he's so tough it would take the whole damn police force to throw him out."

I looked towards the microphone and raised my eyebrows.

"That's okay," Kincaid said. "I gotta feed 'em something to chew on."

He went over to a dirty washbowl in the corner and washed his hands on a scrap of lava soap and dried them on his pocket handkerchief. He was just putting the handkerchief away when the door opened. A small, middle-aged, gray-haired man stood in it, looking at us expressionlessly.

Dolly Kincaid said: "Evening, Chief, anything I can do for you?"

The chief looked at me silently and without pleasure. He had sea-green eyes, a tight, stubborn mouth, a ferret-shaped nose, and an unhealthy skin. He didn't look big enough to be a cop. He nodded very slightly and said: "Who's your friend?"

"He's a friend of my brother-in-law. He's a private dick from L.A. Let's see--" Kincaid gripped desperately in his pocket for my card. He didn't even remember my name.

The chief said sharply: "What's that? A private detective? What's your business here?"

"I didn't say I was here on business," I told him.

"Glad to hear it," he said. "Very glad to hear it. Good night." He opened the door and went out quickly and snapped it shut behind him.

"Chief Anders--one swell guy," Kincaid said loudly. "They don't come any better." He was looking at me like a scared rabbit.

"They never have," I said just as loudly. "In Bay City."

I thought for a moment he was going to faint, but he didn't. We went out in the front of the city hall and got into my car and drove away.

I stopped the car on Altair Street across the way from the residence of Dr. Leland Austrian. The night was windless and there was a little fog under the moon. A faint pleasant smell of brackish water and kelp came up the side of the bluff from the beach. Small riding lights pinpointed the yacht harbor and the shimmering lines of three piers. Quite far out to sea a bigmasted fishing barge had lights strung between its masts and from the mastheads down to the bow and stern. Other things than fishing probably happened on it.

Altair Street in that block was a dead-end, cut off by a tall, ornamental iron fence that walled a big estate. The houses were on the inland side of the street only, on eighty- or hundred foot lots, well spaced. On the seaward side there was a narrow sidewalk and a low wall, beyond which the bluff dropped almost straight down.

Dolly Kincaid was pressed back into the corner of the seat, the red tip of a cigarette glowing at intervals in front of his small blurred face. The Austrian house was dark except for a small light over the embrasure in which the front door was set. It was stucco, with a wall across the front yard, iron gates, the garage outside the wall. A cement walk went from a side door of the garage to a side door of the house. There was a bronze plate set into the wall beside the gates and I knew it would read*Leland M. Austrian, M.D.*

"All right," I said. "Now what was the matter with the Austrian case?"

"Nothing was the matter with it," Kincaid said slowly. "Except you're going to get me in a jam."

"Why?"

"Somebody must have heard you mention Austrian's address over that mike. That's why Chief Anders came in to look at you."

"De Spain might have figured me for a dick--just on looks. He might have tipped him off."

"No. De Spain hates the chief's guts. Hell, he was a detective lieutenant up to a week ago. Anders don't want the Austrian case monkeyed with. He wouldn't let us write it up."

"Swell press you got in Bay City."

"We got a swell climate--and the press is a bunch of stooges."

"Okay," I said. "You got a brother-in-law who's a homicide dick in the sheriff's office. All the L.A. papers but one are strong for the sheriff. This town is where he lives, though, and like a lot of other guys he don't keep his own yard clean. So you're scared, huh?"

Dolly Kincaid threw his cigarette out of the window. I watched it fall in a small red arc and lie faintly pink on the narrow sidewalk. I leaned forward and pressed on the starter button. "Excuse it, please," I said. "I won't bother you any more."

I meshed the gears and the car crawled forward a couple of yards before Kincaid leaned over and jerked the parking brake on. "I'm not yellow," he said sharply. "What do you wanta know?"

I cut the motor again and leaned back with my hands on the wheel. "First off, why did Matson lose his licence. He's my client."

"Oh--Matson. They said he tried to put the bite on Dr. Austrian. And they not only took his licence, they run him out of town. A couple of guys with guns shoved him into a car one night and roughed him around and told him to skip the burg or else. He reported it down at headquarters and you could have heard them laugh for blocks. But I don't think it was cops."

"Do you know anybody called Big Chin?"

Dolly Kincaid thought. "No. The mayor's driver, a goof called Moss Lorenz, has a chin you could balance a piano on. But I never heard him called Big Chin. He used to work for Vance Conried. Ever hear of Conried?"

"I'm all caught up on that angle," I said. "Then if this Conried wanted to bump somebody off that was bothering him, and especially somebody that had made a little trouble here in Bay City, this Lorenz would be just the guy. Because the mayor would have to cover for him--up to a point, anyway."

Dolly Kincaid said, "Bump who off?" and his voice was suddenly thick and tense.

"They didn't only run Matson out of town," I told him. "They traced him to an apartment house in L.A. and some guy called Big Chin gave him the works. Matson must have been working still on whatever it was he was working on."

"Geez," Dolly Kincaid whispered. "I didn't get a word on that."

"The L.A. cops neither--when I left. Did you know Matson?"

"A little. Not well."

"Would you call him honest?"

"Well, as honest as--well, yeah, I guess he was all right. Geez, bumped off, huh?"

"As honest as a private dick usually is?" I said.

He giggled, from sudden strain and nervousness and shock--very little from amusement. A car turned into the end of the street and stopped by the curb and its lights went out. Nobody got out.

"How about Dr. Austrian," I said. "Where was he when his wife was murdered?"

241

Dolly Kincaid jumped. "Jeepers, who said she was murdered?" he gasped.

"I think Matson was trying to say so. But he was trying to get paid for not saying it even harder than he was trying to say it. Either way would have got him disliked, but his way got him chilled with a piece of lead pipe. My hunch is that Conried would have that done because he would not like to have anybody make the pay sign at him, except in the way of legitimate graft. But on the other hand it would be a little better for Conried's club to have Dr. Austrian murder his wife than for her to do a Dutch on account of losing all her dough at Conried's roulette tables. Maybe not a lot better, but some better. So I can't figure why Conried would have Matson bumped off for talking about murder. I figure he could have been talking about something else as well."

"Does all this figuring ever get you anywhere?" Dolly Kincaid asked politely.

"No. It's just something to do while I'm patting the cold cream into my face at night. Now about this lab man that made the blood sample. Who was he?"

Kincaid lit another cigarette and looked down the block at the car that had stopped in front of the end house. Its lights had gone on again now and it was moving forward slowly.

"A guy named Greb," he said. "He has a small place in the Physicians and Surgeons Building and works for the doctors."

"Not official, huh?"

"No, but they don't run to lab men down here. And the undertakers all take turns being coroner for a week, so what the hell. The chief handles it the way he likes."

"Why would he want to handle it at all?"

"I guess maybe he might get orders from the mayor, who might get a hint from the gambling boys that Vance Conried works for, or from Vance Conried direct. Conried might not like his bosses to know he was mixed up with a dead frill in a way to make a kickback on the club."

"Right," I said. "That guy down the block don't know where he lives."

The car was still crawling forward along the curb. Its lights were out again, but it was still moving.

"And while I'm still healthy," Dolly Kincaid said, "you might as well know that Doc Austrian's office nurse used to be Matson's wife. She's a redheaded man-eater with no looks but a lot of outside curve."

"I like a well-crowded stocking myself," I said. "Get out of that door and in the back of the car and lie down and make it fast."

"Geez--"

"Do what I say!" I snapped. "Fast!"

The door on the right clicked open and the little man slid out like a wisp of smoke. The door clicked shut. I heard the rear door open and sneaked a look back and saw a dark shape haunched on the floor of the car. I slid over to the right side myself and opened the door again and stepped out on the narrow sidewalk that ran along the rim of the bluff.

The other car was close now. Its lights flared up again and I ducked. The lights swerved so that they swept my car, then swerved back and the car stopped opposite and went quietly dark. It was a small black coupe. Nothing happened for a minute, then its left door opened and a chunky man stepped out and started to stroll over towards my side of the side-paved street. I took my gun from under my arm and tucked it in my belt and buttoned the bottom button of my coat. Then I walked around the rear end of my car to meet him.

He stopped dead when he saw me. His hands hung empty at his sides. There was a cigar in his mouth. "Police," he said briefly. His right hand shaded back slowly towards his right hip. "Nice night ain't it?"

"Swell," I said. "A little foggy, but I like fog. It softens the air up and--"

He cut in on me sharply: "Where's the other guy?"

"Huh?"

"Don't kid me, stranger. I saw a cigarette on the right side of your car."

"That was me," I said. "I didn't know it was against the law to smoke on the right side of a car."

"Oh, a smart monkey. Who are you and what's your business here?" His heavy, greasy face reflected the sifted light in the soft misty air.

"The name's O'Brien," I said. "Just down from San Mateo on a little pleasure trip."

His hand was very close to his hip now. "I'll look at your driver's licence," he said. He came close enough to reach it, if we both stretched out our arms to each other.

"I'll look at what gives you the right to look at it," I said.

His right hand made an abrupt movement. Mine flicked the gun out of my belt and pointed it at his stomach. His hand stopped as though it had been frozen in a block of ice.

"Maybe you're a stick-up," I said. "It's still being done with nickel badges."

He stood there, paralyzed, hardly breathing. He said thickly: "Got a licence for that heater?"

244

"Every day in the week," I said. "Let's see your badge and I'll put it away. You don't wear the buzzer where you sit down, do you?"

He stood for another frozen minute. Then he looked along the block as if he hoped another car might arrive. Behind me, in the back of my car, there was a soft, sibilant breathing. I didn't know whether the chunky man heard it or not. His own breathing was heavy enough to iron a shirt with.

"Aw, quit your kiddin'," he snarled out with sudden ferocity. "You're nothin' but a lousy two-bit shamus from L.A."

"I upped the rate," I said. "I get thirty cents now."

"Go to hell. We don't want you nosin' around here, see. This time I'm just tellin' you."

He turned on his heel and walked back to his coupe and put a foot on the running board. His thick neck turned slowly and his greasy skin showed again. "Go to hell," he said, "before we send you there in a basket."

"So long, Greasy-Puss," I said. "Nice to have met you with your pants down."

He slammed into his car, started it with a jerk and lurched it around. He was gone down the block in a flash.

I jumped into mine and was only a block behind him when he made the stop for Arguello Boulevard. He turned right. I turned left. Dolly Kincaid came up and put his chin on the back of the seat beside my shoulder.

"Know who that was?" he croaked. "That was Trigger Weems, the chief's right bower. He might have shot you."

"Fanny Brice might have had a pug nose," I said. "It was that close."

I rode around a few blocks and stopped to let him get in beside me. "Where's your car?" I said.

He took his crumpled reporter's hat off and smacked it on his knee and put it back on again. "Why, down at the city hall. In the police yard."

"Too bad," I said. "You'll have to take the bus to L.A. You ought to spend a night with your sister once in a while. Especially tonight."

Four--Redheaded Woman

The road twisted, dipped, soared along the flank of the foothills, a scatter of lights to the northwest and a carpet of them to the south. The three piers seemed remote from this point, thin pencils of light laid out on a pad of black velvet. There was fog in the canyons and a smell of wild growth, but no fog on the high ground between the canyons.

I swung past a small, dim service station, closed up for the night, down into another wide canyon, up past half a mile of expensive wire fence walling in some invisible estate. Then the scattered houses got still more scattered along the hills and the air smelled strongly of the sea. I turned left past a house with a round white turret and drove out between the only electroliers in miles to a big stucco building on a point above the coast highway. Light leaked from draped windows and along an arched stucco colonnade, and shone dimly on a thick cluster of cars parked in diagonal slots around an oval lawn.

This was the Club Conried. I didn't know exactly what I was going to do there, but it seemed to be one of the places where I had to go. Dr. Austrian was still wandering in unknown parts of the town visiting unnamed patients. The Physicians' Exchange said he usually called in about eleven. It was now about ten-fifteen.

I parked in a vacant slot and walked along the arched colonnade. A six-foot-six Negro, in the uniform of a comic-opera South American field marshal, opened one half of a wide grilled door from the inside and said: "Card, please, suh."

I tucked a dollar's worth of folding money into his lilac-colored palm. Enormous ebony knuckles closed over it like a dragline over a bucketful of gravel. His other hand picked a piece of lint off my left shoulder and left a metal tag down behind my show handkerchief in the outside breast pocket of my jacket.

"New floor boss kinda tough," he whispered. "I thank you, suh."

"You mean sucker," I said, and went in past him.

The lobby--they called it a foyer--looked like an MGM set for a night club in the Broadway Melody of 1980. Under the artificial light, it looked as if it had cost about a million dollars and took up enough space for a polo field. The carpet didn't quite tickle my ankles. At the back there was a chromium gangway like a ship's gangway going up to the dining-room entrance, and at the top of this a chubby Italian captain of waiters stood with a set smile and a two-inch satin stripe on his pants and a bunch of gold-plated menus under his arm.

There was a free-arched stairway with banisters like white-enameled sleigh rails. This would go up to the second-floor gambling rooms. The ceiling had stars in it and they twinkled. Beside the bar entrance, which was dark and vaguely purple, like a half-remembered nightmare, there was a huge round mirror set back in a white tunnel with an Egyptian headdress over the top of it. In front of this a lady in green was preening her metallic blond hair. Her evening gown was cut so low at the back that she was wearing a black beauty patch on her lumbar muscle, about an inch below where her pants would have been, if she had been wearing any pants.

A check girl in peach-bloom pajamas with small black dragons on them came over to take my hat and disapprove of my clothes. She had eyes as black and shiny and expressionless as the toes of patent-leather pumps. I gave her a quarter and kept my hat. A cigarette girl with a tray the size of a five-pound candy box came down the gangway. She wore feathers in her hair, enough clothes to hide behind a three-cent stamp, and one of her long, beautiful, naked legs was gilded and the other was silvered. She had the cold, disdainful expression of a dame who is dated so far ahead that she would have to think twice before accepting a knock down to a maharajah with a basket of rubies under his arm.

I went into the soft purple twilight of the bar. Glasses tinkled gently. There were quiet voices, chords on a piano off in a corner, and a pansy tenor singing "My Little Buckeroo" as confidentially as a bartender mixing a Mickey Finn. Little by little the purple light got to be something I could see by. The bar was fairly full but not crowded. A man laughed off-key and the pianist expressed his annoyance by doing an Eddie Duchin ripple down the keyboard with his thumbnail.

I spotted an empty table and went and sat behind it, against the cushioned wall. The light grew still brighter for me. I could even see the buckeroo singer now. He had wavy red hair that looked hennaed. The girl at the table next to me had red hair too. It was parted in the middle and strained back as if she hated it. She had large, dark, hungry eyes, awkward features and no make-up except a mouth that glared like a neon sign. Her street suit had too-wide shoulders, too-flaring lapels. An orange under sweater snuggled her neck and there was a black-and-orange quill in her Robin Hood hat, crooked on the back of her head. She smiled at me and her teeth were as thin and sharp as a pauper's Christmas. I didn't smile back.

She emptied her glass and rattled it on the tabletop. A waiter in a neat mess jacket slipped out of nowhere and stood in front of me.

"Scotch and soda," the girl snapped. She had a hard, angular voice with a liquor slur in it.

The waiter looked at her, barely moved his chin and looked back at me. I said: "Bacardi and grenadine."

He went away. The girl said: "That'll make you sicky, big boy."

I didn't look at her. "So you don't want to play," she said loosely. I lit a cigarette and blew a ring in the soft purplish air. "Go chase yourself," the girl said. "I could pick up a dozen gorillas like you on every block on Hollywood Boulevard. Hollywood Boulevard, my foot. A lot of bit players out of work and fish-faced blondes trying to shake a hangover out of their teeth."

"Who said anything about Hollywood Boulevard?" I asked.

"You did. Nobody but a guy from Hollywood Boulevard wouldn't talk back to a girl that insulted him civilly."

A man and a girl at a nearby table turned their heads and stared. The man gave me a short, sympathetic grin. "That goes for you, too," the girl said to him.

"You didn't insult me yet," he said.

249

"Nature beat me to it, handsome."

The waiter came back with the drinks. He gave me mine first. The girl said loudly: "I guess you're not used to waiting on ladies."

The waiter gave her her Scotch and soda. "I beg your pardon, madam," he said in an icy tone.

"Sure. Come around sometime and I'll give you a manicure, if I can borrow a hoe. Boy friend's paying the ticket on this."

The waiter looked at me. I gave him a bill and a lift of my right shoulder. He made change, took his tip, and faded off among the tables.

The girl picked her drink up and came over to my table. She put her elbows on the table and cupped her chin in her hands. "Well, well, a spender," she said. "I didn't know they made them any more. How do you like me?"

"I'm thinking it over," I said. "Keep your voice down or they'll throw you out."

"I doubt it," she said, "As long as I don't break any mirrors. Besides, me and their boss are like that." She held up two fingers close together. "That is we would be if I could meet him." She laughed tinnily, drank a little of her drink. "Where've I seen you around?"

"Most anywhere."

"Where've you seen me?"

"Hundreds of places."

"Yes," she said. "Just like that. A girl can't hang on to her individuality any more."

"She can't get it back out of a bottle," I said.

"The heck you say. I could name you plenty of big names that go to sleep with a bottle in each hand. And have to get pushed in the arm so they won't wake up yelling."

"Yeah?" I said. "Movie soaks, huh?"

"Yeah. I work for a guy that pushes them in the arm-
-at ten bucks a push. Sometimes twenty-five or fifty."

"Sounds like a nice racket," I said.

"If it lasts. You think it'll last?"

"You can always go to Palm Springs when they run
you out of here."

"Who's going to run who out of where?"

"I don't know," I said. "What were we talking
about?"

She had red hair. She was not good-looking, but she
had curves. And she worked for a man who pushed
people in the arm. I licked my lips.

A big dark man came through the entrance door and
stood just inside it, waiting for his eyes to get used to
the light. Then he started to look the place over
without haste. His glance traveled to the table where I
was sitting. He leaned his big body forward and started
to walk our way.

"Oh, oh," the girl said. "The bouncer. Can you take
it?"

I didn't answer. She stroked her colorless cheek with
a strong pale hand and leered at me. The man at the
piano struck some chords and began to whine about
"We Can Still Dream, Can't We?"

The big, dark man stopped with his hand on the chair
across the table from me. He pulled his eyes off the
girl and smiled at me. She was the one he had been
looking at. She was the one he had come down the
room to get near. But I was the one he looked at from
now on. His hair was smooth and dark and shiny above
cold gray eyes and eyebrows that looked as if they
were penciled, and a handsome actorish mouth and a

nose that had been broken but well set. He spoke liplessly.

"Haven't seen you around for some time--or is my memory bad?"

"I don't know," I said. "What are you trying to remember?"

"Your name, doc."

I said: "Quit trying. We never met." I fished the metal tag out of my breast pocket and tossed it down. "Here's my ticket in from the drum major on the wicket." I got a card out of my wallet and tossed that down. "Here's my name, age, height, weight, scars if any, and how many times convicted. And my business is to see Conried."

He ignored the tag and read the card twice, turned it over and looked at the back, then looked at the front again, hooked an arm over the chair-back and gave me a mealy smile. He didn't look at the girl then or ever. He racked the card edge across the tabletop and made a faint squeak, like a very young mouse. The girl stared at the ceiling and pretended to yawn.

He said dryly: "So you're one of those guys. So sorry. Mr. Conried had to go north on a little business trip. Caught an early plane."

The girl said: "That must have been his stand-in I saw this afternoon at Sunset and Vine, in a gray Cord sedan."

He didn't look at her. He smiled faintly. "Mr. Conried doesn't have a gray Cord sedan."

The girl said: "Don't let him kid you. I bet he's upstairs crooking a roulette wheel right this minute."

The dark man didn't look at her. His not looking at her was more emphatic than if he had slapped her face. I saw her whiten a little, very slowly, and stay white.

I said: "He's not here, he's not here. Thanks for listening. Maybe some other time."

"Oh sure. But we don't use any private eyes in here. So sorry."

"Say that 'so sorry' again and I'll scream. So help me," the red-haired girl said.

The black-haired man put my card in the casual outer pocket of his dinner jacket. He pushed his chair back and stood up.

"You know how it is," he said. "So--"

The girl cackled and threw her drink in his face.

The dark man stepped back jarringly and swept a crisp white handkerchief from his pocket. He mopped his face swiftly, shaking his head. When he lowered the handkerchief there was a big soaked spot on his shirt, limp above the black pearl stud. His collar was a ruin.

"So sorry," the girl said. "Thought you were a spittoon."

He dropped his hand and his teeth glinted edgily. "Get her out," he purred. "Get her out fast."

He turned and walked off very quickly among the tables, holding his handkerchief against his mouth. Two waiters in mess jackets came up close and stood looking at us. Everybody in the place was looking at us.

"Round one," the girl said. "A little slow. Both fighters were cautious."

"I'd hate to be with you when you'd take a chance," I said.

Her head jerked. In that queer purple light the extreme whiteness of her face seemed to leap at me. Even her rouged lips had a drained look. Her hand went up to her mouth, stiff and clawlike. She coughed

253

dryly like a consumptive and reached for my glass. She gulped the bacardi and grenadine down in bubbling swallows. Then she began to shake. She reached for her bag and pushed it over the edge of the table to the floor. It fell open and some stuff came out. A gilt-metal cigarette case slid under my chair. I had to get up and move the chair to reach it. One of the waiters was behind me.

"Can I help?" he asked suavely.

I was stooped over when the glass the girl had drunk from rolled over the edge of the table and hit the floor beside my hand. I picked up the cigarette case, looked at it casually, and saw that a hand-tinted photo of a big-boned, dark man decorated the front of it. I put it back in her bag and took hold of the girl's arm and the waiter who had spoken to me slid around and took her other arm. She looked at us blankly, moving her head from side to side as if trying to limber up a stiff neck.

"Mama's about to pass out," she croaked, and we started down the room with her. She put her feet out crazily, threw her weight from one side to the other as if trying to upset us. The waiter swore steadily to himself in a monotonous whisper. We came out of the purple light into the bright lobby.

"Ladies' Room," the waiter grunted, and pointed with his chin at a door which looked like the side entrance to the Taj Mahal. "There's a colored heavyweight in there can handle anything."

"Nuts to the Ladies' Room," the girl said nastily. "And leggo of my arm, steward. Boy friend's all the transportation I need."

"He's not your boy friend, madam. He don't even know you."

"Beat it, wop. You're either too polite or not polite enough. Beat it before I lose my culture and bong you."

"Okay," I told him. "I'll set her out to cool. She come in alone?"

"I couldn't think of any reason why not," he said, and stepped away. The captain of waiters came halfway down his gangplank and stood glowering, and the vision at the checkroom looked as bored as the referee of a four-round opener.

I pushed my new friend out into the cold, misty air, walked her along the colonnade and felt her body come controlled and steady on my arm.

"You're a nice guy," she said dully. "I played that about as smooth as a handful of tacks. You're a nice guy, mister. I didn't think I'd ever get out of there alive."

"Why?"

"I had a wrong idea about making some money. Forget it. Let it lay with all the other wrong ideas I've been having all my life. Do I get a ride? I came in a cab."

"Sure. Do I get told your name?"

"Helen Matson," she said.

I didn't get any kick out of that now. I had guessed it long ago.

She still leaned on me a little as we walked down the strip of paved road past the parked cans. When we came to mine I unlocked it and held the door for her and she climbed in and fell back in the corner with her head on the cushion.

I shut the door and then I opened it again and said: "Would you tell me something else? Who's that mug on the cigarette case you carry? Seems to me I've seen him somewhere."

She opened her eyes. "An old sweet," she said, "that wore out. He--" Her eyes widened and her mouth snapped open and I barely heard the faint rustle behind me as something hard dug into my back and a muffled voice said: "Hold it, buddy. This is a heist."

Then a naval gun went off in my ear and my head was a large pink firework exploding into the vault of the sky and scattering and falling slow and pale, and then dank, into the waves. Blackness ate me up.

Five--My Dead Neighbor

I smelled of gin. Not just casually, as if I had taken a few drinks, but as if the Pacific Ocean was pure gin and I had been swimming in it with my clothes on. The gin was on my hair, on my eyebrows, on my face and under my chin on my shirt. My coat was off and I was lying flat on somebody's carpet and I was looking up at a framed photograph on the end of a plaster mantel. The frame was some kind of grained wood and the photo was intended to be arty, with a highlight on a long, thin, unhappy face, but all the highlight did was make the face look just that--long and thin and unhappy under some kind of flat, pale hair that might have been paint on a dried skull. There was writing across the corner of the photo behind the glass, but I couldn't read that.

I reached up and pressed the side of my head and I could feel a shoot of pain clear to the soles of my feet. I groaned and made a grunt out of the groan, from professional pride, and then I rolled over slowly and carefully and looked at the foot of a pulled-down twin wall bed. The other twin was still up in the wall with a flourish of design painted on the enameled wood.

When I rolled, a gin bottle rolled off my chest and hit the floor. It was water-white, empty. I thought there couldn't have been that much gin in just one bottle.

I got my knees under me and stayed on all fours for a while, sniffing like a dog who can't finish his dinner and yet hates to leave it. I moved my head around on my neck. It hurt. I moved it some more and it still hurt, so I got up on my feet and discovered that I didn't have any shoes on.

It seemed like a nice apartment, not too cheap and not too expensive--the usual furniture, the usual drum lamp, the usual durable carpet. On the bed, which was down, a girl was lying, clothed in a pair of tan silk stockings. There were deep scratches that had bled and there was a thick bath towel across her middle, wadded up almost into a roll. Her eyes were open. The red hair that had been parted and strained back as if she hated it was still that way. But she didn't hate it any more.

She was dead.

Above and inside her left breast there was a scorched place the size of the palm of a man's hand, and in the middle of that there was a thimbleful of blazed blood. Blood had run down her side, but it had dried now.

I saw clothes on a davenport, mostly hers, but including my coat. There were shoes on the floor-- mine and hers. I went over, stepping on the balls of my feet as though on very thin ice, and picked up my coat and felt through the pockets. They still held everything I could remember having put in them. The holster that was still strapped around my body was empty, of course. I put my shoes and coat on, pushed the empty holster around under my arm and went over to the bed and lifted the heavy bath towel. A gun fell out of it-- my gun. I wiped some blood off the barrel, sniffed the muzzle for no reason at all, and quietly put the gun back under my arm.

Heavy feet came along the corridor outside the apartment door and stopped. There was a mutter of voices, then somebody knocked, a quick, hard, impatient rapping. I looked at the door and wondered how long it would be before they tried it, and if the spring lock would be set so they could walk in, and if it wasn't set how long it would take to get the manager up with a passkey if he wasn't there already. I was still wondering when a hand tried the door. It was locked.

That was very funny. I almost laughed out loud.

I stepped over to another door and glanced into a bathroom. There were two wash rugs on the floor, a bath mat folded neatly over the edge of the tub, a pebbled glass window above it. I eased the bathroom door shut quietly and stood on the edge of the bathtub and pushed up the lower sash of the bathroom window. I put my head out and looked down about six floors to the darkness of a side street lined with trees. To do this I had to look out through a slot formed by two short blank walls, hardly more than an air shaft The windows were in pairs, all in the same end wall opposite the open end of the slot. I leaned farther out and decided I could make the next window if I tried. I wondered if it was unlocked, and if it would do me any good, and if I'd have time before they could get the door open.

Behind me, beyond the closed bathroom door, the pounding was a little louder and harder and a voice was growling out: "Open it up or we'll bust it in."

That didn't mean anything. That was just routine cop stuff. They wouldn't break it down because they could get a key, and kicking that kind of door in without a fire axe is a lot of work and tough on the feet.

I shut the lower half of the window and pulled down the upper half and took a towel off the rack. Then I opened the bathroom door again and my eyes were looking straight at the face in the photo frame on the mantel. I had to read the inscription on that photo before I left. I went over and scanned it while the pounding on the door went on angrily. The inscription said--*With all my love--Leland.*

That made a sap out of Dr. Austrian, without anything else. I grabbed the photo and went back into the bathroom and shut the door again. Then I shoved the photo under the dirty towels and linen in the cupboard under the bathroom closet. It would take them a little while to find it, if they were good cops. If we were in Bay City, they probably wouldn't find it at all. I didn't know of any reason why we should be in Bay City, except that Helen Matson would very likely live there and the air outside the bathroom window seemed to be beach air.

I squeezed out through the upper half of the window with the towel in my hand and swung my body across to the next window, holding on to the sash of the one I had left. I could reach just far enough to push the next window up, if it was unlocked. It wasn't unlocked. I swung my foot and kicked the glass in just over the catch. It made a noise that ought to have been heard a mile. The distant pounding went on monotonously.

I wrapped the towel around my left hand and stretched my arms for all they had in them and shoved my hand in through the broken place and turned the window catch. Then I swung over to the other sill and reached back to push up the window I had come out of.

They could have the fingerprints. I didn't expect to be able to prove I hadn't been in Helen Matson's apartment. All I wanted was a chance to prove how I had got there.

I looked down at the street. A man was getting into a car. He didn't even look up at me. No light had gone on in the apartment I was breaking into. I got the window down and climbed in. There was a lot of broken glass in the bathtub. I got down to the floor and switched the light on and picked the glass out of the bathtub and wrapped it in my towel and hid it. I used somebody else's towel to wipe off the sill and the edge of the bathtub where I'd stood. Then I took my gun out and opened the bathroom door.

This was a larger apartment. The room I was looking at had twin beds with pink dust covers. They were made up nicely and they were empty. Beyond the bedroom there was a living room. All the windows were shut and the place had a close, dusty smell. I lit a floor lamp, then I ran a finger along the arm of a chain and looked at dust on it. There was an armchair radio, a book rack built like a hod, a big bookcase full of novels with the jackets still on them, a dank wood highboy with a siphon and a decanter of liquor on it, and four striped glasses upside down. I sniffed the liquor, which was Scotch, and used a little of it. It made my head feel worse but it made me feel better.

I left the light on and went back to the bedroom and poked into bureau and closets. There were male clothes in one closet, tailor-made, and the name written on the label by the tailor was George Talbot. George's clothes looked a little small for me. I tried the bureau and found a pair of pajamas I thought would do. The closet gave me a bathrobe and slippers. I stripped to the skin.

When I came out of the shower I smelled only faintly of gin. There was no noise or pounding going on anywhere now, so I knew they were in Helen Matson's apartment with their little pieces of chalk and string. I put Mr. Talbot's pajamas and slippers and bathrobe on, used some of Mr. Talbot's tonic on my hair and his brush and comb to tidy up. I hoped Mr. and Mrs. Talbot were having a good time wherever they were and that they would not have to hurry home.

I went back to the living room, used some more Talbot Scotch and lit one of his cigarettes. Then I unlocked the entrance door. A man coughed close by in the hall. I opened the door and leaned against the jamb and looked out. A uniformed man was leaning against the opposite wall--a smallish, blond, sharp-eyed man. His blue trousers were edged like a knife and he looked neat, clean, competent and nosy.

I yawned and said: "What goes on, officer?"

He stared at me with sharp reddish-brown eyes flecked with gold, a colon you seldom see with blond hair. "A little trouble next door to you. Hear anything?" His voice was mildly sarcastic.

"The carrot-top?" I said. "Haw, haw. Just the usual big-game hunt. Drink?"

The cop went on with his careful stare. Then he called down the hallway: "Hey, Al!"

A man stepped out of an open door. He was about six feet, weighed around two hundred, and he had coarse black hair and deep-set expressionless eyes. It was Al De Spain whom I had met that evening at Bay City headquarters.

He came down the hall without haste. The uniformed cop said: "Here's the guy lives next door."

De Spain came close to me and looked into my eyes. His own held no more expression than pieces of black slate. He spoke almost softly.

"Name?"

"George Talbot," I said. I didn't quite squeak.

"Hear any noises? I mean, before we got here?"

"Oh, a brawl, I guess. Around midnight. That's nothing new in there." I jerked a thumb towards the dead girl's apartment.

"That so? Acquainted with the dame?"

"No. Doubt if I'd want to know her."

"You won't have to," De Spain said. "She's croaked."

He put a big, hard hand against my chest and pushed me back very gently through the door into the apartment. He kept his hand against my chest and his eyes flicked down sharply to the side pockets of the bathrobe, then back to my face again. When he had me eight feet from the door he said over his shoulder: "Come in and shut the door, Shorty."

Shorty came and shut the door, small, sharp eyes gleaming. "Quite a gag," De Spain said, very casually. "Put a gun on him, Shorty."

Shorty flicked his black belt holster open and had a police gun in his hand like lightning. He licked his lips. "Oh boy," he said softly. "Oh boy." He snapped his handcuff holder open and half drew the cuffs out. "How'd you know, Al?"

"Know what?" De Spain kept his eyes on my eyes. He spoke to me gently. "What was you goin' to do--go down and buy a paper?"

"Yah," Shorty said. "He's the killer, sure. He come in through the bathroom window and put on clothes belonging to the guy that lives here. The folks are away. Look at the dust. No windows open. Dead air in the place."

De Spain said softly: "Shorty's a scientific cop. Don't let him get you down. He's got to be wrong some day."

I said: "What for is he in uniform, if he's so hot?"

Shorty reddened, De Spain said: "Find his clothes, Shorty. And his gun. And make it fast. This is our pinch, if we make it fast."

"You ain't detailed on the case even," Shorty said.

"What can I lose?"

"I can lose this here uniform."

"Take a chance, boy. That lug Reed next door couldn't catch a moth in a shoe box."

Shorty scuttled into the bedroom. De Spain and I stood motionless, except that he took his hand off my chest and dropped it to his side. "Don't tell me," he drawled. "Just let me guess."

We heard Shorty fussing around opening doors. Then we heard a yelp like a terrier's yelp when he smells a rathole. Shorty came back into the room with my gun in his right hand and my wallet in his left. He held the gun by the fore sight, with a handkerchief. "The gat's been fired," he said. "And this guy ain't called Talbot."

De Spain didn't turn his head on change expression. He smiled at me thinly, moving only the extreme corners of his wide, rather brutal mouth.

"You don't say," he said. "You don't say." He pushed me away from him with a hand as hard as a piece of tool steel. "Get dressed, sweetheart--and don't fuss with your necktie. Places want us to go to them."

Six--I Get My Gun Back

We went out of the apartment and along the hall. Light still came from the open door of Helen Matson's apartment. Two men with a basket stood outside it smoking. There was a sound of wrangling voices inside the dead woman's place.

We went around a bend of the hall and started down the stairs, floor after floor, until we came out in the lobby. Half a dozen people stood around bug-eyed-- three women in bathrobes, a bald-headed man with a green eyeshade, like a city editor, two more who hung back in the shadows. Another uniformed man walked up and down just inside the front door, whistling under his breath. We went out past him. He looked completely uninterested. A knot of people clustered on the sidewalk outside.

De Spain said: "This is a big night in our little town."

We walked along to a black sedan that had no police insignia on it and De Spain slid in behind the wheel and motioned me to get in beside him. Shorty got in the back. He'd had his gun back in his holster long since, but he left the flap unbuttoned, and kept his hand close to it.

De Spain put the car into motion with a jerk that threw me back against the cushions. We made the nearest corner on two wheels, going east. A big black car with twin red spotlights was only half a block away and coming fast as we made the turn.

De Spain spat out of the window and drawled: "That's the chief. He'll be late for his own funeral. Boy, did we skin his nose on this one."

Shorty said disgustedly from the back seat: "Yeah-- for a thirty-day lay-off."

De Spain said: "Keep that mush of yours in low and you might get back on Homicide."

"I'd rather wear buttons and eat," Shorty said.

De Spain drove the car hard for ten blocks, then slowed a little. Shorty said: "This ain't the way to headquarters."

De Spain said: "Don't be an ass."

He let the car slow to a crawl, turned it left into a quiet, dank, residential street lined with coniferous trees and small exact houses set back from small exact lawns. He braked the car gently, coasted it oven to the curb and switched the motor off. Then he threw an arm over the back of the seat and turned to look at the small "sharp-eyed" uniformed man.

"You think this guy plugged her, Shorty?"

"His gun went off."

"Get that big flash outa the pocket and look at the back of his head."

Shorty snorted, fussed around in the back of the car, and then metal clicked and the blinding white beam of a large bell-topped flashlight sprayed over my head. I heard the little man's close breathing. He reached out and pressed the sore place on the back of my head. I yelped. The light went off and the blackness of the dark Street jumped at us again.

Shorty said: "I guess he was sapped."

De Spain said without emotion: "So was the girl. It didn't show much but it's there. She was sapped so she could have her clothes pulled off and be clawed up before she was shot, so the scratches would bleed and look like you know what. Then she was shot with a bath towel around the gun. Nobody heard the shot. Who reported it, Shorty?"

"How the hell would I know? A guy called up two-three minutes before you came into the Hall, while

Reed was still looking for a cameraman. A guy with a thick voice, the operator said."

"Okay. If you done it, Shorty, how would you get out of there?"

"I'd walk out," Shorty said. "Why not? Hey," he banked at me, "why didn't you?"

I said: "I have to have my little secrets."

De Spain said tonelessly: "You wouldn't climb across no air shaft, would you, Shorty? You wouldn't crash into the next apartment and pretend to be the guy that lived there, would you? And you wouldn't call no law and tell them to take it up there in high and they'd catch the killer, would you?"

"Hell," Shorty said, "this guy call up? No, I wouldn't do any of them things."

"Neither did the killer," De Spain said, "except the last one, He called up."

"Them sex fiends do funny things," Shorty said. "This guy could have had help and the other guy tried to put him in the middle after knocking him out with a sap."

De Spain laughed harshly. "Hello, sex fiend," he said, and poked me in the ribs with a finger as hard as a gun barrel. "Look at us saps, just sitting here and throwing our jobs away--that is, the one of us that has a job--and arguing it out when you, the guy that knows all the answers, ain't told us a damn thing. We don't even know who the dame was."

"A redhead I picked up in the bar of the Club Conried," I said. "No, she picked me up."

"No name or anything?"

"No. She was tight, I helped her out into the air and she asked me to take her away from there and while I was putting her into my car somebody sapped mc. I came to on the floor of the apartment and the girl was dead."

De Spain said: "What was you doing in the bar of the Club Conried?"

"Getting my hair cut," I said. "What do you do in a bar? This redhead was tight and seemed scared about something and she threw a drink in the floor boss's face. I felt a little sorry for her."

"I always feel sorry for a redhead, too," De Spain said. "This guy that sapped you must have been an elephant, if he carried you up to that apartment."

I said: "Have you ever been sapped?"

"No," De Spain said. "Have you, Shorty?"

Shorty said he had never been sapped either. He said it unpleasantly.

"All right," I said. "It's like an alcohol drunk. I probably came to in the car and the fellow would have a gun and that would keep me quiet. He would walk me up to the apartment with the girl. The girl may have known him. And when he had me up there he would sap me again and I wouldn't remember anything that happened in between the two sappings."

"I've heard of it," De Spain said. "But I never believed it."

"Well, it's true," I said. "It's got to be true. Because I don't remember and the guy couldn't have carried me up there without help."

"I could," De Spain said. "I've carried heavier guys than you."

"All right," I said. "He carried me up. Now what do we do?"

Shorty said: "I don't get why he went to all that trouble."

"Sapping a guy ain't trouble," De Spain said. "Pass oven that heater and wallet."

Shorty hesitated, then passed them over. De Spain smelled the gun and dropped it carelessly into his side pocket, the one next to mc. He flipped the wallet open and held it down under the dash light and then put it away. He started the car, turned it in the middle of the block, and shot back up Arguello Boulevard, turned east on that and pulled up in front of a liquor store with a red neon sign. The place was wide open, even at that hour of the night.

De Spain said over his shoulder: "Run inside and phone the desk, Shorty. Tell the sarge we got a hot lead and we're on our way to pick up a suspect in the Brayton Avenue killing. Tell him to tell the chief his shirt is out."

Shorty got out of the car, slammed the rear door, started to say something, then walked fast across the sidewalk into the store.

De Spain jerked the car into motion and hit forty in the first block. He laughed deep down in his chest. He made it fifty in the next block and then began to turn in and out of streets and finally he pulled to a stop again under a pepper tree outside a schoolhouse.

I got the gun when he reached forward for the parking brake. He laughed dryly and spat out of the open window.

"Okay," he said. "That's why I put it there. I talked to Violets M'Gee. That kid reporter called me up from L.A. They've found Matson. They're sweating some apartment house guy right now."

I slid away from him over to my corner of the car and held the gun loosely between my knees. "We're outside the limits of Bay City, copper," I told him. "What did M'Gee say?"

"He said he gave you a lead to Matson, but he didn't know whether you had contacted him or not. This apartment house guy--I didn't hear his name--was trying to dump a stiff in the alley when a couple of alcoholics jumped him. M'Gee said if you had contacted Matson and heard his story you would be down here getting in a jam, and would likely wake up sapped beside some stiff."

"I didn't contact Matson," I said.

I could feel De Spain staring at me under his dark craggy brows. "But you're down here in a jam," he said.

I got a cigarette out of my pocket with my left hand and lit it with the dash lighten. I kept my right hand on the gun. I said: "I got the idea you were on the way out down here. That you weren't even detailed on this killing. Now you've taken a prisoner across the city line. What does that make you?"

"A bucket of mud--unless I deliver something good."

"That's what I am," I said. "I guess we ought to team up and break these three killings."

"Three?"

"Yeah. Helen Matson, Harry Matson and Doc Austrian's wife. They all go together."

"I ditched Shorty," De Spain said quietly, "because he's a little guy and the chief likes little guys and Shorty can put the blame on me. Where do we start?"

"We might start by finding a man named Greb who runs a laboratory in the Physicians and Surgeons Building. I think he turned in a phony report on the Austrian death. Suppose they put out an alarm for you?"

269

"They use the L.A. air. They won't use that to pick up one of their own cops."

He leaned forward and started the can again.

"You might give me my wallet," I said. "So I can put this gun away."

He laughed harshly and gave it to me.

Seven--Big Chin

The lab man lived on Ninth Street, on the wrong side of town. The house was a shapeless frame bungalow. A large dusty hydrangea bush and some small undernourished plants along the path looked like the work of a man who had spent his life trying to make something out of nothing.

De Spain doused the lights as we glided up front and said: "Whistle, if you need help. If any cops should crowd us, skin oven to Tenth and I'll circle the block and pick you up. I don't think they will, though. All they're thinking of tonight is that dame on Brayton Avenue."

I looked up and down the quiet block, walked across the street in foggy moonlight and up the walk to the house. The front door was set at night angles to the street in a front projection that looked like a room which had been added as an afterthought to the nest of the house. I pushed a bell and heard it ring somewhere in the back. No answer. I rang it twice more and tried the front door. It was locked.

I went down off the little porch and around the north side of the house towards a small garage on the back lot. Its doors were shut and locked with a padlock you could break with a strong breath. I bent over and shot my pocket flash under the loose doors. The wheels of a car showed. I went back to the front door of the house and knocked this time--plenty loud.

The window in the front room creaked and came down slowly from the top, about halfway. There was a shade pulled down behind the window and dankness behind the shade. A thick, hoarse voice said: "Yeah?"

"Mr. Greb?"

"Yeah."

"I'd like to speak to you--on important business."

"I gotta get my sleep, mister. Come back tomorrow."

The voice didn't sound like the voice of a laboratory technician. It sounded like a voice I had heard over the telephone once, a long time ago, early in the evening at the Tennyson Arms Apartments.

I said: "Well, I'll come to your office then, Mr. Greb. What's the address again?"

The voice didn't speak for a moment. Then it said: "Aw, go on, beat it before I come out there and paste you one."

"That's no way to get business, Mr. Greb," I said. "Are you sure you couldn't give me just a few moments, now you're up?"

"Pipe down. You'll wake the wife. She's sick. If I gotta come out there--"

"Good night, Mr. Greb," I said.

I went back down the walk in the soft, foggy moonlight. When I got across to the far side of the dark parked car I said: "It's a two-man job. Some tough guy is in there. I think it's the man I heard called Big Chin over the phone in L.A."

"Geez. The guy that killed Matson, huh?" De Spain came over to my side of the car and stuck his head out and spat clear oven a fireplug that must have been eight feet away. I didn't say anything.

De Spain said: "If this guy you call Big Chin is Moss Lorenz, I'll know him. We might get in. On maybe we walk ourselves into some hot lead."

"Just like the coppers do on the radio," I said.

"You scared?"

"Me?" I said. "Sure I'm scared. The car's in the garage, so either he's got Greb in there and is trying to make up his mind what to do with him--"

"If it's Moss Lorenz, he don't have a mind," De Spain growled. "That guy is screwy except in two places--behind a gun and behind the wheel of a car."

"And behind a piece of lead pipe," I said. "What I was saying was, Greb might be out without his can and this Big Chin--"

De Spain bent over to look at the clock on the dash. "My guess would be he's skipped. He'd be home by now. He's got a tip to scram out of some trouble."

"Will you go in there or won't you?" I snapped. "Who would tip him?"

"Whoever fixed him in the fist place, if he was fixed." De Spain clicked the door open and slid out of the car, stood looking oven it across the street. He opened his coat and loosened the gun in his shoulder clip. "Maybe I could kid him," he said. "Keep your hands showing and empty. It's our best chance."

We went back across the street and up the walk, up on the porch. De Spain leaned on the bell.

The voice came growling at us again from the half-open window, behind the frayed dank green shade.

"Yeah?"

"Hello, Moss," De Spain said.

"Huh?"

"This is Al De Spain, Moss. I'm in on the play."

Silence--a long, murderous silence. Then the thick, hoarse voice said: "Who's that with you?"

"A pal from L.A. He's okay." More silence, then, "What's the angle?"

"You alone in there?"

"Except for a dame. She can't hear you."

"Where's Greb?"

"Yeah--where is he? What's the angle, copper? Snap it up!"

De Spain spoke as calmly as though he had been at home in an armchair, beside the radio. "We're workin' for the same guy, Moss."

"Haw, haw," Big Chin said.

"Matson's been found dead in L.A., and those city dicks have already connected him with the Austrian dame. We gotta step fast. The big shot's up north alibiing himself, but what does that do for us?"

The voice said, "Aw, baloney," but there was a note of doubt in it.

"It looks like a stink," De Spain said. "Come on, open up. You can see we don't have anything to hold on you."

"By the time I got around to the door you would have," Big Chin said.

"You ain't that yellow," De Spain sneered.

The shade rustled at the window as if a hand had let go of it and the sash moved up into place. My hand started up.

De Spain growled: "Don't be a sap. This guy is our case. We want him all in one piece."

Faint steps sounded inside the house. A lock turned in the front door and it opened and a figure stood there, shadowed, a big Colt in his hand. Big Chin was a good name for him. His big, broad jaw stuck out from his face like a cowcatcher. He was a bigger man than De Spain--a good deal bigger.

"Snap it up," he said, and started to move back.

De Spain, his hands hanging loose and empty, palms turned out, took a quiet step forward on his left foot and kicked Big Chin in the groin--just like that--without the slightest hesitation, and against a gun.

Big Chin was still fighting--inside himself--when we got our guns out. His right hand was fighting to press the trigger and hold the gun up. His sense of pain was fighting down everything else but the desire to double up and yell. That internal struggle of his wasted a split second and he had neither shot nor yelled when we slammed him. De Spain hit him on the head and I hit him on the right wrist. I wanted to hit his chin--it fascinated me--but his wrist was nearest the gun. The gun dropped and Big Chin dropped, almost as suddenly, then plunged forward against us. We caught and held him and his breath blew hot and rank in our faces, then his knees went to pieces and we fell into the hallway on top of him.

De Spain grunted and struggled to his feet and shut the door. Then he rolled the big, groaning, half-conscious man over and dragged his hands behind him and snapped cuffs on his wrists.

We went down the hall. There was a dim light in the room to the left, from a small table lamp with a newspaper over it. De Spain lifted the paper off and we looked at the woman on the bed. At least he hadn't murdered her. She lay in sleazy pajamas with her eyes wide open and staring and half mad with fear. Mouth, wrists, ankles and knees were taped and the ends of thick wads of cotton stuck out of her ears. A vague bubbling sound came from behind the slab of two-inch adhesive that plastered her mouth shut. De Spain bent the lampshade a little. Her face was mottled. She had bleached hair, dark at the roots, and a thin, scraped look about the bones of her face.

De Spain said: "I'm a police officer. Are you Mrs. Greb?"

The woman jerked and stared at him agonizingly. I pulled the cotton out of her ears and said: "Try again."

"Are you Mrs. Greb?"

She nodded.

De Spain took hold of the tape at the side of her mouth. Her eyes winced and he jerked it hard and capped a hand down oven her mouth at once. He stood there, bending over, the tape in his left hand--a big, dark, dead-pan copper who didn't seem to have any more nerves than a cement mixer.

"Promise not to scream?" he said.

The woman forced a nod and he took his hand away. "Where's Greb?" he asked.

He pulled the rest of the tape off her.

She swallowed and took hold of her forehead with her red-nailed hand and shook her head. "I don't know. He hasn't been home."

"What talk was there when the gorilla came in?"

"There wasn't any," she said dully, "The bell rang and I opened the door and he walked in and grabbed mc. Then the big brute tied me up and asked me where my husband was and I said I didn't know and he slapped my face a few times, but after a while he seemed to believe me. He asked me why my husband didn't have the car and I said he always walked to work and never took the car. Then he just sat in the corner and didn't move or speak. He didn't even smoke."

"Did he use the telephone?" De Spain asked.

"No."

"You ever seen him before?"

"No."

"Get dressed," De Spain said. "You gotta find some friends you can go to for the rest of the night."

She stared at him and sat up slowly on the bed and rumpled her hair. Then her mouth opened and De Spain clapped his hand over it again, hard.

"Hold it," he said sharply. "Nothing's happened to him that we know of. But I guess you wouldn't be too damn surprised if it did.

The woman pushed his hand away and stood up off the bed and walked around it to a bureau and took out a pint of whisky. She unscrewed the top and drank from the bottle. "Yeah," she said in a strong, coarse voice. "What would you do, if you had to soap a bunch of doctors for every nickel you made and there was damn few nickels to be made at that?" She took another drink.

De Spain said: "I might switch blood samples."

The woman stared at him blankly. He looked at me and shrugged. "Maybe it's happy powder," he said. "Maybe he peddles a little of that. It must be damn little, to go by how he lives." He looked around the room contemptuously. "Get dressed, lady."

We went out of the room and shut the door. De Spain bent down oven Big Chin, lying on his back and half on his side on the floor. The big man groaned steadily with his mouth open, neither completely out nor fully aware of what was going on around him. De Spain, still bending down in the dim light he'd put on in the hall, looked at the piece of adhesive in the palm of his hand and laughed suddenly. He slammed the tape hard over Big Chin's mouth.

276

"Think we can make him walk?" he asked. "I'd hate like hell to have to carry him."

"I don't know," I said. "I'm just the swamper on this route. Walk to where?"

"Up in the hills where it's quiet and the birds sing," De Spain said grimly.

I sat on the running board of the car with the big bell-shaped flashlight hanging down between my knees. The light wasn't too good, but it seemed to be good enough for what De Spain was doing to Big Chin. A roofed reservoir was just above us and the ground sloped away from that into a deep canyon. There were two hilltop houses about half a mile away, both dark, with a glisten of moonlight on their stucco walls. It was cold up there in the hills, but the air was clean and the stars were like pieces of polished chromium. The light haze over Bay City seemed to be fan off, as if in another county, but it was only a fast ten-minute drive.

De Spain had his coat off. His shirt-sleeves were rolled up and his wrists and his big hairless arms looked enormous in the faint hard light. His coat lay on the ground between him and Big Chin. His gun holster lay on the coat, with the gun in the holster, and the butt towards Big Chin. The coat was a little to one side so that between De Spain and Big Chin there was a small space of scuffed moonlit gravel. The gun was to Big Chin's right and to De Spain's left

After a long silence thick with breathing De Spain said: "Try again." He spoke casually, as if he were talking to a man playing a pinball game.

Big Chin's face was a mass of blood. I couldn't see it as red, but I had put the flash on it a time or two and I knew it was there. His hands were free and what the kick in the groin had done to him was long ago, on the far side of oceans of pain. He made a croaking noise and turned his left hip suddenly against De Spain and went down on his right knee and lunged for the gun.

De Spain kicked him in the face.

Big Chin rolled back on the gravel and clawed at his face with both hands and a wailing sound came through his fingers. De Spain stepped over and kicked him on the ankle. Big Chin howled. De Spain stepped back to his original position beyond the coat and the holstered gun. Big Chin rolled a little and came up on his knees and shook his head. Big dank drops fell from his face to the gravelly ground. He got up to his feet slowly and stayed hunched over a little.

De Spain said: "Come on up. You're a tough guy. You got Vance Conried behind you and he's got the syndicate behind him. You maybe got Chief Anders behind you. I'm a lousy flatfoot with a ticket to nowhere in my pants. Come up. Let's put on a show."

Big Chin shot out in a diving lunge for the gun. His hand touched the butt but only slewed it around. De Spain came down hard on the hand with his heel and screwed his heel. Big Chin yelled. De Spain jumped back and said wearily: "You ain't overmatched, are you, sweetheart?"

I said thickly: "For God's sake, why don't you let him talk?"

"He don't want to talk," De Spain said. "He ain't the talking kind. He's a tough guy."

"Well, let's shoot the poor devil then."

"Not a chance. I'm not that kind of cop. Hey, Moss, this guy thinks I'm just one of those sadistic cops that has to smack a head with a piece of lead pipe every so often to keep from getting nervous indigestion. You

278

ain't going to let him think that, are you? This is a square fight. You got me shaded twenty pounds and look where the gun is."

Big Chin mumbled: "Suppose I got it. Your pal would blast me."

"Not a chance. Come on, big boy. Just once more. You got a lot of stuff left."

Big Chin got up on his feet again. He got up so slowly that he seemed like a man climbing up a wall. He swayed and wiped blood off his face with his hand. My head ached. I felt sick at my stomach.

Big Chin swung his right foot very suddenly. It looked like something for a fraction of a second, then De Spain picked the foot out of the air and stepped back, pulled on it. He held the leg taut and the big bruiser swayed on his other foot trying to hold his balance.

De Spain said conversationally: "That was okay when I did it because you had plenty of gun in your mitt and I didn't have any gun and you didn't figure on me taking a chance like that. Now you see how wrong the play is in this spot."

He twisted the foot quickly, with both hands. Big Chin's body seemed to leap into the air and dive sideways, and his shoulder and face smashed into the ground, but De Spain held on to the foot. He kept on turning it. Big Chin began to thresh around on the ground and make harsh animal sounds, half stifled in the gravel. De Spain gave the foot a sudden hard wrench. Big Chin screamed like a dozen sheets tearing.

De Spain lunged forward and stepped on the ankle of Big Chin's other foot. He put his weight against the foot he held in his hands and spread Big Chin's legs. Big Chin tried to gasp and yell at the same time and made a sound something like a very large and very old dog barking.

De Spain said: "Guys get paid money for what I'm doing. Not nickels--real dough. I oughta look into it."

Big Chin yelled: "Lemme up! I'll talk! I'll talk!"

De Spain spread the legs some more. He did something to the foot and Big Chin suddenly went limp. It was like a sea lion fainting. It staggered De Spain and he reeled to one side as the leg smacked the ground. Then he reached a handkerchief out of his pocket and slowly mopped his face and hands.

"Soft," he said. "Too much beer. The guy looked healthy. Maybe it's always having his fanny under a wheel."

"And his hand under a gun," I said.

"That's an idea," De Spain said. "We don't want to lose him his self-respect."

He stepped oven and kicked Big Chin in the ribs. After the third kick there was a grunt and a glistening where the blankness of Big Chin's eyelids had been.

"Get up," De Spain said. "I ain't goin' to hurt you no more."

Big Chin got up. It took him a whole minute to get up. His mouth--what was left of it--was strained wide open. It made me think of another man's mouth and I stopped having pity for him. He pawed the air with his hands, looking for something to lean against.

De Spain said: "My pal here says you're soft without a gun in your hand. I wouldn't want a strong guy like you to be soft. Help yourself to my gat." He kicked the holster lightly so that it slid off the coat and close to Big Chin's foot. Big Chin bowed his shoulders to look down at it. He couldn't bend his neck any more.

"I'll talk," he grunted.

"Nobody asked you to talk. I asked you to get that gun in your hand. Don't make me cave you in again to make you do it. See--the gun in your hand."

Big Chin staggered down to his knees and his hand folded slowly over the butt of the gun. De Spain watched without moving a muscle.

"Attaboy. Now you got a gun. Now you're tough again. Now you can bump off some more women. Pull it outa the clip."

Very slowly, with what seemed to be enormous effort, Big Chin drew the gun out of the holster and knelt there with it dangling down between his legs.

"What, ain't you going to bump anybody off?" De Spain taunted him.

Big Chin dropped the gun out of his hand and sobbed.

"Hey, you!" De Spain banked. "Put that gun back where you got it, I want that gun clean, like I always keep it myself."

Big Chin's hand fumbled for the gun and got hold of it and slowly pushed it home in the leather sheath. The effort took all his remaining strength. He fell flat on his face oven the holster.

De Spain lifted him by an arm and rolled him over on his back and picked the holster up off the ground. He rubbed the butt of the gun with his hand and strapped the holster around his chest. Then he picked up his coat and put it on.

"Now we'll let him spill his guts," he said. "I don't believe in makin' a guy talk when he don't want to talk. Got a cigarette?"

I reached a pack out of my pocket with my left hand and shook a cigarette loose and held the pack out. I clicked the big flash on and held it on the projecting cigarette and on his big fingers as they came forward to take it.

"I don't need that," he said. He fumbled for a match and struck it and drew smoke slowly into his lungs. I doused the flash again. De Spain looked down the hill towards the sea and the curve of the shore and the lighted piers. "Kind of nice up here," he added.

"Cold," I said. "Even in summer. I could use a drink."

"Me too," De Spain said. "Only I can't work on the stuff."

Eight--Needle-Pusher

De Spain stopped the car in front of the Physicians and Surgeons Building and looked up at a lighted window on the sixth floor. The building was designed in a series of radiating wings so that all the offices had an outside exposure.

"Good grief," De Spain said. "He's up there right now. That guy don't never sleep at all, I guess. Take a look at that heap down the line."

I got up and walked down in front of the dark drugstore that flanked the lobby entrance of the building on one side. There was a long black sedan parked diagonally and correctly in one of the ruled spaces, as though it had been high noon instead of almost three in the morning. The sedan had a doctor's emblem beside the front license plate, the staff of Hippocrates and the serpents twisted around it. I put my flash into the car and read part of the name on the license holder and snapped the light off again. I went back to De Spain.

"Check," I said. "How did you know that was his window and what would he be doing here at this time of night?"

282

"Loading up his little needles," he said. "I've watched the guy some is how I know."

"Watched him why?"

He looked at me and said nothing. Then he looked back over his shoulder into the back part of the car. "How you doin', pal?"

A thick sound that might be trying to be a voice came from under a rug on the floor of the car. "He likes riding," De Spain said. "All these hard guys like riding around in cars. Okay. I'll tuck the heap in the alley and we'll go up."

He slid around the corner of the building without lights and the car sound died in the moonlit darkness. Across the street a row of enormous eucalyptus trees fringed a set of public tennis courts. The smell of kelp came up along the boulevard from the ocean.

De Spain came back around the corner of the building and we went up to the locked lobby door and knocked on the heavy plate glass. Far back there was light from an open elevator beyond a big bronze mailbox. An old man came out of the elevator and along the corridor to the door and stood looking out at us with keys in his hand. De Spain held up his police shield. The old man squinted at it and unlocked the door and locked it after us without saying a word. He went back along the hall to the elevator and rearranged the homemade cushion on the stool and moved his false teeth around with his tongue and said: "What you want?"

He had a long gray face that grumbled even when it didn't say anything. His trousers were frayed at the cuffs and one of his heel worn black shoes contained an obvious bunion. His blue uniform coat fitted him the way a stall fits a horse.

De Spain said: "Doc Austrian is upstairs, ain't he?"

"I wouldn't be surprised."

"I ain't trying to surprise you," De Spain said. "I'd have worn my pink tights."

"Yeah, he's up there," the old man said sourly.

"What time you last see Greb, the laboratory man on Four?"

"Didn't see him."

"What time you come on, Pop?"

"Seven."

"Okay. Take us up to Six."

The old man whooshed the doors shut and rode us up slowly and gingerly and whooshed the doors open again and sat like a piece of gray driftwood carved to look like a man.

De Spain reached up and lifted down the passkey that hung over the old man's head.

"Hey, you can't do that," the old man said.

"Who says I can't?"

The old man shook his head angrily, said nothing.

"How old are you, Pop?" De Spain said.

"Goin' on sixty."

"Goin' on sixty hell. You're a good juicy seventy. How come you got an elevator licence?"

The old man didn't say anything. He clicked his false teeth. "That's better," De Spain said. "Just keep the old trap buttoned that way and everything will be wicky-wacky. Take her down, Pop."

We got out of the elevator and it dropped quietly in the enclosed shaft and De Spain stood looking down the hallway, jiggling the loose passkey on the ring. "Now listen," he said. "His suite is at the end, four rooms. There's a reception room made out of an office cut in half to make two reception rooms for adjoining

284

suites. Out of that there's a narrow hall inside the wall of this hall, a couple small rooms and the doc's room. Got that?"

"Yeah," I said. "What did you plan to do--burgle it?"

"I kept an eye on the guy for a while, after his wife died."

"Too bad you didn't keep an eye on the redheaded office nurse," I said. "The one that got bumped off tonight."

He looked at me slowly, out of his deep black eyes, out of his dead-pan face.

"Maybe I did," he said. "As much as I had a chance."

"Hell, you didn't even know her name," I said, and stared at him. "I had to tell you."

He thought that over. "Well, seeing her in a white office uniform and seeing her naked and dead on a bed is kind of different, I guess."

"Sure," I said, and kept on looking at him.

"Okay. Now--you knock at the doc's office, which is the third door from the end, and when he opens up I'll sneak in at the reception room and come along inside and get an earful of whatever he says."

"It sounds all right," I said. "But I don't feel lucky."

We went down the corridor. The doors were solid wood and well fitted and no light showed behind any of them. I put my ear against the one De Spain indicated and heard faint movement inside. I nodded to De Spain down at the end of the hall. He fitted the passkey slowly into the lock and I rapped hard on the door and saw him go in out of the tail of my eye. The door shut behind him almost at once. I rapped on my door again.

It opened almost suddenly then, and a tall man was standing about a foot away from me with the ceiling light glinting on his pale sand-colored hair. He was in his shirtsleeves and he held a flat leather case in his hand. He was rail-thin, with dun eyebrows and unhappy eyes. He had beautiful hands, long and slim, with square but not blunt fingertips. The nails were highly polished and cut very close.

I said: "Dr. Austrian?"

He nodded. His Adam's apple moved vaguely in his lean throat.

"This is a funny hour for me to come calling," I said, "but you're a hard man to catch up with. I'm a private detective from Los Angeles. I have a client named Harry Matson."

He was either not startled or so used to hiding his feelings that it didn't make any difference. His Adam's apple moved around again and his hand moved the leather case he was holding, and he looked at it in a puzzled sort of way and then stepped back.

"I have no time to talk to you now," he said. "Come back tomorrow."

"That's what Greb told me," I said.

He got a jolt out of that. He didn't scream on fall down in a fit but I could see it jarred him. "Come in," he said thickly.

I went in and he shut the door. There was a desk that seemed to be made of black glass. The chains were chromium tubing with rough wool upholstery. The door to the next room was half open and the room was dark. I could see the stretched white sheet on an examination table and the stirrup-like things at the foot of it. I didn't hear any sound from that direction.

On top of the black glass desk a clean towel was laid out and on the towel a dozen on so hypodermic syringes lay with needles separate. There was an electric sterilizing cabinet on the wall and inside there must have been another dozen needles and syringes. The juice was turned on. I went over and looked at the thing while the tall, nail-thin man walked around behind his desk and sat down.

"That's a lot of needles working," I said, and pulled one of the chairs near the desk.

"What's your business with mc?" His voice was still thick.

"Maybe I could do you some good about your wife's death," I said.

"That's very kind of you," he said calmly. "What kind of good?"

"I might be able to tell you who murdered her," I said.

His teeth glinted in a queer, unnatural half-smile. Then he shrugged and when he spoke his voice was no more dramatic than if we had been discussing the weather. "That would be kind of you. I had thought she committed suicide. The coroner and the police seemed to agree with me. But of course a private detective--"

"Greb didn't think so," I said, without any particular attempt at the truth. "The lab man who switched a sample of your wife's blood for a sample from a real monoxide case."

He stared at me levelly, out of deep, sad, remote eyes under the dun-colored eyebrows. "You haven't seen Greb," he said, almost with an inner amusement. "I happen to know he went East this noon. His father died in Ohio." He got up and went to the electric sterilizer and looked at his strap watch and then switched the juice off. He came back to the desk then and opened a flat box of cigarettes and put one in his mouth and pushed the box across the desk. I reached and took one. I half glanced at the dark examination room, but I saw nothing that I hadn't seen the last time I looked at it.

"That's funny," I said. "His wife didn't know that. Big Chin didn't know it. He was sitting there with her all tied up on the bed tonight, waiting for Greb to come back home, so he could bump him off."

Dr. Austrian looked at me vaguely now. He pawed around on his desk for a match and then opened a side drawer and took out a small white-handled automatic, and held it on the flat of his hand. Then he tossed a packet of matches at me with his other hand.

"You won't need the gun," I said. "This is a business talk which I'm going to show you it will pay to keep a business talk."

He took the cigarette out of his mouth and dropped it on the desk. "I don't smoke," he said. "That was just what one might call the necessary gesture. I'm glad to hear I won't need the gun. But I'd rather be holding it and not need it than be needing it and not hold it. Now, who is Big Chin, and what else important have you to say before I call the police?"

"Let me tell you," I said. "That's what I'm here for. Your wife played a lot of roulette at Vance Conried's club and lost the money you made with your little needles almost as fast as you made it. There's some talk she was going around with Conried in an intimate way also. You maybe didn't care about that, being out all night and too busy to bother being much of a husband to her. But you probably did care about the money, because you were risking a lot to get it. I'll come to that later.

"On the night your wife died she got hysterical over at Conried's and you were sent for and went over and needled her in the arm to quiet hen. Conried took her home. You phoned your office nurse, Helen Matson-- Matson's ex-wife--to go into your house and see if she was all right. Then later on Matson found her dead under the car in the garage and got hold of you, and you got hold of the chief of police, and there was a hush put on it that would have made a Southern senator sound like a deaf mute asking for a second plate of mush. But Matson, the first guy on the scene, had something. He didn't have any luck trying to peddle it to you, because you in your quiet way have a lot of guts. And perhaps your friend, Chief Anders, told you it wasn't evidence. So Matson tried to put the bite on Conried, figuring that if the case got opened up before the tough grand jury that's sitting now it would all bounce back on Conried's gambling joint, and he would be closed up tighter than a frozen piston, and the people behind him might get sore at him and take his polo ponies away from him.

"So Conried didn't like that idea and he told a mug named Moss Lorenz, the mayor's chauffeur now but formerly a strongarm for Conried--he's the fellow I called Big Chin--to take care of Matson. And Matson lost his licence and was run out of Bay City. But he had his own brand of guts too, and he holed up in an apartment house in L.A. and kept on trying. The apartment house manager got wise to him somehow--I don't know how but the L.A. police will find out--and put him on the spot, and tonight Big Chin went up to town and bumped Matson off."

I stopped talking and looked at the thin, tall man. Nothing had changed in his face. His eyes flicked a couple of times and he turned the gun over on his hand. The office was very silent. I listened for breathing from the next room but I didn't hear anything.

"Matson is dead?" Dr. Austrian said very slowly. "I hope you don't think I had anything to do with that." His face glistened a little.

"Well, I don't know," I said. "Greb was the weak link in your setup and somebody got him to leave town today--fast--before Matson was killed, if it was at noon. And probably somebody gave him money, because I saw where he lived and it didn't look like the home of a fellow who was taking in any dough."

Dr. Austrian said very swiftly. "Conried, damn him! He called me up early this morning and told me to get Greb out of town. I gave him the money to go, but--" he stopped talking and looked mad at himself and then looked down at the gun again.

"But you didn't know what was up. I believe you, Doc. I really do. Put that gun down, won't you, just for a little while?"

"Go on," he said tensely. "Go on with your story."

"Okay," I said. "There's plenty more. First off the L.A. police have found Matson's body but they won't be down here before tomorrow; first, because it's too late, and second, because when they put the story together they won't want to bust the case. The Club Conried is within the L.A. city limits and the grand jury I was telling you about would just love that. They'll get Moss Lorenz and Moss will cop a plea and take a few years up in Quentin. That's the way those things are handled when the law wants to handle them. Next point is how I know what Big Chin did. He told us. A pal and I went around to see Greb and Big Chin was squatting there in the dark with Mrs. Greb all taped up on the bed and we took him. We took him up in the hills and gave him the boot and he talked. I felt kind of sorry for the poor guy. Two murders and he didn't even get paid."

"Two murders?" Dr. Austrian said queerly.

"I'll get to that after a while. Now you see where you stand. In a little while you are going to tell me who murdered your wife. And the funny thing is I am not going to believe you."

"My God!" he whispered. "My God!" He pointed the gun at me and immediately dropped it again, before I had time to start dodging.

"I'm a miracle man," I said. "I'm the great American detective--unpaid. I never talked to Matson, although he was trying to hire me. Now I'm going to tell you what he had on you, and how your wife was murdered, and why you didn't do it. All from a pinch of dust, just like the Vienna police."

He was not amused. He sighed between still lips and his face was old and gray and drawn under the pale sand-colored hair that painted his bony skull.

"Matson had a green velvet slipper on you," I said. "It was made for your wife by Verschoyle of Hollywood--custom-made, with her last number on it. It was brand-new and had never been worn. They made her two pairs exactly the same. She had it on one of her feet when Matson found her. And you know where he found her--on the floor of a garage to get to which she had to go along a concrete path from a side door of the house. So she couldn't have walked in that slipper. So she was carried. So she was murdered. Whoever put the slippers on her got one that had been worn and one that had not. And Matson spotted it and swiped the slipper. And when you sent him into the house to phone the chief you sneaked up and got the other worn slipper and put it on her bare foot. You knew Matson must have swiped that slipper. I don't know whether you told anybody or not. Okay?"

He moved his head half an inch downward. He shivered slightly, but the hand holding the bone-handled automatic didn't shiver.

"This is how she was murdered. Greb was dangerous to somebody, which proves she did *not* die of monoxide poisoning. She was dead when she was put under the car. She died of morphine. That's guessing. I admit, but it's a swell guess, because that would be the only way to kill her which would force you to cover up for the killer. And it was easy, to somebody who had the morphine and got a chance to use it. All they had to do was give her a second fatal dose in the same spot where you had shot her earlier in the evening. Then you came home and found her dead. And you had to cover up because you knew how she had died and you couldn't have that come out. You're in the morphine business."

He smiled now. The smile hung at the corners of his mouth like cobwebs in the corners of an old ceiling. He didn't even know it was there. "You interest me," he said. "I am going to kill you, I think, but you interest me."

I pointed to the electric sterilizer. "There are a couple dozen medicos like you around Hollywood--needle-pushers. They run around at night with leather cases full of loaded hypodermics. They keep dopes and drunks from going screwy--for a while. Once in a while one of them becomes an addict and then there's trouble. Maybe most of the people you fix up would land in the hoosegow or the psycho ward, if you didn't take cane of them. It's a cinch they would lose their jobs, if they have jobs. And some of them have pretty big jobs. But it's dangerous because any sorehead can stick the Feds onto you and once they start checking your patients they'll find one that will talk. You try to protect yourself. Part of the way by not getting all of your dope through legitimate channels. I'd say Conried got some of it for you, and that was why you had to let him take your wife and your money."

Dr. Austrian said almost politely: "You don't hold very much back, do you?"

"Why should I? This is just a man-to-man talk. I can't prove any of it. That slipper Matson stole is good for a buildup, but it wouldn't be worth a nickel in court. And any defense attorney would make a monkey out of a little squirt like this Greb, even if they ever brought him back to testify. But it might cost you a lot of money to keep your medical licence."

"So it would be better for me to give you part of it now. Is that it?" he asked softly.

"No. Keep your money to buy life insurance. I have one more point to make. Will you admit, just man to man, that you killed your wife?"

"Yes," he said. He said it simply and directly, as though I had asked him if he had a cigarette.

"I thought you would," I said. "But you don't have to. You see the party that did kill your wife, because your wife was wasting money somebody else could have fun spending, also knew what Matson knew and was trying to shake Conried down herself. So she got bumped off--last night, on Brayton Avenue, and you don't have to cover up for her any more. I saw your photo on her mantel--*With all my love--Leland*--and I hid it. But you don't have to cover up for her any more. Helen Matson is dead."

I went sideways out of the chair as the gun went off. I had kidded myself by this time that he wouldn't try to shoot mc, but there must have been part of me that wasn't sold on the idea. The chair tipped over and I was on my hands and knees on the floor, and then another much louder gun went off from the dark room with the examination table in it.

De Spain stepped through the door with the smoking police gun in his big right hand. "Boy, was that a shot," he said, and stood there grinning.

I came up on my feet and looked across the desk. Dr. Austrian sat there perfectly still, holding his night hand with his left, shaking it gently. There was no gun in his hand. I looked along the floor and saw it at the corner of the desk.

"Geez, I didn't even hit him," De Spain said. "All I hit was the gun."

"That's perfectly lovely," I said. "Suppose all he had hit was my head?"

De Spain looked at me levelly and the grin left his face. "You put him through it, I will say that for you," he growled. "But what was the idea of holding out on me on that green-slipper angle?"

"I got tired of being your stooge," I said. "I wanted a little play out of my own hand."

"How much of it was true?"

"Matson had the slipper. It must have meant something. Now that I've made it up I think it's all true."

Dr. Austrian got up slowly out of his chair and De Spain swung the gun on him. The thin, haggard man shook his head slowly and walked over to the wall and leaned against it.

"I killed her," he said in a dead voice to nobody at all. "Not Helen. I killed hen. Call the police."

De Spain's face twisted and he stooped down and picked up the gun with the bone handle and dropped it into his pocket. He put his police gun back under his arm and sat down at the desk and pulled the phone towards him.

"Watch me get Chief of Homicide out of this," he drawled.

Nine--A Guy With Guts

The little chief of police came in springily, with his hat on the back of his head and his hands in the pockets of a thin dank overcoat. There was something in the right-hand overcoat pocket that he was holding on to, something large and heavy. There were two plainclothes men behind him and one of them was Weems, the chunky fat-faced man who had followed me over to Altair Street. Shorty, the uniformed cop we had ditched on Arguello Boulevard, brought up the rear.

Chief Anders stopped a little way inside the door and smiled at me unpleasantly. "So you've had a lot of fun in our town, I hear. Put the cuffs on him, Weems."

The fat-faced man stepped around him and pulled handcuffs out of his left hip pocket. "Nice to meet you again--with your pants down," he told me in an oily voice.

De Spain leaned against the wall beyond the door of the examination room. He rolled a match across his lips and stared silently. Dr. Austrian was in his desk chain again, holding his head in his hands, staring at the polished black top of the desk and the towel of hypodermic needles and the small black perpetual calendar and the pen set and the hero doodads that were on the desk. His face was stone pale and he sat without moving, without even seeming to breathe.

De Spain said: "Don't be in too much of a hurry, Chief. This lad has friends in L.A. who are working on the Matson kill night now. And that kid reporter has a brother-in-law who is a cop. You didn't know that."

The chief made a vague motion with his chin. "Wait a minute, Weems." He turned to De Spain. "You mean they know in town that Helen Matson has been murdered?"

Dr. Austrian's face jerked up, haggard and drawn. Then he dropped it into his hands and covered his whole face with his long fingers.

De Spain said: "I meant Harry Matson, Chief. He was bumped off in L.A. tonight--last night--now--by Moss Lorenz."

The chief seemed to pull his thin lips back into his mouth, almost out of sight. He spoke with them like that. "How do you know that?"

"The shamus and me picked off Moss. He was hiding out in the house of a man named Greb, the lab man who did a job on the Austrian death. He was hiding there because it looked like somebody was going to open up the Austrian case wide enough for the mayor to think it was a new boulevard and come out with a bunch of flowers and make a speech. That is, if Greb and the Matsons didn't get took care of. It seems the Matsons were workin' together, in spite of being divorced, shaking Conried down, and Conried put the pencil on them."

The chief turned his head and snarled at his stooges. "Get out in the hall and wait."

The plainclothes man I didn't know opened the door and went out, and after a slight hesitation Weems followed him. Shorty had his hand on the door when De Spain said: "I want Shorty to stay. Shorty's a decent cop--not like them two vice squad grafters you been sleepin' with lately."

Shorty let go of the door and went and leaned against the wall and smiled behind his hand. The chief's face colored. "Who detailed you to the Brayton Avenue death?" he barked.

"I detailed myself, Chief. I was in the dicks' room a minute or so after the call come in and I went over with Reed. He picked Shorty up too. Shorty and me was both off duty."

De Spain grinned, a hard, lazy grin that was neither amused nor triumphant. It was just a grin.

The chief jerked a gun out of his overcoat pocket. It was a foot long, a regular hogleg, but he seemed to know how to hold it. He said tightly: "Where's Lorenz?"

"He's hid. We got him all ready for you. I had to bruise him a little, but he talked. That right, shamus?"

I said: "He says something that might be yes or no, but he makes the sounds in the right places."

"That's the way I like to hear a guy talk," De Spain said. "You oughtn't to be wasting your strength on that homicide stuff, Chief. And them toy dicks you run around with don't know nothing about police work except to go through apartment houses and shake down all the women that live alone. Now, you give me back my job and eight men and I'll show you some homicide work."

The chief looked down at his big gun and then he looked at Dr. Austrian's bowed head. "So he killed his wife," he said softly. "I knew there was a chance of it, but I didn't believe it."

"Don't believe it now," I said. "Helen Matson killed her. Dr. Austrian knows that. He covered up for her, and you covered up for him, and he's still willing to cover up for her. Love is like that with some people. And this is some town, Chief, where a gal can commit a murder, get her friends and the police to cover it, and then start out to blackmail the very people that kept her out of trouble."

The chief bit his lip. His eyes were nasty, but he was thinking--thinking hand. "No wonder she got rubbed out," he said quietly. "Lorenz--"

I said: "Take a minute to think. Lorenz didn't kill Helen Matson. He said he did, but De Spain beat him up to the point where he would have confessed shooting McKinley."

De Spain straightened from the wall. He had both hands lazily in the pockets of his suit coat. He kept them there. He stood straight on wide-planted feet, a wick of black hair showing under the side of his hat.

"Huh?" he said almost gently. "What was that?"

I said: "Lorenz didn't kill Helen Matson for several reasons. It was too fussy a job for his type of mind. He'd have knocked her off and let her lay. Second, he didn't know Greb was leaving town, tipped off by Dr. Austrian who was tipped off, in turn, by Vance Conried, who is now up north providing himself with all the necessary alibis. And if Lorenz didn't know that much, he didn't know anything about Helen Matson. Especially as Helen Matson had never really got to Conried at all. She had just tried to. She told me that and she was drunk enough to be telling the truth. So Conried wouldn't have taken the silly risk of having her knocked off in her own apartment by the sort of man anybody would remember seeing if they saw him anywhere near that apartment. Knocking off Matson up in L.A. was something else again. That was way off the home grounds."

The chief said tightly: "The Club Conried is in L.A."

"Legally," I admitted. "But by position and clientele it's just outside Bay City. It's part of Bay City--and it helps to run Bay City."

Shorty said: "That ain't no way to talk to the chief."

"Let him alone," the chief said. "It's so long since I heard a guy think I didn't know they did it any more."

I said: "Ask De Spain who killed Helen Matson."

De Spain laughed harshly. He said: "Sure. I killed her."

Dr. Austrian lifted his face off his hands and turned his head slowly and looked at De Spain. His face was as dead, as expressionless as the big dead-pan copper's. Then he reached over and opened the night-hand drawer of his desk. Shorty flipped his gun out and said: "Hold it, Doe."

Dr. Austrian shrugged and quietly took a wide-mouthed bottle with a glass stopper out of the drawer. He loosened the stopper and held the bottle close to his nose. "Just smelling salts," he said dully.

Shorty relaxed and dropped the gun to his side. The chief stared at me and chewed his lip. De Spain stared at nothing, at nobody. He grinned loosely, kept on grinning.

I said: "He thinks I'm kidding. You think I'm kidding. I'm not kidding. He knew Helen--well enough to give her a gilt cigarette case with his photo on it. I saw it. It was a small hand-tinted photo and not very good and I had only seen him once. She told me it was an old sweet that wore out. Afterwards it came back to me who that photo was. But he concealed the fact that he knew her and he didn't act very much like a copper tonight, in a lot of ways. He didn't get me out of a jam and run around with me in order to be nice. He did it to find out what I knew before I was put under the lamps down at headquarters. He didn't beat Lorenz half to death just in order to make Lorenz tell the truth. He did it to make Lorenz tell anything De Spain wanted him to tell, including confessing to the murder of the Matson girl whom Lorenz probably didn't even know.

"Who called up headquarters and tipped the boys about the murder? De Spain. Who walked in there immediately afterwards and horned in on the investigation? De Spain. Who scratched the girl's body up in a fit of jealous rage because she had ditched him for a better prospect? De Spain. Who still has blood and cuticle under the nails of his night hand which a good police chemist can do a lot with? De Spain. Take a look. I took several."

The chief turned his head very slowly, as if it were on a pivot. He whistled and the door opened and the other men came back into the room. De Spain didn't move. The grin stayed on his face, carved there, a meaningless hollow grin that meant and looked as if it would never go away again.

He said quietly: "And you the guy I thought was my pal. Well, you have some wild ideas, shamus. I will say that for you."

The chief said sharply: "It doesn't make sense. If De Spain did kill her, then he was the one who tried to put you in a frame and the one that got you out of it. How come?"

I said: "Listen. You can find out if De Spain knew the girl and how well. You can find out how much of his time tonight is not accounted for and make him

300

account for it. You can find out if there is blood and cuticle under his nails and, within limits, whether it is or could be the girl's blood and the girl's skin. And whether it was there before De Spain hit Moss Lorenz, before he hit anybody. And he didn't scratch Lorenz. That's all you need and all you can use--except a confession. And I don't think you'll get that.

"As to the frame, I would say De Spain followed the girl over to the Club Conried, or knew she had gone there and went oven himself. He saw her come out with me and he saw me put her in my car. That made him mad. He sapped me and the girl was too scared not to help him get me to her apartment and up into it. I don't remember any of that. It would be nice if I did, but I don't. They got me up there somehow, and they had a fight, and De Spain knocked her out and then he deliberately murdered her. He had some clumsy idea of making it look like a rape murder and making me the fall guy. Then he beat it, turned in an alarm, horned in on the investigation, and I got out of the apartment before I was caught there.

"He realized by this time that he had done a foolish thing. He knew I was a private dick from L.A., that I had talked to Dolly Kincaid, and from the girl he probably knew that I had gone to see Conried. And he may easily have known I was interested in the Austrian case. Okay. He turned a foolish play into a smart one by stringing along with me on the investigation I was trying to make, helping me on it, getting my story, and then finding himself another and much better fall guy for the murder of the Matson girl."

De Spain said tonelessly: "I'm goin' to start climbing on this guy in a minute, Chief. Okay?"

The chief said: "Just a minute. What made you suspect De Spain at all?"

"The blood and skin under his nails, and the brutal way he handled Lorenz, and the fact that the girl told me he had been her sweet and he pretended not to know who she was. What the hell more would I want?"

De Spain said: "This."

He shot from his pocket with the white-handled gun he had taken from Dr. Austrian. Shooting from the pocket takes a lot of practice of a kind cops don't get. The slug went a foot over my head and I sat down on the floor and Dr. Austrian stood up very quickly and swung his right hand into De Spain's face, the hand that held the wide-mouthed brown bottle. A colorless liquid splashed into his eyes and smoked down his face. Any other man would have screamed. De Spain pawed the air with his left hand and the gun in his pocket banged three times more and Dr. Austrian fell sideways across the end of the desk and then collapsed to the floor, out of range. The gun went on banging.

The other men in the room had all dropped to their knees. The chief jerked his hogleg up and shot De Spain twice in the body. Once would have been enough with that gun. De Spain's body twisted in the air and hit the floor like a safe. The chief went over and knelt beside him and looked at him silently. He stood up and came back around the desk, then went back and stooped over Dr. Austrian.

"This one's alive," he snapped. "Get on the phone, Weems." The chunky, fat-faced man went around the far side of the desk and scooped the telephone towards him and started to dial. There was a sharp smell of acid and scorched flesh in the air, a nasty smell. We were standing up again now, and the little police chief was looking at me bleakly.

"He oughtn't to have shot at you," he said. "You couldn't have proved a thing. We wouldn't have let you."

I didn't say anything. Weems put the phone down and looked at Dr. Austrian again.

"I think he's croaked," he said, from behind the desk.

The chief kept on looking at me. "You take some awful chances, Mr. Dalmas. I don't know what your game is, but I hope you like your chips."

"I'm satisfied," I said. "I'd like to have had a chance to talk to my client before he was bumped off, but I guess I've done all I could for him. The hell of it is I liked De Spain. He had all the guts they ever made."

The chief said: "If you want to know about guts, try being a small-town chief of police some day."

I said: "Yeah. Tell somebody to tie a handkerchief around De Spain's night hand, Chief. You kind of need the evidence yourself now."

A siren wailed distantly on Arguello Boulevard. The sound came faintly through the closed windows, like a coyote howling in the hills.

1

There was a desert wind blowing that night. It was one of those hot dry Santa Anas that come down through the mountain passes and curl your hair and make your nerves jump and your skin itch. On nights like that every booze party ends in a fight. Meek little wives feel the edge of the carving knife and study their husbands' necks. Anything can happen. You can even get a full glass of beer at a cocktail lounge.

I was getting one in a flossy new place across the street from the apartment house where I lived. It had been open about a week and it wasn't doing any business. The kid behind the bar was in his early twenties and looked as if he had never had a drink in his life.

There was only one other customer, a souse on a bar stool with his back to the door. He had a pile of dimes stacked neatly in front of him, about two dollars' worth. He was drinking straight rye in small glasses and he was all by himself in a world of his own.

I sat farther along the bar and got my glass of beer and said: "You sure cut the clouds off them, buddy. I will say that for you."

"We just opened up," the kid said. "We got to build up trade. Been in before, haven't you, mister?"

"Uh-huh."

"Live around here?"

"In the Berglund Apartments across the street," I said. "And the name is Philip Marlowe."

"Thanks, mister. Mine's Lew Petrolle." He leaned close to me across the polished dark bar. "Know that guy?"

"No."

"He ought to go home, kind of. I ought to call a taxi and send him home. He's doing his next week's drinking too soon."

"A night like this," I said. "Let him alone."

"It's not good for him," the kid said, scowling at me.

"Rye!" the drunk croaked, without looking up. He snapped his fingers so as not to disturb his piles of dimes by banging on the bar.

The kid looked at me and shrugged. "Should I?"

"Whose stomach is it? Not mine."

The kid poured him another straight rye and I think he doctored it with water down behind the bar because when he came up with it he looked as guilty as if he'd kicked his grandmother. The drunk paid no attention. He lifted coins off his pile with the exact care of a crack surgeon operating on a brain tumor.

The kid came back and put more beer in my glass. Outside the wind howled. Every once in a while it blew the stained-glass door open a few inches. It was a heavy door.

The kid said: "I don't like drunks in the first place and in the second place I don't like them getting drunk in here, and in the third place I don't like them in the first place."

"Warner Brothers could use that," I said.

"They did."

Just then we had another customer. A car squeaked to a stop outside and the swinging door came open. A fellow came in who looked a little in a hurry. He held the door and ranged the place quickly with flat, shiny,

305

dark eyes. He was well set up, dark, good-looking in a narrow-faced, tight-lipped way. His clothes were dark and a white handkerchief peeped coyly from his pocket and he looked cool as well as under a tension of some sort. I guessed it was the hot wind. I felt a bit the same myself only not cool.

He looked at the drunk's back. The drunk was playing checkers with his empty glasses. The new customer looked at me, then he looked along the line of half-booths at the other side of the place. They were all empty. He came on in--down past where the drunk sat swaying and muttering to himself--and spoke to the bar kid.

"Seen a lady in here, buddy? Tall, pretty, brown hair, in a print bolero jacket over a blue crêpe silk dress. Wearing a wide brimmed straw hat with a velvet band." He had a tight voice I didn't like.

"No, sir. Nobody like that's been in," the bar kid said.

"Thanks. Straight Scotch. Make it fast, will you?"

The kid gave it to him and the fellow paid and put the drink down in a gulp and started to go out. He took three or four steps and stopped, facing the drunk. The drunk was grinning. He swept a gun from somewhere so fast that it was just a blur coming out. He held it steady and he didn't look any drunker than I was. The tall dark guy stood quite still and then his head jerked back a little and then he was still again.

A car tore by outside. The drunk's gun was a .22 target automatic, with a large front sight. It made a couple of hard snaps and a little smoke curled--very little.

"So long, Waldo," the drunk said.

Then he put the gun on the barman and me.

The dark guy took a week to fall down. He stumbled, caught himself, waved one arm, stumbled again. His hat fell off, and then he hit the floor with his face. After he hit it he might have been poured concrete for all the fuss he made.

The drunk slid down off the stool and scooped his dimes into a pocket and slid towards the door. He turned sideways, holding the gun across his body. I didn't have a gun. I hadn't thought I needed one to buy a glass of beer. The kid behind the bar didn't move or make the slightest sound.

The drunk felt the door lightly with his shoulder, keeping his eyes on us, then pushed through it backwards. When it was wide a hard gust of air slammed in and lifted the hair of the man on the floor. The drunk said: "Poor Waldo. I bet I made his nose bleed."

The door swung shut. I started to rush it--from long practice in doing the wrong thing. In this case it didn't matter. The car outside let out a roar and when I got onto the sidewalk it was flicking a red smear of taillight around the nearby corner. I got its license number the way I got my first million.

There were people and cars up and down the block as usual. Nobody acted as if a gun had gone off. The wind was making enough noise to make the hard quick rap of .22 ammunition sound like a slammed door, even if anyone heard it. I went back into the cocktail bar.

The kid hadn't moved, even yet. He just stood with his hands flat on the bar, leaning over a little and looking down at the dark guy's back. The dark guy hadn't moved either. I bent down and felt his neck artery. He wouldn't move--ever.

The kid's face had as much expression as a cut of round steak and was about the same color. His eyes were more angry than shocked.

I lit a cigarette and blew smoke at the ceiling and said shortly: "Get on the phone."

"Maybe he's not dead," the kid said.

"When they use a twenty-two that means they don't make mistakes. Where's the phone?"

"I don't have one. I got enough expenses without that. Boy, can I kick eight hundred bucks in the face!"

"You own this place?"

"I did till this happened."

He pulled his white coat off and his apron and came around the inner end of the bar. "I'm locking this door," he said, taking keys out.

He went out, swung the door to and jiggled the lock from the outside until the bolt clicked into place. I bent down and rolled Waldo over. At first I couldn't even see where the shots went in. Then I could. A couple of tiny holes in his coat, over his heart. There was a little blood on his shirt.

The drunk was everything you could ask--as a killer.

The prowl-car boys came in about eight minutes. The kid, Lew Petrolle, was back behind the bar by then. He had his white coat on again and he was counting his money in the register and putting it in his pocket and making notes in a little book.

I sat at the edge of one of the half-booths and smoked cigarettes and watched Waldo's face get deader and deader. I wondered who the girl in the print coat was, why Waldo had left the engine of his car running outside, why he was in a hurry, whether the drunk had been waiting for him or just happened to be there.

The prowl-car boys came in perspiring. They were the usual large size and one of them had a flower stuck under his cap and his cap on a bit crooked. When he saw the dead man he got rid of the flower and leaned down to feel Waldo's pulse.

"Seems to be dead," he said, and rolled him around a little more. "Oh yeah, I see where they went in. Nice clean work. You two see him get it?"

I said yes. The kid behind the bar said nothing. I told them about it, that the killer seemed to have left in Waldo's car.

The cop yanked Waldo's wallet out, went through it rapidly and whistled. "Plenty jack and no driver's license." He put the wallet away. "O.K., we didn't touch him, see? Just a chance we could find did he have a car and put it on the air."

"The hell you didn't touch him," Lew Patrolle said.

The cop gave him one of those looks. "O.K., pal," he said softly. "We touched him."

The kid picked up a clean highball glass and began to polish it. He polished it all the rest of the time we were there.

In another minute a homicide fast-wagon sirened up and screeched to a stop outside the door and four men came in, two dicks, a photographer and a laboratory man. I didn't know either of the dicks. You can be in the detecting business a long time and not know all the men on a big city force.

One of them was a short, smooth, dark, quiet, smiling man, with curly black hair and soft intelligent eyes. The other was big, raw-boned, long-jawed, with a veined nose and glassy eyes. He looked like a heavy drinker. He looked tough, but he looked as if he thought he was a little tougher than he was. He shooed me into the last booth against the wall and his partner got the kid up front and the bluecoats went out. The fingerprint man and photographer set about their work.

A medical examiner came, stayed just long enough to get sore because there was no phone for him to call the morgue wagon.

The short dick emptied Waldo's pockets and then emptied his wallet and dumped everything into a large handkerchief on a booth table. I saw a lot of currency, keys, cigarettes, another handkerchief, very little else.

The big dick pushed me back into the end of the half-booth. "Give," he said. "I'm Copernik, Detective Lieutenant."

I put my wallet in front of him. He looked at it, went through it, tossed it back, made a note in a book.

"Philip Marlowe, huh? A shamus. You here on business?"

"Drinking business," I said. "I live just across the street in the Berglund."

"Know this kid up front?"

"I've been in here once since he opened up."

"See anything funny about him now?"

"No."

"Takes it too light for a young fellow, don't he? Never mind answering. Just tell the story."

I told it--three times. Once for him to get the outline, once for him to get the details and once for him to see if I had it too pat. At the end he said: "This dame interests me. And the killer called the guy Waldo, yet didn't seem to be anyways sure he would be in. I mean, if Waldo wasn't sure the dame would be here, nobody could be sure Waldo would be here."

"That's pretty deep," I said.

He studied me. I wasn't smiling. "Sounds like a grudge job, don't it? Don't sound planned. No getaway except by accident. A guy don't leave his car unlocked much in this town. And the killer works in front of two good witnesses. I don't like that."

"I don't like being a witness," I said. "The pay's too low."

He grinned. His teeth had a freckled look. "Was the killer drunk really?"

"With that shooting? No."

"Me too. Well, it's a simple job. The guy will have a record and he's left plenty prints. Even if we don't have his mug here we'll make him in hours. He had something on Waldo, but he wasn't meeting Waldo tonight. Waldo just dropped in to ask about a dame he had a date with and had missed connections on. It's a hot night and this wind would kill a girl's face. She'd be apt to drop in somewhere to wait. So the killer feeds Waldo two in the right place and scrams and don't worry about you boys at all. It's that simple."

"Yeah," I said.

"It's so simple it stinks," Copernik said.

He took his felt hat off and tousled up his ratty blond hair and leaned his head on his hands. He had a long mean horse face. He got a handkerchief out and mopped it, and the back of his neck and the back of his hands. He got a comb out and combed his hair--he looked worse with it combed--and put his hat back on.

"I was just thinking," I said.

"Yeah? What?"

"This Waldo knew just how the girl was dressed. So he must already have been with her tonight."

"So, what? Maybe he had to go to the can. And when he came back she's gone. Maybe she changed her mind about him."

"That's right," I said.

But that wasn't what I was thinking at all. I was thinking that Waldo had described the girl's clothes in a way the ordinary man wouldn't know how to describe them. Printed bolero jacket over blue crêpe silk dress. I didn't even know what a bolero jacket was, And I might have said blue dress or even blue silk dress, but never blue crêpe silk dress.

After a while two men came with a basket. Lew Petrolle was still polishing his glass and talking to the short dark dick.

We all went down to Headquarters.

Lew Petrolle was all right when they checked on him. His father had a grape ranch near Antioch in Contra Costa County. He had given Lew a thousand dollars to go into business and Lew had opened the cocktail bar, neon sign and all, on eight hundred flat.

They let him go and told him to keep the bar closed until they were sure they didn't want to do any more printing. He shook hands all around and grinned and said he guessed the killing would be good for business after all, because nobody believed a newspaper account of anything and people would come to him for the story and buy drinks while he was telling it.

"There's a guy won't ever do any worrying," Copernik said, when he was gone. "Over anybody else."

"Poor Waldo," I said. "The prints any good?"

"Kind of smudged," Copernik said sourly. "But we'll get a classification and teletype it to Washington some

312

time tonight. If it don't click, you'll be in for a day on the steel picture racks downstairs."

I shook hands with him and his partner, whose name was Ybarra, and left. They didn't know who Waldo was yet either. Nothing in his pockets told.

2

I got back to my street about 9 P.M. I looked up and down the block before I went into the Berglund. The cocktail bar was farther down on the other side, dark, with a nose or two against the glass, but no real crowd. People had seen the law and the morgue wagon, but they didn't know what had happened. Except the boys playing pinball games in the drugstore on the corner. They know everything, except how to hold a job.

The wind was still blowing, oven-hot, swirling dust and torn paper up against the walls.

I went into the lobby of the apartment house and rode the automatic elevator up to the fourth floor. I unwound the doors and stepped out and there was a tall girl standing there waiting for the car.

She had brown wavy hair under a wide-brimmed straw hat with a velvet band and loose bow. She had wide blue eyes and eyelashes that didn't quite reach her chin. She wore a blue dress that might have been crêpe silk, simple in lines but not missing any curves. Over it she wore what might have been a print bolero jacket.

I said: "Is that a bolero jacket?"

She gave me a distant glance and made a motion as if to brush a cobweb out of the way.

"Yes. Would you mind--I'm rather in a hurry. I'd like--"

I didn't move. I blocked her off from the elevator. We stared at each other and she flushed very slowly.

"Better not go out on the street in those clothes," I said.

"Why, how dare you--"

The elevator clanked and started down again. I didn't know what she was going to say. Her voice lacked the edgy twang of a beer-parlor frill. It had a soft light sound, like spring rain.

"It's not a make," I said. "You're in trouble. If they come to this floor in the elevator, you have just that much time to get off the hall. First take off the hat and jacket--and snap it up!"

She didn't move. Her face seemed to whiten a little behind the not-too-heavy make-up.

"Cops," I said, "are looking for you. In those clothes. Give me the chance and I'll tell you why."

She turned her head swiftly and looked back along the corridor. With her looks I didn't blame her for trying one more bluff.

"You're impertinent, whoever you are. I'm Mrs. Leroy in Apartment Thirty-one. I can assure--"

"That you're on the wrong floor," I said. "This is the fourth." The elevator had stopped down below. The sound of doors being wrenched open came up the shaft.

"Off!" I rapped. "Now!"

She switched her hat off and slipped out of the bolero jacket, fast. I grabbed them and wadded them into a mess under my arm. I took her elbow and turned her and we were going down the hall.

"I live in Forty-two. The front one across from yours, just a floor up. Take your choice. Once again-- I'm not on the make."

She smoothed her hair with that quick gesture, like a bird preening itself. Ten thousand years of practice behind it.

"Mine," she said, and tucked her bag under her arm and strode down the hall fast. The elevator stopped at the floor below. She stopped when it stopped. She turned and faced me.

"The stairs are back by the elevator shaft," I said gently.

"I don't have an apartment," she said.

"I didn't think you had."

"Are they searching for me?"

"Yes, but they won't start gouging the block stone by stone before tomorrow. And then only if they don't make Waldo."

She stared at me. "Waldo?"

"Oh, you don't know Waldo," I said.

She shook her head slowly. The elevator started down in the shaft again. Panic flicked in her blue eyes like a ripple on water.

"No," she said breathlessly, "but take me out of this hall."

We were almost at my door. I jammed the key in and shook the lock around and heaved the door inward. I reached in far enough to switch lights on. She went in past me like a wave. Sandalwood floated on the air, very faint.

I shut the door, threw my hat into a chair and watched her stroll over to a card table on which I had a chess problem set out that I couldn't solve. Once inside, with the door locked, her panic had left her.

"So you're a chess player," she said, in that guarded tone, as if she had come to look at my etchings. I wished she had.

We both stood still then and listened to the distant clang of elevator doors and then steps--going the other way.

I grinned, but with strain, not pleasure, went out into the kitchenette and started to fumble with a couple of glasses and then realized I still had her hat and bolero jacket under my arm. I went into the dressing room behind the wall bed and stuffed them into a drawer, went back out to the kitchenette, dug out some extra-fine Scotch and made a couple of highballs.

When I went in with the drinks she had a gun in her hand. It was a small automatic with a pearl grip. It jumped up at me and her eyes were full of horror.

I stopped, with a glass in each hand, and said: "Maybe this hot wind has got you crazy too. I'm a private detective. I'll prove it if you let me."

She nodded slightly and her face was white. I went over slowly and put a glass down beside her, and went back and set mine down and got a card out that had no bent corners. She was sitting down, smoothing one blue knee with her left hand, and holding the gun on the other. I put the card down beside her drink and sat with mine.

"Never let a guy get that close to you," I said. "Not if you mean business. And your safety catch is on."

She flashed her eyes down, shivered, and put the gun back in her bag. She drank half the drink without stopping, put the glass down hard and picked the card up.

"I don't give many people that liquor," I said. "I can't afford to."

Her lips curled. "I supposed you would want money."

"Huh?"

She didn't say anything. Her hand was close to her bag again.

"Don't forget the safety catch," I said. Her hand stopped. I went on: "This fellow I called Waldo is quite tall, say five eleven, slim, dark, brown eyes with a lot of glitter. Nose and mouth too thin. Dark suit, white handkerchief showing, and in a hurry to find you. Am I getting anywhere?"

She took her glass again. "So that's Waldo," she said. "Well, what about him?" Her voice seemed to have a slight liquor edge now.

"Well, a funny thing. There's a cocktail bar across the street...Say, where have you been all evening?"

"Sitting in my car," she said coldly, "most of the time."

"Didn't you see a fuss across the street up the block?"

Her eyes tried to say no and missed. Her lips said: "I knew there was some kind of disturbance. I saw policemen and red searchlights. I supposed someone had been hurt."

"Someone was. And this Waldo was looking for you before that. In the cocktail bar. He described you and your clothes."

Her eyes were set like rivets now and had the same amount of expression. Her mouth began to tremble and kept on trembling.

"I was in there," I said, "talking to the kid that runs it. There was nobody in there but a drunk on a stool and the kid and myself. The drunk wasn't paying any attention to anything. Then Waldo came in and asked about you and we said no, we hadn't seen you and he started to leave."

I sipped my drink. I like an effect as well as the next fellow. Her eyes ate me.

"Just started to leave. Then this drunk that wasn't paying any attention to anyone called him Waldo and took a gun out. He shot him twice--I snapped my fingers twice--"like that. Dead."

She fooled me. She laughed in my face. "So my husband hired you to spy on me," she said. "I might have known the whole thing was an act. You and your Waldo."

I gawked at her.

"I never thought of him as jealous," she snapped. "Not of a man who had been our chauffeur anyhow. A little about Stan, of course--that's natural. But Joseph Coates--"

I made motions in the air. "Lady, one of us has this book open at the wrong page," I grunted. "I don't know anybody named Stan or Joseph Coates. So help me, I didn't even know you had a chauffeur. People around here don't run to them. As for husbands--yeah, we do have a husband once in a while. Not often enough."

She shook her head slowly and her hand stayed near her bag and her blue eyes had glitters in them.

"Not good enough, Mr. Marlowe. No, not nearly good enough. I know you private detectives. You're all rotten. You tricked me into your apartment, if it is your apartment. More likely it's the apartment of some horrible man who will swear anything for a few dollars. Now you're trying to scare me. So you can blackmail me--as well as get money from my husband. All right," she said breathlessly, "how much do I have to pay?"

I put my empty glass aside and leaned back. "Pardon me if I light a cigarette," I said. "My nerves are frayed."

I lit it while she watched me without enough fear for any real guilt to be under it. "So Joseph Coates is his name," I said. "The guy that killed him in the cocktail bar called him Waldo."

She smiled a bit disgustedly, but almost tolerantly. "Don't stall. How much?"

"Why were you trying to meet this Joseph Coates?"

"I was going to buy something he stole from me, of course. Something that's valuable in the ordinary way too. Almost fifteen thousand dollars. The man I loved gave it to me. He's dead. There! He's dead! He died in a burning plane. Now, go back and tell my husband that, you slimy little rat!"

"I'm not little and I'm not a rat," I said.

"You're still slimy. And don't bother about telling my husband. I'll tell him myself. He probably knows anyway."

I grinned. "That's smart. Just what was I supposed to find out?"

She grabbed her glass and finished what was left of her drink. "So he thinks I'm meeting Joseph. Well, perhaps I was. But not to make love. Not with a chauffeur. Not with a bum I picked off the front step and gave a job to. I don't have to dig down that far, if I want to play around."

"Lady," I said, "you don't indeed."

"Now, I'm going," she said. "You just try and stop me." She snatched the pearl-handled gun out of her bag. I didn't move.

"Why, you nasty little string of nothing," she stormed. "How do I know you're a private detective at all? You might be a crook. This card you gave me doesn't mean anything. Anybody can have cards printed."

"Sure," I said. "And I suppose I'm smart enough to live here two years because you were going to move in today so I could blackmail you for not meeting a man named Joseph Coates who was bumped off across the street under the name of Waldo. Have you got the money to buy this something that cost fifteen grand?"

"Oh! You think you'll hold me up, I suppose!"

"Oh!" I mimicked her, "I'm a stick-up artist now, am I? Lady, will you please either put that gun away or take the safety catch off? It hurts my professional feelings to see a nice gun made a monkey of that way."

"You're a full portion of what I don't like," she said. "Get out of my way."

I didn't move. She didn't move. We were both sitting down--and not even close to each other.

"Let me in on one secret before you go," I pleaded. "What in hell did you take the apartment down on the floor below for? Just to meet a guy down on the street?"

"Stop being silly," she snapped. "I didn't. I lied. It's his apartment."

"Joseph Coates'?"

She nodded sharply.

"Does my description of Waldo sound like Joseph Coates?"

She nodded sharply again.

"All right. That's one fact learned at last. Don't you realize Waldo described your clothes before he was shot--when he was looking for you--that the description was passed on to the police--that the police don't know who Waldo is--and are looking for somebody in those clothes to help tell them? Don't you get that much?"

The gun suddenly started to shake in her hand. She looked down at it, sort of vacantly, and slowly put it back in her bag.

"I'm a fool," she whispered, "to be even talking to you." She stared at me for a long time, then pulled in a deep breath. "He told me where he was staying. He didn't seem afraid. I guess blackmailers are like that. He was to meet me on the street, but I was late. It was full of police when I got here. So I went back and sat in my car for a while. Then I came up to Joseph's apartment and knocked. Then I went back to my car and waited again. I came up here three times in all. The last time I walked up a flight to take the elevator. I had already been seen twice on the third floor. I met you. That's all."

"You said something about a husband," I grunted. "Where is he?"

"He's at a meeting."

"Oh, a meeting," I said, nastily.

"My husband's a very important man. He has lots of meetings. He's a hydroelectric engineer. He's been all over the world. I'd have you know--"

"Skip it," I said. "I'll take him to lunch some day and have him tell me himself. Whatever Joseph had on you is dead stock now. Like Joseph."

"He's really dead?" she whispered. "Really?"

"He's dead," I said. "Dead, dead, dead. Lady, he's dead."

She believed it at last. I hadn't thought she ever would somehow. In the silence, the elevator stopped at my floor.

I heard steps coming down the hall. We all have hunches. I put my finger to my lips. She didn't move now. Her face had a frozen look. Her big blue eyes were as black as the shadows below them. The hot wind boomed against the shut windows. Windows have to be shut when a Santa Ana blows, heat or no heat.

The steps that came down the hall were the casual ordinary steps of one man. But they stopped outside my door, and somebody knocked.

I pointed to the dressing room behind the wall bed. She stood up without a sound, her bag clenched against her side. I pointed again, to her glass. She lifted it swiftly, slid across the carpet, through the door, drew the door quietly shut after her.

I didn't know just what I was going to all this trouble for.

The knocking sounded again. The backs of my hands were wet. I creaked my chair and stood up and made a loud yawning sound. Then I went over and opened the door--without a gun. That was a mistake.

3

I didn't know him at first. Perhaps for the opposite reason Waldo hadn't seemed to know him. He'd had a hat on all the time over at the cocktail bar and he didn't have one on now. His hair ended completely and exactly where his hat would start. Above that line was hard white sweatless skin almost as glaring as scar tissue. He wasn't just twenty years older. He was a different man.

But I knew the gun he was holding, the .22 target automatic with the big front sight. And I knew his eyes. Bright, brittle, shallow eyes like the eyes of a lizard.

He was alone. He put the gun against my face very lightly and said between his teeth: "Yeah, me. Let's go on in."

I backed in just far enough and stopped. Just the way he would want me to, so he could shut the door without moving much. I knew from his eyes that he would want me to do just that.

I wasn't scared. I was paralyzed.

When he had the door shut he backed me some more, slowly, until there was something against the back of my legs. His eyes looked into mine.

"That's a card table," he said. "Some goon here plays chess. You?"

I swallowed. "I don't exactly play it. I just fool around."

"That means two," he said with a kind of hoarse softness, as if some cop had hit him across the windpipe with a blackjack once, in a third-degree session.

"It's a problem," I said. "Not a game. Look at the pieces."

"I wouldn't know."

"Well, I'm alone," I said, and my voice shook just enough.

"It don't make any difference," he said. "I'm washed up anyway. Some nose puts the bulls on me tomorrow, next week, what the hell? I just didn't like your map, pal. And that smug-faced pansy in the bar coat that played left tackle for Fordham or something. To hell with guys like you guys."

I didn't speak or move. The big front sight raked my cheek lightly almost caressingly. The man smiled.

"It's kind of good business too," he said. "Just in case. An old con like me don't make good prints, all I got against me is two witnesses. The hell with it."

"What did Waldo do to you?" I tried to make it sound as if I wanted to know, instead of just not wanting to shake too hard.

"Stooled on a bank job in Michigan and got me four years. Got himself a nolle prosse. Four years in Michigan ain't no summer cruise. They make you be good in them lifer states."

"How'd you know he'd come in there?" I croaked.

"I didn't. Oh yeah, I was lookin' for him. I was wanting to see him all right. I got a flash of him on the street night before last but I lost him. Up to then I wasn't lookin' for him. Then I was. A cute guy, Waldo. How is he?"

"Dead," I said.

"I'm still good," he chuckled. "Drunk or sober. Well, that don't make no doughnuts for me now. They make me downtown yet?"

I didn't answer him quick enough. He jabbed the gun into my throat and I choked and almost grabbed for it by instinct.

"Naw," he cautioned me softly. "Naw. You ain't that dumb."

I put my hands back, down at my sides, open, the palms towards him. He would want them that way. He hadn't touched me, except with the gun. He didn't seem to care whether I might have one too. He wouldn't--if he just meant the one thing.

He didn't seem to care very much about anything, coming back on that block. Perhaps the hot wind did something to him. It was booming against my shut windows like the surf under a pier.

"They got prints," I said. "I don't know how good."

"They'll be good enough--but not for teletype work. Take 'em airmail time to Washington and back to check 'em right. Tell me why I came here, pal."

"You heard the kid and me talking in the bar. I told him my name, where I lived."

"That's how, pal. I said why." He smiled at me. It was a lousy smile to be the last one you might see.

"Skip it," I said. "The hangman won't ask you to guess why he's there."

"Say, you're tough at that. After you, I visit that kid. I tailed him home from Headquarters, but I figure you're the guy to put the bee on first. I tail him home from the city hall, in the rent car Waldo had. From Headquarters, pal. Them funny dicks. You can sit in their laps and they don't know you. Start runnin' for a streetcar and they open up with machine guns and bump two pedestrians, a hacker asleep in his cab, and an old scrubwoman on the second floor workin' a mop. And they miss the guy they're after. Them funny lousy dicks."

He twisted the gun muzzle in my neck. His eyes looked madder than before.

"I got time," he said. "Waldo's rent car don't get a report right away. And they don't make Waldo very soon. I know Waldo. Smart he was. A smooth boy, Waldo."

"I'm going to vomit," I said, "if you don't take that gun out of my throat."

He smiled and moved the gun down to my heart. "This about right? Say when."

I must have spoken louder than I meant to. The door of the dressing-room by the wall bed showed a crack of darkness. Then an inch. Then four inches. I saw

325

eyes, but didn't look at them. I stared hard into the bald-headed man's eyes. Very hard. I didn't want him to take his eyes off mine.

"Scared?" he asked softly.

I leaned against his gun and began to shake. I thought he would enjoy seeing me shake. The girl came out through the door. She had her gun in her hand again. I was sorry as hell for her. She'd try to make the door--or scream. Either way it would be curtains--for both of us.

"Well, don't take all night about it," I bleated. My voice sounded far away, like a voice on a radio on the other side of a street.

"I like this, pal," he smiled. "I'm like that."

The girl floated in the air, somewhere behind him. Nothing was ever more soundless than the way she moved. It wouldn't do any good though. He wouldn't fool around with her at all. I had known him all my life but I had been looking into his eyes for only five minutes.

"Suppose I yell," I said.

"Yeah, suppose you yell. Go ahead and yell," he said with his killer's smile.

She didn't go near the door. She was right behind him.

"Well--here's where I yell," I said.

As if that was the cue, she jabbed the little gun hard into his short ribs, without a single sound.

He had to react. It was like a knee reflex. His mouth snapped open and both his arms jumped out from his sides and he arched his back just a little. The gun was pointing at my right eye.

I sank and kneed him with all my strength, in the groin.

His chin came down and I hit it. I hit it as if I was driving the last spike on the first transcontinental railroad. I can still feel it when I flex my knuckles.

His gun raked the side of my face but it didn't go off. He was already limp. He writhed down gasping, his left side against the floor. I kicked his right shoulder-- hard. The gun jumped away from him, skidded on the carpet, under a chair. I heard the chessmen tinkling on the floor behind me somewhere.

The girl stood over him, looking down. Then her wide dark horrified eyes came up and fastened on mine.

"That buys me," I said. "Anything I have is yours-- now and forever."

She didn't hear me. Her eyes were strained open so hard that the whites showed under the vivid blue iris. She backed quickly to the door with her little gun up, felt behind her for the knob and twisted it. She pulled the door open and slipped out.

The door shut.

She was bareheaded and without her bolero jacket.

She had only the gun, and the safety catch on that was still set so that she couldn't fire it.

It was silent in the room then, in spite of the wind. Then I heard him gasping on the floor. His face had a greenish pallor. I moved behind him and pawed him for more guns, and didn't find any. I got a pair of store cuffs out of my desk and pulled his arms in front of him and snapped them on his wrists. They would hold if he didn't shake them too hard.

His eyes measured me for a coffin, in spite of their suffering. He lay in the middle of the floor, still on his left side, a twisted, wizened, bald-headed little guy with drawn-back lips and teeth spotted with cheap silver fillings. His mouth looked like a black pit and his breath came in little waves, choked, stopped, came on again, limping.

I went into the dressing room and opened the drawer of the chest. Her hat and jacket lay there on my shirts. I put them underneath, at the back, and smoothed the shirts over them. Then I went out to the kitchenette and poured a stiff jolt of whiskey and put it down and stood a moment listening to the hot wind howl against the window glass. A garage door banged, and a power-line wire with too much play between the insulators thumped the side of the building with a sound like somebody beating a carpet.

The drink worked on me. I went back into the living room and opened a window. The guy on the floor hadn't smelled her sandalwood, but somebody else might.

I shut the window again, wiped the palms of my hands and used the phone to dial Headquarters.

Copernik was still there. His smart-aleck voice said: "Yeah? Marlowe? Don't tell me. I bet you got an idea."

"Make that killer yet?"

"We're not saying, Marlowe. Sorry as all hell and so on. You know how it is."

"O.K., I don't care who he is. Just come and get him off the floor of my apartment."

"Holy Christ!" Then his voice hushed and went down low. "Wait a minute, now. Wait a minute." A long way off I seemed to hear a door shut. Then his voice again. "Shoot," he said softly.

"Handcuffed," I said. "All yours. I had to knee him, but he'll be all right. He came here to eliminate a witness."

Another pause. The voice was full of honey. "Now listen, boy, who else is in this with you?"

"Who else? Nobody. Just me."

"Keep it that way, boy. All quiet. O.K.?"

"Think I want all the bums in the neighborhood in here sightseeing?"

"Take it easy, boy. Easy. Just sit tight and sit still. I'm practically there. No touch nothing. Get me?"

"Yeah." I gave him the address and apartment number again to save him time.

I could see his big bony face glisten. I got the .22 target gun from under the chair and sat holding it until feet hit the hallway outside my door and knuckles did a quiet tattoo on the door panel.

Copernik was alone. He filled the doorway quickly, pushed me back into the room with a tight grin and shut the door. He stood with his back to it, his hand under the left side of his coat. A big hard bony man with flat cruel eyes.

He lowered them slowly and looked at the man on the floor. The man's neck was twitching a little. His eyes moved in short stabs--sick eyes.

"Sure it's the guy?" Copernik's voice was hoarse.

"Positive. Where's Ybarra?"

"Oh, he was busy." He didn't look at me when he said that. "Those your cuffs?"

"Yeah."

"Key."

I tossed it to him. He went down swiftly on one knee beside the killer and took my cuffs off his wrists, tossed them to one side. He got his own off his hip, twisted the bald man's hands behind him and snapped the cuffs on.

"All right, you bastard," the killer said tonelessly.

Copernik grinned and balled his fist and hit the handcuffed man in the mouth a terrific blow. His head snapped back almost enough to break his neck. Blood dribbled from the lower corner of his mouth.

"Get a towel," Copernik ordered.

I got a hand towel and gave it to him. He stuffed it between the handcuffed man's teeth, viciously, stood up and rubbed his bony fingers through his ratty blond hair.

"All right. Tell it."

I told it--leaving the girl out completely. It sounded a little funny. Copernik watched me, said nothing. He rubbed the side of his veined nose. Then he got his comb out and worked on his hair just as he had done earlier in the evening, in the cocktail bar.

I went over and gave him the gun. He looked at it casually, dropped it into his side pocket. His eyes had something in them and his face moved in a hard bright grin.

I bent down and began picking up my chessmen and dropping them into the box. I put the box on the mantel, straightened out a leg of the card table, played around for a while. All the time Copernik watched me. I wanted him to think something out.

At last he came out with it. "This guy uses a twenty-two," he said. "He uses it because he's good enough to get by with that much gun. That means he's good. He knocks at your door, pokes that gat in your belly, walks you back into the room, says he's here to close your mouth for keeps--and yet you take him. You not having any gun. You take him alone. You're kind of good yourself, pal."

"Listen," I said, and looked at the floor. I picked up another chessman and twisted it between my fingers. "I was doing a chess problem," I said "Trying to forget things."

"You got something on your mind, pal," Copernik said softly. "You wouldn't try to fool an old copper, would you, boy?"

"It's a swell pinch and I'm giving it to you," I said. "What the hell more do you want?"

The man on the floor made a vague sound behind the towel. His bald head glistened with sweat.

"What's the matter, pal? You been up to something?" Copernik almost whispered.

I looked at him quickly, looked away again. "All right," I said. "You know damn well I couldn't take him alone. He had the gun on me and he shoots where he looks."

Copernik closed one eye and squinted at me amiably with the other. "Go on, pal. I kind of thought of that too."

I shuffled around a little more, to make it look good. I said, slowly: "There was a kid here who pulled a job over in Boyle Heights, a heist job. It didn't take. A two-bit service station stick-up. I know his family. He's not really bad. He was here trying to beg train money off me. When the knock came he sneaked in-- there."

I pointed at the wall bed and the door beside. Copernik's head swiveled slowly, swiveled back. His eyes winked again. "And this kid had a gun," he said.

I nodded. "And he got behind him. That takes guts, Copernik. You've got to give the kid a break. You've got to let him stay out of it."

"Tag out for this kid?" Copernik asked softly.

"Not yet, he says. He's scared there will be."

Copernik smiled. "I'm a homicide man," he said. "I wouldn't know--or care."

I pointed down at the gagged and handcuffed man on the floor. "You took him, didn't you?" I said gently.

Copernik kept on smiling. A big whitish tongue came out and massaged his thick lower lip. "How'd I do it?" he whispered.

"Get the slugs out of Waldo?"

"Sure. Long twenty-two's. One smashed a rib, one good."

"You're a careful guy. You don't miss any angles. You know anything about me? You dropped in on me to see what guns I had."

Copernik got up and went down on one knee again beside the killer. "Can you hear me, guy?" he asked with his face close to the face of the man on the floor.

The man made some vague sound. Copernik stood up and yawned. "Who the hell cares what he says? Go on, pal."

"You wouldn't expect to find I had anything, but you wanted to look around my place. And while you were mousing around in there"--I pointed to the dressing room--"and me not saying anything, being a little sore, maybe, a knock came on the door. So he came in. So after a while you sneaked out and took him."

"Ah," Copernik grinned widely, with as many teeth as a horse. "You're on, pal. I socked him and I kneed him and I took him. You didn't have no gun and the guy swiveled on me pretty sharp and I left-hooked him down the backstairs. O.K.?"

"O.K.," I said.

"You'll tell it like that downtown?"

"Yeah," I said.

"I'll protect you, pal. Treat me right and I'll always play ball. Forget about that kid. Let me know if he needs a break."

He came over and held out his hand. I shook it. It was as clammy as a dead fish. Clammy hands and the people who own them make me sick.

"There's just one thing," I said. "This partner of yours-- Ybarra. Won't he be a bit sore you didn't bring him along on this?"

Copernik tousled his hair and wiped his hatband with a large yellowish silk handkerchief.

"That guinea?" he sneered. "To hell with him!" He came close to me and breathed in my face. "No mistakes, pal--about that story of ours."

His breath was bad. It would be.

4

There were just five of us in the chief-of-detective's office when Copernik laid it before them. A stenographer, the chief, Copernik, myself, Ybarra. Ybarra sat on a chair tilted against the side wall. His hat was down over his eyes but their softness loomed underneath, and the small still smile hung at the corners of the clean-cut Latin lips. He didn't look directly at Copernik. Copernik didn't look at him at all.

Outside in the corridor there had been photos of Copernik shaking hands with me, Copernik with his hat on straight and his gun in his hand and a stern, purposeful look on his face.

They said they knew who Waldo was, but they wouldn't tell me. I didn't believe they knew, because the chief-of-detectives had a morgue photo of Waldo on his desk. A beautiful job, his hair combed, his tie straight, the light hitting his eyes just right to make them glisten. Nobody would have known it was a photo of a dead man with two bullet holes in his heart. He looked like a dance-hall sheik making up his mind whether to take the blonde or the redhead.

It was about midnight when I got home. The apartment door was locked and while I was fumbling for my keys a low voice spoke to me out of the darkness.

All it said was: "Please!" but I knew it. I turned and looked at a dark Cadillac coupe parked just off the loading zone. It had no lights. Light from the street touched the brightness of a woman's eyes.

I went over there. "You're a darn fool," I said.

She said: "Get in."

I climbed in and she started the car and drove it a block and a half along Franklin and turned down Kingsley Drive. The hot wind still burned and blustered. A radio lilted from an open, sheltered side window of an apartment house. There were a lot of parked cars but she found a vacant space behind a small brand-new Packard cabriolet that had the dealer's sticker on the windshield glass. After she'd jockeyed us up to the curb she leaned back in the corner with her gloved hands on the wheel.

She was all in black now, or dark brown, with a small foolish hat. I smelled the sandalwood in her perfume.

"I wasn't very nice to you, was I?" she said.

"All you did was save my life."

"What happened?"

"I called the law and fed a few lies to a cop I don't like and gave him all the credit for the pinch and that was that. That guy you took away from me was the man who killed Waldo."

"You mean--you didn't tell them about me?"

"Lady," I said again, "all you did was save my life. What else do you want done? I'm ready, willing, and I'll try to be able."

She didn't say anything, or move.

"Nobody learned who you are from me," I said. "Incidentally, I don't know myself."

"I'm Mrs. Frank C. Barsaly, Two-twelve Fremont Place, Olympia Two-four-five-nine-six. Is that what you wanted?"

"Thanks," I mumbled, and rolled a dry unlit cigarette around in my fingers. "Why did you come back?" Then I snapped the fingers of my left hand. "The hat and jacket," I said. "I'll go up and get them."

"It's more than that," she said. "I want my pearls." I might have jumped a little. It seemed as if there had been enough without pearls.

A car tore by down the street going twice as fast as it should. A thin bitter cloud of dust lifted in the streetlights and whirled and vanished. The girl ran the window up quickly against it.

"All right," I said. "Tell me about the pearls. We have had a murder and a mystery woman and a mad killer and a heroic rescue and a police detective framed into making a false report. Now we will have pearls. All right--feed it to me."

"I was to buy them for five thousand dollars. From the man you call Waldo and I call Joseph Coates. He should have had them."

"No pearls," I said. "I saw what came out of his pockets. A lot of money, but no pearls."

"Could they be hidden in his apartment?"

"Yes," I said. "So far as I know he could have had them hidden anywhere in California except in his pockets. How's Mr. Barsaly this hot night?"

"He's still downtown at his meeting. Otherwise I couldn't have come."

"Well, you could have brought him," I said. "He could have sat in the rumble seat."

"Oh, I don't know," she said. "Frank weighs two hundred pounds and he's pretty solid. I don't think he would like to sit in the rumble seat, Mr. Marlowe."

"What the hell are we talking about anyway?"

She didn't answer. Her gloved hands tapped lightly, provokingly on the rim of the slender wheel. I threw the unlit cigarette out the window, turned a little and took hold of her.

When I let go of her, she pulled as far away from me as she could against the side of the car and rubbed the back of her glove against her mouth. I sat quite still.

We didn't speak for some time. Then she said very slowly: "I meant you to do that. But I wasn't always that way. It's only been since Stan Phillips was killed in his plane. If it hadn't been for that, I'd be Mrs. Phillips now. Stan gave me the pearls. They cost fifteen thousand dollars, he said once. White pearls, forty-one of them, the largest about a third of an inch across. I don't know how many grains. I never had them appraised or showed them to a jeweler, so I don't know those things. But I loved them on Stan's account. I loved Stan. The way you do just the one time. Can you understand?"

"What's your first name?" I asked.

"Lola."

"Go on talking, Lola." I got another dry cigarette out of my pocket and fumbled it between my fingers just to give them something to do.

"They had a simple silver clasp in the shape of a two-bladed propeller. There was one small diamond where the boss would be. I told Frank they were store pearls I had bought myself. He didn't know the difference. It's not so easy to tell, I dare say. You see-- Frank is pretty jealous."

In the darkness she came closer to me and her side touched my side. But I didn't move this time. The wind howled and the trees shook. I kept on rolling the cigarette around in my fingers.

"I suppose you've read that story," she said. "About the wife and the real pearls and her telling her husband they were false?"

"I've read it," I said, "Maugham."

"I hired Joseph. My husband was in Argentina at the time. I was pretty lonely."

"*You* should be lonely," I said.

"Joseph and I went driving a good deal. Sometimes we had a drink or two together. But that's all. I don't go around--"

"You told him about the pearls," I said. "And when your two hundred pounds of beef came back from Argentina and kicked him out--he took the pearls, because he knew they were real. And then offered them back to you for five grand."

"Yes," she said simply. "Of course I didn't want to go to the police. And of course in the circumstance Joseph wasn't afraid of my knowing where he lived."

"Poor Waldo," I said. "I feel kind of sorry for him. It was a hell of a time to run into an old friend that had a down on you."

I struck a match on my shoe sole and lit the cigarette. The tobacco was so dry from the hot wind that it burned like grass. The girl sat quietly beside me, her hands on the wheel again.

"Hell with women--these fliers," I said. "And you're still in love with him, or think you are. Where did you keep the pearls?"

"In a Russian malachite jewelry box on my dressing table. With some other costume jewelry. I had to, if I ever wanted to wear them."

"And they were worth fifteen grand. And you think Joseph might have hidden them in his apartment. Thirty-one, wasn't it?"

"Yes," she said. "I guess it's a lot to ask."

I opened the door and got out of the car. "I've been paid," I said. "I'll go look. The doors in my apartment are not very obstinate. The cops will find out where Waldo lived when they publish his photo, but not tonight, I guess."

"It's awfully sweet of you," she said. "Shall I wait here?"

I stood with a foot on the running board, leaning in, looking at her. I didn't answer her question. I just stood there looking in at the shine of her eyes. Then I shut the car door and walked up the street towards Franklin.

Even with the wind shriveling my face I could still smell the sandalwood in her hair. And feel her lips.

I unlocked the Berglund door, walked through the silent lobby to the elevator, and rode up to Three. Then I soft-footed along the silent corridor and peered down at the sill of Apartment 31. No light. I rapped--the old light, confidential tattoo of the bootlegger with the big smile and the extra-deep hip pockets. No answer. I took the piece of thick hard celluloid that pretended to

be a window over the driver's license in my wallet, and
eased it between the lock and the jamb, leaning hard
on the knob, pushing it toward the hinges. The edge of
the celluloid caught the slope of the spring lock and
snapped it back with a small brittle sound, like an
icicle breaking. The door yielded and I went into near
darkness. Street light filtered in and touched a high
spot here and there.

I shut the door and snapped the light on and just
stood. There was a queer smell in the air. I made it in a
moment-- the smell of dark-cured tobacco. I prowled
over to a smoking stand by the window and looked
down at four brown butts-- Mexican or South
American cigarettes.

Upstairs, on my floor, feet hit the carpet and
somebody went into a bathroom. I heard the toilet
flush. I went into the bathroom of Apartment 31. A
little rubbish, nothing, no place to hide anything. The
kitchenette was a longer job, but I only half searched. I
knew there were no pearls in that apartment. I knew
Waldo had been on his way out and that he was in a
hurry and that something was riding him when he
turned and took two bullets from an old friend.

I went back to the living room and swung the wall
bed and looked past its mirror side into the dressing
room for signs of still current occupancy. Swinging the
bed farther I was no longer looking for pearls. I was
looking at a man.

He was small, middle-aged, iron-gray at the temples,
with a very dark skin, dressed in a fawn-colored suit
with a wine-colored tie. His neat little brown hands
hung limply by his sides. His small feet, in pointed
polished shoes, pointed almost at the floor.

He was hanging by a belt around his neck from the metal top of the bed. His tongue stuck out farther than I thought it possible for a tongue to stick out.

He swung a little and I didn't like that, so I pulled the bed shut and he nestled quietly between the two clamped pillows. I didn't touch him yet. I didn't have to touch him to know that he would be cold as ice.

I went around him into the dressing room and used my handkerchief on drawer knobs. The place was stripped clean except for the light litter of a man living alone.

I came out of there and began on the man. No wallet. Waldo would have taken that and ditched it. A flat box of cigarettes, half full, stamped in gold: "Louis Tapia y Cia, Calle de Paysandü, 19, Montevideo." Matches from the Spezia Club. An under-arm holster of dark-grained leather and in it a 9-millimeter Mauser.

The Mauser made him a professional, so I didn't feel so badly. But not a very good professional, or bare hands would not have finished him, with the Mauser--a gun you can blast through a wall with--undrawn in his shoulder holster.

I made a little sense of it, not much. Four of the brown cigarettes had been smoked, so there had been either waiting or discussion. Somewhere along the line Waldo had got the little man by the throat and held him in just the right way to make him pass out in a matter of seconds. The Mauser had been less useful to him than a toothpick. Then Waldo had hung him up by the strap, probably dead already. That would account for haste, cleaning out the apartment, for Waldo's anxiety about the girl. It would account for the car left unlocked outside the cocktail bar.

That is, it would account for these things if Waldo had killed him, if this was really Waldo's apartment--if I wasn't just being kidded.

I examined some more pockets. In the left trouser one I found a gold penknife, some silver. In the left hip pocket a handkerchief, folded, scented. On the right hip another, unfolded but clean. In the right leg pocket four or five tissue handkerchiefs. A clean little guy. He didn't like to blow his nose on his handkerchief. Under these there was a small new keytainer holding four new keys--car keys. Stamped in gold on the keytainer was: Compliments of R. K. Vogelsang, Inc. "The Packard House."

I put everything as I had found it, swung the bed back, used my handkerchief on knobs and other projections, and flat surfaces, killed the light and poked my nose out the door. The hall was empty. I went down to the street and around the corner to Kingsley Drive. The Cadillac hadn't moved.

I opened the car door and leaned on it. She didn't seem to have moved, either. It was hard to see any expression on her face. Hard to see anything but her eyes and chin, but not hard to smell the sandalwood.

"That perfume," I said, "would drive a deacon nuts...no pearls."

"Well, thanks for trying," she said in a low, soft vibrant voice. "I guess I can stand it. Shall I...Do we...Or...?"

"You go on home now," I said. "And whatever happens you never saw me before. Whatever happens. Just as you may never see me again."

"I'd hate that."

"Good luck, Lola." I shut the car door and stepped back.

The lights blazed on, the motor turned over. Against the wind at the corner the big coupe made a slow contemptuous turn and was gone. I stood there by the vacant space at the curb where it had been.

It was quite dark there now. Windows, had become blanks in the apartment where the radio sounded. I stood looking at the back of a Packard cabriolet which seemed to be brand new. I had seen it before--before I went upstairs, in the same place, in front of Lola's car. Parked, dark, silent, with a blue sticker pasted to the right-hand corner of the shiny windshield.

And in my mind I was looking at something else, a set of brand-new car keys in a keytainer stamped: "The Packard House," upstairs, in a dead man's pocket.

I went up to the front of the cabriolet and put a small pocket flash on the blue slip. It was the same dealer all right. Written in ink below his name and slogan was a name and address-- Eugenie Kolchenko, 5315 Arvieda Street, West Los Angeles.

It was crazy. I went back up to Apartment 31, jimmied the door as I had done before, stepped in behind the wall bed and took the keytainer from the trousers pocket of the neat brown dangling corpse. I was back down on the street beside the cabriolet in five minutes. The keys fitted.

5

It was a small house, near a canyon rim out beyond Sawtelle, with a circle of writhing eucalyptus trees in front of it. Beyond that, on the other side of the street, one of those parties was going on where they come out and smash bottles on the sidewalk with a whoop like Yale making a touchdown against Princeton.

There was a wire fence at my number and some rose trees, and a flagged walk and a garage that was wide open and had no car in it. There was no car in front of the house either. I rang the bell. There was a long wait, then the door opened rather suddenly.

I wasn't the man she had been expecting. I could see it in her glittering kohl-rimmed eyes. Then I couldn't see anything in them. She just stood and looked at me, a long, lean, hungry brunette, with rouged cheekbones, thick black hair parted in the middle, a mouth made for three-decker sandwiches, coral-and-gold pajamas, sandals--and gilded toenails. Under her ear lobes a couple of miniature temple bells gonged lightly in the breeze. She made a slow disdainful motion with a cigarette in a holder as long as a baseball bat.

"We-el, what ees it, little man? You want sometheeng? You are lost from the bee-ootiful party across the street, hem?"

"Ha-ha," I said. "Quite a party, isn't it? No, I just brought your car home. Lost it, didn't you?"

Across the street somebody had delirium tremens in the front yard and a mixed quartet tore what was left of the night into small strips and did what they could to make the strips miserable. While this was going on the exotic brunette didn't move more than one eyelash.

She wasn't beautiful, she wasn't even pretty, but she looked as if things would happen where she was.

"You have said what?" she got out, at last, in a voice as silky as a burnt crust of toast.

"Your car." I pointed over my shoulder and kept my eyes on her. She was the type that uses a knife.

The long cigarette holder dropped very slowly to her side and the cigarette fell out of it. I stamped it out, and that put me in the hall. She backed away from me and I shut the door.

The hall was like the long hall of a railroad flat. Lamps glowed pinkly in iron brackets. There was a bead curtain at the end, a tiger skin on the floor. The place went with her.

"You're Miss Kolchenko?" I asked, not getting any more action.

"Ye-es. I am Mees Kolchenko. What the 'ell you want?"

She was looking at me now as if I had come to wash the windows, but at an inconvenient time.

I got a card out with my left hand, held it out to her. She read it in my hand, moving her head just enough. "A detective?" she breathed.

"Yeah."

She said something in a spitting language. Then in English: "Come in! Thees damn wind dry up my skeen like so much teesue paper."

"We're in," I said. "I just shut the door. Snap out of it, Nazimova. Who was he? The little guy?"

Beyond the bead curtain a man coughed. She jumped as if she had been stuck with an oyster fork. Then she tried to smile. It wasn't very successful.

"A reward," she said softly. "You weel wait 'ere? Ten dollars it is fair to pay, no?"

"No," I said.

I reached a finger towards her slowly and added: "He's dead."

She jumped about three feet and let out a yell.

A chair creaked harshly. Feet pounded beyond the bead curtain, a large hand plunged into view and snatched it aside, and a big hard-looking blond man was with us. He had a purple robe over his pajamas, his right hand held something in his robe pocket. He stood quite still as soon as he was through the curtain, his feet planted solidly, his jaw out, his colorless eyes like gray ice. He looked like a man who would be hard to take out on an off-tackle play.

"What's the matter, honey?" He had a solid, burring voice, with just the right sappy tone to belong to a guy who would go for a woman with gilded toenails.

"I came about Miss Kolchenko's car," I said.

"Well, you could take your hat off," he said. "Just for a light workout."

I took it off and apologized.

"O.K. ," he said, and kept his right hand shoved down hard in the purple pocket. "So you came about Miss Kolchenko's car. Take it from there."

I pushed past the woman and went closer to him. She shrank back against the wall and flattened her palms against it. Camille in a high-school play. The long holder lay empty at her toes.

When I was six feet from the big man he said easily: "I can hear you from there. Just take it easy. I've got a gun in this pocket and I've had to learn to use one. Now about the car?"

"The man who borrowed it couldn't bring it," I said, and pushed the card I was still holding towards his face. He barely glanced at it. He looked back at me.

"So what?" he said.

"Are you always this tough?" I asked. "Or only when you have your pajamas on?"

"So why couldn't he bring it himself?" he asked. "And skip the mushy talk."

The dark woman made a stuffed sound at my elbow.

"It's all right, honeybunch," the man said. "I'll handle this. Go on."

She slid past both of us and flicked through the bead curtain.

I waited a little while. The big man didn't move a muscle. He didn't look any more bothered than a toad in the sun.

"He couldn't bring it because somebody bumped him off," I said. "Let's see you handle that."

"Yeah?" he said. "Did you bring him with you to prove it?"

"No," I said. "But if you put your tie and crush hat on, I'll take you down and show you."

"Who the hell did you say you were, now?"

"I didn't say. I thought maybe you could read." I held the card at him some more.

"Oh, that's right," he said. "Philip Marlowe, Private Investigator. Well, well. So I should go with you to look at who, why?"

"Maybe he stole the car," I said.

The big man nodded. "That's a thought. Maybe he did. Who?"

"The little brown guy who had the keys to it in his pocket, and had it parked around the corner from the Berglund Apartments."

He thought that over, without any apparent embarrassment. "You've got something there," he said. "Not much. But a little. I guess this must be the night of the Police Smoker. So you're doing all their work for them."

"Huh?"

"The card says private detective to me," he said. "Have you got some cops outside that were too shy to come in?"

"No, I'm alone."

He grinned. The grin showed white ridges in his tanned skin. "So you find somebody dead and take some keys and find a car and come riding out here--all alone. No cops. Am I right?"

"Correct."

He sighed. "Let's go inside," he said. He yanked the bead curtain aside and made an opening for me to go through. "It might be you have an idea I ought to hear."

I went past him and he turned, keeping his heavy pocket towards me. I hadn't noticed until I got quite close that there were beads of sweat on his face. It might have been the hot wind but I didn't think so.

We were in the living room of the house.

We sat down and looked at each other across a dark floor, on which a few Navajo rugs and a few dark Turkish rugs made a decorating combination with some well-used overstuffed furniture. There was a fireplace, a small baby grand, a Chinese screen, a tall Chinese lantern on a teakwood pedestal, and gold net curtains against lattice windows. The windows to the south were open. A fruit tree with a whitewashed trunk whipped about outside the screen, adding its bit to the noise from across the street.

The big man eased back into a brocaded chair and put his slippered feet on a footstool. He kept his right hand where it had been since I met him--on his gun.

The brunette hung around in the shadows and a bottle gurgled and her temple bells gonged in her ears.

"It's all right, honeybunch," the man said. "It's all under control. Somebody bumped somebody off and this lad thinks we're interested. Just sit down and relax."

The girl tilted her head and poured half a tumbler of whiskey down her throat. She sighed, said, "Goddam," in a casual voice, and curled up on a davenport. It took all of the davenport. She had plenty of legs. Her gilded toenails winked at me from the shadowy corner where she kept herself quiet from then on.

I got a cigarette out without being shot at, lit it and went into my story. It wasn't all true, but some of it was. I told them about the Berglund Apartments and that I had lived there and that Waldo was living there in Apartment 31 on the floor below mine and that I had been keeping an eye on him for business reasons.

"Waldo what?" the blond man put in. "And what business reasons?"

"Mister," I said, "have you no secrets?" He reddened slightly.

I told him about the cocktail lounge across the street from the Berglund and what had happened there. I didn't tell him about the printed bolero jacket or the girl who had worn it. I left her out of the story altogether.

"It was an undercover job--from my angle," I said. "If you know what I mean." He reddened again, bit his teeth. I went on: "I got back from the city hall without telling anybody I knew Waldo. In due time, when I decided they couldn't find out where he lived that night, I took the liberty of examining his apartment."

"Looking for what?" the big man said thickly.

"For some letters. I might mention in passing there was nothing there at all--except a dead man. Strangled and hanging by a belt to the top of the wall bed--well out of sight. A small man, about forty-five, Mexican or South American, well-dressed in a fawn-colored--.

"That's enough," the big man said. "I'll bite, Marlowe. Was it a blackmail job you were on?"

"Yeah. The funny part was this little brown man had plenty of gun under his arm."

"He wouldn't have five hundred bucks in twenties in his pocket, of course? Or are you saying?"

"He wouldn't. But Waldo had over seven hundred in currency when he was killed in the cocktail bar."

"Looks like I underrated this Waldo," the big man said calmly. "He took my guy and his pay-off money, gun and all. Waldo have a gun?"

"Not on him."

"Get us a drink, honeybunch," the big man said. "Yes, I certainly did sell this Waldo person shorter than a bargain counter shirt."

The brunette unwound her legs and made two drinks with soda and ice. She took herself another gill without trimmings, wound herself back on the davenport. Her big glittering black eyes watched me solemnly.

"Well, here's how," the big man said, lifting his glass in salute. "I haven't murdered anybody, but I've got a divorce suit on my hands from now on. You haven't murdered anybody, the way you tell it, but you laid an egg down at police Headquarters. What the hell! Life's a lot of trouble, anyway you look at it. I've still got honeybunch here. She's a white Russian I met in Shanghai. She's safe as a vault and she looks as if she could cut your throat for a nickel. That's what I like about her. You get the glamor without the risk."

"You talk damn foolish," the girl spat him.

"You look O.K. to me," the big man went on ignoring her. "That is, for a keyhole peeper. Is there an out?"

"Yeah. But it will cost a little money."

"I expected that. How much?"

"Say another five hundred."

"Goddam, thees hot wind make me dry like the ashes of love," the Russian girl said bitterly.

"Five hundred might do," the blond man said. "What do I get for it?"

"If I swing it--you get left out of the story. If I don't-- you don't pay."

He thought it over. His face looked lined and tired now. The small beads of sweat twinkled in his short blond hair.

"This murder will make you talk," he grumbled. "The second one, I mean. And I don't have what I was going to buy. And if it's a hush, I'd rather buy it direct."

"Who was the little brown man?" I asked.

"Name's Leon Valesanos, a Uruguayan. Another of my importations. I'm in a business that takes me a lot of places. He was working in the Spezzia Club in Chiseltown--you know, the strip of Sunset next to Beverly Hills. Working on roulette, I think. I gave him the five hundred to go down to this--this Waldo--and buy back some bills for stuff Miss Kolchenko had charged to my account and delivered here. That wasn't bright, was it? I had them in my briefcase and this Waldo got a chance to steal them. What's your hunch about what happened?"

I sipped my drink and looked at him down my nose. "Your Uruguayan pal probably talked curt and Waldo didn't listen good. Then the little guy thought maybe that Mauser might help his argument--and Waldo was too quick for him. I wouldn't say Waldo was a killer-- not by intention. A blackmailer seldom is. Maybe he lost his temper and maybe he just held on to the little guy's neck too long. Then he had to take it on the lam. But he had another date, with more money coming up.

And he worked the neighborhood looking for the party. And accidentally he ran into a pal who was hostile enough and drunk enough to blow him down."

"There's a hell of a lot of coincidence in all this business," the big man said.

"It's the hot wind," I grinned. "Everybody's screwy tonight."

"For the five hundred you guarantee nothing? If I don't get my cover-up, you don't get your dough. Is that it?"

"That's it," I said, smiling at him.

"Screwy is right," he said, and drained his highball. "I'm taking you up on it."

"There are just two things," I said softly, leaning forward in my chair. "Waldo had a getaway car parked outside the cocktail bar where he was killed, unlocked with the motor running. The killer took it. There's always the chance of a kickback from that direction. You see, all Waldo's stuff must have been in that car."

"Including my bills, and your letters."

"Yeah. But the police are reasonable about things like that--unless you're good for a lot of publicity. If you're not, I think I can eat some stale dog downtown and get by. If you are-- that's the second thing. What did you say your name was?"

The answer was a long time coming. When it came I didn't get as much kick out of it as I thought I would. All at once it was too logical.

"Frank C. Barsaly," he said.

After a while the Russian girl called me a taxi. When I left, the party across the street was doing all that a party could do. I noticed the walls of the house were still standing. That seemed a pity.

6

When I unlocked the glass entrance door of the Berglund I smelled policeman. I looked at my wrist watch. It was nearly 3 AM. In the dark corner of the lobby a man dozed in a chair with a newspaper over his face. Large feet stretched out before him. A corner of the paper lifted an inch, dropped again. The man made no other movement.

I went on along the hall to the elevator and rode up to my floor. I soft-footed along the hallway, unlocked my door, pushed it wide and reached in for the light switch.

A chain switch tinkled and light glared from a standing lamp by the easy chair, beyond the card table on which my chessmen were still scattered.

Copernik sat there with a stiff unpleasant grin on his face. The short dark man, Ybarra, sat across the room from him, on my left, silent, half smiling as usual.

Copernik showed more of his big yellow horse teeth and said: "Hi. Long time no see. Been out with the girls?"

I shut the door and took my hat off and wiped the back of my neck slowly, over and over again. Copernik went on grinning. Ybarra looked at nothing with his soft dark eyes.

"Take a seat, pal," Copernik drawled. "Make yourself to home. We got pow-wow to make. Boy, do I hate this night sleuthing. Did you know you were low on hooch?"

"I could have guessed it," I said. I leaned against the wall.

Copernik kept on grinning. "I always did hate private dicks," he said, "but I never had a chance to twist one like I got tonight."

He reached down lazily beside his chair and picked up a printed bolero jacket, tossed it on the card table. He reached down again and put a wide-brimmed hat beside it.

"I bet you look cuter than all hell with these on," he said.

I took hold of a straight chair, twisted it around and straddled it, leaned my folded arms on the chair and looked at Copernik.

He got up very slowly--with an elaborate slowness, walked across the room and stood in front of me smoothing his coat down. Then he lifted his open right hand and hit me across the face with it--hard. It stung but I didn't move.

Ybarra looked at the wall, looked at the floor, looked at nothing.

"Shame on you, pal," Copernik said lazily. "The way you was taking care of this nice exclusive merchandise. Wadded down behind your old shirts. You punk peepers always did make me sick."

He stood there over me for a moment. I didn't move or speak. I looked into his glazed drinker's eyes. He doubled a fist at his side, then shrugged and turned and went back to the chair.

"O.K.," he said. "The rest will keep. Where did you get these things?"

"They belong to a lady."

"Do tell. They belong to a lady. Ain't you the lighthearted bastard! I'll tell you what lady they belong to. They belong to the lady a guy named Waldo asked about in a bar across the street--about two minutes before he got shot kind of dead. Or would that have slipped your mind?"

I didn't say anything.

"You was curious about her yourself," Copernik sneered on. "But you were smart, pal. You fooled me."

"That wouldn't make me smart," I said.

His face twisted suddenly and he started to get up. Ybarra laughed, suddenly and softly, almost under his breath. Copernik's eyes swung on him, hung there. Then he faced me again, bland-eyed.

"The guinea likes you," he said. "He thinks you're good."

The smile left Ybarra's face, but no expression took its place. No expression at all.

Copernik said: "You knew who the dame was all the time. You knew who Waldo was and where he lived. Right across the hall a floor below you. You knew this Waldo person had bumped a guy off and started to lam, only this broad came into his plans somewhere and he was anxious to meet up with her before he went away. Only he never got the chance. A heist guy from back East named Al Tessilore took care of that by taking care of Waldo. So you met the gal and hid her clothes and sent her on her way and kept your trap glued. That's the way guys like you make your beans. Am I right?"

"Yeah," I said. "Except that I only knew these things very recently. Who was Waldo?"

Copernik bared his teeth at me. Red spots burned high on his sallow cheeks. Ybarra, looking down at the floor, said very softly: "Waldo Ratigan. We got him from Washington by Teletype. He was a two-bit porch climber with a few small terms on him. He drove a car in a bank stick-up job in Detroit. He turned the gang in later and got a nolle prosse. One of the gang was this Al Tessilore. He hasn't talked a word, but we think the meeting across the street was purely accidental."

Ybarra spoke in the soft quiet modulated voice of a man for whom sounds have a meaning. I said: "Thanks, Ybarra. Can I smoke--or would Copernik kick it out of my mouth?"

Ybarra smiled suddenly. "You may smoke, sure," he said.

"The guinea likes you all right," Copernik jeered. "You never know what a guinea will like, do you?"

I lit a cigarette. Ybarra looked at Copernik and said very softly: "The word guinea--you overwork it. I don't like it so well applied to me."

"The hell with what you like, guinea."

Ybarra smiled a little more. "You are making a mistake," he said. He took a pocket nail file out and began to use it, looking down.

Copernik blared: "I smelled something rotten on you from the start, Marlowe. So when we make these two mugs, Ybarra and me think we'll drift over and dabble a few more words with you. I bring one of Waldo's morgue photos--nice work, the light just right in his eyes, his tie all straight and a white handkerchief showing just right in his pocket. Nice work. So on the way up, just as a matter of routine, we rout out the manager here and let him lamp it. And he knows the guy. He's here as A. B. Hummel, Apartment Thirty-one. So we go in there and find a stiff. Then we go round and round with that. Nobody knows him yet, but he's got some swell finger bruises under that strap and I hear they fit Waldo's fingers very nicely."

"That's something," I said. "I thought maybe I murdered him."

Copernik stared at me a long time. His face had stopped grinning and was just a hard brutal face now. "Yeah. We got something else even," he said. "We got Waldo's getaway car--and what Waldo had in it to take with him."

I blew cigarette smoke jerkily. The wind pounded the shut windows. The air in the room was foul.

"Oh, we're bright boys," Copernik sneered. "We never figured you with that much guts. Take a look at this."

He plunged his bony hand into his coat pocket and drew something up slowly over the edge of the card table, drew it along the green top and left it there stretched out, gleaming. A string of white pearls with a clasp like a two-bladed propeller. They shimmered softly in the thick smoky air.

Lola Barsaly's pearls. The pearls the flier had given her. The guy who was dead, the guy she still loved.

I stared at them, but I didn't move. After a long moment Copernik said almost gravely: "Nice, ain't they? Would you feel like telling us a story about now, Mister Marlowe?"

I stood up and pushed the chair from under me, walked slowly across the room and stood looking down at the pearls. The largest was perhaps a third of an inch across. They were pure white, iridescent, with a mellow softness. I lifted them slowly off the card table from beside her clothes. They felt heavy, smooth, fine.

"Nice," I said. "A lot of the trouble was about these. Yeah, I'll talk now. They must be worth a lot of money."

Ybarra laughed behind me. It was a very gentle laugh. "About a hundred dollars," he said. "They're good phonies--but they're phony."

I lifted the pearls again. Copernik's glassy eyes gloated at me. "How do you tell?" I asked.

"I know pearls," Ybarra said. "These are good stuff, the kind women very often have made on purpose, as a kind of insurance. But they are slick like glass. Real pearls are gritty between the edges of the teeth. Try."

I put two or three of them between my teeth and moved my teeth back and forth, then sideways. Not quite biting them. The beads were hard and slick.

"Yes. They are very good," Ybarra said. "Several even have little waves and flat spots, as real pearls might have."

"Would they cost fifteen grand--if they were real?" I asked.

"Si. Probably. That's hard to say. It depends on a lot of things."

"This Waldo wasn't so bad," I said.

Copernik stood up quickly, but I didn't see him swing. I was still looking down at the pearls. His fist caught me on the side of the face, against the molars. I tasted blood at once. I staggered back and made it look like a worse blow than it was.

"Sit down and talk, you bastard!" Copernik almost whispered.

I sat down and used a handkerchief to pat my cheek. I licked at the cut inside my mouth. Then I got up again and went over and picked up the cigarette he had knocked out of my mouth. I crushed it out in a tray and sat down again.

Ybarra filed at his nails and held one up against the lamp. There were beads of sweat on Copernik's eyebrows, at the inner ends.

"You found the beads in Waldo's car," I said, looking at Ybarra. "Find any papers?"

He shook his head without looking up.

"I'd believe you," I said. "Here it is. I never saw Waldo until he stepped into the cocktail bar tonight and asked about the girl. I knew nothing I didn't tell. When I got home and stepped out of the elevator this girl, in the printed bolero jacket and the wide hat and the blue silk crêpe dress--all as he had described them--was waiting for the elevator, here on my floor. And she looked like a nice girl."

Copernik laughed jeeringly. It didn't make any difference to me. I had him cold. All he had to do was know that. He was going to know it now, very soon.

"I knew what she was up against as a police witness," I said. "And I suspected there was something else to it. But I didn't suspect for a minute that there was anything wrong with her. She was just a nice girl in a jam--and she didn't even know she was in a jam. I got her in here. She pulled a gun on me. But she didn't mean to use it."

Copernik sat up very suddenly and he began to lick his lips. His face had a stony look now. A look like wet gray stone. He didn't make a sound.

"Waldo had been her chauffeur," I went on. "His name was then Joseph Coates. Her name is Mrs. Frank C. Barsaly. Her husband is a big hydroelectric engineer. Some guy gave her the pearls once and she told her husband they were just store pearls. Waldo got wise somehow there was a romance behind them and when Barsaly came home from South America and fired him, because he was too good-looking, he lifted the pearls."

Ybarra lifted his head suddenly and his teeth flashed. "You mean he didn't know they were phony?"

"I thought he fenced the real ones and had imitations fixed up," I said.

Ybarra nodded. "It's possible."

"He lifted something else," I said. "Some stuff from Barsaly's briefcase that showed he was keeping a woman--out in Brentwood. He was blackmailing wife and husband both, without either knowing about the other. Get it so far?"

"I get it," Copernik said harshly, between his tight lips. His face was still wet gray stone. "Get the hell on with it."

"Waldo wasn't afraid of them," I said. "He didn't conceal where he lived. That was foolish, but it saved a lot of finagling, if he was willing to risk it. The girl came down here tonight with five grand to buy back her pearls. She didn't find Waldo. She came here to look for him and walked up a floor before she went back down. A woman's idea of being cagey. So I met her. So I brought her in here. So she was in that dressing room when Al Tessilore visited me to rub out a witness." I pointed to the dressing-room door. "So she came out with her little gun and stuck it in his back and saved my life," I said.

Copernik didn't move. There was something horrible in his face now. Ybarra slipped his nail file into a small leather case and slowly tucked it into his pocket.

"Is that all?" he said gently.

I nodded. "Except that she told me where Waldo's apartment was and I went in there and looked for the pearls. I found the dead man. In his pocket I found new car keys in a case from a Packard agency. And down on the street I found the Packard and took it to where it came from. Barsaly's kept woman. Barsaly had sent a friend from the Spezzia Club down to buy something and he had tried to buy it with his gun instead of the money Barsaly gave him. And Waldo beat him to the punch."

"Is that all?" Ybarra said softly.

"That's all," I said licking the torn place on the inside of my cheek.

Ybarra said slowly: "What do you want?"

Copernik's face convulsed and he slapped his long hard thigh. "This guy's good," he jeered. "He falls for a stray broad and breaks every law in the book and you ask him what does he want? I'll give him what he wants, guinea!"

Ybarra turned his head slowly and looked at him. "I don't think you will," he said. "I think you'll give him a clean bill of health and anything else he wants. He's giving you a lesson in police work."

Copernik didn't move or make a sound for a long minute. None of us moved. Then Copernik leaned forward and his coat fell open. The butt of his service gun looked out of his underarm holster.

"So what do you want?" he asked me.

"What's on the card table there. The jacket and hat and the phony pearls. And some names kept away from the papers. Is that too much?"

"Yeah--it's too much," Copernik said almost gently. He swayed sideways and his gun jumped neatly into his hand. He rested his forearm on his thigh and pointed the gun at my stomach.

"I like better that you get a slug in the guts resisting arrest," he said. "I like that better, because of a report I made out on Al Tessilore's arrest and how I made the pinch. Because of some photos of me that are in the morning sheets going out about now. I like it better that you don't live long enough to laugh about that baby."

My mouth felt suddenly hot and dry. Far off I heard the wind booming. It seemed like the sound of guns.

Ybarra moved his feet on the floor and said coldly: "You've got a couple of cases all solved, policeman. All you do for it is leave some junk here and keep some names from the papers. Which means from the D.A. If he gets them anyway, too bad for you."

Copernik said: "I like the other way." The blue gun in his hand was like a rock. "And God help you, if you don't back me up on it."

Ybarra said: "If the woman is brought out into the open, you'll be a liar on a police report and a chisler on your own partner. In a week they won't even speak your name at Headquarters. The taste of it would make them sick."

The hammer clicked back on Copernik's gun and I watched his big finger slide in farther around the trigger.

Ybarra stood up. The gun jumped at him. He said: "We'll see how yellow a guinea is. I'm telling you to put that gun up, Sam."

He started to move. He moved four even steps. Copernik was a man without a breath of movement, a stone man.

Ybarra took one more step and quite suddenly the gun began to shake.

Ybarra spoke evenly: "Put it up, Sam. If you keep your head everything lies the way it is. If you don't-- you're gone."

He took one more step. Copernik's mouth opened wide and made a gasping sound and then he sagged in the chair as if he had been hit on the head. His eyelids dropped.

Ybarra jerked the gun out of his hand with a movement so quick it was no movement at all. He stepped back quickly, held the gun low at his side.

"It's the hot wind, Sam. Let's forget it," he said in the same even, almost dainty voice.

Copernik's shoulders sagged lower and he put his face in his hands. "O.K.," he said between his fingers.

Ybarra went softly across the room and opened the door. He looked at me with lazy, half-closed eyes. "I'd do a lot for a woman who saved my life, too," he said. "I'm eating this dish, but as a cop you can't expect me to like it."

I said: "The little man in the bed is called Leon Valesanos. He was a croupier at the Spezzia Club."

"Thanks," Ybarra said. "Let's go, Sam."

Copernik got up heavily and walked across the room and out of the open door and out of my sight. Ybarra stepped through the door after him and started to close it.

I said: "Wait a minute."

He turned his head slowly, his left hand on the door, the blue gun hanging down close to his right side.

"I'm not in this for money," I said. "The Barsalys live at Two-twelve Fremont Place. You can take the pearls to her. If Barsaly's name stays out of the paper, I get five C's. It goes to the Police Fund. I'm not so damn smart as you think. It just happened that way-- and you had a heel for a partner."

Ybarra looked across the room at the pearls on the card table. His eyes glistened. "You take them," he said. "The five hundred's O.K. I think the fund has it coming."

He shut the door quietly and in a moment I heard the elevator doors clang.

7

I opened a window and stuck my head out into the wind and watched the squad car tool off down the block. The wind blew in hard and I let it blow. A picture fell off the wall and two chessmen rolled off the card table. The material of Lola Barsaly's bolero jacket lifted and shook.

I went out to the kitchenette and drank some Scotch and went back into the living room and called her--late as it was.

She answered the phone herself, very quickly, with no sleep in her voice.

"Marlowe," I said. "O.K. your end?"

"Yes...yes," she said. "I'm alone."

"I found something," I said. "Or rather the police did. But your dark boy gypped you. I have a string of pearls. They're not real. He sold the real ones, I guess, and made you up a string of ringers, with your clasp."

She was silent for a long time. Then, a little faintly: "The police found them?"

"In Waldo's car. But they're not telling. We have a deal. Look at the papers in the morning and you'll be able to figure out why."

"There doesn't seem to be anything more to say," she said. "Can I have the clasp?"

"Yes. Can you meet me tomorrow at four in the Club Esquire bar?"

"You're really rather sweet," she said in a dragged out voice. "I can. Frank is still at his meeting."

"Those meetings--they take it out of a guy," I said. We said goodbye.

I called a West Los Angeles number. He was still there, with the Russian girl.

"You can send me a check for five hundred in the morning," I told him. "Made out to the Police Relief Fund, if you want to. Because that's where it's going."

Copernik made the third page of the morning papers with two photos and a nice half-column. The little brown man in Apartment 31 didn't make the paper at all. The Apartment House Association has a good lobby too.

I went out after breakfast and the wind was all gone. It was soft, cool, a little foggy. The sky was close and comfortable and gray. I rode down to the boulevard and picked out the best jewelry store on it and laid a string of pearls on a black velvet mat under a daylight-blue lamp. A man in a wing collar and striped trousers looked down at them languidly.

"How good?" I asked.

"I'm sorry, sir. We don't make appraisals. I can give you the name of an appraiser."

"Don't kid me," I said. "They're Dutch."

He focused the light a little and leaned down and toyed with a few inches of the string.

"I want a string just like them, fitted to that clasp, and in a hurry," I added.

"How, like them?" He didn't look up. "And they're not Dutch. They're Bohemian."

"O.K., can you duplicate them?"

He shook his head and pushed the velvet pad away as if it soiled him. "In three months, perhaps. We don't

364

blow glass like that in this country. If you wanted them matched--three months at least. And this house would not do that sort of thing at all."

"It must be swell to be that snooty," I said. I put a card under his black sleeve. "Give me a name that will--and not in three months--and maybe not exactly like them."

He shrugged, went away with the card, came back in five minutes and handed it back to me. There was something written on the back.

The old Levantine had a shop on Melrose, a junk shop with everything in the window from a folding baby carriage to a French horn, from a mother-of-pearl lorgnette in a faded plush case to one of those .44 Special Single Action six-shooters they still make for Western peace officers whose grandfathers were tough.

The old Levantine wore a skull cap and two pairs of glasses and a full beard. He studied my pearls, shook his head sadly, and said: "For twenty dollars, almost so good. Not so good, you understand. Not so good glass."

"How alike will they look?"

He spread his firm strong hands. "I am telling you the truth," he said. "They would not fool a baby."

"Make them up," I said. "With this clasp. And I want the others back, too, of course."

"Yah. Two o'clock," he said.

Leon Valesanos, the little brown man from Uruguay, made the afternoon papers. He had been found hanging in an unnamed apartment. The police were investigating.

At four o'clock I walked into the long cool bar of the Club Esquire and prowled along the row of booths until I found one where a woman sat alone. She wore a hat like a shallow soup plate with a very wide edge, a brown tailor-made suit with a severe mannish shirt and tie.

I sat down beside her and slipped a parcel along the seat. "You don't open that," I said. "In fact you can slip it into the incinerator as is, if you want to."

She looked at me with dark tired eyes. Her fingers twisted a thin glass that smelled of peppermint. "Thanks." Her face was very pale.

I ordered a highball and the waiter went away. "Read the papers?"

"Yes."

"You understand now about this fellow Copernik who stole your act? That's why they won't change the story or bring you into it."

"It doesn't matter now," she said. "Thank you, all the same. Please--please show them to me."

I pulled the string of pearls out of the loosely wrapped tissue paper in my pocket and slid them across to her. The silver propeller clasp winked in the light of the wall bracket. The little diamond winked. The pearls were as dull as white soap. They didn't even match in size.

"You were right," she said tonelessly. "They are not my pearls."

The waiter came with my drink and she put her bag on them deftly. When he was gone she fingered them slowly once more, dropped them into the bag and gave me a dry mirthless smile.

I stood there a moment with a hand hard on the table.

"As you said--I'll keep the clasp."

I said slowly: "You don't know anything about me. You saved my life last night and we had a moment, but it was just a moment. You still don't know anything about me. There's a detective downtown named Ybarra, a Mexican of the nice sort, who was on the job when the pearls were found in Waldo's suitcase. That is in case you would like to make sure--"

She said: "Don't be silly. It's all finished. It was a memory. I'm too young to nurse memories. It may be for the best. I loved Stan Phillips--but he's gone--long gone."

I stared at her, didn't say anything.

She added quietly: "This morning my husband told me something I hadn't known. We are to separate. So I have very little to laugh about today."

"I'm sorry," I said lamely. "There's nothing to say. I may see you sometime. Maybe not. I don't move much in your circle. Good luck."

I stood up. We looked at each other for a moment. "You haven't touched your drink," she said.

"You drink it. That peppermint stuff will just make you sick."

I stood there a moment with a hand on the table.

"If anybody ever bothers you," I said, "let me know."

I went out of the bar without looking back at her, got into my car and drove west on Sunset and down all the way to the Coast Highway. Everywhere along the way gardens were full of withered and blackened leaves and flowers which the hot wind had burned.

But the ocean looked cool and languid and just the same as ever. I drove on almost to Malibu and then parked and went and sat on a big rock that was inside somebody's wire fence. It was about half-tide and coming in. The air smelled of kelp. I watched the water for a while and then I pulled a string of Bohemian glass imitation pearls out of my pocket and cut the knot at one end and slipped the pearls off one by one.

When I had them all loose in my left hand I held them like that for a while and thought. There wasn't really anything to think about. I was sure.

"To the memory of Mr. Stan Phillips," I said aloud. "Just another four-flusher."

I flipped her pearls out into the water one by one at the floating seagulls They made little splashes and the seagulls rose off the water and swooped at the splashes.

THE END

CPSIA information can be obtained
at www.ICGtesting.com
Printed in the USA
LVHW011015130620
657889LV00010B/2122